AF488716

THE BLOOD, THE BONE, AND FRAGMENTS OF THE SOUL

SM HYUN

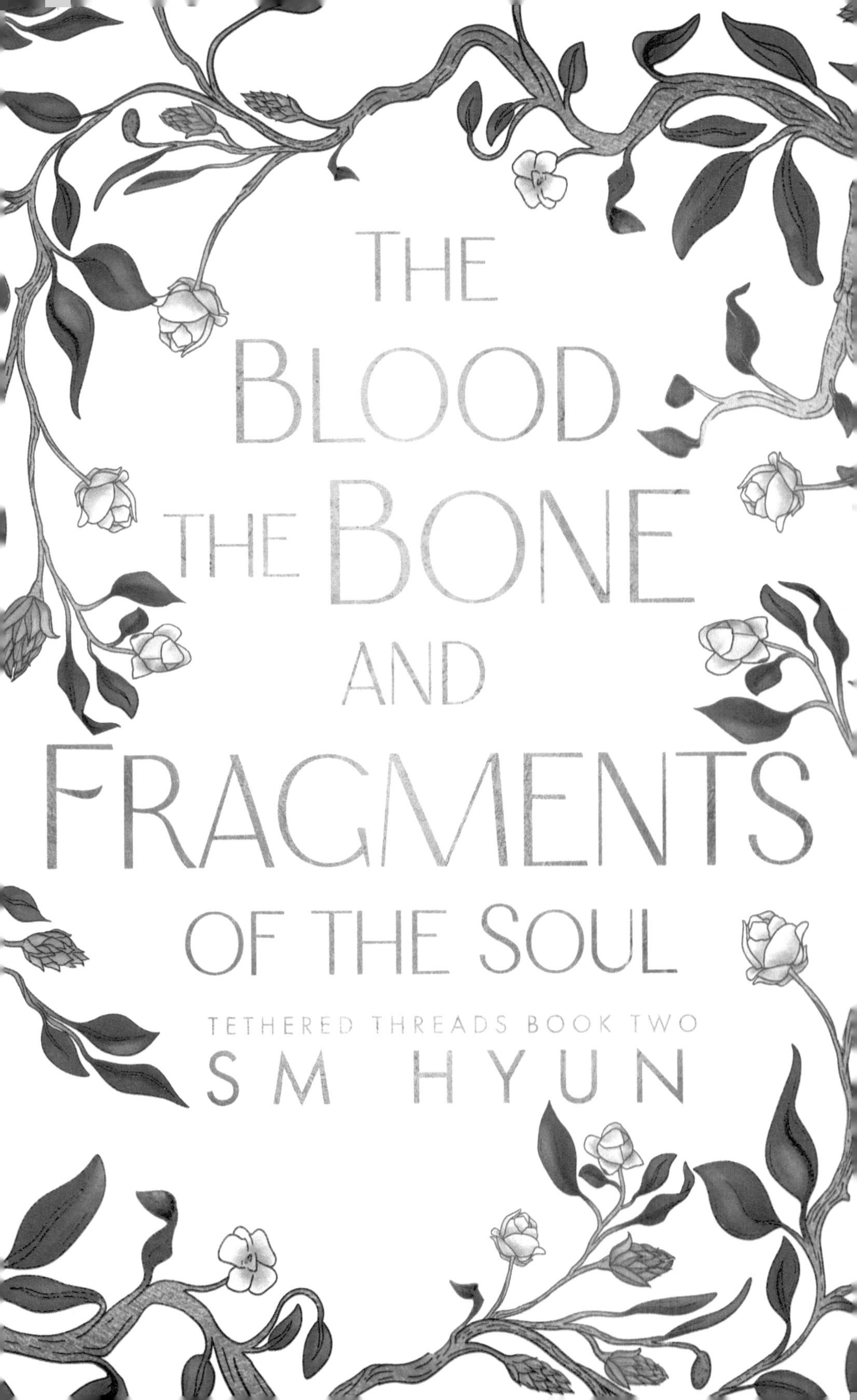

THE
BLOOD
THE BONE
AND
FRAGMENTS
OF THE SOUL
TETHERED THREADS BOOK TWO
SM HYUN

THE BLOOD, THE BONE, AND FRAGMENTS OF THE SOUL
TETHERED THREADS BOOK 2

Copyright © 2026 SM Hyun
All rights reserved.
ISBN: 979-8-9928209-6-6

No part of this work may be reproduced, distributed, or transmitted in any form or by any means, electronic, mechanical, photocopying, recording, scanning, or otherwise, without written permission from the author, except in the case of brief quotations in a book review where the author is cited.

The characters and events portrayed in this book are fictitious or are used fictitiously. Any similarity to real persons, living or dead, is purely coincidental and not intended by the author.

NO AI TRAINING: Without in any way limiting the author's exclusive rights under copyright, any use of this publication to "train" generative artificial intelligence (AI) technologies to generate text is expressly prohibited.

Cover design, interior design, and formatted by Rena Violet
(Coversbyviolet.com, @violet.book.design)

Chapter illustrations by Tadd Galusha
(taddgalusha.com, @taddgalusha)

Line Editing by Holly at Bird and Bear Editorial Services

*This book is dedicated to every person who has ever wondered
what those strawberry candies were called.*

Chapter Fourteen is for you, my friends.

*(p.s. There's a glossary in the back of each book,
if you didn't catch that in the first book.)*

AUTHOR'S NOTE

As a portion of this book takes place in Alaska, I have briefly addressed the Missing and Murdered Indigenous Women Crisis *that has been ongoing in the United States. I do not go in-depth into this subject; however, it was important to me to bring attention to the crisis and not casually attribute magical means to the women who have gone missing and/or lost their lives when this book is an Urban Fantasy set in contemporary times. This problem is one embedded in a tragic history of the intergenerational trauma that has resulted from the colonization and genocide of Alaska Natives.*

To learn more about this topic, you can visit:

National Indigenous Women's Resource Center
https://www.niwrc.org/policy-center/mmiwr

Alaska Native Women's Resource Center
https://www.aknwrc.org/resources/

CONTENT WARNINGS

- Suicidality
- Violent deaths
- Postpartum depression—briefly mentioned
- Torture

PROLOGUE

He quailed under the silence of the god's regard, retreating deep within his mind. A spiral of private admonishments ran wild within him, quietly reminding his selves of the end goal. Every one of his minds paused to take the opportunity to self-flagellate the life decisions that had landed him in this position.

While chaos reigned within himself, his body remained still, his face stoic. Nothing betrayed his inner thoughts to the deity who dictated his life.

The *kami* took a moment to check in with the present and found nothing of value in the god's speech. It was nothing he hadn't already heard, this obsession of the god's. He latched onto the opportunity to assess the barrier surrounding his heart. It was still holding firm, despite being pierced by the *haetae* a few months ago. He felt a sigh of relief echo within his mind. He had put it up as a precautionary measure once upon a time, before this plan had been put into effect. Now, the need to check on it was an insistent thrum that he couldn't ignore, a worm of fear that burrowed deeper into his thoughts with every passing moment. It was his final act of rebellion.

Despite the fact he, himself, was also a deity, he held no power here.

All Orochi had ever wanted was his Thread. When his old friend—turned enemy—had told him of the *onna uo's* prophetic words, his thoughts singularly focused on protecting his Thread at any cost.

If he had known what would have befallen them over these centuries past, he didn't know if he would choose this path again. To blindly put his trust in his oldest friend's words.

Those words had stripped him of everything he had held dear.

CHAPTER ONE

There was nothing like the ripe smell of decomposing flesh being pulled out of a river in the middle of a heat wave.

Especially when you were supposedly *blessed* with heightened senses.

"Who's such a good girl? You're the good girl! Who's the bestest girl ever? You're the bestest girl!"

I coughed to cover up my laugh as Aidan cooed to Yumi while they played tug-of-war over a platypus.

The lab mix was still rebuilding her confidence after the events from a few months ago, and I wouldn't be the one to discourage her, even if I was technically laughing at Aidan. She was one of our most successful cadaver water-search K9s, and this was her first underwater SAR since her injuries in the spring.

"My God, what is that *smell?*" A sheriff's deputy leaned over his watercraft and promptly lost his lunch. A pungent odor of rotting fish accompanied the smell of death. They would likely associate it with the river, but I knew better.

"Forget the smell, what *happened* to it?" Another deputy turned green as the bloated body was pulled into their craft. Bite marks—likely from the sea lions that swam up the Columbia River—had ripped huge chunks of flesh from the body, mutilating it beyond simple decomposition. Its skin had begun to slough off due to the time it had spent underwater, but what remained was an unnatural white and gray.

"Who would kill an *iwana bōzu*?" Aidan murmured to me. "They harm no one."

No, but the peace-inclined fish were incredibly principled and could be considered self-righteous when they encountered anyone who they believed to be overfishing.

"Is this your guy?" I asked Sheriff Danly, who was in the boat with us.

Jeff Danly had been scrutinizing the body closely as it had been pulled up from the depths in front of the Bonneville Dam. At my question, he ran his hand through his thick, sandy-colored hair and sighed. "Hard to tell with the decomp, but what clothing is left on the body matches the description of our missing person." He eyed us. "You're certain it's an *iwana bōzu*?"

Aidan and I both nodded.

"Well, fuck me sideways. Then, yeah, it's probably, like, a ninety-eight percent chance. It's not like I can actually submit a DNA test. And there's fuckall left of the body for fingerprints."

He didn't need to mention the missing head for the lack of dental records. Not that any of the Abstruse ever went to the dentist. I enjoyed a brief mental image of Reika going to get her tooth pulled with her rows of serrated teeth and tusks.

It would serve her right after all she'd put me through recently.

The divers who had assisted with the SAR over the past few days climbed back into the crafts idling around the site, and we began to make our way back to the boat launch. As the smell filtered back to us, I held back a reflexive gag. I hated the smell of fish. Dead bodies, I could do all day. Fish, I couldn't stand.

"Tish is going to love this. Yet another case for her to investigate." Jeff winced subconsciously.

Tisha was his wife. One of my best friends. Skamania County's prosecuting attorney and county coroner. And she was also a *kitsune* who became cranky as hell when her caseload piled up.

"Imagine if she had been a big fancy-pants district attorney like her parents wanted instead of a lowly county prosecutor for Skamania," Aidan teased. "You'd definitely be dead by now and she'd be disbarred."

"That's why we got Ruby," Jeff grumbled. "She was supposed to be her stress reliever."

We all snickered. The Danlys' corgi had immediately glued herself to Jeff when they brought her home, and it had been all over from there.

"This is, what, the sixth death since June?" Aidan asked. I struggled to keep my face neutral, not enjoying the reminder of that time in my life. It was August now and my life had been relatively peaceful since the wild ride I had been on in spring. I was keeping my fingers crossed that it stayed that way.

Aidan and I had gone missing in May. We had been kidnapped by someone I had mistakenly put my trust in…who ended up using me for his own purposes. I had lost weeks to a temporal snare. Then I lost even more time to the turmoil that followed. By the time I'd returned to the Quote realm and Skamania, summer had arrived and it was mid-June.

But I couldn't complain too much. It had brought someone I had thought dead back into my life.

"Seventh since May. Don't forget the call-out while you were in Neskowin."

"Oh, that's right. The missing child that turned out to be the *curupira*." Aidan blanched. "*Kamis'* alive, the poor Abstruse."

Unlike Aidan, I hadn't forgotten. I wish I could. The missing guardian had been found in our forests. A location too far away from his home to make any sense, as he rarely left his territory. Instead of forgetting, I could perfectly recall the dread that had filled my body in anticipation of telling Anhangá the news when I finally returned. My breath caught in my throat as I remembered the cold stillness that had emanated from him when he had arrived to identify the body, the only time I had seen him take a human form. It had been an experience nearly as devastating as when he had lost control of his power.

The *curupira* was found beaten and had been the first of this rash of decapitations. At least the first one we knew of so far. Given the wounds, combined with the *ki* found on the body, a *yōkai* was clearly the culprit behind his death. Not knowing differently, it had been ruled an animal attack by the Quotes. By the time the fourth death hit the area, panic had already started to bloom among the Quotidians of Skamania and its neighboring counties, and the reports began to make national news. Previously popular hikes were abandoned as people sought trails in safer territories.

Now, it was only clueless tourists, hikers with no sense of preservation, true crime aficionados, and cryptid hunters who lost themselves in the Gifford Pinchot National Forest. Which made for a remarkably busy season for Blue Bear Search and Rescue, despite the overall decline.

"We're still trying to identify who filed the missing persons report," Jeff remarked. There was no compassion or empathy in his tone, only a grim sense of determination with an undercurrent of anger. "They were clearly shifted, and they shed the appearance they wore after leaving the station. No one seems to be able to accurately recall their description, even after watching the CCTV footage. As soon as you glance away from the screen, it's like a filter is placed over your memory."

"Like every report filed for these murders," I added softly.

Jeff inclined his head in confirmation. "Every report. They change up their appearances, they remain androgynous—each witness account varies in whether they are male, female, or nonbinary. Their ethnicity remains ambiguous. It's the one thing that ties all the reports together, beyond the bodies themselves."

All of the Abstruse could glamour. But most of us had limitations dictated by our ancestry. I could change small aspects of my appearance, enough to pass as a relative when I needed to switch identities in the Quotidian world, but I still looked East Asian.

"So that leaves...what?" Danly asked, throttling back the craft to reduce our speed as we began approaching the launch. "Gods, *doekkabi*, *tanukis*, skinwalkers...."

"*Tanukis* retain their basic features through each shift," I countered. "Both the Uncles keep the color of their hair in any form they take, regardless of if it has hair or not."

"What about Reika?" Aidan asked. "She pulled off that switch on Toyotama. Made her not only look like an entirely different person but rendered her a Quote."

"She was still Japanese though," Danly pointed out.

I refocused on a different tangent from Danly's prior comments. "Whoever is behind the disappearances of the guardians was taunting us. Still is. Calling attention to the *curupira* while we were searching for Toyotama? The bodies? Very few of us die from decapitation. They are flaunting the ability to kill without destroying each Abstruse's source of *ki*. Which lends more strength to the theory that it's a god. I'm one of the few Abbies who can kill indiscriminately, but there's nothing left of the body after I do. They are both taunting and distracting us from focusing on finding *them*."

"A *doekkabi* could," Aidan noted.

"Only if they had racked up enough karmic imbalance to warrant it," I tossed back.

Aidan gave me a look. The thought of it being Theo was so antithetical to me that my stomach immediately churned.

"So…why now?" Jeff asked, exhaustion lining his face.

"Because Rafael pulled us into the game. That's the major change." Aidan let out a heavy breath as the realization hit him. Hit all of us.

We sat in silence while the implications cycled through our minds. We hadn't had the opportunity to put our heads together since this all began, thanks to the frenetic nature of these searches and subsequent investigations. To say nothing of all the additional SARs scattered between them. We'd hardly had a chance to breathe, let alone talk.

In the midst of all that had happened this year, several of my friends and I had been recruited by Rafael's ancestral grandfather to find out who was behind the guardians of the realms disappearing or dying out. Except, Rafael was gone now, ripped to wherever Orochi had escaped to by the slave bands encircling his forearms.

"Is it because Rafael pulled you guys into the game, or is it because he pulled *Cam* into the game?" Danly's tone was grim.

"Fuck if I know." I scrubbed my face with my hands as if it could reset my brain. I had gone on a wild ride of emotions this past summer in a futile attempt to come to terms with my feelings around the *kariudo* and all he represented to me. Despite the fact it had been months, betrayal and regret surged within me at the reminder. Getting over something so significant when there was no opportunity for closure felt insurmountable on top of everything else that had happened. Rafael saving my life made it that much more difficult.

"Speaking of the male, how is your personal search going?" Despite the roar of the motors, Jeff had kept his voice quiet so no one else would be able to hear. The boat idled as we lingered behind the crafts being loaded onto trailers. As the motor quieted, a clamor of shouts began to overtake the river.

I sent a dark look at the crush of reporters vying to get past the line of deputies holding them back. News vans had been taking over the parking areas since our search for the *iwana bōzu* began. The vultures were ruthless as they fought each other for the latest scoop on the deaths.

When my gaze returned to my present company, Aidan looked pained. My heart tugged at me, and I felt the pieces scattering throughout my body as I recalled Jeff's question. I tried my best to keep my feelings concealed. Apparently failing, based on the sympathy radiating from Jeff. "It's not," I admitted quietly. "We have no way to trace Orochi. He used a masking spell over his magic trail, and even if he hadn't, Max can't search *under* the water, only over. So there's jackshit that a Point Last Seen can do for us. Theo hasn't been able to pick up on his karmic trail either, due to how unusual his case is."

The sheriff grimaced as he carefully steered the craft to the trailer waiting at the bottom of the boat launch. "You sure you want to find this huntsman guy, Cam? He sounds like a fast track to heartbreak and grief."

Unfortunately, Danly's warning came several months too late for me.

Aidan snorted in agreement while I laughed bitterly. "We need him, Jeff; we have no idea what we're doing without him."

"Hmm" was his only response.

"Anhangá basically let him have free rein over this issue while he focused on his own territory. This whole debacle has been the quintessential example of the right hand knowing jackall about what the left hand is doing." Once I had returned to Oregon, I scoured the journal made of *onna uo* skin for clues, but it only contained the ravings of a *kami* who had lost control—there was nothing to be found about the genocides he had ordered.

"Welp, if anyone's going to find him, it'll be you and your crew, Cam." The small craft bumped against the sides of the boat launch as Jeff maneuvered it, turning off the engine when we slid into place. Aidan tossed the ropes to the waiting deputy, and we were gently guided to the trailer waiting for us. The two of us climbed over the side of the craft while Yumi hopped out neatly, like she had been born to water.

Jeff threw his arm behind his seat and stared me down with a knowing look. "Don't let this consume you, Cam. If you can't find him, you can't find him. Adapt, work around the barrier, and let him go."

The effort it took to smile weakly was exhausting. "Sure, Beauty. I'm a pro at letting go of things at my age. Until next time." I turned to walk up the ramp, leaving him and the artificial smile on my face behind.

CHAPTER TWO

Microphones and cameras were shoved in our faces as Aidan and I shouldered through the throng of reporters with grim determination. Aidan quickly climbed into the passenger seat of my vehicle, slumping in his seat with relief that he'd made it through. Yumi, who had jumped in first, narrowly missed being sat on as she happily leapt into the backseat.

Gale popped out from dashboard, their natural glamour hiding them from Quotes unless they chose to be revealed. The little gremlin chattered with so much excitement I could barely understand them. I opened the door a crack and squeezed through, wanting to leave no opportunity for a reporter to get inside. I ignored the cry of protest as I slammed the door on a mike, then slammed it again as the owner of the microphone quickly retracted it. I wasn't worried about potential damage to the 4Runner since I had a whole host of gremlins back at BBSR's facility. Especially not when Gale clapped their hands in excitement upon seeing the scratches in the paint.

I cringed as I sat in the driver's seat, the leather squeaking in protest and burning the fuck out of my ass, even through the fabric of my pants. You would think something like a hot leather seat in a record-setting heat wave wouldn't be able to affect someone who could control fire, but *no*. I had to suffer like everyone else.

Well. *Almost* everyone else. The littlest of the gremlins, used to the blistering heat of engines, was unaffected by the hotbox they had been in for hours, and climbed my shoulder, gesturing wildly at my new stereo system with pride. Every now and then, if the work on a vehicle didn't require engine repair, the gremlins liked to come along for a ride to see their work in action. I smiled tiredly at Gale, this smile genuine, while Aidan snorted.

"I'm pretty sure you're the only creature in existence that would revert a perfectly functional modern stereo back to a cassette player."

I put the SUV in reverse. The press scattered like roaches as I gunned it out of the parking lot. I mentally wished Danly luck with them before I stabbed a finger in Aidan's direction. "Listen. I have had to completely redo my music collection too many times in my long life. No more. It's too damn expensive."

"But cassettes, Cam? Really? They're, like, the least practical option." Gale opined their agreement with Aidan. *Traitor.* But so long as they kept… *down*-dating my stereos, I would keep on loving them.

"Records are less practical. They're too big in a car if you're trying to put a new record in or change sides. And CDs? With how often they scratch? Absolutely not. We won't talk about all the other options that have been around."

"Scratches? Please. How often do you have to respool your tapes?" He motioned to my floorboards. "And you can't tell me they don't take up a shit ton of space."

The conversation was eerily reminiscent of one I had had with Rafael. I wondered briefly if the huntsman had known how well he would have blended with my team if he had been given time, and I shoved the thought down as quickly as it had appeared.

Instead, I lifted my chin and shifted into drive. "Since when does space matter when you have *magic*?"

Gale's hands landed on their hips as they glared at me. I corrected myself, "Okay, a *gremlin* with magic who can create a pocket in the liminal sera for storage."

Aidan shook his head and reached back to begin riffling through said pocket for music. "Bluetooth? Streaming?"

I scoffed and slapped his hand. "Magical Fixer of My Stereo gets to pick my music, since Pea isn't here." A squeaky whoop sounded, and Gale dived into the back. "Why would I want my music on something intangible like a goddamn *cloud*, Aidan? Clouds vaporize and vanish in thin air. I'm not having the digital version of that happen to my music collection."

"You are a *dinosaur*. You don't text, you don't use streaming services—"

"I use streaming services on my TV!"

"Oooooh, watch out world! Cam is finally entering the twenty-first century!"

I shoved his shoulder affectionately as Gale inserted a tape into their newly installed stereo. "Shadows" by Cannons began playing softly throughout the vehicle. The magical amplification Gale had added made the experience an immersive one. I did my best to ignore the lyrics, not wanting a reminder of other shadows currently absent from my life.

Aidan sighed happily. "At least you and Gale have good taste." He held a hand out to the gremlin, who gave him a high five before scampering into the back to snuggle up with Yumi. "Speaking of shadows…"

A groan squeezed out of me. So much for ignoring the lyrics. "Are we talking the *kariudo*, the giant ass of an entity, or Toyotama? Well, technically Toyo doesn't have that kind of *ki*, but the dead do like to yank her around."

"I'm sorry…*what?*"

I waved him off. "Remember the issues we had with the scent disappearing when we were searching for"—I coughed—"Misaki Aoki, otherwise known as Toyotama-hime?"

"Yeah, but I thought that was Rafael transporting her all over the place to fuck up our search."

"Good assumption, but no. He was only in America for the tail end of our search and was responsible for her appearing in the forest. She disappeared on her own when she fell off the cliff, but Rafael was still able to collect her since she dropped into Yomi," I explained. "Remember the rumors of the *bijin* and how she would vanish mysteriously?"

We now knew the *bijin* had been Toyo. Aidan nodded, the light beginning to turn on in his brain.

"Well, all her disappearances over the past century couldn't have been due to the *kariudo*," I pointed out, as the wards that hid the small Abstruse town of Blue Bear washed over me. I ignored the sensation of prickles all over my body. "The sickness that Ryūjin—the real *kami*, not the imposter—had been trying to cure his daughter of was the power the dead have over her. They can yank her into Yomi whenever they so please, then jettison her back out of the underworld."

Horror suffused Aidan's face. I shrugged as I left Main Street and headed toward Aidan's small cabin a few miles away from my home. "Toyotama, the *kami* and princess of the sea god, was used to it and had some level of control over it. Misaki did not. Toyo thought she had simply gone mad when she had been trapped in a Quotidian body."

"That sounds *awful*." A shudder passed through his body. "I can't imagine having no control over what realm I was in."

"Eh. Live with it for tens of thousands of years and you get used to it, according to her. But if she's recently returned from the underworld, try to be extra nice to her or avoid her altogether. It makes her cranky. And no one wants a cranky crocodilian on their hands." She was still in Ryūgū-jō anyway, and had yet to come to America since she regained her *ki*. I suspected she was in full avoidance mode and mired in grief. I couldn't blame her—I would want to avoid this place, too, after living a fake life for so long.

"Anyway, no I wasn't talking about the sea princess. I was referring to *Rafael*." He drew out the huntsman's name with relish and stabbed a finger in my face. "What are you planning to do when you find him?"

I batted his finger away. Fingers in your face were the worst. That's why I used them. "We have to get those slave bands off before we can do anything with him." And that prospect was what I hated most of all. Not because he would be free, but because of what I would have to do in the process.

"You know that's not what I meant. Stop avoiding the topic, Cam. You *liiiiiked* him. You wanted to get freaky in the sack with him. You wanted to bear that demi-entity's children."

Why. Why me? I sagged into my seat. Sadly, the leather had cooled off with the air conditioning, thus rendering it incapable of burning me to ashes and subsequently leaving me to endure this conversation.

"Why am I even friends with you? Quotes' sake, I even *slept* with you." My face thudded into the steering wheel repeatedly while I waited for a car to turn at the stop sign.

"Exactly. You slept with me. Multiple times. So I know better than most what your tells are."

The *kamis*-damned finger was back in my face. I bit it. Naturally.

Aidan yelped and said finger recoiled rapidly into his own mouth. "You can't fool me. Cam and Rafael, sitting in a tree, *K-I-S—*"

"If you want to remain in the land of the living, you will shut your mouth now," I grumbled, cutting his garbled song off. The 4Runner heaved as we went in and over the potholes that pitted Aidan's road. "The male betrayed me in so many different ways. There will be no *kissing*. And there will be no children. With anyone. *Ever.*" I shuddered at the thought.

"Mm-hmm. And yet, you still fought by his side and went along with the plan. Kind of. Okay, you didn't go along with the plan at all. *Anyway.* He saved your life. I see that look in your eyes whenever his name is brought up."

Aidan's beautiful log cabin loomed in front of us, and I parked with great relief. "Out of the car. Write your report. And we will never speak of this again."

Cackles of glee erupted from him as he opened the door for Yumi to leap out. Before shutting it, he poked his head back in. "You know what happens to things that are rigid, right?"

"They get off?"

"They *break*. Just think about it, Cam. You're going to have to face the male sooner or later." On that note, he shut the door and cheerfully made his way to his home with Yumi trotting at his side. I watched him closely until they were safely behind his doors. I was glad he was able to rib me and laugh—I would willingly be the butt of any of his jokes if it could wipe the heaviness that lurked in his gaze. But only time would be capable of that.

Just think about it, the male had said. As if I thought about anything else. My nightmares of *Hyakki Yagyō* had since been replaced with images of Rafael betraying me. The look on his face when he was dragged away from me by the bands encircling his forearms. His slight gasp of breath whenever I touched him. That slight flash of desire in his eyes. How could I not think about the male when he haunted my waking thoughts and visited me in my dreams? I shook my head as I pulled the 4Runner into a three-point turn and headed for home.

CHAPTER THREE

A dilapidated purple Geo Metro was parked in my usual spot when I pulled into my drive. The color was barely recognizable under the mud, dents, and scratches that littered the body. Four cracks spanned the entire windshield with multiple chips pitting the glass. The side mirrors were duct-taped back to the car. Forget about the rearview mirror—that was missing altogether. Not that a rearview mirror would be helpful with a backseat filled to the brim with odds and ends that most would consider garbage.

"Fuck," I muttered to Gale, cringing. "I forgot what day it was."

The little gremlin snickered from where they sat on my dashboard as they stared longingly at the car. I'm sure they were fantasizing about all the work they could do on it. Alas, Reika would never let the gremlins touch her car. The rest of society just had to be aware of the danger she posed whenever she took the trash heap on the road. Gale would have to settle for my air conditioner. The poor unit had been working overtime during this heat wave and had taken its last breath last night.

I took my time getting out of my vehicle, Gale now perched on my head. I dawdled while inspecting each and every piece of my gear before unloading it. Dragged my feet to check my mail. Anything to put off facing being a complete and utter disappointment to the *yamauba*.

"This is stupid," I said aloud. "Why am I hesitating to enter my own home?"

"I wasn't going to question it, but you do look pretty stupid." Out of the mouths of gremlin babes. I would have glared at the voice coming from the top of my head, but alas, they were out of my range of sight. Pea always sat on my head for the exact same reason.

With that in mind, because I was a *strong, empowered, female who wasn't afraid of no powerful witch,* I entered the sauna that was my home with false bravado, shuffling through the mail like it was a shield and pretending to be unaffected by the wall of heat that slammed into me. My house in which there was a conspicuous absence of a certain *yamauba.* The lack of her presence only ratcheted up my apprehension. It was like waiting for a jack-in-the-box to spring at you, except, instead of a freaky puppet head on a spring, it was an old, crochety, vicious hag.

I threw the mail on the couch and made my way into the living room, tension building with every step. A barrage of chirps and hisses hit my ears as Pea admonished me for nearly nailing her with the bundle of letters. She was burrowed in the nest she had made out of my clothes, pillow, and... *were those sticks she had added since I last saw her?*

"I love you, Pea, but no sticks on the couch," I said with fondness, but worry plagued me and I winced as I felt a pang in my chest. Ever since I had shifted on Mount St. Helens and had come back slightly...wrong, the fragments of my body liked to drift and jump around when I experienced any negative emotions. The subsequent shifts I had done shortly after hadn't helped the situation at all. Apparently, it wasn't enough to have my mind spiraling, my body had to as well.

That wasn't all that had changed about me. But I didn't want to think about the *other* foreign invasion of my person. I had successfully kept thoughts of it stuffed in the dusty corner of my mind all day and I wasn't about to let it out now.

A cold nose shoved its way through Pea's tightly curled body. Her heavy tail whacked Woodrow across the snout in reprimand, but he kept forcing his way past her barriers until she finally uncurled and stood, hissing at the malamute.

"Quit that. He's only worried about you. You've barely left this nest, except to gather more objects for it, since we returned to Blue Bear." A quiet thumping, accompanied by a rhythmic swishing, added Vicky and Max's agreement with my words from their dog pile at the base of the couch. "I know it wasn't actually Ryūjin, but seeing him as if he were still alive and going back to Ryūgū-jō was like losing him all over again." I sighed. "I wish I could stay on this couch with you and not leave either." A warm breeze brushed over our group, generated from the stand fan working its ass off in the corner to keep the living room tolerable. Vicky and Max slept directly in front of the box fan aimed at the couch, preventing any air from reaching the rest of us.

After I eyed my surroundings and found myself satisfied by the continued absence of Reika, I stuffed myself next to Pea, lifting Woody's massive paws and head and settling them back over my lap so I could fit on the sofa between the two of them. It may have been sweltering outside, but puppy cuddles were worth the heatstroke. The mail crunched and wrinkled underneath me, but I wasn't up for caring about it tonight. Gale leapt from my head and landed on Pea, who snapped her jaws at the gremlin before the little immortal opossum sniffed and turned her back to us, returning to a tiny ball of grief and depression. I wasn't much better as I stroked Woody's soft ears and stuffed my feet under the dog pile below us.

"You're late."

Fuck. Gale and I jumped at the sound of Reika's voice coming from immediately behind my ear. Everyone else remained content in their spots, used to the comings and goings of the witch.

"Boundaries!" I admonished Reika while choking around the segment of heart that had lodged itself in my throat.

"You get boundaries when you master the *ki* within you." She spat on the ground in disgust. I returned her disgust as my upper lip curled at the sight of a loogie on my beautiful hardwood floors.

If she made me swallow *that* to see if we could work Ryūjin's *ki*, then I was fetching my *tamatebako* from its pocket in the liminal sera and opening it to end my existence. If not to escape the torture Reika was putting me under, then out of spite so she didn't get what she wanted.

"At least you aren't as lazy as the other one. *Psh.* Girl hasn't even shown up once."

Girl. Toyo was eons older than this harridan. I had a feeling Reika was a big reason why she hadn't returned from Ryūgū-jō yet.

Reika was gearing up to spit on my floor again. "Don't you fucking dare. I don't spit in your cave, you don't spit in my home. If you're not going to hold to my boundaries, then you *will* hold to basic manners. There are more ways to express your disgust with us than *spitting on my goddamn floors.*"

She waved me off. "What progress have you made? And why is it so warm in this room, can you not afford a better fan?"

I stared at her. "Since you were here two days ago? None. I've been working. Which I told you I would be doing when you left. Which I told you I would continue to do when you first demanded this of me months ago." I ignored her question about the temperature and my finances.

Before she could respond, a voice echoed all around us. The one and only time I would be grateful for this entity's invasion of my privacy. Apparently, doors in my home were utterly unnecessary now. Why would they be needed when everyone assumed they were open anyway?

"We have a lead."

I didn't even react as my home rattled with the supernatural equivalent of surround sound, not bothering to turn from the glare I aimed at Reika. Vicky's tail wagged slightly in my peripherals. Figures. She was in love with Rafael; of course she'd love his ancestral grandfather.

"What now?" I asked, turning to the entity as Reika's face contorted into a sneer.

"You! You are the reason why she is always distracted. You and that boy of yours."

The giant stag bared fangs at Reika. I startled at the sight of them—I wasn't sure when he had added those to his repertoire.

"After I took you to Korea for our last lead, I encountered some of your delightful Siberian musk deer. You like?"

"Sure. Fangs are the new black. Why are you here this time?" I asked warily.

"He finally surfaced."

I eyed the hooves scratching up my floors. One day, after this was all over, I was going to have to have these floors completely refinished. Dog claws had nothing on deer hooves or *yamauba* spit. "You've said that before, only for nothing to pan out. I'm not holding my breath."

"Yes, *deer*. She has much more important things to do. Like live. How is she supposed to rescue your little grandson if she's dead?"

Eh. Living was overrated. So was Rafael.

One of the deer hooves stomped. A frame fell off the wall as my house shuddered again. I cringed internally at the damage my house was suffering. "Those were possible sightings of Orochi's human form. But this time, there have been reported findings of a land formation in Wrangell–St. Elias National Park." The hoof vanished into a cloud of dark mist that hovered over my remote control before turning on the news.

New Mountain Range Discovered in Alaska, Three Scientists Presumed Dead ran across the news ticker at the bottom of the screen. I sat up slowly as the shot panned out to show several mountain peaks.

Eight peaks. And eight valleys, to be exact.

Reika muttered something under her breath, so softly I couldn't make out the words, before raising her voice, "What is that *baka* doing? The idiot is going to reveal us to the Quotes."

I didn't disagree, but I had more pressing matters on my mind. I moved out from under Woody, leaving him grumbling and resettling on the couch, and carefully stepped over the two K9s at my feet so I could move closer to the TV. "Whiz?"

The gremlin materialized out of the TV. Gale squealed in delight. Meanwhile, the golden stag's face grimaced, baring its curved fangs again. It was unsettling. Musk deer fangs were one thing…these were more like straight-up tusks. "That is entirely unnatural," he said with disdain.

"Says the death entity who dissipates into a black mist and randomly decided to sport fangs," the *yamauba* said wryly. I was glad I wasn't alone, even if it was Reika agreeing with me.

"I am part of the natural order. Technology is not."

I ignored his commentary and gestured to the TV. "Whiz, do you have any intel on this?"

The nine-and-five-eighths-inch tall gremlin had wrapped a bright green circuit board around himself like a wrap dress, the copper traces gleaming in the light. We weren't allowed to say nine-and-a-half inches. That eighth of an inch had to be recognized. And you know what? As a fellow short person, I could empathize. Standing next to their father, it was apparent that Gale would mature into a combination of the archetypal World War II gremlins, like Whiz, and the pop culture version of Gizmo. Tulpas were fun like that.

While I had been talking to the stag, Gale had excitedly leapt off the couch at the sight of their father. Whiz squinted at the screen while chewing on the flash drive in his mouth and patted his child on the head. "Gimme a sec. Wanna go for a ride, kiddo?" Gale nodded with a wide grin on their face.

Gale had the natural talent for machinery that all gremlins had, but as Whiz's child, they loved every opportunity to explore the digital world to build upon their skills.

The two of them vanished from sight, leaving me alone with Anhangá and Reika once again. I refused to contemplate his news as a possible lead until we had more information. We had been burned enough in the past few months.

"Some optimism wouldn't kill you, little guardian."

"So sayeth the one enshrouded in black mist and dealing in souls," I muttered.

"Black is slimming and beautiful."

I scoffed. It wasn't like Anhangá needed it. I had seen him take a human form exactly once, and I now knew where Rafael had gotten his height and strong facial features.

"We will find them."

"How do you know this," Reika challenged.

"Really, hag. Where else in the world is a new mountain range popping up? One specifically with *eight peaks and eight valleys.* It's like I am surrounded by incompetence. Of course it's Orochi, and wherever that *kami* is, Rafael will be found."

My gut tightened at the thought. I both wanted to see the huntsman and dreaded it at the same time. Rationally, I understood the reason behind his actions. Emotionally? Betrayal wasn't so easy an emotion to get over, even if he had saved my life. Could that even count toward balancing the scales when he had been the one to put me in this situation to begin with? Then there were the nightmares that only served to complicate my feelings further.

You're the one who went off script, said the annoying voice in the back of my head. I shoved it down again, uncomfortable with facing the thought.

Who could say whether we would have been better or worse off if we had followed Rafael and Anhangá's plan? That trail of thought led to monsters in the depths of my mind.

"Do you ever *not* think?" asked Anhangá. "No wonder you and my grandson are perpetually stressed."

The glare I shot him went unnoticed, as had every other glare I'd ever given him. He continued instead, "Have you been successful in deciding our next steps when my grandson is retrieved?" A pointed look was aimed at the hidden scars that decorated my forearms.

And therein lay one of the major reasons why I wasn't looking forward to finding Orochi and Rafael. Because I would have to beg from someone I desperately didn't want to beseech.

"You will have to get over this annoying avoidance trait of yours at some point, little *haetae,* if we are to make any progress."

"You're the entire reason why he has the slave bands in the first place," I replied, venom dripping from my voice as I recalled what I had seen from Rafael's life.

"Yes, well, they served their purpose then. Now they are inhibiting us from moving forward."

I couldn't even. I opened my mouth, ready to eviscerate the entity, only to have the other equally irritating presence in my life interrupt me.

"She doesn't have time to go gallivanting around the globe on your little tasks. Ryūjin's *ki* must be made whole. I would ask if you even cared, but you obviously don't know how."

"Aw, Reika. I had no idea you cared. I just figured you enjoyed coming up with new disgusting ways to make me suffer for being *lazy*." I felt like the child of a custody battle where neither parent actually wanted the child but still fought over who got to keep them out of spite.

I was taking glee in her inability to respond when the gremlins leapt back out of the TV and put a halt to the tirade she was brewing. Maybe karma was on my side after all. Then again, maybe not, based on the grim looks on their faces.

"The new mountain range was discovered about six weeks ago," Whiz reported. "A team of researchers was sent out to investigate it since no unusual seismic activity had been identified. They stopped reporting about two weeks ago. The news is understating it for once. The entire team is missing, not just three scientists. Anyone who has been sent on a SAR is also missing. Whoever is trying to keep this under wraps has done an excellent job. Gale has uploaded everything we found on the topic to the servers." The gremlin looked exhausted. The magic he had utilized to find out the information had obviously been immense. His skin, normally a dark forest-green, had faded like the color had been leeched out of it and he was now a pale version of his formerly rich hue.

I tensed at Whiz's news. Alaska's SAR teams were excellent. They had to be, considering the deadly terrain they navigated and the sheer number of people who went missing in their state. For their teams to also go missing was concerning.

Gale dashed back up to my shoulder so they could be better heard. "The damning evidence is that the formations keep *shifting*, Cam. The range changes position every few days." Their eyes made contact with their father before they continued. "We think this might be the real deal this time."

Anhangá nodded in satisfaction. "I told you it was legitimate this time."

I inclined my head stiffly in return. "So you did." And that meant I needed to get off my ass and prepare for whatever scene greeted us when we finally found the *kariudo*. I sighed in defeat. "At least we have a location to start from, rather than having to search for a ten-million-acre-sized haystack." I turned to Anhangá. "Can you take me to Cheuksin?"

A wicked smile overtook the stag, and darkness obscured my vision before I could offer my gratitude to the gremlins. Or do anything about the *yamauba* in my house. The awful sensation of my body being disassembled overwhelmed me as we dematerialized from Blue Bear and reappeared in my Neskowin kitchen.

CHAPTER FOUR

Before I could fully take form, a thick fibrous cord wrapped around my neck and yanked me off my feet, sending me crashing to the floor as the rest of the cells making up my body settled into their places. A small figure kneeled menacingly over me, their face shielded by a thick curtain of black hair.

Fucking Anhangá. I held up my hands in submission as three light coughs sounded from behind me, tinged with amusement. I just knew the bastard had a cervid look of glee on his face at the sight of me on the floor.

The cord slowly unwound itself from my neck and the black curtain shrank back to its normal length to reveal Cheuksin. The comfortably cool air in the home felt amazing and I sucked it in greedily. It would take a few days for the bruising around my neck to heal without Pea around, the injury not being severe enough to warrant magical intervention.

"Why would you just drop into this house after everything this territory went through a few short months ago," the tiny goddess hissed at Anhangá. "Use the gods-damned door and *knock* like a normal person."

"Why be normal when I can be me?"

Cheuksin and I snorted at the same time as she held out a hand to help me to my feet.

"Fuck, I hate traveling like that," I muttered, adjusting my position in an attempt to find a drop of comfort in my own body. I gave up and rubbed my throat.

"Ah, but it beats Portland traffic." A flash of concern lit Anhangá's eyes for a fraction of a second before he reverted back to his amused stare. "You don't have many shifts left, little *haetae*. Have you shifted since I last saw you?"

I grimaced. "Maybe."

Only two week ago, I had encountered a family of *onikuma* that had fully descended into delirium from the starvation they had endured in Ryūgū-jo during a SAR in Southern Oregon. My impending death wasn't something I wanted to dwell on right now. I shoved the thoughts of the battle to the back of my head, not wanting additional commentary about it, and faced Cheuksin instead. "We think we've found them."

A host of emotions skewed her face. "And now we have to go through with it, don't we?"

"We do. I'm so sorry."

She sighed and took a seat on one of the stools. "Why do I care about saving a world hell-bent on destroying itself?"

"To be fair, much of that is due to whoever is pulling the puppet strings and destroying the guardians," Anhangá said wryly.

"Like I said…why do I care? The fact the world even needs guardians to prevent the Quotes from destroying this place and each other says enough."

She wasn't wrong.

"Perhaps because all of the realms are tied with Earth's continued existence, and if Earth fails, the sera feeding all the realms will bleed out and doom the rest to the same fate?" The stag raised an eyebrow.

"Oh yes. That detail." Cheuksin's lip curled. "Fine. I will break my silence with my family and summon Seokga."

A bead of sweat dripped between my shoulder blades. Anhangá dipped his head once again and vanished in a cloud of black mist. The task of breaking my slave bands had nearly killed me. I had no idea what it would do to Rafael. The male was close to being eternal, but as the Quotes liked to say—close only counted in horseshoes and hand grenades.

Cheuksin glanced at the clock as the last particles of Anhangá vanished and shook her head. "We'll give it a few more hours. Seokga likes to start his days late. We'll only be asking for his ire if we summon him now."

The relief at having the ordeal put off until evening was stupidly immense. I tried to hide the physical signs of it and asked, "How have the refugees been settling in?"

Her shoulders sagged with frustration and a touch of fatigue. "The factions have already formed. The Abbies who were already here had naturally segregated themselves by region. Now they're segregating themselves even further—by type of *yōkai*, how they arrived to the States, age, region…you name it, they'll find a reason to do it."

I rubbed my face with the palms of my hands, digging into my eyes like the motion was a magical cure to my stress. It was a natural occurrence, cultural and language differences being what they were. But beyond that, immortal beings were gold medal champions in holding grudges. When an atrocity happened to you, as opposed to an ancestor, it was hard to let go of that level of well-deserved resentment. It wasn't generational trauma. No, it was lived trauma that accumulated and compounded upon itself. A body can't heal when a wound is constantly being reopened. The mind was no exception to the rule.

Cheuksin dipped her head and leaned it against my shoulder. "The Uncles are on it. If anyone can do it, it'll be them."

"The Uncles will find some way to unite them through a shared love of erotica," I said fondly. The goddess shook my body as she vibrated with snickers.

"Probably." The affection in her eyes for the Uncles was even greater now after they had gone through their shared experience of defending the Neskowin territory. Well, one Uncle did anyway. Aidan and his boisterous uncle had been whisked away to safety by Rafael after Orochi had set a *kotengu* on them.

Yet another reason to be grateful to the *kariudo*, despite his actions that spoke otherwise.

"What will you need to do to summon Seokga?" I was curious despite myself. I wasn't a goddess—I had to go through the entire *gut* ritual when I had sought to break my own bands. Food and drink I could do, but my skill at song and dance had offended many before Seokga had been willing to help me out of sheer amusement.

"I'm going to call him, Cam. On the phone." She looked at me like I was crazy. "How else would I get a hold of him?"

"I—"

"Oh my gods. You did the *gut* ritual didn't you?" Cackles erupted from my terrible friend. "*You* sang and danced? *Aish*. The male is going to ask you for a repeat performance as soon as he realizes you're here."

Fuck my life.

"Over my dead and decaying body."

Still cackling, albeit less intensely, Cheuky shook her head and went about the kitchen, ingredients seemingly appearing out of thin air. She began washing the uncooked rice that had dropped onto the counter.

"It's been far too hot. We're having *samgyetang*. You'll need your salt replenished if you're going to be singing and dancing in this heat," she said as she moved on to rinsing the Cornish game hens and began stuffing them with the rice and smashed garlic cloves. "It was also one of Seokga's favorite dishes, if I recall correctly."

I wouldn't be singing and dancing again if I could help it, but I appreciated Cheuky's knowledge of the trickster god. Perhaps we'd get off easy on the tasks we needed to free Rafael. And perhaps I was made of cotton candy and would dissolve with the next rainfall.

Cheuksin tied off the hens and tossed them in the stockpot that had landed on the stove, along with some ginseng, red dates, and green onions. Once filled with water, she set the lid on to allow the ingredients to come to boil. Washing her hands, she continued, "You're lucky. Seokga is one of the few members of my family I can still somewhat stand. He set you on my path to freedom, after all."

Pain flashed through her features. Her brows furrowed slightly and her shoulders crept up as she recalled her past. I came around the counter and gave her a hug. "And he gave me one of my best friends as a result. Even if you tried to kill me on our very first meeting, and have continued to try ever since." I shuddered internally at the memory of the STIs she had inflicted on me in that first meeting. Abbies were supposed to be immune to that sort of thing, but not when it came to Cheuky. It made the infections so much worse, because Abbies had no way to treat something that wasn't supposed to impact them.

She smiled weakly. "Good thing you're so damn hard to kill." She booped my nose and slipped my embrace to dry off her hands. It was subtle and well-done, but a gesture we both appreciated. Neither of us were good with prolonged physical touch.

"Now. How are *you* doing, Cam?" Concern laced her tone. "The only times I've seen you since June have been filled with getting shit settled for the refugees of Ryūgū-jō. We haven't actually sat down and talked." Evidently this was becoming a theme in my life. The deity continued, "I can't believe you managed to hide your identity as the last *haetae* from all of us for so long. To say nothing of you being Threaded. You can't possibly be okay after everything."

I sighed. The female was excellent at holding her silences, but when she decided something needed digging, she didn't let up. I stared into the pot of game hens, willing it to boil, if only to give me something to do. "I'm not great."

A guffaw erupted from my friend. "*Not great.* I'm pretty sure that'd be the understatement of the decade."

"Probably," I agreed. "I haven't slept well since before May."

"Nightmares?"

"Nightmares." My confirmation came with the need to sit, and I pulled a stool to the other side of the counter so we could face each other for this conversation. "Except these ones are new. Because the thing I needed most was more nightmare fodder."

"About the *incident?*"

"Sure, the *incident*, since that seems to be what everybody is calling that clusterfuck of a situation, but moreso…" I hesitated.

"Moreso…" The silence that followed Cheuksin's pause was heavy with expectation.

"The *kariudo*," I blurted.

"Mm-hmm. And *what* about the *kariudo*."

My leg bounced under the counter, betraying my agitation over this subject. Thank the *kamis* it was out of sight. Though I was sure there were other physical signs giving it away.

"I was starting to…*like* him?"

"Are you asking me if you liked him?" Amusement filled Cheuksin's voice as her lips lifted slightly in a wry smile. "Pretty sure only you could tell me whether or not you did."

"Fucking fine. I liked the male."

"Liked? Or *like-liked*?"

"Oh my gods. Are we middle school Quotes, female?"

The little bitch snickered. "You really think I couldn't tell, Cam? Of course you liked the huntsman. It was apparent to all of us. You had a look when you interacted with him that no one has ever seen before. We all knew you wanted to jump his bones. Does he even truly have bones?" she mused.

Embarrassment flooded my body and heated my cheeks. I hid them in my hands and groaned. "Cheuksin, tell me that's not true."

"As if. I'm not about to encourage your lies to yourself."

"Ugh. *Fine*. I *like-liked* the male, to use your words."

"And he's taken a starring role in your nights. Oh my, Cam. How absolutely scandalous." Her eyes practically sparkled as she teased me.

"I hate you." *And Aidan*, I added in my head. Quotes above, had I been so obvious that not only one but *two* of my friends were giving me shit over this?

"No, but for real, Cam. That must have made his betrayal that much worse."

My feet dropped from the rung on the stool as my entire body let go of the tension it was carrying. "It really did," I admitted.

"Is he the first male since… I know you've slept with others, but I never had an impression they were more than a casual lay."

"Because they weren't."

"So he was different. What made him different?"

I hesitated. Every time I thought about Rafael, I did my best to shove him back out of my brain. Doing the opposite felt unnatural and far too easy all at once.

"The way he took the time to ask about Vicky and listened to what I had to say about her. No, actually—the way he listened, *period*. The way my K9s loved him, even Woody at the end. The way he came to love Pea and tried to take care of her. His moral compass, which is in direct opposition to what he's had to do in life. The way he saved Olly. His gods-damned *forearms*. And his ass. Cheuky, no ass should look that good in trekking pants."

The goddess threw her head back and laughed.

"It *is* a mighty fine peach. Did you want to take a bite?"

I reached over the counter and punched her shoulder. "Cheuky!"

Then, "Maybe."

"I knew it. What are you going to do when you see him again?"

The stockpot and its contents began boiling at last and I got up to skim the broth. "Aidan asked me the same thing," I admitted.

"Ha. I told you we could all tell. Let me guess…you didn't answer."

"Because I don't *know*. I don't think I'll know for sure until I see him again."

"That's valid as hell, Cam. Maybe leave the weapons at home in case your first reaction is to kill him though."

"Anhangá would just bring him back," I muttered.

"Well, how many times do you think you'd have to kill him to feel better about it? You already have once, from what you've told me."

"I don't want to kill him!"

"Okay, so that's one option off the table. You gonna kiss him?"

"No!"

"So that's two options gone now. Look at you go."

"Ugh, you are the *worst*."

"And proud of it. In all reality, you don't need to know how you're going to react ahead of time. But at least take the time to riffle through your feelings first so they don't hit you all at once."

It wasn't bad advice, but I wanted to hide under a rock with the idea of having to feel my feelings. My skin crawled at the thought.

"There's something else, too," I confessed.

Cheuky's eyebrow raised.

"I…I think I died in Ryūgū-jō." I hadn't admitted that to anyone who hadn't been there yet. Cheuky's already fair skin paled to an ashen gray.

"You're not allowed to die," she finally said, firmly.

"It's not my death that's been bothering me. I've been anticipating it— no, before you protest, let me finish. I always knew Death was imminent after I realized what Ryū's *ki* was doing to me, just not *when* it would happen. But this was different. All I knew was that I had been poisoned by the hemlock sap and fading, then suddenly I was back again. But with something…extra."

Her nose scrunched. "What do you mean by *extra*? Did you come back possessed or something?"

"No. I'm pretty sure I came back with… Fuck this sounds crazy, Cheuks."

"We're Abbies. Everything that happens around us seems crazy," she replied matter-of-factly. "Spit it out already. You're killing me. No pun intended."

"I think I came back with some of Rafael *in* me."

I realized too late how that sounded and Cheuky wheezed with laughter.

I frowned at the Outhouse Goddess. "Not like *that* and you damn well know it. No, now when I drop my glamours, there's a black matter, similar to Rafael's *ki*, that rises from my scars. I can see it when I look in the mirror, too."

I'd nearly screamed after the first shower I took when I got home and wiped the steam from the mirror.

"How do you know it's Rafael and not the natural progression of your illness?"

I paused, considering. "Because it feels like him. I don't know how to describe it, but if you could condense his entire personality and all his masks into an incorporeal substance, it would feel like this. Not only that but..."

Cheuksin waited patiently.

"But...I can feel emotions that aren't mine. And Cheuksin. I can feel overwhelming *pain* in addition to my own. If it is a piece of Rafael, he's not doing well."

The pain was one thing. I'd lived with pain so long that I was used to placing it on a shelf and slamming the door shut on it for the most part. The absolute emptiness that seized my heart's fragments was entirely different. Anhangá had confirmed that Rafael's soul had reached him several times since being recalled to the *kami*. But the magic binding the *kariudo* would snatch him back as soon as his soul had the slightest of tethers again, preventing Rafael from saying anything to his grandfather.

"How the hell do you get yourself in these situations, Cam?"

"Hey! Don't blame the victim," I protested. "It's not like I asked these males to leave a li'l something extra in me. I did not consent here."

"No, but here we are. Yet again." She sighed.

"I don't know what you want me to do about it. It's not like I had any control over Ryūjin and Rafael's actions."

"*Males.*"

Truer words have never been spoken.

Cheuksin shuffled over to check the *samgyetang*, then herded me out of the kitchen. "On that note, go wash up before dinner. You smell like dead fish."

"Thanks. It's my new perfume. *Eau de iwana bōzu.* You like?"

"It's positively delightful. Only second to *eau de* outhouse. Now shoo before it embeds itself into the walls of this kitchen, and go enjoy the finer things this time period has to offer, like running water."

CHAPTER FIVE

lone at last. I sighed with relief as I entered my bedroom. A hot breeze blowing gently through an open window carried hints of the ocean air. It had been over forty-eight hours since I'd last been by myself. I loved my friends, I did. But I enjoyed silence even more. Pea recognized this and would often round up and drive the K9s away to play elsewhere when I needed to recharge. Or fall into a pit of grief and depression. Those had been fewer and farther between until recent months.

Pea was currently drowning in her own ocean of melancholy though, and our roles had reversed. I frowned as I entered my bathroom, pulling my shirt up and over my head and dropping it on the floor while I crossed the threshold. I wasn't used to her absence, and I wasn't sure how to support my friend as she fought through her grief. The last time she had been embroiled in it, I had been right there with her.

This time, grief took a backseat in my mind. Instead, all I could feel was rage when I thought of my Thread. An all-encompassing inferno of anger, resentment, and fury.

I was pissed and there was nothing I could do about it, because Ryūjin had died over a century ago, ruining not just my life but his entire kingdom's. My vision began to drift into a sea of molecules as my thoughts spiraled. I took a deep breath and shook out my hands, doing my best to calm down and make a concerted effort to pull my mind back to the present. As my vision returned to normal, I unbuttoned my pants and stepped out of them. If only I could shed the past as easily.

A thin limb, mottled like the color of a rotting wound, caught my eye as it slipped behind my shower door.

A shriek left my mouth before I could control myself, and I snapped the towel from the rack to wrap around my mostly bare body, tripping over the pants I had dropped to the floor. I caught myself on the towel bar, managing to wrench the whole thing out of the wall with my weight, just barely gaining enough traction to right myself again. I was only minimally grateful that I still wore a bra and underwear as I ripped the shower door open, towel bar with protruding screws held high, ignoring the crash as the door bounced off the wall and slammed back into me.

A young *akaname* crouched in my shower, perched on the two digits of each hand and foot, staring at me with their single wide eye. Their thick, greasy hair fell to the middle of their back. A long tongue retracted slowly from the drain, a small tangle of hair wrapped around it, gnarled with accumulated scum.

I fought off my cringe from the sight and nodded to the small *yōkai*. They looked at me quizzically, their eye darting from my face to the towel bar. Pushing aside my bafflement that Cheuky would allow a bathroom to become dirty enough to attract an *akaname*, I bent down as if imparting a great secret and whispered, "Thank you for attending to my bath, but seek out the public bathrooms down at the state park. Be careful not to get caught while you're in the Quote realm."

Their eye widened and they nodded with excitement, rapping their knuckles on the toilet before scrambling out of the bathroom and through the open bedroom window. The toilet rattled as another, smaller *akaname* shot up and out of the tank, the lid clattering to the tile floor, and darted after them. I shook my head and shut the bedroom window behind them. Ocean breeze or not, I preferred privacy for my shower. I laid the bar on the counter as I reentered the bathroom and threw my towel in the hamper, not wanting to use a towel contaminated with the smell of death and fish to dry myself off. I started the water and bent down to replace the tank lid on the toilet. I was just grateful it hadn't shattered upon impact.

Steam began to fill the small room while I removed the rest of my clothing and stepped into the shower. I held my breath for a few seconds and relaxed when nothing formed out of the steam. Leaning my head against the shower wall, I allowed the accumulated fatigue and tension of the past few days to bleed out of me.

I'd had maybe eight minutes to myself, tops, when the temperature of my shower dropped drastically. The steam intensified with the temperature change and shaped itself into the form of a petite Korean female. A female with a gaping wound where her liver should have been. It was a battle to tear my eyes away from the necrotic void left in the vapor.

"Hello, *Eomma*."

My dead mother had started dropping in on me ever since Rafael tethered the fragments of my soul back to my body and left a piece of himself behind. Before, I could only see the spirits left behind that turned into the *yōkai* and ghosts with unfinished business. But now? Like everyone else in my life, my *eomma* dropped by with abandon and zero sense of decorum whenever I was alone.

The face in the steam frowned at my body and began making hand gesticulations. "*Aigoo*, this body? What have you done to it?"

"We go through this every time you show up." One might have thought she was referring to the broken state of my body. But no. My word to the ears of Abstruse gods, I did not have the patience for this today. "I am not fat; I am as healthy as I can get in my condition," I continued in English. The first time my mother had appeared in front of me, she insisted she wanted to practice her English after she got done berating me for screaming at the sight of her. So sue me for not expecting my long since murdered mother to suddenly show up while I was taking a shit.

Her vaporous hands fell to her hips as she glared at me. "You need to eat." She bustled around the shower as if she was looking for ingredients.

Did mothers across the world have specific mannerisms downloaded to their brain after giving birth? "You can*not* berate me for being fat, then tell me I need to eat in the next breath!"

She waved me off with an opaque hand that faded into wisps at the end of the motion. "Eat *right*. Not this American food you eat here. I have seen what you eat when I watch."

I pinched the bridge of my nose. "*Eomma.* What are you even looking for? We're in a *shower.*" I ignored the fact that I was fully nude—communal baths had been the norm when my mother had been murdered—it was the thought of eating food procured from a bathroom that held my focus.

Eomma turned to face me. "You make friends with Cheuksin, yes?"

I nodded.

"So how come no ginseng in this house?"

"Because, I repeat, we are in the bathroom. Not the kitchen."

"*Aish.* I am not looking in bathroom. You think your *eomma* stupid? What kind of child did I raise? This body can do many things now. Like *look in kitchen* when I am here." She pointed at the shower floor with a look on her face that clearly indicated that she thought her daughter was the stupid one. "And there is no ginseng."

"*Eomma,*" I said as gently as I could. "Ginseng is not going to fix this body and glue it back together. And Cheuksin probably used her current stock of ginseng for the *samgyetang* she's making."

She made a small sound of protest and shook the finger that had previously been pointing at the floor at me instead, to emphasize her point.

I reached out for her hands before I remembered that she was made of steam and let them drop again. "*Eomma.* I am going to die eventually. It's okay."

"Is *not.* You *haetae.* Strong, not...*this.* Not my daughter." Distress riddled her body, droplets of water forming from the empty space where her eyes should be before rolling down the steam shaping her face to join the cooling water of the shower. I turned the water off and reached for one of the unsoiled towels and wrapped it around myself, grateful that I had at least finished washing the stench from my body before she had shown up.

"We all die eventually. I have made my peace with it." She muttered some unsavory curses about Ryūjin under her breath, which I ignored. "Why have you come to visit?"

"Should I not visit my only child? Is my child so ungrateful that they do not appreciate seeing their dead *eomma?*"

The sigh I would sigh right now if it wouldn't get me into even more trouble with my mother. It was too bad I couldn't sic her on Orochi; she would have him corralled within three sentences.

"Of course I am happy to see you." *I just become riddled with more and more guilt over my failure to save you with every visit.* I pulled my gaze back from where it had drifted to her wound and went into the bedroom to find new clothes. She floated behind me. "But if you have something you need, I want to make sure I take care of that too, so I can be a good daughter."

One did not survive to adulthood with Asian parental figures without earning a PhD in tact. As it turned out, you could miss your parents with every passing moment after their deaths, but as soon as they turn back up, you get assaulted with all the reminders of why it was difficult to get along with them. At least when they were alive, things like walls and doors were barriers that afforded you an escape. My mother had transcended those barriers now.

Speaking of parents. "Why do you come but not *Appa*?" I asked as I slipped into a pair of lounge pants. I hadn't seen my father once since gaining this new ability.

She wrinkled her nose. "He say we should leave alone." She threw her hands up in exasperation. "He say, *we should leave to the 'natural order.'*" She dramatically mimed air quotations and scoffed. "What kind of parent is he? Letting his only child die. Shameful. He say we see you when you pass into the next world and join us, like it should be."

I winced. I didn't know if they knew I wouldn't be passing into any realm after this due to the state of my soul.

"He all the time forget once his daughter is gone, she is *gone*. You will not be joining us. *Michyeosseo.*"

Nope. Guess they knew. I wasn't sure if she was calling my father crazy for being in denial or commenting on the fact that I wouldn't pass into the next life.

A look of concern flashed across her face, and she pointed northwest. "We have not seen the *kariudo*. You must save him. He key to your life."

My eyes narrowed. "You know where he is?"

She shook her head, her form becoming more and more transparent as the steam evaporated. "*Ani.* No. The spirits who know him all look but cannot find. But he becoming smaller. Thinner. Like air." She motioned to her body, which was beginning to dissipate without the shower to keep the moisture in the air. "But spirits notice a new—what you call in

English—*presence* that way. The Japanese ones tell Izanami, who tell your father, who tell me today it feel like what they remember Orochi feel like."

I nodded, slowly pulling a tank top over my head, foregoing a bra in this weather. The Japanese Goddess of Creation and Death had to be thrilled that she had been made into a messenger. But, it made sense. Since I began working with Anhangá, I'd discovered that spirits were restricted to communicating with whomever reigned over the dead in their birthland, which was how Anhangá got his information. The only exception to this rule was when the deities and entities that oversaw Death visited a colleague's realm.

"You must hurry," my mother reiterated as her presence faded with the last of the vapors. "Otherwise, you too late."

CHAPTER SIX

Termites were burrowing through his body. Fire ants chewed through the remnants of his back. Baki's band of gremlins pounded away with abandon from the inside of his skull.

Rafael groaned as he woke and reality set back in. He was lying on his back—a back that was failing terribly at repairing itself. He sucked in a breath at the pain as he attempted to roll, forgetting that the act of breathing was as good as drowning. The thought of coughing was horrifying, but his body forced him through it to relieve his lungs of the blood accumulating in them.

He wasn't healing. He'd been through pain before. He'd even healed slowly in the past. But never *this* slowly, especially with the carousel of injuries that were laid upon his body on any given day. He would never take Abstruse healing for granted again. He wished these injuries were severe enough to kill him, so he had a chance to return whole for a brief respite before it began all over again. Then again, coming back healed meant his nerves also healed…and subsequently felt the full brunt of any new injuries.

There was no way to know how long he had been out this time. The forest cover was too dense for light to filter through, let alone into the cave he was trapped in. For all he knew, only a day could have passed in the eternity of his existence in this dark place. He only had the comfort of knowing that he wasn't in a temporal snare and potentially losing centuries of time. Or experiencing centuries of torture in the span of a day.

No. He wasn't in a temporal snare at all. He was hidden within a cave, somewhere in the forests and mountains of Orochi's body. The *kami* had discovered some of Rafael's secrets in the process of his torture. Not from Rafael's words, but through sheer observation. After he had killed him the first few times, Orochi had delighted in knowing that his *kariudo* was *unkillable*.

But it was all worth it.

Worth it to see some of the madness leave the *kami's* eyes as Camellia had attempted to pierce his heart. Worth it if only for the fact that he had been able to save her life.

Rafael shuddered as he was haunted by the image of Camellia lying so still. His fingers twitched as he felt the absence of her heartbeat under them once again. His *ki* strained against its bonds as they fought to tie the fragments of her soul that tried to dissolve into the ether.

She's not here. She is still alive. He could tell himself this until the *bitan* came home, but making himself *believe* it without being able to see her whole in front of him was another story.

His nightmares never let him forget. It was a relief when he lost consciousness due to the severity of his injuries, or when he died, yet again. It was the only respite from the memory.

She would have died either way once he had been set upon his task of tracking Dr. Ao—*Toyotama*, he mentally corrected himself. As soon as he had surfaced in Washington, the brand that ingrained Orochi's orders into his being had burned, activating in the presence of a *haetae*. At least he had been able to control the outcome and twist it to save the guardian.

He glanced down his torso through swollen eyes. Baki had died. The tattoo had faded to gray with her death. Even though she had risen again, for all intents and purposes, the last *haetae* had been killed.

It was absolutely fucking worth it.

She was still in danger, but she was no longer in danger from *him*. The *kami* wouldn't be able to command him to do anything related to *haetae* anymore, the magic in his slave bands now convinced that the species was eradicated. The comfort he gleaned from that knowledge was the only thing making the pain bearable.

Eyes blinked at him from the rock formation that made up the cave. "How long?" Rafael asked futilely.

The *shikigami* trapped in the rocks rolled its eyes, clearly communicating, *I have no mouth, why do you persist in asking me questions.*

"Who knows, maybe since the last time the *kami* flayed me, he was good enough to give *you* a mouth and *me* some company."

The eyes only narrowed at him in response.

Rafael sagged, wincing as the exposed muscles of his back protested the movement, tearing the newly formed scabs. New tattoos littered his chest, their orders entrenched in his soul, regardless of whether or not the tattoo was stripped from his body when the *kami* flayed his skin. They simply reappeared when his skin regrew.

Tattoos preventing him from leaving his cave. Tattoos forcing him to speak the truth. Blocking his ability to heal. His ability to shift forms. Tattoos that strengthened the geas that choked his ability to speak on any topics the *kami* deemed forbidden.

Orochi had well and truly leashed him.

The scars around the bands that gave the *kami* power over him also remained. A testament to the number of times he had tried to free himself over the decades, despite his promise to his grandfather.

His mind flickered back to Baki. The deep scars she had shown him around her forearms had left far more of an impact on his mind than the scars from her Thread being severed. Because it meant that freedom *was* possible.

It had left him with the *kamis*-damned feeling of hope. And hope was Death to someone like him. He had been far better off when he had been resigned to his fate.

Light footsteps approached the cave and the *shikigami* quickly closed its eyes, camouflaging itself as a darker shadow filled the entrance of the cave.

Where Ryūjin had been lithe and muscular, this *kami* was broader in the chest, thicker through the legs, his body coiled with power. His black hair was thick and wavy with a red gleam to it, like an ember in the night. His steps were quiet despite his bulk. Rafael knew he only heard the *kami's* approach because Orochi had wanted him to tense with anticipation.

Rafael forced his body to remain relaxed as he calmly looked back at the *kami* who had been the cause of so much chaos and destruction. A thin scar encircled his neck. A memento from one of the times the god had been decapitated, Rafael assumed.

Madness still glinted in the *kami's* eyes, although it was nowhere near the extreme it had been prior to Cam's attempt to take him down. Which was to Rafael's detriment—the commands given by Orochi were notably more ironclad with little room for interpretation.

"Where is the *haetae?*" Orochi hissed, his words echoing through the space despite his low tones.

Rafael remained still and responded, "The *haetae* perished." It was the truth and yet not.

A strike echoed through his body, the pain muffled through all the other noise screaming in him from his injuries.

"I know she is alive," a growl proclaimed. "Where is Camellia Kimoto?"

"I don't know." Yet another truth.

And that was the beauty of it all. He wasn't omniscient. He couldn't know where Baki was at this moment in time. For all he knew, she was deployed to search a natural disaster in another country. There was no room for interpretation in the *kami's* order to only be told the truth, which meant Rafael couldn't *guess.*

It was another consolation. At least he could still protect Baki in this way.

Another thorny vine whipped against his flesh and flayed a strip from it.

"I cannot tell you what I don't know," he said tranquilly in response to Orochi's temper.

Rafael knew better than to fight back as the *kami* rained his temper down on him. Even without the commands throttling Rafael's power, the being in front of him was simply a projection of the *kami's* minds. No, nothing he could do would harm the *kami,* because Orochi wasn't here.

He forced himself to remain calm. Because while he didn't know where *Cam* was precisely, he *did* know the location of the piece of himself that had sheared from him when he had fought to bring the *haetae* back to life.

And he suspected that shard had adhered itself to her soul.

CHAPTER SEVEN

After my mother dissipated, I wandered down the stairs and out onto the back porch, enjoying the sun setting over the Pacific Ocean as I dried my hair in a towel. Her parting words rang in my mind.

"You could have warned me about the *akaname* in my bathroom," I called through the open doors.

"And miss your delightful screams?" a deep, gravelly voice asked from behind my shoulder.

I stifled a shriek yet again as tension vibrated through my body. "You got here quickly," I responded carefully.

"Ah yes. Well, when dear Cheuksin throws in her *samgyetang* as incentive, one would be stupid to not accept the invite, no? I do admit, hearing your caterwauling while your muscles seized again may be equal to it."

I eyed Seokga as he settled into one of the Adirondack chairs, pulling his slacks up at the knees to maintain their pressed look. He looked as beautiful as one would expect a god to look. A thick lock of pitch-black hair fell over his forehead, a thick and slightly curled lock that would drive anyone with a preference for males to brush it back. I fought the urge to look down but failed as the god crossed an ankle over his knee, a knowing smirk on his face. The deity wore neon pink socks with upside-down pineapples and alicorns. Subtle. I watched as his eyes dragged from my toes to my hair, his gaze lingering on my hips and chest, and I fought the urge to squirm.

He had chosen the same chair Rafael had sat in when he had been here. I deliberately selected a different seat from the one I had sat in then to avoid a minor recreation of the scene. The absence of my K9s and Pea helped.

So did the new burn scars that streaked down the chairs. Yet another consequence of the spring's events.

"Cheuksin tells me you need to break another set of slave bands. As a god of trickery, I do so enjoy the situations you find yourself in." He eyed my glamoured arms with anticipation.

"They're not mine."

"Oh? And why should I be inclined to help with the removal of bands for someone I don't even know? Perhaps they deserve them."

I bristled immediately.

He raised a hand. "Easy, *haetae*. I only say this to test you. I don't believe such things. How can mayhem ensue with such tightly controlled binds?"

"Did you conveniently forget that you contributed to their creation?" I asked in disbelief.

Seokga shrugged. "They were fun the first few centuries, but the novelty quickly wore off the more they were used. No one was *creative* about how they used them."

I could feel a muscle tick in my jaw. This was why I hated talking to this deity. Actually, the majority of deities, Cheuksin excepted, had little to no respect for their creations.

"Now, who is it that needs the bands broken?" he asked.

I chose my words carefully, trying to pick the right combination to intrigue the rebellious side of him.

"It is the *kariudo* of Yamata no Orochi."

"Ah. Yes, the unveiling of Orochi shook the Eastern realms. Everyone is suspicious of whether or not they are who they say they are." He shivered with delight. "It's been wonderful. Nobody knew such magic existed. I only wish I had thought of it myself."

His response could be suggestive of one or two possibilities. He might be eager to release Rafael to see what further chaos might be caused by such an event. Or he might be on the side of Orochi and whoever puppeted him, because of the trickery *they* had wrought, and he wanted to see how it would play out as is. There were probably more scenarios, but my brain was broken from lack of sleep.

I banked on his desire to participate in the chaos himself and leaned toward the god. "Imagine how much more chaos could be invoked if you became involved and freed the puppet's puppet. You would wreak havoc on puppet inception."

A gleam of anticipation ensnared Seokga's gaze. Intrigue had him bending toward me, as I had hoped it would. "Do you not mean free the puppet from its puppet *master*?"

I sat back in my chair and inspected my nails, hoping I wasn't making the situation worse. "You didn't hear? The *kami* is only one piece of the puzzle in the downfall of the guardians in this world."

"And you know this how?"

I lifted a shoulder in fake casualness. "I pierced his heart. How else? Or should I say, I *tried* to pierce his heart. He has a wall of magic protecting the organ against Evil. He's fighting back."

"And why should I not want to see how it might play out if the *kami* should fall to Evil?"

"Please. That's too predictable for you. Instead of allowing Orochi to fall to Evil and the full influence of his controller, imagine what might happen if he was freed from that influence and sought vengeance instead?" I leaned toward him like I was about to divulge a particularly juicy bit of gossip. "Consider the level of potential destruction Orochi could unleash."

"Hmm." Seokga leaned back in his chair and tapped his chin. "That might prove entertaining. But how does freeing the huntsman come into play?"

"Well, we would need to undermine the *kami* in order to release Rafael from his master. Orochi's too powerful otherwise. And what better way than by removing the one carrying out the *kami's* commands."

"I do so enjoy when you try to be devious in an attempt to woo me to your ways, *haetae*."

Fuck. My spine went rigid at his chuckle.

His ankle circled round and round while he stroked the rough bristles of his short beard in thought.

"I will humor you. But I will require three tasks from you, not this *kariudo*. In good faith, I will allow you to break these bands before completing them. You proved yourself trustworthy when you released yourself from your own slavery."

It was like someone opened a valve to my body that released all my tension at once, while simultaneously filling it with the greasy feel of dread. There was no limit to what he might ask for.

"First, you will fix this situation." He motioned to my chest, where my scars were visible over the neck of my shirt. "That Thread of yours did you dirty, and the deities from your Korean heritage are a bit upset over what he has wrought on one of our guardians. You weren't broken like this when we last met. You will find a way to resolve this issue, because this is an unacceptable condition for a guardian to be in. You will complete this task, or this deal will be considered forfeit. I suggest that you not fall into any temporal snares as you did on your last adventure."

I stared at Seokga, my mouth slightly agape. Like I *hadn't* been trying to fix the situation that was my shattered body over the past century? I wasn't sure how he intended I "fix" the *issue* of my failing body. Maybe I would need to drink ginseng after all.

"Second, you will remove the influence that is presently controlling Orochi."

"You really decided not to hold back when it comes to these tasks, didn't you?"

"Did you not suggest this very situation to incentivize me? Come now, *haetae*. You mustn't make suggestions you are unable to make good on. Bad things happen to beings who do."

"Nope. No, no, I'm all good with this plan." I cringed, trying to think of who I'd need to recruit. I would definitely fail if I had to do this on my own. "You said three though, and you have only mentioned two."

"Ah. Yes. A *gut* will be required to release the *kariudo*."

I stifled my grimace and nodded. "I accept."

"Excellent," he said, pleased with himself, and held out a hand to pull me out of my chair. "Let's eat."

CHEUKSIN LOOKED APPROPRIATELY concerned about the tasks set forth for me as we ate our soup. Until Seokga detailed the last one. She nearly choked on a piece of chicken as she cackled.

"Oh, please tell me I can be there for this."

I flipped her the finger as I used my other hand to add a generous portion of the salt and pepper that sat in a small dish to my soup. "Absolutely not."

"Oh, no, I think an audience should be necessary this time around," Seokga responded, amused.

There wasn't a particular ritual to null a set of bands. They were specific to the being wearing the bands, and releasing them could only be accomplished by a major Korean deity. Life would have been so much easier if I could have asked Cheuky. But as a minor household goddess—to say nothing of the residue from her curse—she didn't have the power to accomplish the task. Seokga had slid in and tweaked the power required to both embed and release bands at the last moment to add to the divisiveness between the gods and goddesses.

These rules were why the slave bands were so effective once they were donned. The *kamis* had completely and utterly taken advantage of the situation and stolen sets whenever they had the opportunity for their own use. Since the *kamis* had no power to remove the bands, there was no incentive for the enslaved to rebel against their owner in a bid to free themselves.

"Now"—the god rubbed his hands together—"tell me about the *kariudo*."

I hesitated for a split second before I shrugged off my concern. Seokga would require knowing all that I knew of the *kariudo* and his powers. Rafael's secrets would have to be revealed for this to be successful. I thought it was a light consequence for what Rafael had done to me. After all, he would win his freedom for it.

"The *kariudo* is a direct relation to Anhangá." I didn't need to specify who the death entity was or what powers he held. All the deities knew of each other. "He started life out as a half-Perigean and half-*oni* before Anhangá invoked Rafael's birthright, changing him from a Peri to what I assume is a half-Eternal entity."

Seokga's thick, well-manicured eyebrows arched as he blew the steam away from his spoonful of soup. "You used your powers on him, now did you? *Tsk, tsk.* That was in poor form, *haetae.* I thought we had learned restraint."

"Yeah, well sue a bitch when she lashes out because she has been betrayed."

Cheuksin shook her head. "Sure. Lash out by hexing him to experience soggy cuffs for the rest of his life. Death is too easy."

I went on to describe the power of Rafael's *ki* I had both witnessed firsthand and experienced through his past. Seokga questioned me on his character, and I felt acute discomfort as I recalled the moral compass the huntsman had possessed.

Silence passed for a few moments as he decided on the course to be taken. I finished my soup and set the bowl aside. The silence was interrupted by a brief clatter of dishes as Cheuksin called upon her power to clean the space.

"I think a variation of *Ssitgim-gut* will suit nicely here considering his association with death and the purification of a soul tainted by the acts demanded by Orochi. It will necessitate his death, but as he does not remain dead, that should have little bearing." He held up a hand and an assortment of the items needed for the ritual landed softly on the counter.

"You must make sure to complete the *gut* within twenty minutes of his death. Otherwise, the backlash might bind him even more tightly to the *kami.*"

"And if it does take longer than twenty minutes?" I asked, my voice tight.

"Freeing him may no longer be possible."

CHAPTER EIGHT

Despite the severe consequences we could be facing with these tasks, it was difficult to focus on Seokga as he droned on. It was like listening to someone list all the safety disclosures in a pharmaceutical ad. *Do not take if allergic. Potential side effects include loss of body parts and possible death. Blah, blah, blah.* While my mind entertained itself, Anhangá formed in my kitchen. I eyed him suspiciously.

Had he actually been here this entire time?

The deer huffed and interrupted Seokga's monologue. "I do have a life and responsibilities outside of you and my grandson, *haetae*."

"How lonely your life must be." I couldn't resist prodding the entity. There must be some malfunctioning component in my brain.

"I prefer it."

I admitted to myself there were long stretches in my life where I would have, too. But I refused to say so out loud. Didn't matter. He knew my thoughts anyway, judging by the smirk on his face.

"You have much to accomplish in very little time. I suggest you get started immediately, considering your three-month deadline," Seokga interjected, the thick lock of hair falling back into his eyes when he gave the stag a brief nod before vanishing from sight without further comment. I couldn't decide whether I should be relieved by his absence, or worried that he left before adding something critical for me to know. Considering

I couldn't recall him saying anything about a time limit for my tasks until just now, the chances were strong.

Ah well, too late now. If he had left something out, I would need to improvise. The amount of coordination that this would take was intimidating, but I had accomplished worse under stricter timelines in the past.

"Give us until morning to make arrangements for this territory," I told Anhangá.

"I'll give you until three a.m. It'll technically be morning. We don't have time to waste. Not with the guardians continuing to disappear."

Exasperation ran through my body and I wanted to bash my head against the countertop, but I knew any argument would be pointless, so I waved him off instead. He faded out with tendrils of mist trailing after him.

"What fresh hell is this?" I asked Cheuksin, my head in my hands.

"The kind of fresh hell that only you are capable of." She linked her arm through the crook of my elbow and led me out the back door, an unconscious mirror of what Seokga had done with me. She dropped my arm like it was a molten Hot Pocket when we hit the wall of heat waiting for us outdoors, her lip curled in disgust at the weather. As we made our way to her car, the slight smile that was almost perpetually on her face dipped into a frown. "I don't like what this ritual requires of you."

I shrugged while getting into the passenger side and hissed as the hot leather seared the back of my legs through my thin pants. "I have been losing pieces of me for well over a century. A few more pieces aren't going to make a difference at this point. It's not like they're keeping me alive. I'm pretty sure I lost bits of my flesh to your car just now, as a matter of fact."

"Cam. You're sacrificing your blood, of which you have barely any left, a bone from somewhere in your body, and a fragment of your soul. All for a male you aren't sure if you even like. This is madness."

At that, I dropped my glamours and twisted to face her fully as she turned the key in the ignition. A tiny tendril of black mist swirled and caressed my body, looping in and out of the crevices that were ever widening. She froze in the act of shifting the old Subaru out of park. Shock took over the frown on her face before grief overpowered it. She reached out as if to touch me, but let her hand fall back to her side.

"Cam."

"It is what it is, Cheuksin." I stared down at my body and lifted my hands before my face. Even the little finger was fragmented, the center phalange broken into two and freely rotating in opposition of one another now. I prodded it with my right hand and watched as the pieces flew apart, before snapping back into the wrong placement. The mist immediately wrapped itself around the two pieces, forming a near solid cast around them. It was crazy, but it almost felt as if the substance was admonishing me for not treating my body with due respect.

"What good are these bones to me anyway? They are clearly not responsible for holding me together," I continued, a level of protectiveness and fierceness surging into my voice. "It doesn't matter if I hate this male or like him, Cheuksin. No one should be subjected to what Rafael has endured." I shook my head in an attempt to get rid of the images of his life that flashed before me. In the past, the memories of the souls I had judged would begin to fade to an unopened box in my mind, unless triggered by an event. The *kariudo's* stayed with me as fresh as the day I had pierced his heart.

"He should have a chance to live his life for himself. Not for this bastard of a *kami*. Not for his grandfather. But for *himself*." A sigh gusted out of me as I began to carefully construct my glamours once again. "I can't judge him for his actions while under the *kami's* control."

It was a truth I had acknowledged weeks ago. But it didn't rid me of the betrayal I still felt.

"Your feelings are valid, regardless," Cheuksin pointed out.

"They may be valid, but they're also unfair to Rafael," I admitted. The idea was hard to swallow. It was a realization that had come to me as Seokga had detailed the requirements of the ritual and I had experienced no hesitation in accepting the terms. I stared at my hands, hands that looked normal once more. "When I look at his actions as a whole, the good outweighs the bad. He saved my life, Cheuksin. If he had truly betrayed me, he would have left me to the *kami* and allowed me to die. Instead, he exposed his secrets to me. What have I ever done to warrant that?"

Cheuksin had been making her way down the pitted drive, but a hand flew out to smack me in the chest. "*Aish*. I will not stand for this self-deprecation. You have done so much to warrant saving. The fact that he could do good though, does that not refute the control he actually has?"

"But does he have any control? Cheuksin, he willingly accepted enslavement at his grandfather's due. He spent his entire life living it for other people. Even as a young child, his focus was on his ailing mother. Were any of his decisions truly his own?"

"They were still choices."

My gaze rose over the trees passing us by, up to the blue skies above us. Sweat rolled down my neck from the heat. I blinked away the sting as a drop fell into my eyes. It might be cooler on the coast, but the heat was still overpowering, and now humid, too. "It's easy to consider them choices at first glance, but how much choice does a child trying to survive truly have? How much choice does one have in such an unequal power dynamic? He is a victim of his circumstances doing his best to survive."

"It doesn't excuse his actions," Cheuksin insisted.

"I never said it was an excuse. The truth is…I think I've already forgiven him. That doesn't mean I trust him while he has those bands on though. When they come off, we'll see."

The months apart since the betrayal had allowed me that clarity, at the very least, and given me the space I had needed.

We approached an enormous Sitka spruce that sprawled across an area equivalent to a city block. Exposed roots had been delicately trained to form the words *Shore Inn*. A warm yellow light glowed from its interior. Large, enclosed platforms hung beneath the umbrellas of the spruce needles, branches entwined together to create rooms the Abstruse could rent. Unlike the Hairy Inn and Dalton's crochety personality, Shore Inn radiated a welcoming ambiance that enticed you to stay in the tree homes that boasted either a view of the ocean or the forests.

Well. It was *normally* welcoming. Cheuksin and I exchanged glances as bellows filtered through the open car windows. We hastily exited and headed for the mouth of the tree.

An *ushi oni* faced off against an Uncle.

An arachnid claw waves a piece of Tamayori's body in the air like some sort of twisted trophy.

I shook my head hard to get rid of the flashback that came on too easily these days and did my best to focus on the situation at hand. Uncle had also taken the shape of an *ushi oni*. It was that iridescent shimmer that gleamed against the black coat of one of the beings that allowed me to recognize him as a *tanuki* taking the shape of another.

Not that it would have been difficult to determine which *yōkai* was the cause of the scene before us.

The *ushi oni's* body was twisted in the worst possible case of lordosis I had seen in all my years alive. Her oxen head nearly reached the opposite end of her arachnid body, her horns millimeters from puncturing her own abdomen. Four of her legs flailed in the air, uselessly mimicking the scurrying motion of the remaining four on the ground. The state of her starvation was evident in the way her body had drawn into itself so tightly that I could see the outline of her digestive system. Her coat, which should have been sleek and smooth, was instead patchy and dull, with several extensive areas missing fur and covered with oozing sores as her body ate away at her own flesh. A wicked lash of vicarious pain whipped through my body as my brain tried to fathom the suffering she was enduring.

Uncle's deep melodic voice rang out over the area, soothing and mellow, his pedipalps patting the air in an imitation of the universal gesture that all was well and to calm down. Several Abbies crowded around the base of the inn, blocked from the entrance by the scene in front of them. It didn't matter *what* Uncle said, it only mattered what his tone conveyed.

Cheuksin and I didn't dare intervene, not wanting to disrupt Uncle's attempt at deescalating the *ushi oni*. Abruptly, his Thread came skidding to a stop next to us, his sides heaving as he held a small object in his mouth. His whiskers twitched rapidly in worry as he transformed from a raccoon dog into his human form, and the object fell from his mouth into his hand. He bent at the waist, heaving in air, his hands fisted at his knees. He gave us a brief nod in acknowledgment before he shifted again, this time into an *ushi oni* with a salt-and-pepper coat, the object now grasped between his pedipalps as he slowly approached his Thread.

The *ushi oni* bellowed in pain, nearly deafening us all, before it abruptly focused on the new arrival, turning around so her head could face the Uncles. Her forelegs and pedipalps reached for the object, but failed due to the way her body contorted.

Uncle nodded gravely and he cautiously moved past his Thread, who was continuing to murmur in a soothing tone, before setting the object in front of the *ushi oni*.

A *tamatebako.*

The small box was made of mahogany, its color deep and rich. Ivory embellished its sides with depictions of *ushi oni*. The ivory would have been harvested from her horns at birth. A heavy pall of gravity filled the area with the sight of the *tamatebako*. I resisted the urge to rip a hole in the liminal sera to access the pocket that had been created for the purpose of securing my own where no other could reach it.

Uncle met her eyes briefly, ascertaining this was what she wanted, though she was so far gone from starvation she could no longer form coherent thoughts. A shudder rippled through his body before he carefully touched her *tamatebako* to her horns, the action springing the lid open.

Everyone in the clearing bowed their heads in respect as *ki* first filled the air then rushed to surround the *ushi oni*. Motes flitted through the air as her body broke down, back to ash. Several moments passed before the *ki* dispersed as though it had never been there to begin with, peace replacing the anxiety that had overwhelmed the space. Slowly, everyone's gazes began to lift again. The Uncles reverted to their human forms, their postures heavy with grief. Nothing remained before them, the essence of the *ushi oni* and her *tamatebako* having returned to Nature and her soul to the Afterlife.

CHAPTER NINE

A minute passed by in silence, then two. Slowly, the Abbies began to move quietly among themselves, continuing whatever they had intended on doing prior to the *ushi oni's* passing. Cheuksin and I approached the Uncles, who had an arm wrapped around each other's waist, their heads tipped together, sharing their grief through their bond.

Not only grief, but rage. A level of anger that was palpable in the air around them.

"How many?" I asked quietly, after giving each of them a hug.

They exchanged a weary glance between them and shook their heads, heavy with the weight of the losses. Icy hands gripped my lungs at the movement and *squeezed*, my breath stuttering at the implication.

Uncle's Thread sighed and stepped out from under Uncle's brawny arm, disheveling his salt-and-pepper hair in the process. "We have managed to retrieve six *tamatebakos* to release the souls of those *kis*. But there are dozens more who are lost to starvation, and we have no good way to house them."

I winced. The challenges of trying to soothe and deescalate the *yōkai* who were desperate due to the pain, starvation, and the delirium that eventually took them all. The attempts to console grieving families when they were unable to save their loved ones. I was the one who put the Uncles through that. I had made that choice.

I should have been here.

"Don't." The heaviness of Uncle's tone was further emphasized as he crossed his arms across his broad chest. "I know what you're thinking—"

"—and you are only one person," his Thread finished for him, his lithe form rising to his full height. "So stop it. No matter how difficult this is, we are standing strong."

"These deaths may be devastating, but it is an *honor* that you entrusted this community to us and we are able to release these tormented souls to a life of peace in the Afterlife. It is the least they deserve. This is not your fault. The blame rests solely on the ones who put these plays into motion." Uncle's body virtually vibrated with his conviction.

I glanced over at Cheuksin to evaluate her silence. Sorrow was written across her face, in the depths of her eyes, in the furrow of her brow, and in the defeated posture that she wore. The Uncles' gazes followed mine.

"And you," Uncle's voice boomed through the clearing as he shook his finger at her, his thick forearm looking ridiculous when shaken at the tiny form that was the goddess. "You have nothing to feel guilty for. You take care of *all* of us. Just because the families of the lost entrust us with this task does not diminish your worth. Strengthen that spine and be proud. You cannot leap over millennia of bad blood and warring nations in a single bound."

A flash of doubt flickered across Cheuky's face, but before she could get a word out, his Thread's finger smashed against her lips. "Ah! We accept no slander of our family members. Especially when it's self-directed."

She sighed in defeat and shot me a look. I shrugged. There was no arguing with the Uncles; I learned that lesson long ago. They won every time, if not through reasoning, then through a war of attrition. A war where they simply wore down your every argument until you had none left and gave up for the sake of your own sanity.

"Now." Uncle gently grasped his Thread's finger and pushed it down, entwining their hands together as he went. "I know you didn't come here to witness a tragedy. How can we help?"

Quotes damn it all. I felt his last statement ring throughout my body and I fought against the urge to cry. Not, *what do you want?* Not, *seriously? You haven't asked enough of us already?* But a simple, *how can we help?*

A pair of slender arms wrapped around my shoulders, and I was drawn against a broad chest as both Uncles offered the comfort of a hug.

Grumbling noises rang in the undercurrent of the breeze as Cheuksin was dragged into the hug against her will. I still saw the gleam of tears in her eyes though. She struggled as much as I did with accepting love from others. The Uncles may not have been related to us by blood, but they claimed us as their own anyway.

"We think we may have found him," I said softly from my cocoon of love and security. Of family. "Or our best chance at finding Rafael, at least. I am taking Cheuksin away from you for some time."

Uncle pulled away from me and Cheuksin, a salt-and-pepper lock of hair falling into his eyes with the movement, "Don't you worry about us. We have this small little community locked down."

I smiled weakly. "I know you do." And I did. But it was one thing to know something in your mind, and an entirely different thing to convince my ruined heart that I wasn't abandoning my family.

Cheuky wrapped her arms around the Uncles' waists and led them into the inn. "Come. Let's discuss what you'll need to take over in my absence. Cam has other tasks she needs to take care of before we leave."

As their forms disappeared into the warm glow of the shore pine, I watched the sun settle beyond the reach of the ocean, leaving behind shades of blue and fading pinks. "Whiz?" I called into the night, shrugging off the melancholy that had settled over my shoulders.

A disembodied voice answered me, echoing around us, as well as in my mind. "Are you incapable of handling anything on your own?"

I snorted. "You know none of us would be able to function without you. Can you call Lala in from the search in PDX and tell her to meet us at the facility at 0300? Actually, loop in Theo and Yuri, too."

Silence greeted my request but I knew the gremlin was already on it. I started down the path to the sandy beach as I waited.

A few moments later, his voice returned. "Lala says thank you times a thousand, since she's working with that cop she hates. To actually quote her, she said 'I fucking love you, Cam. Fuck this job, fuck that man, and fuck my life.' Theo's response was, 'The hell I will; what kind of time is that?' Yuri nodded. They'll be there in the early morning once they wrap up what they're doing now." With every response, Whiz imitated the Abbie in question. A smile broke across my face as he threw his hip out to the side and gave me a middle finger while mimicking Theo.

"Appreciate it, Whiz." I had left my nanos on during my talk with Seokga, so I knew Whiz was fully up-to-date and diving into data so we could deploy on this unconventional SAR with as much information as possible. We truly couldn't function without the gremlin.

"Gale plans to go with the crew this time," Whiz's voice warned in my mind.

"We'll be glad to have them. Hands-on mechanical and technical gremlin *ki* during the SAR? We couldn't ask for anything more."

"Oh. And that deer with the fangs is here playing with the K9s. Best as I can tell, they're playing chase."

I couldn't hold back my laugh as Whiz sent me video of the three K9s attempting to tackle the entity, only for him to vanish into a black mist and reappear several feet away on the bank of the creek that ran through my property. Except he startled the *hanzaki*, who had grown like a weed in the past few months and was now the size of a small vehicle. A quick whip of the giant salamander's tail sent a veritable tsunami of creek water over the stag, leaving him drenched. I cackled as the image faded away in my brain while Whiz disengaged with my nanos to continue his data mining.

A life and responsibilities outside of me and his grandson, my ass.

CHAPTER TEN

Waves lapped gently at my feet as I met the ocean and waded into the water. At least I didn't have to worry about Quotidian tourists. The sheer influx of Abbies that had come with the exodus from Ryūgū-jō had tripled the size of the Neskowin realm as it expanded to accommodate the *ki* within it. The small territory now overlapped with the Neskowin of the Quotes' realm, making my life infinitely easier as I slipped from one area to the next.

I dove beneath the waves and resurfaced in the newly warded territory that encompassed our small corner of the world. Aquatic Abbies swam past me. Some looked happy and healthy, chattering in family or friend groups. Others—the *yōkai* who had arrived mere months ago—had slowly fading expressions of shell shock, their gaunt features finally beginning to fill out with adequate sustenance and rest in an environment that wasn't filled with threats.

Taking a moment to myself, I leaned back and allowed myself to float while staring at the stars in this realm. The same constellations, and yet so very different. They were much brighter, giving one the sense that they were near as opposed to so far away. Their brilliance began to fade as a bluish glow began to expand over my gaze and ancient avian skeletons took the place of the stars in the skies.

"Need a taxi?" A large, rolling wave moved me several feet away before dragging me back a few inches. Bones rattled across my body as a large prehistoric fish was swept up in the motion that announced Murry's arrival. I took a deep breath and dipped back underwater before resurfacing, coming face-to-face with a giant eye filled with black fire.

"How'd you guess?"

"Oh, I don't know, it's only been about the only thing we've done whenever you've been out here." The giant undead whale spouted water through his spiracles, sending an undead fish soaring through the air. "Are you finally going to try to convince her to come back over?"

I had Anhangá and Cheuksin on my side. But a *kami* wouldn't be unwelcome. Particularly one who had been Threaded to the *kami* we were hunting down.

"I am," I admitted, snagging a hold of the spinous process of one of his vertebrae.

"Well, good luck with that. She hasn't so much as budged an inch since she regained herself."

Well. At least Pea and I weren't the only ones stuck in a cycle of grief. The Quotes did like to say that misery loved company.

We flowed smoothly through the water and began approaching an unnaturally dark patch. Only two beings were keyed to this century-old spatial snare. The combination of the backlash of Pea's severed bond and the *ki* Murry had expended to make himself corporeal long enough to get two unconscious bodies to safety gave them their access. The limited accessibility of spatial snares was one of many benefits to them, as it controlled who had access where.

As Murry and I entered the space, the ocean blues transitioned into utter darkness. It was a place where silence rang through your ears. No smells. No taste. Even the perception of my grip on Murry vanished, something that always made the pieces of my heart tremor with anxiety. Finally, we were thrust back into the shocking sensory experience of the real world.

Into a realm that was still dying.

I desperately needed to figure out the foreign *ki* within me so that I could give the power back to Ryūgū-jō. The fear that I might fail paralyzed me in my lessons with Reika, leaving me worse off every time.

A weak shudder of warmth greeted me as I let go of Murry and gently landed on the ground. It reminded me of the hesitant, pain-ridden wag of Vicky's tail when I had first found her. Despair burdened my shoulders as

I wrapped my arms around myself. Ryūgū-jō's joy in my presence was undeniable, even as life leaked out of it. The bleached white had overtaken even more of the palace since my last visit. All that was left were striations of crimson streaking across the coral like trails of blood, and I had done nothing to stay the damage. I didn't deserve the happiness the realm offered me.

A lone female sat on a coral bench in the gardens, staring into the distance as she absently stroked a thin band of red running through the coral. A faint pulse rang through the air with each touch, but quickly faded, Ryūgū-jō no longer able to maintain a consistent level of *ki*. Whispers carried on the light breeze, too quiet for me to make out, even as Murry and I approached. I wasn't sure if she was talking to the realm or the dead.

"I'm not going back," Toyotama said, her back still facing us. Before we could say anything, she continued, "What if…" She swallowed. "What if these are my last moments with Ryūgū-jō? I can't abandon them to die alone. I can't lose someone else." The last sentence came out as a hushed breath. Her voice was desolate, ringing with grief. She had already lost so much; deaths that were a hundred years in the past for me were fresh wounds to her.

Before I could respond, her head snapped to the empty space on her left. "It's not the same," she snarled.

"I don't want to make you leave." My voice was soft. Cautious. I lowered myself to the bench and looked out at the landscape of death with her. "I wish I could wave a so-called magic wand and fix all of this. We don't have that luxury though. Ryūgū doesn't have that luxury."

I didn't say it aloud. We both knew that she had been remiss in her promise to Reika. How could I blame her though? With everything she had gone through, I wouldn't want to leave the last place I had seen my sister alive either. We were both failing the realm in our own separate ways.

Toyo faced me, her nictitating membrane blinking several times in a futile effort to hold back tears. She was ashen, even more pale than she typically was, and she had lost weight, giving her lithe form a ghostly presence. Murry's bioluminescence only emphasized the appearance further, her pearlescent skin reflecting his blue glow.

"How did you keep going? After… After." She ended without needing to say more.

"What makes you think I have?" I refuted. I was definitively *not* the poster child for healthy grieving. As if there was such a thing.

We sat on the bench in silence for a few minutes, Murry hovering silently in the background, respecting our space, his undulating shadow protecting us from the afternoon sun that was high in the sky in this part of the realm. I couldn't decide if the sunshine was a mockery or a mercy as the warm beams highlighted the death that surrounded us in the gardens, creating a stark contrast of warmth and chilling bleakness.

I bumped the *kami* with my shoulder. "Tama would give you never-ending shit if she knew Reika turned you into a Quote and it took you over a century to figure it out."

Toyo gave a weak and congested laugh. "She would. That bitch." She took a deep breath, gathering her courage. Her right shoulder twitched like she wanted to shrug something off. "How did she die? I can't remember. And that's what's killing me most of all—I remember *nothing* from that night."

I cringed as if the reaction could repress the memories that came roaring back in full force. "That might be something to be grateful for."

"It's not though," she whispered. "I feel like I have a hole in me, Cam. A hole in my mind. Another in my heart. Because I have no idea what happened. And I can't help but think it was fucking Reika's fault for the magic she wove over me. That's the other reason I haven't gone back, because I don't think I can see that hag without killing her at first sight. She took my *life* away from me."

She wasn't wrong. Even though a century was a drop in time for us, it was still over a hundred years just…gone.

"I wasn't there." My grief rose like bile, choking me as it resurfaced. "I can't give you the answers you're hoping for. All I found as I fought my way to Ryū were your bodies. You had shifted, and Tama's body was beneath you as you tried to protect—"

"And failed to do so, abysmally," she interrupted.

"Your own father didn't survive that night," I snapped. "The *kami* of the seas and weather died that night, too. If he couldn't take down whoever it was killing the *kamis* and the guardians, what the hell makes you think you could have done any better?" Oh, how the tables had turned. Now I was the one giving the lecture instead of receiving it.

"You're still alive," she pointed out. "You made it out. Why? Because my *father*—" She spit out the title like it was something foul on her tongue. Imprints of fingertips suddenly formed on her arms, then dragged down, leaving deep, red impressions—the dead trying to hold the tide of her anger back. She shook her arms out, unable to be bothered with the dead as her rage crashed over us. "Because he *knew* what was going to happen that night and planned in advance to spare your life, but he did *nothing* to save the life of his favorite daughter."

Toyotama pounded a small fist against her chest. "Why *me*? Why did he have Reika spare my life with a transformation spell and render me as a Quotidian? That's what I'm stuck on. Tama was the good daughter. The perfect daughter who could do no wrong. I was the broken, mentally ill child that he discarded in his efforts to create a better daughter. He *broke* me, Cam. He chose to break me when he severed my Thread, and again with my sister's death."

I sighed, my shoulders folding in as my breath left me. Truth be told, I was still just as angry at him as Toyo was now.

"You both would have died that night." Murry's deep voice resonated through the gardens. "Ryūjin knew he had the impossible choice of deciding which daughter would live and which would die. He chose *you*, Toyo. He chose you, because ultimately, he knew Tama had lived a good life, and he wanted you have the chance to have one as well."

A pit formed deep within me at this new information. Not about Ryūjin's decision to make the impossible choice, but the reminder, yet again, that Murry had *known* the entire time.

"Well, my father chose wrong," Toyo snapped, her face contorted with rage and pain, scarlet tinting her previously pale cheeks. "Tama was all that was good and right in this world. She was bright; a ray of sunshine in the dark. I am none of that. My own *Thread*, the one soul who should've loved me above all others, rejected me. I am worth *nothing*. He should have chosen the daughter who actually enjoyed living. Not the one who is constantly being dragged into Yomi by the dead. I was already halfway there."

"I can't excuse his choices, but we don't know what the *onna uo* revealed to him." My voice was tight as I attempted to find another way to forgive my Thread. Murry remained silent on the matter.

Toyo scoffed and turned to face the gardens again. The path our conversation had led us down made me feel like absolute shit for what I was about to say. "Despite everything, I need you, Toyo. I need you back in the Quote realm. I need your help tracking down Orochi."

CHAPTER ELEVEN

The way her body stiffened wasn't immediate but a slow progression, like watching ice freeze over water as her spine drew her taller. "Absolutely the fuck not," she hissed.

"He is your Thread. You can trace him," I said softly. In reality, we could have found Rafael much earlier had we pulled Toyo in. But Murry and I had known it was too soon to ask. Despite the suffering Rafael was likely going through, he wouldn't die his last Death, not so long as Anhangá continued to retether his soul. "Even severed, the frayed bonds you share give you something to work with. I wouldn't ask, except I have a countdown now."

"What do you mean *a countdown,*" came a whisper, soft and deadly.

It was my turn to draw a deep breath for courage. "I bargained with Seokga."

"*Are you mad?*" Murry thundered.

"Probably."

"Cam! No one should bargain with the gods. Ask me how I know? Because *I am one.* How fucking stupid can you be?" Toyo shouted, her arms flinging out to emphasize her point, nearly catching me full in the face.

"The guardians are dying," I threw back at her. "If I don't get Rafael freed from Orochi, they will continue to do so, until all the realms are destroyed without their protectors in place. I have survived Seokga's tasks once before; I can do it again."

"Why is this *kariudo* so *kamis*-damned important? It's not like you can't solve this puzzle without him," Murry tried to reason.

"We could, but we'd be starting from square one, whereas he's been at this for decades. We don't have the luxury of time with so few guardians remaining." *And because the* kariudo *didn't deserve to be in his position after sacrificing himself for me.* I had questions for him after everything had played out. So many questions.

"And how far did that get him?" Toyo asked pointedly. "Enslaved and tortured, and that was before he even served your liver up on a platter. The fact that the *kariudo* has been working at this for decades isn't a real big endorsement for him right now," she added, the sarcasm practically dripping from her words.

"It's not like any of us even knew that the missing guardians had anything to do with Orochi until Rafael inserted himself into our lives." I threw out. "We could, I don't know, work together or something crazy like that, so I don't have to cover ground that has already been established! For the love of all things unholy, Toyo, Ryūgū-jō doesn't have that long."

The barest hint of a shiver shook the bench under us. The weakness of Ryūgū-jō's response placed a heavy weight on the importance of expediency. That, more than anything I could have said, hit Toyo like a *kanabō* of common sense to the brain.

"Fuuuuuck." She dragged a hand down her face. "I hate you for this."

I nodded. "I'm aware."

"You're going to owe me *so* big."

I raised an eyebrow.

"Okay. Fine. You still have favors built up. But I get to be cranky, and no one is going to judge me for it."

A pressure wave washed over us as Murry *harrumphed* at Toyo's last statement. "As if you're ever not cranky."

"Shush, whale. Don't think we've forgotten that you had some knowledge of these events and didn't bother to tell anyone at any point in time," the *kami* scolded.

The black fire consuming Murry's eye socket flickered in return.

Toyo's nose crinkled in distaste as she stood. "You don't have to be so excited about this," she snapped over her left shoulder. Murry and I knew she wasn't speaking to us and followed quietly behind her while she continued muttering to sights unseen on her way into the palace. At the very least, it was good to see that she had regained far more control since returning to her original form. I left Murry hovering at the palace doors and wandered the expansive halls, keeping light contact with the realm as I ran my fingers gently against the walls while I waited for Toyo to collect whatever she would need.

"Where is your marsupial cling-on?" Toyo called, her voice resonating through the space.

The art on the walls rattled as the realm echoed her query.

"Grieving," I replied simply, standing before a mural of a *chīnouya*, one who bore a strong resemblance to the one I had persuaded to leave this realm and join us in Neskowin. The painting morphed subtly as I watched. The female spirit settled beneath a tree and began to weep as she nursed the ghost of a child. I traced the trail of tears and nodded. "We're all grieving." My words were quiet. I knew Toyo would hear, but these words were meant for Ryūgū-jō. The *chīnouya's* head turned slowly and gave me a slight nod, as if gravity weighed her down.

A thud sounded and I turned away from the painting. A *shhhushhh*ing sound filled the hall, followed by another thud and a shhhushhh. After a minute, Toyo came into view. Her right foot, clad in a combat boot, kicked a duffle bag, which slid across the floor. Gone were the practical shoes that Misaki had worn, back was the rebellious fashionista I had once known.

"You like?" Toyo stuck a toe out and twisted her foot back and forth for me to admire. They were an ochre yellow with bright purple splattered across them. Laces in a vibrant green were threaded all the way to her knees. Black knit knee-high socks peeked over the top of the boots, then transitioned into green leggings that matched the laces.

"We definitely won't have to worry about your visibility in the woods," I teased.

"That's one thing I don't mind about this era. The colors are so much more vibrant." Her tone was approving as she admired her boots before she hauled her leg back and launched the duffle bag straight out the palace doors with one solid kick. Cursing followed shortly.

"Who the fuck is assaulting me with projectiles?" Murry yelled.

"You're dead!" Toyo shouted back. "A duffle bag isn't going to hurt you. Not to mention, you're like…a million times bigger than that duffle."

"I should have guessed," the whale muttered. "You took out my fish!"

"They're dead, too," was her cheerful response.

I shook my head and made my way back out the doors and into the gardens. Three prehistoric fish floated belly-up near Murry's indignant eye. *Not my circus.*

Toyo trailed behind me, the *kami* and *bakekujira* trading insults as we made our way back to the spatial snare. I snickered to myself.

Nah. They were definitely part of my circus.

Night still held firm on this side of the world as we resurfaced in Neskowin where Cheuky and the Uncles waited on shore.

"Thank you for the ride, old friend." I gave the bones of his flipper an affectionate hug. "Until we return."

Murry rocked from side to side, generating a small rolling wave. "You're not leaving me here. There's still some power left in the wards you painted on me during your last trip to Neskowin a few weeks ago. I'll meet you up there so you have more than one escape path if needed."

I eyed the cetacean, my gaze scanning the length of his skeleton as if I could still see the *hanja* that had sunk into his bones the moment the last character had been written. The wards were good for four weeks at most; the length of time varied, depending on how often Murry took advantage of having them. It had been a little over two and a half weeks since I last applied them. It would be another eight before I could reapply the *hanja*, or the wards would begin to lose their efficacy. The average humpback took six to eight weeks to migrate between Alaska and Oregon, but Murry didn't have sheer mass slowing him down. He could probably make it in three days, with the assistance of his *ki* and his undead friends creating a slipstream for him.

Murry's fluke slapped against the water. "I am fine, Tsubaki. I have only made two trips. But I'd rather be there, just in case."

I shook my head. "We can't risk it, I'm sorry."

Toyo pulled my hand, dragging me to shore. "Come on. It's Murry. He's nearly as old as you; he'll be fine."

I grimaced as I pulled my arm back to swim through the waves, Murry following behind. "I don't know how long we'll be in Alaska, but the timing doesn't work out. Even if you get there in three days, Murry, that gives us about four days to not only hike out to where the researchers went missing, but to find and rescue Rafael, and then make the return trip before you would have to swim back. I know you want to help, but you will be worth so much more here, in case we need to access the spatial snare."

Murry's fluke slapped the water with his frustration and my heart bled for how restricted he was for a creature meant to wander great distances.

"I'm sorry, my friend. I wish circumstances were different, but this is where we're at right now."

Water blew from his spiracles, a sigh leaving his form, as he raised a fluke in farewell and rolled to swim back to deeper waters.

Toyo stepped onto shore and echoed the conversation I had had with Cheuksin earlier. "Maybe Quotes deserve Murry's kind of power. Look at the state of the world now."

Cheuky laughed as she stepped forward. "She's not wrong. It's good to meet you, Toyotama. I've heard plenty about you."

Toyo's nose wrinkled. "Toyo please, and I'm assuming it's all been bad." She winked at the goddess.

"Well, it definitely hasn't been good." I snorted as I gave the Uncles hugs. "You guys all set?"

They exchanged glances. "As ready as we'll ever be," they chorused.

"Besides, how boring would life be without a challenge?" Uncle grinned as a shock of salt-and-pepper hair fell over his forehead, which earned him a smack from his Thread.

"Eh! Am I not challenge enough for you?" His Thread scowled.

Uncle wrapped a slender arm around the broad shoulders and leaned in for a sound kiss. "No."

His Thread shoved him good-naturedly before addressing me again. "We're good." He thought about his statement for a moment, then shook his dark head vigorously. "Not him. But I am."

Toyo watched them with a faint hint of amusement tugging at her lips, though her eyes rang with sadness.

Cheuky rubbed her mouth, unsuccessfully hiding the smile behind her hand. "Come on, let's get you guys back up to the house so you can get at least a few hours of shut-eye before we leave again."

I cringed internally. "Could we not and say we did?"

"No," everyone chorused.

"Fine," I grumbled and headed up the shore. Because there was nothing quite like the knowledge that horrors were waiting for you the moment you closed your eyes and dropped into the realm of dreams.

CHAPTER TWELVE

I tossed the sweat-soaked covers off my clammy body and padded out the bedroom and down the stairs, the routine as familiar to me as the back of my hand by this point. I slid open my back door and stepped onto the wood planks that made up my porch for the hundredth time since June. The figure in my chair was expected at this point. As was his pensive stare into the forest. My eyes roamed his body, against my better judgment.

"You again." The words fell out of my mouth in a sigh. Fatigue overwhelmed me despite the fact I was asleep. Taking a step forward felt like trudging through mudflats, and I was damned if I could summon the energy to be pissed.

"Me again," he agreed without turning.

"What did I do to my subconscious to deserve you in my dreams every time I close my eyes, regardless of the time of day?"

"I'm afraid you're going to have to take that up with your brain instead of me."

"I just don't understand what my brain is trying to tell me," I mused to myself, propping my body against the railing. I didn't want to sit next to Dream Rafael, but staying upright required assistance.

"That you have masochistic and self-harm tendencies?" The *kariudo* turned to face me at last, revealing a wry expression on his face.

My face flushed. "There is no self-harming happening here."

"What would you call it when you have gone…how many days without sleep at this point?"

"Self-preservation."

"Mmm." He didn't elaborate.

"Listen. Cheuky can call me out. The Uncles can get away with it. Toyo earned the right. But you? Even if you're my brain's manifestation of some deep unknown terror and not *actually* Rafael, you still don't get to do that."

"What would it take to earn that right?"

Disbelief contorted my face and I somehow knew that my physical face would be imitating the expression in my sleep. "You want to *earn* the right to call me a masochist? My guy, that's all kinds of fucked up."

I knew what he actually meant, but it really *was* all kinds of fucked up to ask my own self what it would take to call out my tendency toward self-sabotage. I didn't dwell on it. That road led to madness.

He sighed deeply and returned his gaze to the forest. I fidgeted, my left foot tapping like it was trying to power the entire neighborhood with its excess of energy. We were a few days shy of a full moon and I desperately wanted to walk down the moonlit trail in front of me, but prior experience had taught me that I couldn't leave the porch once I stepped onto it.

"Why so broody?" I snapped when the silence became too heavy to bear.

The silence stood firm for another eternity. There was nothing I could do but wait it out unless something woke me up. I could feel my agitation growing, clearing my mind of its fatigue, and I stood to pace the length of the porch. If I couldn't walk in the woods, at least I had some square footage that would allow me that level of peace. The thick atmosphere just burned off more of my restless energy.

"Why are you still searching for me, Baki?"

I was at the far end of the deck when the words spilled from his mouth. They didn't surprise me—he asked every time we saw each other this way. I knew it was nothing more than my heart questioning why I was willing to stick my neck out for a male who had already betrayed me while my brain rationalized all the reasons we needed to find the *kariudo*.

Before I could respond with my usual rhetoric, he spoke again. "I didn't betray you only for you to turn around and put yourself right back into Orochi's reach."

I frowned. There was a new tone underpinning his words that hadn't been present in any of my past nightmares. It wasn't so much worry as it was unease.

"I've avoided this scenario for over a century and where did that get me?" I countered. "I managed to end up within his reach anyway. Why should it matter at this point?"

"Because you are valued."

"And you're not?"

"Baki. I've done far too much damage in this world to be worth the effort. There are exactly zero people in this world who would miss me when I'm gone."

"So you're going to give up?" That was what pissed me off the most. That, and the fact that I would miss him for some *kamis*-forsaken reason. I didn't know if it was the actual male I would miss, or the lost potential of what could have been had he had a chance.

"You're just going to hang up your boots and call it good and leave the world in the state it's in without even *trying* to make it better? You know what? You're right. If that's going to be your attitude, why bother?"

Rafael visibly flinched when my words hit their mark. If I was ashamed of berating someone who so wholly felt worthless, I shoved it down deep where it couldn't rise again.

I didn't know why or when it had become my mission for him to see his own self-worth when I was still so angry, but I stormed back to him and got in his face. "Except your grandfather says otherwise. So *get off your ass* and start fucking fighting already."

A vein throbbed in his forehead, and I watched, fascinated, as his neck corded with the effort to hold back his anger.

Good. If he could still feel anger, there was still hope.

"How dare you," he hissed through his clenched teeth. "You have no idea what lengths I have gone through to keep you and yours safe. How hard I've fought to circumvent so many deaths that Orochi ordered." He raised himself out of his seat and leaned into my face. "*Fuck you.*"

I settled back against the railing and nodded. "Then why quit now?"

He collapsed back into his chair. "Because I'm fucking tired, Baki. What do you want me to say? My life has been nothing but violence, and I can't bring myself to care about continuing it."

I could relate to that, at least. "Then let us help you break this cycle."

He smiled wryly. "Baki, the Incarnation of Second Chances herself. Don't you ever get tired of saving everyone?"

I snorted. "I hardly save everyone." My body count far exceeded his given the length of my life.

Our conversation fell to silence, and I contemplated the path that had led me to this moment. Quotes only knew what was on Rafael's mind.

"Where are you, Rafael?" The question fell out of my mouth, as it did every time I slept, as though I had no control over my words. I regretted the question immediately, knowing what would happen next. The fragments of my heart fell to the depths of my body as I braced myself, and I wished with every fiber of my being to take the question back.

Rafael's mouth opened as if to answer, but his words quickly morphed into a scream. His face contorted in pain and blood sprayed across my deck, despite a lack of visible wounds on the *kariudo*. He fell out of the chair into the fetal position and began to seize. I tried to hurry to him, but my legs might as well have been mired in concrete, the effort it took to lift a leg monumental. A sharp crack rang through the air as his femur snapped. By the time I was able to take half a step forward, he vanished.

A FANGED STAG stood next to my bed as I woke mid-yell. "*Kamis* above. What the hell are you doing in my room? We keep talking about this. Boundaries are important."

Anhangá shook his head. "Did you kill my grandson again?"

I eyed him warily. "Not that I'm aware of." I hoped I hadn't anyway. I wasn't sure how my nightmares could manifest someone's death.

Anhangá huffed. "You reek of guilt. No matter. It's time."

I groaned. I swear I was more tired now than I was before I tried to get some decent sleep. "Be right down."

I bolted for the bathroom to splash cold water on my face, enjoying the feel of the dried sweat being stripped from my body. I silently wished that it could wash away the growing pit in my chest.

Rafael's fine, I tried to convince myself. *It was just a dream. They're always just dreams.*

I gave the shower a longing look but knew that was too much to ask for. I opted to brush my teeth and quickly wiped down my body with a damp cloth instead.

Anhangá nodded approvingly when I stepped out of the bathroom moments later, and we headed down the stairs. I hoped that watching a cervid navigate the stairs would always be weird to me.

If it wasn't, it would mean I had spent far too much time with the stag.

"You would be so lucky to spend that much time in my company," Anhangá said with a sniff as we stepped into my living room.

"Ah. Our ride has arrived," Cheuksin said with a faint hint of malice.

"Anhangá Air, at your service," he intoned snidely, bending a foreleg into a bow.

A *kami* was conspicuously missing from our group.

"Toyo?" I asked Cheuksin.

She shook her head. "She couldn't sleep, so she took one of the vehicles and drove to Blue Bear. She should be arriving any moment."

"And on that note…" Anhangá stepped forward, and a moment later our bodies ceased to be whole.

CHAPTER THIRTEEN

Screams, excited barks, and howls greeted us as soon as we materialized in the Blue Bear Search and Rescue facility.

The screams were courtesy of Lala. A duffle bag suddenly shot through the entrance. Toyo walked through the door a moment later, and only a slight widening of her eyes betrayed her nonchalance at the Perigean's screams. Theo and Yuriko barely reacted. The former had a cup of coffee raised to his lips and Gale on his shoulder. The latter sat on a desk chair, her legs crossed, an eyebrow raised, and Pea curled around her neck.

All of which I saw from the vantage point of the floor beneath a pile of wriggling K9s. Pea picked up her head at our arrival and bolted down Yuri, bypassing me, and launching herself straight up Toyo's body. I shoved the flare of jealousy as far down as it could go. I was just happy to see her experiencing something other than grief.

"Jesus Christ." Lala pressed a hand to her chest. "I don't need those years you shaved off my life or anything like that. Don't worry about me. I have the lifespan of a Perigean. It's not like I was gonna find the cure for cancer or bring about world peace. It's cool. I didn't need those years anyway."

"You're late," Yuri said calmly.

"So sorry. I took some time to wash my face and brush my teeth," I said, without a hint of remorse. I hadn't yet recovered from the nightmare and was immediately flung into chaos. Overstimulation, thy name is Camellia. I took a moment to try to regulate my breathing and ground myself.

Theo chucked a red fifty-liter backpack at Toyo. "Pack what you can into this. The pack has the supplies you'll need for the trip." A colorful row of backpacks were leaning against the wall behind the *dokkaebi*. Pea hissed at him as Toyo nearly dropped her in her effort to catch the pack before it landed on the *shikigami*. Cheuky walked over and snagged one before he could lob another at her.

Ah. My people. The kind who gave exactly zero fucks about royalty or gods being in their mix. "Everyone, Toyotama-*hime*." I added extra emphasis on the princess portion of her name, while I hugged Woody and Max with each arm. Vicky sat in my lap, her tail thumping happily on the tile. Toyo shot me a nasty look for the emphasis on her title, which she hated. "Toyo, meet Theo and Lala. You already know Yuriko from the past. And it looks like Emma and Hideki are here, too, if I'm right about who's in the conference room."

"They're taking the decapitation cases off our hands while we're gone," Lala announced. "Another missing person was called in last night while you were in Neskowin."

I cocked my head at a more extreme angle so I could see into the room better. Emma's body was hard at work, pounding away at a keyboard, while her head was suspended in front of the projected display. Her reading glasses remained propped on top of her head, forgotten. Visual deficits weren't a serious enough condition to trigger Abbie healing at first—if you didn't treat your eyes kindly, they continued to deteriorate until you went blind, and then your healing kicked in to start the cycle all over again with perfect vision. Knowing Emma, she was so engrossed in trying to pull together the twists and turns of the decapitations, she probably didn't even hear us arrive, despite the ruckus the K9s had made.

Hideki stood catty-corner to Emma's floating head with one hand on his hip, and the other rubbing the back of his neck in exhaustion. Luna laid at his feet, finally back to work after tearing her cruciate ligament this past winter. The injury itself had been repaired as soon as Pea got to her. Her confidence walking over rubble, less so. Hideki's hands had been full with rehabbing the black lab's confidence, and he and Aidan had spent most of the summer trading ideas. He caught my eye and raised his hand in greeting before turning back to his work. The wall before him was covered in maps, sticky notes, pins, and gruesome photos of the murders that Whiz had procured for the team.

Lala nodded toward them. "They're looking for any potential links with the new call-out and the cases that have been called in so far." If anyone was going to find a link, it would be Emma. Lala made her way into the conference room, Phally trotting at her heels. Theo and Cheuky followed her in.

"What's up, gang?" A voice whistled as the front door slammed open again, before the rest of us could join the five in the conference room. A shock of auburn hair poked his head through the doorway, accompanied by a chocolate-brown head of fur. "My Uncles called. You didn't really think you could leave without me, did you?" He glared at Anhangá, who joined the group as he entered. Aidan leaned against the doorframe with his arms crossed. Dark circles underlined his eyes, and his hair looked like it had gone through a cyclone.

"You're gonna go bald if you keep pulling your hair like that," I noted. He snorted and held out his arms for a hug, which I obliged, finally getting up from my dog pile. He kissed the top of my head and squeezed hard.

Aidan and Anhangá had gotten off on the wrong foot in the spring. But then again, Anhangá generally had that effect on everyone upon meeting him. It was a competition between Reika, Cheuksin, and Aidan on who disliked the entity the most.

The stag merely lifted his head and stared him down. "You are an unnecessary accessory to a serious operation. We have no need of your presence."

"Listen—" Aidan began, his face turning red.

I interrupted him before the fireworks could begin and smiled up at him gratefully. "Thanks for coming, Aidan. You're the last for this search though. Jeff needs the rest of the crew here in case another Abbie goes missing. Are you coming off last night's call-out now?"

He ran his hand through his already wild hair. "Got home about an hour ago, got clean, got the message from my Uncles, and got my ass over here before you could leave me behind."

I swatted his arm. "You could have stayed back and gotten some sleep in the middle of all those *gots* you just mentioned. The cases here are just as important."

Aidan shrugged. "What can I say? I liked the guy. Figured I'd help him out, if I could, and return the favor. Hideki, Scott, Leilani, and Emma have things covered here."

"Do we know who the call-out is for this time?" I asked as the rest of us filed into the conference room.

"To the Quotidian world, a thirty-four-year-old environmental lawyer who disappeared off of Mississippi Street when he got off work. To the Abbie world? He's a leshy. His husband told Portland PD that they had a standing date at the taqueria, and our missing person typically walked there after work," Emma reported.

Whiz popped in, stabbing a flash drive at several black dots on the map of North Portland. "Traffic and security cams show that he was approached by someone." Several different images of the missing Slavic forest guardian talking to someone appeared on the screen. The stills ran the gamut of quality, and they offered a variety of angles of the unknown person.

Gale took over. "Based on his appearance, Portland PD assumed it was a random unhoused person and have been canvassing the usual encampments to see if anyone recognizes who it was. Interestingly enough, they kept their face from being on camera, as if they knew exactly what angles to avoid, so the task force doesn't have much to go on. But…" Gale paused, and one of the images jumped ahead in time then zoomed in rapidly. "After we cleaned up this image as much as we could, we found this partial face. Look familiar anyone?"

Aidan and I nodded grimly as he took the seat next to me. The unknown subject wasn't familiar in the sense of knowing who they were. Rather, what we could see of the face was familiar in its utter ambiguity.

Whiz continued, "We can't be certain it's the same person who reported all the others missing, but they share several of the same characteristics."

Aidan grimaced. I noticed he was making a concentrated effort to avoid looking at Theo and Anhangá. "We don't have a contact in the Portland PD. We're hamstrung when it comes to passing this info along."

"Which could be a good thing, given the increasing certainty that this is an Abstruse-related case," Emma said pointedly. "Portland PD doesn't know that it's likely connected to the decapitation cases as a result, they just know they had a lawyer go missing in the city. It doesn't tie back to the cases here unless you know that he's an Abbie."

"Not even an Abbie, but a guardian, which pretty much seals the deal on it being related," Hideki added.

"Whiz?" I asked. The gremlin nodded, familiar with what I was asking after working with me for so long.

"Gale will be going to Alaska with Cam," he announced. "I'm going to stay back with Emma, Hideki, and the rest of the crew here to see if we can find some way to identify the unknown sub."

"Speaking of Alaska." Lala leaned over the conference table, the chair nearly sliding out from under her. "How are we going to work this situation? We don't have a mutual aid agreement with Alaska, and it's not like this is a natural disaster. Are we just going to…I don't know, fly into Anchorage, catch a bush plane, and then be like '*Hey you guyyyyyyyys?*' if and when we run into the National Guard's search teams?"

CHAPTER FOURTEEN

Yuriko squinted at Lala. "Have the past two decades not passed us by or…?"

"Cam has her cassette tapes, I have *The Goonies*," Lala said defensively.

"I'm not sure how I got dragged into—"

"It's because you're a dinosaur," Toyo said cheerfully to me. Cheuky smirked.

I reached into the candy jar in the middle of the conference table and chucked strawberry bon bons at them. "You two are even older than me. If I'm a dinosaur, what are you? A single-celled organism?"

"Anyway," Theo interrupted. "Do we have flights secured? Or does Gale need to get on that while we compare all the ways we aren't able to adapt to the times." He turned to Aidan. "I didn't pack for you."

Aidan waved off the silent question uncomfortably. He was going to have to work on that, or else Theo was going to catch on to the fact that he was in contention as one of Aidan's leading suspects. "My pack's in the truck. I'm covered." Aidan dropped in a chair, exhaustion underpinning his every movement.

Anhangá ignored Aidan's exchange with Theo, Aidan might not have been in the room with us at all, for all the attention the stag paid to the redhead. "We're not traveling commercially," the stag said matter-of-factly, as though this should have been obvious to everyone. He stood in the doorway, opting to remain in his preferred form over taking on a human persona and taking a seat at the table.

Lala eyed the entity's fangs warily while unwrapping a candy and popping it into her mouth. "Cam. Who is the talking Vambi who hates Aidan standing in our doorway?"

The cackle erupted from me before I could hold it back. The stress over the *ushi oni*, my nightmare, and the lack of sleep—even if I had managed to nap—finally overwhelmed me, and I collapsed in my chair as I laughed until I cried. Up until now, Lala had had the good fortune of missing Anhangá's presence every time he visited.

"Cam," Lala mock-whispered. "It wasn't that funny. Theo, fix her. She's broken."

My chair wheeled a few inches as a toe nudged one of the legs, and I spun slowly as I went. Vicky scrambled up, excited by the movement, and leapt into my lap.

"Sorry, Lalanator. Pretty sure this is a permanent condition. It's called being Camellia Kimoto. I'm afraid it's terminal and I have no cure." Theo's tone was full of dry amusement.

"Vambi," I gasped through my tears. "Stop, Vicky. Stop." I meekly fought off my Heinz-57 dog who braced her front paws against my shoulders and excitedly tried to lick my face. "I'm stealing that. That's what I'm calling you from now on."

Anhangá merely rolled his eyes, which was an entirely unsettling sight on a stag.

"Lala, meet Rafael's ancestral grandfather, Anhangá. Anhangá, Lala." I hugged the unruly K9 to my chest to curtail her wriggling.

"*This* is the being you've been bitching about the whole time? He's a *deer*?" Lala stabbed a finger in his direction.

I shrugged. "His shape wasn't really pertinent to my complaints."

Lala shook her head at me as she began to type. Gale vanished from Theo's shoulder and reappeared next to her. The gremlin hip-checked Lala's arm out of their way and commandeered the keyboard. A moment later, a topographic map of Wrangell–St. Elias National Park was projected on the far wall, leaving Emma and Hideki's work intact. The tip of Gale's tongue poked out while they typed in a quick sequence, and pins dropped on the new range that had appeared.

While we waited, Toyo started pulling everything out of her duffle and the pack she'd been given to reorganize it all. Theo eyed her actions for all of a minute before he gave in to the compulsion to wheel her chair out of his way and began repacking it for her. Pea climbed down from Toyo's neck and settled into a tight ball in her now open lap. Even if it had only been for a few minutes, I was happy to see she had paused to take in a breath of the air around her before drowning in her grief again. She was slowly coming back to us.

"Okay. So we're…'teleporting' there, or whatever the hell it's called when people appear out of thin air. How the hell are we going to explain that if any Quotes happen to be near our arrival site? The odds of that are far higher than usual, considering the search." Lala pointed out.

"There is no need to worry about Quotes when we are arriving in the Abstruse realm," Anhangá said.

"Maybe I need to check my hearing, but it sounded like you said we weren't doing the sane thing and entering Wrangell–St. Elias under the much more reasonable conditions of the Quote realm." Lala steepled her fingers against the tabletop expectantly. If skepticism could be made tangible, hers would be a weapon of mass destruction with the way she wielded it.

"Well, we won't have to worry about flight conditions?" I offered weakly. Yuriko shook her head. Okay, so weather conditions generally weren't something we needed to worry about anyway in alpine regions with a *yuki onna* on our team. Even one who was still recovering from the *futakuchi onna* attack.

"More severe weather conditions, thicker forest growth, territorial and potentially—no, *definitely*—dangerous Abbies, uncharted temporal snares." Lala ticked the risks of arriving in the Abbie realm on her fingers. "Anything else I'm missing?"

"I don't know," Theo commented, not even bothering to look up from Toyo's pack. She sat behind him, a disgruntled expression on her face. "Maybe a pissed-off *kami* that has not one, not two…but *eight* heads that would consider any one of us an M&M in a bag of trail mix? Which makes my job of ensuring you lot stay alive that much harder."

Toyo snorted. "He's a vegetarian; he doesn't eat Abbies or Quotes. He just kills them."

As one, everyone turned to look at Toyo with varying degrees of disbelief and raised eyebrows, except for Yuri.

Toyo pointed at each of us. "Stop that. That's fucking creepy. You're not a hive mind." Woody *woo-woo*ed from where he sat to my right, as if he was agreeing with her. He probably was.

"I'm sorry, but how many women were sacrificed to him before Susano'o intervened?" Theo asked slowly.

"Susano'o is a dick and narcissist of the highest order. He is the *literal* snot from Izanagi's nose. Orochi gave the Quotidian women and Abstruse females who had been callously sacrificed by their villages refuge in his valleys. He never ate them. Most of them still live there, as his dragon form is essentially one massive temporal snare."

"I'm sorry, what?" Aidan asked, voicing the question everyone had in the room, without needing to specify.

Toyo sighed. "He's going to kill me if he finds out I revealed this. Anyone who is pulled into his dimension will not age, due to the level of *ki* he contains in his natural form, essentially creating a temporal snare where time ceases to have meaning. It is neither faster, nor slower, nor is it the same, because time doesn't even exist. His form is, simply put, another dimension that isn't bound within the confines of the liminal space. When he folds into his human form, his longtime residents experience no change. They continue as they always have. His actual dimension is separate from his physical being. Quotes can climb his peaks all day long without ever entering his dimension."

"Well that's about as clear as mud," Aidan muttered.

"Think of it as similar to our liminal space. His physical and his dimensional form run parallel to one another. But you have to be invited, or accompany someone who has been invited, to access it. If that wasn't the case, then people would be going missing far more often."

"And no one has ever noticed a mountain range that appears and disappears into thin air before?" Aidan asked skeptically.

Toyo flicked at something unseen on her shoulder. "He's never taken this form in the Quotidian realm. It's always been in the Abstruse realm, where moving land masses aren't necessarily a cause for concern."

"How did you escape?" Gale asked Yuri in curiosity, successfully inferring from the *yuki onna's* body language that she had been sacrificed to Orochi when the rest of us had remained clueless.

She lifted a shoulder. "I didn't."

"He doesn't hold anyone captive," Toyo tried to explain. "Everyone is free to come and go as they please."

Anhangá grunted. I cocked my head to the side. Toyo flushed. "They used to come and goes as they please." She cleared her throat. "Obviously, circumstances have…changed."

Silence fell over the conference room as everyone digested this information.

"Then…" Lala paused, as she considered how to ask her question. "Then what changed?"

"And why doesn't anyone know about this side of the *kami*?" Theo queried.

Toyo blew out a breath slowly. "Cultivating the image of a fearsome *kami*, one who ate Quotes and Abbies alike for trespassing on him, suited his needs. Until Susano'o happened. After Susano'o attempted to murder Orochi, he turned into a genuine asshole. One I had no recognition of." She added the last statement under her breath.

"Can't blame an Abbie for that," Lala pointed out, a loud crunch sounding through the conference room as she bit through her strawberry bon bon. She unwrapped another one. "So, the *kariudo* has been trapped on the plane of existence that is Orochi, with no sense of time, just an eternal cycle of torture, death, and rebirth?"

Anhangá looked grim as Toyo nodded, knowing exactly how many times Rafael had succumbed to Death. Lala continued, "So then how exactly do we free the *kariudo* and make it back onto Quote land without also becoming a prisoner?"

"That's why Cam dragged you back to this realm, isn't it," Aidan asked Toyo slowly. "You're his Thread, no matter if it was severed or not. You have a free pass to enter and exit at will. And you're going to use that to our advantage."

Toyo smiled slowly, revealing her jagged, crocodilian teeth in response.

The hells hath no fury like an Asian goddess scorned.

CHAPTER FIFTEEN

Sighs of relief surrounded me as we rematerialized into the cool air that graced the rugged beauty of Wrangell–St. Elias. The difference in temperature alone merited an internal debate about moving to Alaska. Even Pea scrambled down my body to revel in the feeling of ice beneath her paws. The crisp blue of the ocean complemented the glacial whites and blues of Tyndall Glacier. The roughly hewn Saint Elias mountains rose around it, accentuating the beautiful but foreboding nature that surrounded us.

It had taken a full day of deliberation, planning, and packing with Anhangá becoming increasingly impatient, but we were here at last. I gave Max a hug and checked the straps of his harness, ensuring that nothing had loosened on the trip. Pea hauled herself up his haunches, settling on his head for the beginning of our trek. Woodrow and Victoria had been incensed, but I left them in the care of Kenichi. We were risking enough on this trip. I didn't need to add them to the list since Max could track *ki*.

Gale appeared a minute later, a yelp escaping them as they registered the ice against their bare feet. They quickly scrambled up Cheuky's shoulder and began working on a small device. In moments, a 3D projection dropped over each of us, overlapping the landmarks of the Quote and Abbie realm. It was our usual protocol on a deployment that involved the Abstruse realm, and it prevented us from being led astray in the wilderness. For the most part, at least. Everyone stopped what they were doing and stood still for a moment as our vision adapted to the vertigo-inducing image.

"Cam," Toyo called, her tone hushed. She motioned to several irregular shapes that dotted the ice. Aidan, Yuri, and Theo were bent over a particularly large one. I followed Max to the one closest to me. His tail tucked between his legs as he let out a mournful whimper, and Pea hissed at the sight. Lala and Cheuky followed behind.

"Is…" Gale's voice was hushed. "Are those…?"

"I guess we know why the *habu kurage* were eager to partake in the torture and murder of so many civilians on behalf of my alleged father," Toyo said grimly. "They were promised the ability to walk on land again."

Except deals with gods never went well, as Toyo had pointed out to me earlier. The jellyfish may have bargained for the ability to walk on land again, but the devil was in the details. They still possessed no skeleton. No shell to protect them from the elements. And most importantly, no ability to process oxygen outside of the sea. What was worse was the sight of varied species dotting the ice. There were thousands who had followed their cousins in vain.

Cheuky shaded her eyes and I turned to see what she was gazing at. Lala gently admonished Phally behind me, who was nosing at the dead moon jelly in front of her.

"The road to Hell…" Cheuky said softly as we watched a group of jellyfish drag themselves out of the water. "All those lives. Gone. For a lie." *Habu kurage*, Lion's Mane, moon jellies—the assortment was wide and varied. Most native to Alaska's waters. I assumed more were attempting the same on their own shores. At the sight of them, Toyo sprinted to the edge, where glacier met water, slipping and sliding on the ice along the way. Before she plunged into the water, she transformed into a massive crocodilian, sending a huge wave over the ice and dragging the new group back into the sea as the water receded.

"I hope they listen," Yuriko said grimly, walking up to us.

"Toyo has a better chance than the rest of us. For all her alleged faults, or perhaps *because* of them, she was beloved by the masses and despised by the upper class. She always took the time to check in with the *habu kurage* and the less aggressive jellyfish in the realm. Toyo always felt her father's punishment had been cruel and wildly unfair," I said, memories of going on walks with Toyo and stopping every thirty feet to talk to someone else. It was likely the reason Ryūjin chose to save her. Though Tamayori was loved by many for her sheer presence and beauty, she never took the time to get to know those below her. Ryūjin was nothing if not observant. He would've chosen the daughter he felt would do the most for his realm.

Only *he* had the knowledge of whether or not he knew how much his decision would hurt his surviving daughter.

Black tendrils of mist whipped wildly around us. I turned to address Anhangá, but found his eyes consumed with blackness, rage radiating from his body. I took a step back, pulling Yuriko, Lala, and Cheuky with me, leery of his power, which had ensnared me back in the dungeons of Ryūgū-jō. Their K9s followed us, recoiling from the threat in their vicinity. Pea quickly threw a shield over us, tinting our world in more shades of blue. Theo and Aidan were safe enough, still a ways out. Theo was crouched over the Lion's Mane he and Yuri had first approached upon our arrival, and was taking samples, which he tucked away in his pack. Aidan straightened and anxiety cascaded over his face as he processed the situation at hand.

"Anhangá." I raised my voice when he didn't respond. "*Anhangá*." The pitch-black of his gaze narrowed in on me, but he didn't respond, the black mist only expanding, beginning to swallow his enormous body.

"*Aish*. Fuck this," Cheuksin muttered, stepping out from under Pea's shield. She marched up to the stag and gave him a mighty slap across his muzzle, one that made me and Lala flinch, while Yuriko looked on. The diminutive goddess grabbed his muzzle firmly in her small hand and jerked his head around to look into his right eye. "You listen to me, you giant asshole of a cervid. The one responsible for this massacre *isn't here*. Unleashing your power serves no one. It only hurts the people who are trying to help. Toyo is doing what she can to spread the word that to walk the land is to find death. You want to get revenge? Then fucking rein it in and hunt that eight-headed douche-canary down and take it out on *him*. Not us."

The entity blinked, the black slowly clearing from his eyes, while the mist that had overtaken the ice around him began to retreat. He shook his head, freeing his snout from her grasp. He tilted his antlers toward her. "Thank you, Toilet Girl." A lip curled up and over a fang in apparent distaste. "It seems losing control around you, little *haetae*, is becoming a habit."

I recoiled. "Please don't let it." The shield around us dropped with a quiet *pop* as Pea let her *ki* go, scolding the entity with violent hisses and clicks. Another whimper sounded from the sorrowful head next to my hip and I dropped to a knee to give the compassionate Saint Bernard another hug. "I know, sweetie. The *ki* is thick and filled with death and pain. I'm sorry for bringing you on this trip with me."

Maxwell had been with Pea and me the longest out of any K9. His ability to understand situations was likely greater than many Quotes at this point. I felt my heart trying to break into smaller fragments at the grief he was absorbing from his surroundings and squeezed him tighter for it. A long, wide tongue made its way across my face as he licked me in reassurance. "I know you'll be okay, but I'm still sorry, buddy."

A massive reptilian head flopped onto the edge of the glacier, sending up a spray of ice from its sheer weight. It was far larger than it had been when she dove in. Claws scrabbled for purchase in the ice as Toyo bellowed from the effort it was taking her to clamber up the edge of the glacier. There was no point in helping her. For one, she was way too large right now for any of us to bear her weight, supernatural strength or not. Second, there was the fact that I knew she would unequivocally refuse it.

"Good goddamn," Lala murmured, moving to stand in front of Phally like she thought Toyo might eat her K9. "Is she related to the dinosaurs? How big is she?"

"Dinosaurs aren't reptiles," Toyo called as she shifted into her human form and laid on the ice, chest heaving for air. "Fuck, I'm out of shape. What did Misaki do to my body?"

"I doubt she was hauling a few tons of crocodile ass out from the sea onto a shelf of ice," Theo remarked as he walked up to us, capping one last specimen and swinging his pack back over his shoulder.

"I can't help if you lot are jealous of my big and beautiful curves," Toyo snarked back, rolling onto her hands and knees and hauling herself back to standing.

Yuriko sighed and gave the *kami* a look. "Shall we move while we still have daylight?"

The summer solstice had already come and gone for the year, and Alaska was rapidly losing light with every passing day, though the days were still a couple hours longer than they had been in Skamania. We split into the three groups we had planned. Icy Bay sat nearly center to the eight peaks that had settled in the area. Each team had an individual that had extrasensory abilities when it came to searches, a traditionally trained K9, and a deity, or someone with near godlike powers. I had Max. Lala joined me with Phally, along with Cheuksin. Theo had his ability to track karmic balances. As a *dokkaebi*, he was nearly as powerful as Anhangá, Toyotama, or Cheuksin. When combined with Yuriko's power, even diminished, they equaled the other two teams, even without an additional member. Yuri's K9, Willa, rounded out their team. Finally, Toyo would be relying on the remnants of her Thread to guide her way, and was joined by Aidan and his K9, Yumi, in order to have someone watching her back.

Anhangá had to return to his lands, unable to leave his responsibilities for long, and Gale would be jumping from one team to the next to help as needed, not being constrained by the same laws of physics as the rest of us.

We completed one last equipment check, doing our best to ignore the death that surrounded us. With that done, we split into our teams and went our separate ways.

"Whoever thought we'd be on our way to rescue that Creepy Abbie in the Woods," Lala commented, as we began tracking to the northeast. Max and Phally led the way over the ice, though still tethered to me and Lala as a precautionary measure. None of us were willing to risk losing them to a crevasse for a better chance of catching a scent. Max sneezed and shook his head several times, trying to rid himself of the intense traces of *ki* that remained in the area.

"Creepy Abbie in the Woods?" Cheuky asked.

"Oh yeah…that's what we dubbed Rafael before we knew who he was. Just showed up out of nowhere to harass Cam, then vanished just as quickly. He earned the name," Lala reassured the goddess.

Cheuky snorted. "Why am I not surprised. That male isn't the best at understanding social graces, and why would he be as a *kariudo*?"

Why would he be indeed? Although it didn't have anything to do with his position in life to me, as I recalled his life to date.

"Is he really that bad?" Gale asked, fascinated. They had opted to stick with our team to start. "He seemed nice enough when I saw him at the facility that one time."

I hesitated. "Bad isn't the right word for Rafael."

"Conflicted," Cheuksin offered. "He's a deeply conflicted Abbie."

I agreed. "He didn't want to do the bad things. Most of the time at least. He usually doesn't have a choice. But sometimes the ends justified the means for him." Orochi and Rafael were the first beings who I had tried to consume that still remained among the living. It was jarring, holding their memories as if I lived them, knowing they were still in this realm. At least with Orochi, I had only partially inhaled the Evil within him. I had consumed *all* of Rafael's, leaving me with an intimate knowledge of all the past experiences that had shaped him into who he was today.

Gale chewed on that information as we continued in silence before disappearing to check on the other teams. Pea abandoned her perch on Max's head to burrow down into the comfort of the pouch on his harness. A few hours later, we had all worked up a sweat, despite the cool temperatures. We were in the middle of the civil twilight as the sun continued to drop beyond the horizon, the alpenglow leaving a pink cast against our surroundings.

"There's a good place to set up camp less than a mile from here," Gale said suddenly as they popped back on Cheuky's shoulder. "You should be able to get there before blue hour passes into night."

"Shit on a stick!" Lala yelled, startled.

"Did you not get my signal that I was coming back?" Gale asked.

"I'm a Peri," she reminded the gremlin. "I require a more obvious signal than these two."

The gremlin flushed a little, their green cheeks darkening. "I forgot about that. Sorry."

Lala waved their concern off. "You're good. I needed that adrenaline to wake me back up."

"How are the other teams doing," I asked.

"Good. Toyo thinks they'll reach their target in a couple days." While my team was looking for Rafael, Toyo's was searching for the essence of the *kami* himself so she could provide a distraction while the rest of us got Rafael out. Theo's team was running the end of the range to cover our bases, and had the furthest to go. "She gave me these to give to you guys."

The little gremlin held out three small Mason jars. A viscous red fluid with a distinct pearlescent sheen filled each, and it had...*stuff* floating in it.

Lala wrinkled her nose. "Is that..."

"Blood," Cheuksin said, frowning at the jar. "Bits of shell, and… scutes? The scales from her crocodilian form?"

Gale nodded. "She said to drink this before you try to enter Orochi's dimension. It contains blood from her human form, shell from her sea turtle, and scutes from her crocodilian hide. The components from each of her forms should grant you entrance."

"What is with all the Abbies who want me to *eat* them lately?" I complained.

Lala waggled her eyebrows suggestively. I swatted her. "That is not what I meant, and you know it." I sighed. "At least Reika has desensitized me to the act. Kind of. Maybe. Okay not at all."

At least we didn't have to do it right now. We arrived in the clearing that Gale had mentioned and there was a collective set of groans as we dropped our packs on the ground, glad to be rid of the weight. Although Cheuksin wasn't part of the agency, setting up camp was still a breeze, as Lala and I were long used to working around one another. Cheuksin busied herself with working with our supplies to make dinner.

"We realize how insane this deployment is, right?" Lala suddenly piped up as she tossed a couple sleeping bags my way to put in the tents I had set up. Pea clicked with displeasure about the sudden movement, poking her head out of my jacket to see what was going on. She had migrated from Max to me for the last half of our trek. The *shikigami* climbed out of my jacket and down my body, opting to resettle on the sleeping bag I had laid out. Lala watched her movements with a quirk to her lips.

"I'm not the only one who recognizes that, right? We're somehow supposed to find *one* being across the span of eight mountain peaks? Valleys included? With no aerial assistance and no motorized vehicles to speed up the search, just three teams on foot?"

"I have access to the aerial searches that are being conducted by the Quotes," Gale reassured Lala. "I can hear everything they're saying and have all of their data. All of the missing people have been localized to one area. My father and I suspect that they've been disappearing anytime they get close to where Rafael is being kept, regardless of whether or not they can enter Orochi's dimension. It's the area that has been pinging with the most unusual seismic activity, along with other oddities. Toyo's connection should help lead her straight to Orochi's actual presence. Nobody expects Theo's team to pick up anything, but we still need to cover all our bases."

"And somehow avoid detection by the Quotes when we switch back into their realm. That should be fun," Lala countered.

I tossed the wadded-up compression sacks that had contained the sleeping bags back at her, the light fabric falling far short of their target. "Since when did you become such a pessimist?"

Lala walked over to pick them up. "Since we started a deployment on *a brand-new mountain range* in *Alaska*. Let's not forget that the mountain range is actually a *deity*. We've done our share of complicated searches, the one for Misaki, a.k.a. Toyo, being a particular highlight. But this? Come on, now; we don't have a chance in hell."

I shrugged. "Good thing we've got a Death entity, a goddess with one foot in Yomi, and another goddess capable of inflicting awful disease on our team then."

Said deity of STIs handed us each a bowl of steaming ramen. Not the instant kind, but the kind with a rich broth base and loaded with extras. All made from ingredients we didn't have in our packs.

"New rule," Lala announced, staring at her bowl in fascination. "We're never going on a call-out again without a household deity. This is fucking amazing, Cheuky."

Cheuky gave a nod to Gale, who sat on a lounging Max, who had already scarfed down his meal. "Thank them. They created a pocket in the liminal sera for me to store ingredients."

"Gale, you are my hero. Both of you are." Lala sighed happily as she drank the broth. Gale gave her a thumbs-up with one hand.

I offered my jammy eggs to Pea, who took each half one at a time, delicately plucking them from my fingers with her one forepaw.

"We'll find him," I said with more confidence than I felt. My mother's warning about being too late echoed in my mind.

I didn't think I had a choice in the matter.

CHAPTER SIXTEEN

Dreams were strange experiences. Because how did I unzip the entrance to my tent and step out to take a piss and end up on my back porch in Neskowin otherwise? The transition from the brisk mid-thirties back into the sweltering heat wave was another mindfuck altogether. I much preferred the reverse, when Anhangá had dropped us off in Alaska.

I didn't bother greeting Rafael this time. Instead, I made my way through the thick atmosphere, padding over the wooden planks in my insulated socks to drop into the chair next to him.

"I'm sorry," I said softly once I settled, busying myself with picking threads out of the pillow. He was only a figment of my imagination, but it always took days to shake the violent images my mind created when these dreams happened. Because I knew somewhere out there, he actually was being tortured.

It was why I did my best to avoid sleep now.

"For what?"

"The question."

I could see his lip curl up out of the corner of my eye. "I know you're not intentionally asking the question, Baki."

I suppose it made sense that my subconscious would know that after all.

"Well, even so. I wish I had more control over it." My head thudded back against the chair and I stared at the stars. The haze created by the heat wave made them shimmer in the night.

"There's a lot of things I wish I had more control over, Baki. I believe you Americans like to say that if wishes were horses—"

"—beggars would ride," I finished. "Horses hate me. They know I'm actually a predator and they start panicking."

"That must have been hard to explain back in early-1900s Oregon."

I laughed. "You have no idea. It was bad enough being a lone Asian woman living in the woods. Now I'm a strange Asian woman in the woods who terrifies horses? Yeah, I spent most of those years in the Abstruse realm so I wouldn't end up burned at the stake as a witch."

"Ah, Quotes. Always so quick to violence against anyone who doesn't look or sound like them."

"Mmm." I was too tired tonight to be contentious. "Have you ever thumb warred?" I asked out of the blue.

I could tell the question took him aback based on the bewilderment on his face and his slowness to respond. "Have I ever…" His voice trailed off.

"Thumb warred," I encouraged. I knew he hadn't. There was no room for gaiety in the life he had led thus far.

"Is this a metaphor for something? Because I'm struggling to understand how thumbs go to war."

"Not at all," I said with as much cheer as I could muster through my fatigue. I grabbed his hand, the rules of cautious touch out with the wind in a dream. I heard a soft intake of air and steadfastly avoided eye contact, while also doing my best to ignore the way his hand felt in my own. Instead, I adjusted his grip, placing our thumbs in the proper position.

"Alright, so here's what we do." I finally looked up. "Your thumb is going to stay upright and we're gonna chant at the same time."

He raised an eyebrow. "Are we performing a spell?"

"No, you dork. We're gonna chant: One, two, three, four, I declare a thumb war."

A grin slowly spread across his face. "One, two, three, four, I declare a thumb war. Got it."

"Then…" I manipulated my thumb and smashed his down against our joined hands. "We're gonna fight to get the other's thumb down first. You don't win by pinning the thumb though. You gotta keep the other's thumb down long enough to chant, 'One, two, three, four, I win thumb-o-war.' *Then* you win," I let his hand go free and mock-cheered, pumping both fists into the air. "I win!"

"I do believe that could be considered cheating," he commented.

"*Psh.* Best three out of five?"

"You're on." An affectionate look entered his eyes, tinged with good humor and delight. It might have been the first time I'd seen actual joy in his eyes.

"Alright, you ready? And *go*." We began the chant together and then all bets were off. First, our arms went wild as we each tried to gain the advantage. Then our entire bodies got involved, as we contorted into any position that might allow us to pin the other's thumb, cackling maniacally as we did. Official rules of thumb war were out the window. It was, as it was called, *war*. Soon, we weren't even limiting ourselves to the one hand—the other got involved as Rafael tried to tickle me, and I tried to jab him in the armpit.

I won the second round after I gave his thigh a wicked horse bite and startled him into a yelp. Rafael caught on quickly and won the next three after he learned that my ribs were the death zone for tickles. We both fell into our chairs panting and shaking with laughter.

It was the most fun I'd had in ages.

We fell into a comfortable silence after we stopped laughing and focused on catching our breath, allowing the moment to linger.

"Why can't you let me go, Baki?" Rafael whispered into the night.

I stared pensively at my hands. The ones that had touched this male playfully just moments ago. With any luck, I would be seeing the real Rafael soon and I needed to be honest with myself.

"You betrayed me, yes," I admitted. "But others have betrayed me far more brutally, and I still found it within myself to forgive them."

It was easier back then. I didn't have to worry about how every shift brought me closer to death. I could see for myself if they were falling to Evil or not, and if they weren't, I couldn't bring myself to continue hating them. Even in cases where I obviously should have.

The *mukwa* I had forged a relationship with being a standout example. He had attempted to slay me the first time he had seen me shifted. I forgave him for it. He was terrified. He didn't know *haetae* actually existed.

And then he had betrayed my family and me to his commanders once he learned what my mother and I truly were. He had been the one to stab my mother in the liver with the ulleungdo hemlock sap.

Rafael's fingers tapped along the leather cuff hiding the bands beneath the material. "I led you to your death."

"You saved me from death," I corrected. "Did you lead me there? Sure. But no matter how many times I look back on that fight, you did everything you could to mitigate my death. I was just too angry to realize it at the time."

"I'm aware," he responded ruefully, rubbing his heart.

I nodded to it and let out a sigh. "I saw your heart, Rafael. I saw your memories. And I regretted my actions almost instantly, even if I didn't want to admit it to myself. You're not an evil male. Is your heart teetering on the edge? Yes. But that is due to Orochi's commands. You haven't tipped into Evil because you are truly disgusted and devastated with every life you take."

"Nearly every life," he corrected. "There have been some that I have been happy to execute. They weren't good males."

No, I thought with a shudder, recalling some of his memories. *They had certainly not been good males.*

I sighed again. "Once I realized that, holding onto my anger was a challenge. I haven't actually hated you for several weeks now. Just myself and my impulsive actions."

"I still can't see how. I haven't even had the opportunity to try to redeem myself, and you're here saying I'm forgiven?"

"You redeemed yourself the moment you saved my life, Rafael. You redeemed yourself when you revealed what you are to Orochi in an effort to protect me, and then sacrificed yourself. You feel the need to do a grand gesture? There's nothing much grander than those actions in my eyes."

I readjusted my chair so I could look him directly in the eyes. "I'm not the one who needs to forgive you. The burden of that responsibility now lies firmly on your shoulders. But if you still feel the need to redeem yourself, I'm not going to say no to a grand gesture after we find you."

I could feel the question rising and slammed a palm over my mouth in an attempt to stymie the words that were trying to pour out. The *kariudo* gave me a sad smile and gently pulled my hand away.

The words fell like an anchor on land. "Tell me where you are, Rafael."

The mountains in Alaska rang with my scream when I woke.

CHAPTER SEVENTEEN

Rafael's consciousness began to return, much to his dismay.

He groaned as he woke up yet again, this time to an unfamiliar sensation on his skin. The ground beneath him felt different. Not as...hard. Or cold. No, the ground under him felt spongy, the softness a luxury he hadn't experienced in an eon. And while he wasn't warm, he could feel warmth upon his body. Which was an unwelcome feeling on the areas missing flesh. A twinge of panic also filled his body, but before he could suss out the reason, feminine voices reached his ears, confusing him further.

"Oh, he's waking!"

He pried an eye open and was immediately blinded. His lids slammed back shut.

The sun. He was in the sun.

Someone held a cup to his mouth and glorious liquid flowed down his throat, relieving some of the fire burning through it. He couldn't remember the last time he had the opportunity to drink something. Maybe the coffee Cam had made in her Neskowin home?

Knowing he was in daylight now, he took his time opening his eyes, cracking them just enough to squint. A bevy of women and females stared down at him. Old, young. Tall, short. Lithe, curvy. Quotes. Abbies.

Maybe he had died for real this time. He couldn't think of any other explanation for the circle of females gazing at his body. He self-consciously tried to cover himself, but his arms wouldn't listen to his brain's commands.

Two of them rolled him onto his stomach before he could say anything, and the most amazing sensation flooded through his body as a cool, soothing blanket covered the raw meat of his back and shielded his wounds from the sun. A groan rang from his lungs before he could stifle it. The feminine chatter above him rose with the sound.

The woman he could most easily see from his peripheral, an elderly auntie, frowned. She made as if to pat him on his shoulder, but stopped short of doing so, to his great relief. He begged her to kill him with his eyes.

However, to the opposite effect, she shook her head in response to his request. His eyes closed in frustration.

Fuck. It really was a versatile word. One that had peppered his thoughts since meeting Cam and her crew. He didn't think he could summon enough energy, nor breath, to explain that A) he wanted to die, and B) he wasn't suicidal, that he had a valid reason for wanting to die.

Guess he was going to be stuck healing Quote-slow until he could escape this body and reform a new one.

Rafael startled when he opened his eyes to find the auntie a few inches away from him, her myopic gaze considering his body. It evidently did not meet her expectations as she shook her head and muttered something under her breath. She *tsked* in a disapproving tone. The tree branch she was using as a walking stick struck the forest ground as if to emphasize her point.

He nodded incrementally, having no idea what he was agreeing with, but kept a wary eye on the woman. Honestly, he was probably more afraid of that branch than Orochi's torture. *Kamis* were one thing, but you never disrespected an auntie. The smaller they were—the *older* they were—the more power they wielded, as if the gods had decided age and size had to have an inverse relationship with strength, all in the name of balance.

"Why aren't you healing?"

He tried to answer but stopped as muscle spasms began to rack his body. Grimacing, he simply answered in Japanese, "Can't." Delight filled the atmosphere with that single word.

A broad smile wreathed the auntie's face at the sound of his voice. "Ah, this is much better," she responded back in kind.

"Where?" he mouthed as his energy began to sap.

She motioned around her. "We are in the forests of Orochi."

Well, damn. He hadn't expected anything else, and yet, the confirmation he remained hostage to the *kami* felt like another blow to his body. However, it didn't explain why he was here and not in the cave where he had spent the past eternity.

The panic flickered again and nausea swirled in his gut, burning as it rose up his throat, leaving a terrible taste in his mouth.

The fire in his throat.

Vines wrap around his neck, restraining and choking him at the same time.

Endless pain, before it suddenly stops.

Floating in and out of consciousness before the kami *returns.*

Rafael furrowed his brow as he questioned whether the next image was anchored in reality or simply a hallucination born out of pain. A hand attempted to smooth out the crinkles in his forehead, admonishing him about wrinkles. But…he heard voices in the memory. American voices that begged and pleaded. And Orochi's voice ringing out above them.

"I'm afraid I will have to evict you from this space, kariudo. *I require larger accommodations for the pesky Quotes. You do understand, yes?"*

Accommodations. As though he had simply been staying at a hotel resort and enjoying all the amenities the *kami* had to offer. Ten percent off your exfoliation treatment for staying with Hotel Orochi indefinitely!

You know… he mused to himself. *I bet Grandfather and Orochi might actually get along, now that I think about it.*

He hadn't seen who had been deposited in the cave or what they looked like—his eyes had been swollen shut—but there had been multiple voices of all genders. He wished he knew where he was in relation to the cave, although it wasn't as if he was in the type of shape where he could go scavenging for information, or freeing other hostages. Which brought his mind back to the hands carefully tending the injuries littered across his body.

Why was Orochi amassing Quotes like they were his personal insect collection?

Rafael was too exhausted to contemplate it now; he'd ask the women more questions after he took a nap. He tried to place the feeling of panic in his system…

And startled himself back into wakefulness. A new energy and a whole lot of fear riddled his body.

Why wasn't Cam in the Pacific Northwest? More to the point—

Why was she nearing his location?

A dark shadow fell over Rafael. He struggled to open his eyes again to determine its origin, but when he did, he found a massive *onna uo* staring back at him. A ripple of water sparkled around her, a rare ward that was designed specifically with water-dwelling Abbies in mind. Rafael had only seen one of its kind in his history. She rose several feet above him, the horns protruding from her human head nearly three feet in length. The *onna uo's* hair puddled on the forest floor. He was unable to see past her to estimate the total breadth of her body, but she had to be far more than fifty feet in length. Fins tipped in claws paddled at the water in her ward, bringing her closer to him.

His gaze narrowed in on the patch of flesh missing on her abdomen. It looked fresh, with the way blood wept from the wound, but he knew better, having wielded a similar weapon in the past. Rafael remembered the fleeting relief he had experienced when Baki had divested him of the blades. Because he bore witness to the effects of wounds that would never heal directly in front of him. Judging by the shape and size of the wound, this was the *onna uo* who had "donated" her flesh to the making of Orochi's journal. The same *onna uo* who had started this quest into madness so long ago.

The same *onna uo* who ominously intoned, "Your time is coming, *kariudo*," in the here and now.

What the flying fuck was that supposed to mean?

CHAPTER EIGHTEEN

"Altitude is a bitch," Lala groaned as we trudged up yet another steep incline.

We were finally off the glacier and had been ascending the latest mountain peak for the past thirty-six hours, stopping at night to rest. I hadn't slept since that first night, not wanting to risk the nightmare again. My ears still resonated with the sound of Rafael's cries of pain, as if they were happening right now. It only made me more determined to find the male once and for all.

Max and Phally were in their element, fresh off their night of sleep, and charged up the mountain side, noses in the air, searching for any hint of Rafael, whether it was his scent or *ki*.

"Why can't we ever get called out for someone missing in, like… Nebraska," Lala said, panting.

"Then you'd be complaining of humid conditions because of the corn sweat," I commented, keeping an eye on the K9s. Pea clicked in agreement, the sound practically vibrating in my ear as she snuggled in closer to my neck.

"What must it be like, having four legs to support your body weight instead of these two stick things," Lala continued to grumble as we began to summit the latest peak.

Cheuksin laughed, making Lala jab a trekking pole in her direction.

"Not a sound out of you. You're like…thirty-five pounds soaking wet. Okay, so maybe I'm exaggerating, but still. You're not hauling up as much weight as this human body who still experiences the terrible feeling of my muscles slowly tearing into shreds because of this incline."

"I have shorter legs, so I have to take more strides," Cheuky pointed out.

"Irrelevant. You're a goddess."

"She has a point," I agreed as my own quads burned. This climb would be so much easier if I could have shifted.

Lala sighed in relief when we reached the summit. I squinted despite the eye protection I wore. We were overlooking a deep basin, carved out by glaciers long since gone, now overtaken by the boreal forests. Goose bumps rippled across my skin—they always did when we were in Alaska for a training or call-out—as I took a moment of silence. The knowledge of how many Alaska Native women had gone missing or murdered in this state never failed to test my faith in humanity.

Because on the rare occasion a woman was found, it was a Quote who had committed the crime. Never an Abbie. Privately, I reflected on whether this world was worth saving after all.

I couldn't help but wonder how many women had lost their lives without anyone ever reporting them missing and fervently hoped those souls had found peace after their lives had been cut short.

"You good?" Cheuksin bumped my shoulder.

"Yep." I swallowed and shook out my hands, as though it could rid me of the eerie feeling that had come over me, and refocused on the land below us. I cringed at the sight of a muskeg—finding our way around the unfamiliar bog would be our safest option.

Most importantly, the overlay of the Quote realm revealed our destination. A vast formation loomed over the basin, instead of the ridge of spines we saw in our realm. Red pins the size of trees dotted the side, near the base. They had to be on the other side of the muskeg, of course. Orochi had settled himself right over the top of an existing range. *Bet that was driving the researchers mad.*

I peered up at the sun, gauging the distance and the sun's position. "We should make it by the end of the day. We'll set up camp in the basin before we try going any further."

It would be suicide to attempt at night.

We carefully picked our way down the rocky terrain and passed the alpine line and into the cover of the trees that made their home in this environment.

As one, we all paused our progress, watching warily as a massive *onikuma* made her way across the basin, three cubs following her playfully. One rolled off their path and sank beneath the deceptive surface of the muskeg. I held my breath, but the cub splashed back out without a problem, tackling one of its siblings, while its mother continued on her path without bothering to check if her offspring followed.

"Quotes above," Cheuksin whispered. "What's wrong with her?"

At Cheuksin's question, I refocused on the *onikuma*. On my second glance, I could see patches of missing fur, the skin beneath it appearing melted. The cubs played as if nothing was wrong with them, but upon closer inspection, one had a foot turned completely backwards. And when another turned to face me, its face was missing half its fur, and an eye was missing from the socket. Only the one who had fallen into the muskeg looked the way I would expect a normal *onikuma* cub to look.

Over the past three days, we had run into several variety of *hanzaki*—one massive salamander had broken through a thin crust of ice to watch us as we passed, before it settled back into place. We had cautiously bypassed a cave system that housed a *tsuchigumo*, nearly falling into its illusion and becoming the spider's meal, if not for Lala noticing the sheen of a web. Gale reported that Theo's team had had to barter with a *yamauba* who had made her territory southeast of the glacier. Apparently, the *yōkai* had shied away from Toyo's presence, as her team had yet to encounter anybody.

Despite our sightings, there was no other indication of life in this basin, beyond the *onikuma* and her cubs. No calls of birds. No movement in the brush from ground-dwelling animals or Abbies, *yōkai* or otherwise.

The reason for the stillness struck us the moment we reached the bottom. A pulse of *wrongness* enveloped us. The hairs on the nape of my neck rose from the sensation of something—*someone*— watching us. A hollow formed in my stomach and my breathing grew difficult, strained. As though an elephant was sitting on my chest doing its best to crush the air out of me. My limbs filled with restless agitation, making me want to run, flail, kick, *anything* to get rid of the feeling. Max howled in distress, a sound I almost never heard from him, and the K9 laid down, frantically pawing at his muzzle like he could physically remove the feeling. Phally cowered between Lala's legs, tail tucked, his entire body trembling. Pea hissed long and low from inside my jacket.

"You guys feel that, right?" Lala asked through gritted teeth, her hands fisted at her sides.

Cheuksin nodded through a grimace. Pea fled down my jacket, as if it could protect her from whatever it was, and a blue shield shimmered over us a moment later, providing relief from the sensation. Max and Phally wouldn't be able to scent, but I didn't give a damn about that.

"If that's how bad it is on this side, imagine how much worse it is in the Quote realm." I sucked in air, trying to recover.

"How did the researchers even cope with this?" Cheuksin rubbed her arms.

"Anything in the name of science, I guess." Lala pulled her hair out of its messy bun and shook her head violently. "God, it's clinging to me. I've never needed a shower so badly. What the hell kind of ward is this? Pea, I think this might be the most I have ever appreciated one of your shields."

I bent to rub my hands along Max's body. The big K9 leaned hard into me, throwing different parts of his body into my hands to make sure I didn't forget them. Pea nudged the elastic at the waist of the jacket aside and clambered onto Max's back. She made her way to his head to peer at the landscape, letting out a soft hiss at invisible wards that surrounded her shield. Lala mimicked my administrations with Phally. Both K9s shook afterward, both sneezing several times in succession before sitting, waiting for us to tell them how to proceed.

"Let's just head toward the pins. We knew we weren't really going to catch a trail outside of Orochi's dimension. I'd rather keep the K9s under the shield," Lala decided, voicing the thoughts running through my head.

"That ward must be the reason for the defects on the *onikuma* and her cubs. But why would they stay in this region," Cheuky wondered out loud.

The sound of bickering voices cut through the air. No, bickering was too kind a word. The opinions of the two individuals were being vociferously made. To make things worse, I realized I recognized both of them. One...somewhat expected. The other? I spun to find Reika and Anhangá mere feet behind us, looking like they were about to go to war upon one another. A gentle electrical buzz lit the air, signaling Gale was on their way, giving Lala ample warning of their arrival.

"What in Yomi are you doing here?" I hissed at Reika, not unlike Pea. I had been looking forward to my mini vacation from the *yamauba*, if one could call trekking through the Alaskan wilderness a vacation. But apparently, I wasn't that lucky. Gale popped into the space at that moment, appearing on Anhangá's withers. None were able to pass through Pea's *ki*.

The hag turned her back to the stag and flung something at my face, making me flinch back when it passed through the shield. Whatever Reika's latest concoction was missed my face and slid down my jacket, leaving a slimy residue behind. Pea snapped her jaws violently at Reika in rage.

"You thought—you *really* thought—that you could leave me behind? Skimp on calling forth Ryūjin's *ki*? Does no one respect their betters anymore?" Reika sniped.

Her wording didn't slip past me. Not elders, but *betters*. The stag snorted in agreement with my thoughts, knowing that four of us in this space had years on Reika.

"The crocodile and Theo have hit the ward, too," Anhangá announced. "Toyotama insisted that we would need this hag to get through the wards to get to Orochi." A hoof stamped the ground, leaving an imprint in the marshy area.

"The *ki* in this area has twisted," Reika informed us. "There's something in the ward that is targeting the amygdala and turning off its survival mechanism for some, disorienting the beings caught in it so that the instinct to flee never happens."

"That seems counterintuitive to a ward," Cheuksin pointed out.

"What part of twisted didn't you hear," she snapped. She held out three bracelets and three collars. "These will help shield you against its effects, so Pea can conserve her *ki*."

Pea reluctantly let down her shield and the soured magic hit us the moment it dropped. We pulled the trinkets out of Gale's hands, and I bent to fasten the collars on Pea and Max before adding my own to my wrist. The pressure faded immediately and I breathed a sigh of relief.

Gale jumped in during the small pause in conversation. "My father and I assessed the muskeg and laid out a safe path for you guys."

A slightly opaque trail dropped over the bog, allowing us to still see the terrain beneath but clearly delineating the areas less likely to trap and drown us. I really didn't know how regular SAR operations functioned without the aid of tech-savvy gremlins. I held my hand to them for a high-five which they reciprocated.

"This cuts so much time for us. Thank you, Gale. You, too, Whiz," I called, knowing that even if he wasn't here, he was always listening.

"You thank the gremlin, but not me?" Reika bared her terrifying teeth at me.

"Of course. Gale is actually likeable. You aren't," I volleyed back at her, still grossed out by the glistening trail of *something* on my clothing.

"Well, shall we?" Lala cut in, gesturing to the land in front of us. She carefully stepped on the bog and relaxed when it held her weight. We both shortened the leads we had on our K9s for tighter control as we forded the muskeg. Before we continued, Anhangá vanished in a swirl of black mist and my tension fell from my shoulders. Having Reika along wasn't my idea of a good time, but listening to her and the death entity bicker the entire time would have been infinitely worse.

Vegetation squished beneath our boots as water, darkened by tannins, seeped over them. A tinge of sulfur imbued the air. Stunted, scruffy junipers and spruce littered the land, lacing the sulfur with a much more pleasant aroma when we passed them. After about an hour of slow, but steady progress, we had crossed the muskeg and reached the first pin. "Anyone on the other side?" I asked Gale.

They shook their head. "The campsite is abandoned. Alaska's teams have already searched the area and moved past it."

"Here goes nothing then."

CHAPTER NINETEEN

The overlay of terrain lifted from our vision the moment we stepped into the researchers' base camp. It was as vertigo-inducing as when it was put in place. I waited a moment, the vertigo affecting my system worse than the others due to my competing *kis*.

At first glance, no one would have ever known that Quotes had been at this campsite recently. The flat area was cleared of all its equipment. The only sign anyone had been here for any length of time was the browned patches of grass. Those would blend in soon enough, now that autumn had hit Alaska. Elsewhere, the ground cover would be transitioning to the vivid ambers and golds of fall. Here, everything was shaded in the dull monotone colors of Death. Pea crawled out from her pouch and let out a long hiss when she beheld the sight in front of us.

"I wonder how the Quotes explained the decay," Cheuksin murmured. That feeling of *wrongness* we had experienced was indeed worse on this side. Like Ryūgū-jō, the muskeg was dying in the Quotidian realm. The water was covered by a thick, tarry substance. The vegetation—withered and brown. Blueberries had been in abundance in the Abstruse realm, yet not one berry was to be found here. Sulfur consumed the senses, overpowering any other scents in the area and leaving a foul taste, even with our mouths closed. Reika's *ki*-filled trinkets might prevent any harmful effects from the twisted magic in this place, but they didn't filter out the air surrounding us.

"At least we know what started Ryūgū-jō's illness," I observed as I fit a mask to Max's muzzle. Reversing the damage done to this place and Ryūgū-jō would be another matter altogether. Pea delicately bit the straps of Max's mask in her mouth, tugging gently and giving me a click of approval.

"Air scenting isn't going to be possible until we get out from under this cloud of gas," Lala pointed out, as she stood from fitting Phally to his own mask. Neither of us wanted our K9s to go nose-blind before we began our search in earnest.

"Hopefully once we gain access to Orochi's forests, the air pollution won't be a factor anymore." I mentally crossed my fingers

"We can't camp here," Cheuky agreed.

"I'm going to go update the others to let them know your change in plans and check in on where they're at," Gale announced. We gave them a thumbs-up before they vanished with a quiet *pop*.

Twisting my pack to my side, I pulled out the jars filled with…*bits* of Toyo, grimacing when they sloshed against the glass with the movement. "If we're not camping here tonight then…bottoms up, I suppose."

At least I'd had practice consuming all things offensive lately, thanks to Reika. Lala went positively green as she peered into her jar.

"Don't look at it too closely," Cheuksin advised her, albeit a little late.

"I hate swallowing aspirin, and now I'm going to be swallowing pieces of a *kami* I just met. What has this world come to?"

I unscrewed the lid while squeezing my eyes shut. With any luck, if I tossed it back at the right angle, maybe it wouldn't hit my tongue, and I could bypass the taste altogether.

No such luck. Lala and I gagged while Cheuksin sipped hers demurely.

"What?" she asked when we both gave her a look. She looked back at the chunky liquid in hand. "This? Please. After living in all manners of outhouses for millennia, this is nothing." The goddess shook her head at us, continuing to sip the concoction leisurely.

ALTHOUGH NIGHT WAS rapidly approaching, we made our way north, our movement becoming more challenging with every step.

"The hell? We're not even moving uphill yet," Lala said. "Why does it feel like we're trying to wade through a waist-deep muskeg?"

"Magic," I panted.

"Magic is stupid," she muttered. Pea gave a click in agreement as Lala bent to pick up Phally, who was struggling with the atmosphere, and hoisted him over her shoulders, settling him so the majority of his weight balanced across her pack. We had been doing our best to traverse the latest muskeg on our path for the past two hours, and the effort it took to cut through the thick, greasy air that was contaminated with *ki* and sulfur was immense.

Max led the way and was faring better than all of us with the little *shikigami* perched on his back blazing a path for him with *ki*. Unfortunately, her power only extended the length of Max's body, unable to withstand the wards for long. The rest of us were left to trudge along.

"Cam? Lala?" The urgency in Cheuksin's voice had us looking up. "You mentioned decapitations before we left."

"Ye…" Lala's voice trailed off before she could finish.

The trees in front of us rattled violently, sending scores of needles flying into the air. Rocks and twigs under our boots trembled with increasing intensity. But that wasn't what had our attention riveted.

"The source of the twisted *ki*," Reika said grimly.

We had found what countless searches had not.

Spanning before us was a veritable wall of heads. Our own heads tilted back as a collective, trying to find its apex, as it stretched over thirty feet into the sky. No end was visible as it extended as far as the eye could see to either side of us. Faces and empty sockets stared back at us, flickering with power. Some from fossilized skulls. Other skulls a shocking white against the sepia hues of the land. And some heads still as fresh as the day they were hacked from their body. Sightless eyes stared at us in varying degrees of decomposition. At me. Judgment for my failure to save them rang through my body. Whether that judgment was from the souls staring at me or generated from the self-hate in my mind was moot.

Although, our focus wasn't on the shock of the heads themselves.

No.

It was the way the skulls *vibrated* with *ki* as they began to shift. Hundreds, thousands of skulls moved as though they had been waiting for our arrival.

Vibrating. Then…rolling into position. Rising. A chattering noise clanged out against the silence of Death in the forest. Skulls worked their jaws to clamber upon one another, sinking their teeth into any remaining flesh to gain purchase and *climb*. One turned, his face still intact, the branches protruding from his skull shaking with the movement. His eyes glowed a haunting vibrant blue before he opened his mouth to scream as another bit down on his cheek to propel itself upward. Soon, he was lost beneath the heads that flowed over one another, gaining fluidity and speed as they went. A new *ki* arose as they began to take the shape of a massive skeleton.

"*Gashadokuro*," I breathed.

CHAPTER TWENTY

"WE are truly and utterly fucked," Cheuksin said, her eyes wide, taking in the sight of the skeleton forming in front of her. Waves of malevolence pulsed through the air, blending with the sulfur of the dying muskeg, creating an unholy combination.

Pea let out an ear-splitting screech and scrambled to the top of Max's head as both K9s snarled at the atrocity growing before us. Phally's mask snapped and hung by one ear as the German shepherd snapped his teeth at the threat to our presence. A blast of orange *ki* sent Phally scrambling to Max's side, his nails leaving drag marks below him, tearing up the decaying plant life as he went. As soon as he reached the Saint Bernard, a solid sheet of blue dropped over the three of them, and the sounds of their snarls muffled.

"Lala!"

"I'm right here," she said through gritted teeth. "I'm trying." The power that made her a Perigean flowed out of her and wrapped around the *gashadokuro*, doing its best to soften the anger and fear that emanated from the new being that had risen, to little effect. The malice that glinted like starlight in its empty eye sockets dimmed slightly. Skulls fell from its body and shattered on the ground as it gained size, only to be replaced by five others as it grew to enormous proportions. Bony hands grasped the stunted trees from the ground and flung them at us.

"This is why I came," Reika hissed, as she ripped a hand now tipped with talons through the air. The atmosphere rent before her, and bags upon bags of salt began to spill out of the pocket in the liminal sera.

"If you knew this was going to happen and said nothing about it, we are going to have words," I shouted, as I dove for the ground and narrowly missed being flattened by a hand the size of a truck. It was like trying to dive into a pool of molasses thanks to the ward that didn't impact the *gashadokuro's* movements, only ours. Cheuksin did the same, slamming against a large boulder as a spray of dirt, rocks, and vegetation rained down upon us.

Reika stood her ground, using her talons, her teeth, her sheer brute will to tear the bags of salt open, creating a small mountain of white, black, pink, and gray. Had the hag bought out the entire stock of salt in southwest Washington? No matter, I was grateful to have it.

The *gashadokuro* rose to its full height, towering above us, casting a shadow across a dying land. We all scattered as it took its first step, but Pea and the K9s weren't fast enough, the *shikigami's* concentration on maintaining the shield instead of cutting through the wards.

My heart fractured as I watched the foot come down on them. "Phally!" Lala shrieked, losing her grip on her power. Malevolence smothered the air as her influence shattered. The ball of *ki* that made up Pea's shield went flying out from under the *gashadokuro's* foot, its force unable to penetrate the shield. I screamed as Pea, Max, and Phally smashed into the muskeg and began to sink.

Before I could move toward them, a force slammed into my chest, forcing all air from my body as it squeezed and lifted me high above the others. I struggled to free myself and stabbed down hard with the claws that manifested on one hand. I ignored the wrenching pain that came with the partial shift and ripped several skulls free. The *gashadokuro* shrieked with outrage, the sound echoing through the vast space, and flung me. I crashed upon a small grove of spruce, decaying skulls pelting my body, my heavy pack cushioning my landing, saving any ribs that weren't already broken.

Stringy hair that was once flame red in life, now the color of dried blood, filled my mouth, and a rheumy eye shifted in its socket to focus on me. The mouth of the *curupira* we had failed creaked open as if to say something, his decomposing skin tearing at the corners. Horror filled me at the sight, and I swallowed a scream rising in my throat, throwing the head from my body, my hands scrambling to rid my mouth of his hair.

"Cheuksin," the *yamauba* snapped. "Now! Be ready, *haetae*."

The household deity slammed her hands together, dodging the skulls that fell from the chest of the skeleton that loomed over her. A rainbow of salt rose into the air and exploded against the *gashadokuro*. Thousands of cries of pain surrounded us as the skulls shrieked in unison.

"Camellia, NOW!" Reika shouted as she launched herself at the *gashadokuro* and used her *deba* to climb the skeleton. The blade stabbed into sockets, jaws, anywhere she could make purchase to help her ascent.

In the blink of an eye, my vision shifted. Of course it had to be fucking salt. Salt didn't like to burn easily. But flesh did. To say nothing of the dying plant matter around us that was tinder to a flame.

My *ki* was sloppy. I didn't give a flying fuck about being careful about what I lit on fire. I slammed my *ki* into the molecules I now saw before me and sent them crashing into one another. All I cared about was getting these Quotes-damned *heads* out of my way so I could get to Pea, Max, and Phally.

The inferno was instantaneous as the flames surrounded the *gashadokuro*. The flames refueled and cycled through me, and I poured more *ki* into them until they began to glow white. Cheuksin hammered the skeleton with salt, my fire turning the grains molten as they crashed into the skeleton and melted bone.

Reika's *deba* lengthened as she reached her target, her blade now honed in such a way that it cut through the skulls with no effort at all. The *yamauba's* arm extended far behind her, and I watched, panting with effort, as the *deba* impaled the *gashadokuro's* back, sliding through a mass of flesh, bone, and cartilage, until the tip of the blade exited through its chest. I had enough sense of mind to keep flames from the hag, but the temptation to let her burn was strong.

Unearthly howls cut through the air as the heads screamed as one. They contained the rage of a death come too soon. The highest pitches carried the agony of never seeing justice served. The bass tones, the grief of leaving loved ones behind.

The discordance rang through my ears, deafening me, as I ran with agonizing slowness through the muskeg, Lala far ahead of me. Pea, Max, and Phally were sinking, the *shikigami's* shield now only half above the tarry substance that made up the water. The only reason they hadn't sunk completely was the sheer viscosity of the fluid, if it could still be called that. They were mere feet away from the path that would have taken us safely to the other side. Because of the twisted *ki* in the air, Pea could only hold her shield. Dropping it in favor of trying to save themselves would require her sacrificing someone, which she would never do. I could feel the strain of her power working to keep the wards out and preventing their group from slipping further into the muskeg.

A tendril of anger lashed through me. Once upon a time, Pea had been powerful enough that she could have easily saved us all. Now, she struggled to save three after the damage Ryūjin had done.

LALA RUMMAGED THROUGH her pack as we ran, pulling out a rope, tying knots with a speed that would put a sailor to shame.

"Pea," I screamed as I skid to a stop when we arrived, sending a spray of mud, leaves, and death everywhere. "Let go of the shield."

Instantly, the bubble popped, leaving us access to the three of them. The muskeg flooded the space left behind. Fear rode the K9s' eyes as they listened to their instincts and remained still, thank the Quotes. Max held Pea by her scruff, refusing to let the little *shikigami* go, the mask he had worn long gone, swallowed by the muskeg somewhere along the way.

"Phally first," I said, cautiously laying across the bog, spreading the weight of my body as much as possible while I inched toward the German shepherd mix. Pain screamed through my chest, as my broken ribs protested the movement.

"You're alright, buddy," Lala's tear-filled voice came from behind me. "You're doing so good. Stay still for Auntie Cam, okay? You'll get all the salmon in the world if you just be the best boy for Auntie Cam."

He watched his mom with intelligent eyes and remained still as I wrapped the rope that Lala had thrust in my hands carefully around his body. The inferno behind us reflected in his wide, terrified eyes. I gently slid my hands underneath his body and with a sucking sound, shifted him, so the K9 lay on his side, rather than on all fours. He struggled in my hands, everything in his brain telling him he needed to be on his feet, not on his side.

"No, no Phally," Lala cried. "Play dead, okay, bud? This is just a game, just play dead."

Trusting her, Phally closed his eyes and went limp, playing dead as she indicated, and I closed the loop of rope around him. I tugged and Lala began to drag his body back with agonizing slowness. Sobs rang out behind me, letting me know he was safe now. I focused on Max, holding his big head between my hands.

"You can let her go now, big guy," I whispered softly. "You did so good."

The gentle giant carefully let the little opossum drop from his maw. Pea scrambled up my arm and sat on my head, as a flurry of clicks, chirps, and hisses were directed at the K9.

I chuckled, despite everything else. "I think you're being scolded, friend. She's already dead. You're not." Pea's tail thumped against my head in agreement.

Now that she was out of the bog and Phally was safe, Pea shifted the focus of power. The wards and twisted *ki* produced by the *gashadokuro* were already lifting, allowing Pea to send a slow, but steady stream of magic, which illuminated the area around us in a gentle orange glow. She lifted the Saint Bernard inch by inch, drying him as he went. Finally, he rose out of the treacherous water with a *pop* and Pea floated him back to the path. I slithered backwards until I joined the rest of them.

Lala threw herself against me, her body heaving with the adrenaline dump she had just gone through. "I fucking hate this place," she sob-laughed.

"May have to pass up any requests for aid for Southeast Alaska for a while," I half joked. Pea clambered up my chest and wrapped herself so tightly around my neck I nearly choked. Despite the stranglehold, I left her as she was, stroking her back in reassurance. I needed the comfort of her presence as much as she needed mine. I looked at our two sludge monsters. "Woodrow would be pretty proud of both of you right now with how dirty you are."

I rose onto my feet and groaned at the thought of walking again. My entire body felt like one massive bruise, and wading through the ward sounded like Yomi on earth. The broken fragments of my ribs resumed the agonizing process of piecing themselves together.

"Do you feel that?" Lala asked. She lifted a hand and moved it through the air. "I think the ward is going dormant."

"Thank fuck for small favors." I breathed with relief, the action slightly easier now as my body tried to repair itself.

CHAPTER TWENTY-ONE

The screams were dying, but fire still raged back on firm land. Cheuksin and Reika stood knee-deep in the muskeg to avoid the flames as we made our way over to them. Exhausted, I reached out with my *ki*, smothering the fire. Now that the wards were down, Pea sent a jolt of power down our bond, refilling my cup, ensuring I wouldn't be on empty if another crisis arose.

A field of skulls remained, some reduced to ash, others charred. A minority of them were fully intact, indicating they had had an affinity for fire in life. I stopped by the *curupira's* skull and lifted it, prepared to call Anhangá so he could call his own back home.

A swirl of ashes began to form in the atmosphere, my *eomma* taking shape with her back to me. Her effervescent shoulders were bowed, and she knelt to the ground, touching the pristine skull in front of her. A dragon's head with a stump in the center of it. The bone itself had fossilized with age.

"Your *imo*," she said softly. "My sister. She vanished before you were ever born."

"*Eomma?*" Lala and Cheuksin looked at me curiously as I uttered the word. Reika was gathering ashes, flesh, and bits of bone from the dead, the ruthless *yamauba* unwilling to let this opportunity to collect rare ingredients pass her by.

My mother stood abruptly and whipped around to face me, a blurred motion as the ashes took a moment to catch up with her movement. "This has been going on far longer that anyone has realized." Her English diction was suddenly perfect, fueled by her anger. "Yeomra!" The summons was clear in her tone. Cheuksin paled next to Lala, grabbing for her hand as the land began to quake once again. My entire being quailed, the urge to run and hide nearly overpowering with the knowledge of who was coming.

One moment, my mother stood before me. In the next breath, her body exploded into a shower of ashes, and a male stood in her place. He looked young and ancient at once, his black-as-pitch hair flowing around him, thick and unruly. It was difficult to focus on him, as his appearance seemed to filter through a thousand personas at once. His narrowed eyes found mine and I fell to my knees.

The ashes resettled in my mother's form, now with the skull of her sister, the *imo* I'd never known I had, in her hands. Lala and Cheuky sucked in a breath as they watched the skull move, seemingly under its own power when my mother shook it at the King of the Korean underworld. However, it no longer held the hostility the *gashadokuro* had projected.

"You! You told me you couldn't find her. That she was missing in all the realms. One of your own *haetae*, who dedicated her life to you, judging souls you couldn't attend to. And this is where she has been? In the Quotidian realm, her body desecrated?" A flurry of Korean curses flew out of her mouth.

The absolute audacity of Korean mothers frightened me.

Yeomra took the skull gently from *Eomma*, tucking it under his arm as he took my mother's flailing hands and held them within his own. He bent from his great height to look her in the eyes. "Would knowing that her body had been desecrated and her soul rendered to become a *gashadokuro* given you any peace? Or would you have neglected your duties to find her, like your young has?"

I flinched at the comment.

"At least I would have *known*," she spat back out at the god. "My daughter has done more for our world than the best of us. I fail to see how she has neglected any duties. If anything, she has taken far more than she should. She is *broken* because of this path in her life, and she is the last."

Anhangá materialized next to Yeomra, two powerful beings who held thrall over the dead in a field of skulls. "She is right, Yeomra," the stag stated flatly. "You should have told her. Perhaps we would have stopped this centuries ago if you had addressed it back then."

"What would you have me do? We knew nothing of what has been happening until these past few months."

Anhangá cocked his head, angling his antlers to the side, as his lip lifted in a sneer. "Did you not notice the near extinction of your *haetae*? Do you not care for those who belong to you? Were you never curious about the cause of their disappearance?"

As they argued, I stood and approached Anhangá quietly, placing the *curupira* before him. He stopped talking and stared down at the skull, the briefest flash of grief filling his eyes. A swirl of mist swept around his body and a svelte male stood in his place, his skin dark. Nose broad. Where Yeomra's hair was wild, Anhangá's fell in a sleek sheet, the color a shade lighter than Rafael's black-brown hair. His body was made of sinew, made all the more obvious by the tension he carried. He carefully lifted the *curupira's* skull between two hands with reverence and gave me a nod of respect.

"Your *haetae* deserved better than what you offered," he said without inflection to Yeomra. "My grandson deserved better than I gave him. I'm learning that as I go. Perhaps we could have saved this world so much suffering had we been willing to do our own jobs."

Color me shocked. Anhangá had been listening.

"I like to think I'm capable of learning, even at my great age." A hint of a smile curled the corner of his lip up, a quirk that followed him no matter what shape he took. "I'm sorry I wasn't here sooner. I was with Theo's team when they ran into their own troubles. I'm pleased to see the canines are okay." He gave Phally and Max a scruff behind their ears, to their pleasure, sending clouds of dried mud in the air. Phally looked a bit confused as to where the stag had gone, but Max had taken it in a stride.

"Theo? Yuri?" Lala asked, fear in her voice.

"They are a bit banged up but fine. They encountered a forest of *koda-ma*. The spirits didn't want to let them pass and the flora put up a fight to keep them out."

He turned back to Yeomra. "You should take the time to listen and learn as well. In the meantime, we have souls to lay to rest." A large hand gestured widely to the field of death before us. "Hag!" he snapped when he noticed what Reika was doing. "Leave these souls alone. They do not deserve desecration after all they have been through."

Reika turned to glare at the entity, her serrated teeth glinting off the light of the full moon. "I will take whatever I can to sort out this one's *ki*. We honor these dead by making sure their deaths had meaning." She waved the leather bag she had been using. "These pieces do not represent those who died. Their souls do. They have no use for this matter anymore."

Black mist whipped angrily around the entity, but Anhangá gave the *yamauba* a terse nod, acknowledging her point. He gave the Korean god a beckoning gesture and began to wade into the sea of skulls.

Before Yeomra acknowledged Anhangá, the Korean god turned to me with a sober expression. "Despite what he has said, you have been remiss in your duties. You must return to them. Now more than ever."

Fire flickered through me, but I tamped it down before it could catch flame. Ashes swirled in an angry cloud as my mother seethed with discontent, her mouth opening to rebuke to deity once more. Fear for my mother's safety, and resentment, had me cutting in ahead of whatever she was going to say. "My *duties* are a little hard to attend to when doing so is literally killing me with every shift."

The god simply raised a thick eyebrow at me. "Since when have the guardians put their own needs before the needs of the realms? What is the point to your existence if you don't follow your purpose?"

The loudest hiss I have ever heard from Pea shattered the air near my ear. A pulse of uncontrolled *ki* shot toward Yeomra, which he absorbed like a gentle breeze. I sucked in a breath through gritted teeth and pulled Pea from my shoulders, hugging her tight to my chest. Her small body shook with rage, clicks and hisses still falling from her maw. I gave him a tight nod in acknowledgement. *So be it.* My death would be imminent, but a world without *haetae* would be better than one who didn't see to her responsibilities apparently. For having no physical form, the look on my mother's face was capable of evisceration. Yeomra waved a hand and her presence vanished from our group.

"Don't give me that look, *haetae*. Your *eomma* is fine. She has earned her place in my realm and no harm will come to her."

The implication that I had not, and therefore was at risk, was heavy. Except the joke was on him; I wouldn't end up in any realm when I died.

"Yeomra," Anhangá snapped. He had returned to his stag form during our brief interaction, and he herded the god toward the carnage that lay before them. "Leave her be. Call Izanami and our other colleagues and let them be on their way. Camellia, I won't be able to follow you to Orochi's forests now. You will be on your own for transportation once you leave."

"Yes, go now," Reika shooed the beings away. "Our time is running out."

"That can't possibly mean anything good," Cheuksin remarked. The look on her face was contorted as she watched them wade into the sea of skulls, the intense temperatures having no effect on the beings. The expression was made of equal parts relief and sadness. Relief that she hadn't had to deal with a relative when her ties to her family were so strained. Sadness that she hadn't had to deal with a relative because they had acted as if she didn't exist.

"So much for *leave no trace*," Lala joked weakly, coming to stand next to us as the gods of the underworlds began appearing one by one. The reactions varied from shock to horror, grief, and apathy as they beheld their task. "At least the land was already dead?"

I cringed. It might have been dead, but it could've eventually come back from the damage done. But now that the land had been salted? It would remain fallow for years to come.

Cheuksin held out a hand and wiggled it a bit. "Forgetting something about me?" The salt began to drain from the land, filtering through the muskeg before piling in front of the deity. "You deal with the salt," she told the *yamauba*. "As the Quotes say, 'pack it in, pack it out.'"

Reika sighed but did as she was told. This time she took time to carefully open her liminal pocket and gestured to Cheuksin to take over. Cheuky shook her head at the *yamauba* and the salt rose in the air once again, the grains separating themselves into types and landing in neat piles, the packaging they came in now ash on the land.

Reika sealed the pocket back up. "I wasn't joking…we must go now. The *kariudo's* time is running out."

"Not that I don't agree with getting a move on, but what do you mean the *kariudo's* time is running out? Can't Vambi tether his soul back to life every time Orochi kills him?" Lala asked, starting on the path that Reika had indicated. Phally hugged her side tightly, still wound tight by the earlier events. I didn't blame him. I was traumatized, too. I ruffled Max's ears at the thought and sent a wave of gratitude to Pea. She nuzzled hard against my cheek in return. I squinted at the sky as storm clouds began to roll in.

A side-eye in conjunction with a sneer of serrated teeth was no joke. "Do you want to explain, or shall I," the *yamauba* asked snidely.

The shards of my body felt like a thousand pounds, weighed down by weariness. "Rafael can return to life as many times as him and his grandfather desire. But the type of trauma that we assume he's enduring has impact on a being. His balance was already teetering on Evil's edge. Eventually that edge will erode if it's not shored up, and he will fall fully into Evil."

Not everyone responded to trauma the same way. Some Quotes are graced with never having to experience it even. Not the Abbies and their long lifespans. Still, there are the Abbies who are generally unaffected by trauma. They tended to be young, not having had the experience of cumulative tragedies over time. There are the Abbies who eventually learn how to cope and deal with each hand they are dealt, though it takes time with every incident that occurs. What that looks like differs for each of them.

And then there are the Abbies who lean into the skills they learned in order to survive the trauma because they know no other way. Skills that made sense at the time of the trauma. Skills that kept them alive. But those skills were too brutal for life outside that environment. The edges that are honed in those Abbies are lethal and cut far too easily. They learn to enjoy it as a matter of self-preservation.

Rafael, without a doubt, would fall into the last category if we didn't pull him out soon.

Reika was right. We were running out of time before the scales could no longer be tipped in his favor.

If we failed, I would have to do Yeomra's bidding and take the huntsman's soul.

CHAPTER TWENTY-TWO

A little over an hour passed in silence as we walked and processed the ordeal we had just endured. My broken bones had mostly reset by now, leaving behind a deep ache, an echo of the pain I had been in.

The storm clouds arrived, blotting out the alpenglow that had settled over the mountains. Lala swore softly as flakes of snow began to pick up speed around us. We began fording a shallow river, the cool water lazily parting around our limbs. Max and Phally bounded across it, tails high in the air. The far-off beating of helicopter rotors that we had noticed half an hour ago was becoming fainter with each breeze that blew by—Alaska's rescue squadrons calling the search due to the weather conditions.

"It's August," Lala said.

"It's late August, in Alaska, in high elevations. That's not even considering Yuriko. Who knows if there are others in this range." I fervently hoped the storm wasn't blowing in because of Yuri.

Max heaved his soggy body out of the water and vanished, sending Phally into frantic barking. A flood of panic would have hit me regardless, but the vanishing act on the heels of seeing Max, Phally, and Pea sinking in the muskeg upped the panic factor exponentially. Pea tightened her tail around my neck, feeding off my anxiety, clicking frantically with worry.

I rushed to where the big Saint Bernard had been, sending sprays of water around me as I did my best to hurry through it. The force I was using to propel myself, in combination with the sudden loss of surface tension, resulted in my body slamming face-first into an invisible wall as I left the river. The gelatinous consistency of the wall bounced me around like a pinball machine then spit me out the other side.

Pea scrambled around my body, managing to avoid being squashed as I landed on my back. Maxwell gave a happy *woof*, looming over where I lay on the mossy ground, water soaking me as it dripped from his thick fur. My panic finally subsided at the sight. A wide doggy grin wreathed his face, and his feathered tail wagged, sending water everywhere.

"You need to stop giving me heart attacks, bud," I choked out. His long tongue did a slow slurp up my face in response. Pea climbed off my chest and scurried off abruptly, her small body waddling at a brisk pace away from us. The reason why became apparent not even a moment later when a feminine shriek rang through the air and Lala tripped over my prone body. She valiantly twisted as she toppled, landing face-first on my chest, leaving me to take the brunt of the fall instead of Phally.

"I love you, Lala, but not like that," I groaned. If a single fragment of my body remained unbruised, I would be shocked. A small hand came precariously close to smashing my chest as she tried to hoist herself off of me. "Careful with the goods! They may be small, but they're still sensitive."

Lala cackled as she opted to roll off to the side instead of trying to climb my body. She lay on her pack and sucked in a huge gulp of air. "I never realize how much I appreciate clean air until it's gone, regardless of whether its due to a cursed bog or a natural disaster." I took my own deep breath in agreement.

Cheuky followed shortly after. Her entrance was full of grace until she tripped over me, then almost caught her balance, only to lose it completely as she went over Lala's body, kicking the Peri in the ribs as she went down.

"I intentionally gave you guys extra time to clear the way," the goddess complained, pushing her long hair back from her face. "And yet, here you two still lay."

"I might stay here forever," Lala said, sprawling her arms out so her back arched across her pack. "This is actually kinda comfy, and I've missed comfy these past few days. Why do I do this job again?"

"Your overinflated savior complex?" I teased, staring up into the clear sky. We had left the storm back in the Quotidian realm. If there was no time here, then why were there stars at night? Maybe there was no day? How did that even work?

Lala gave me a half-hearted kick in the thigh. "*You're* the one with the overinflated savior complex."

"Okay, okay," I conceded. "Because this is the ultimate middle finger to your mother, who sacrificed everything—her homeland, her husband, a child—to bring you to a safe land, only for you to repay her by not becoming a doctor. Or lawyer. Or—*oomph*." Air gusted out of my chest as she aimed her next kick higher and with more force.

Then all humor drained from Lala's face as she quickly sat up and stared at me. "Uh. Cam? Why are you…leaking?" She gestured all around me. I glanced down, shocked to find my glamours had dropped and the black substance was twining all around me.

"Because she carries a piece of the *kariudo's* soul within her," Reika said with disdain as she crossed over, managing to avoid all of us and remain upright in the process.

"Excuse me?" Lala exclaimed. "When were you planning to tell the class about this? First, it's *Surprise!* You're a *haetae*. But you didn't stop there… no. Then you added, oh I don't know, 'Bee-tee-dubs, guys, I was also a Thread to the freaking *kami* that ruled the seas, and I've been in hiding for over a century because another god is out to get me 'cause he wants my freaking liver. Oh. *And* I'm dying because my Thread was a jackass and introduced a foreign *ki* in my body.' Now you have someone else's *soul?* Is there anything else you forgot to tell us about? I thought we were friends."

Hurt rimmed her eyes in a glimmer of silver as she blinked back tears. Cheuky nodded, in accord with Lala's words. She pulled herself upright and wrapped an arm around Lala's shoulders. The two had formed a strong bond over the past few days.

Quotes damn it all, I was awful. I hugged Max's big head to me. "I'm sorry." The whisper could barely be heard on the breeze. "There's no excuse, but…I was—"

Cheuksin's hand slashed through the air. "No. Like you said, no excuses. This isn't about protecting *us*. You insult our intelligence when you make those decisions for us. This is about your complete and utter inability to ask for help when you need it. For fuck's sake, Cam. You bargained with a *god* before you even thought to ask any of us about possibilities that don't involve tying yourself to the gods that forsook you. And not just any god, but *Seokga*. I might still like the asshole, but not only is he a trickster, but he is one of our creators. And I went along with it! Despite knowing firsthand how the gods reciprocate bargains. I have known you for hundreds of years, and still you haven't changed. The Uncles were right, you know. Just say it, Cam. You're on the fast track to suicide because you can't possibly see a way around unsnarling your *kis*."

A sledgehammer to my chest would hurt less than Lala and Cheuksin's judgment. I focused on the brown splotch partially covering Max's muzzle. "I know." The words left my mouth on the smallest of exhales.

A sigh gusted from Lala's general direction. "We don't have time for this." I could feel her eyes surveying me while Cheuksin grumbled, "Just... trust us, okay? That's all we ask. You too, Pea. Let us make the decision to help you or not, instead of freezing us out." She shrugged out of her pack and her jacket. A grimace twisted her face when she unbuckled her helmet from the hip belt. The entire left side had been crushed during the fight with the *gashadokuro*. "Well, that thing's useless now," she muttered.

She set aside the battered head protection and unzipped the bottom of the pack body and rummaged around the space until she pulled out a resealable bag and a few other items. Contained within the plastic was a cuff Rafael had left behind in the apartment I had allocated to him. She waved the object at me. "Well? Are we going to do this or not?"

"Ugh." I gently pushed Max from my lap and dug in the pocket at my hip belt, wrenching a baggie complete with one dirty sock. I wrinkled my nose. "Our job is so glamorous sometimes. Did it have to be a sock, Theo? He left his entire wardrobe for the trip behind."

"Theo obviously loves me more," Lala snickered, the sound having a false ring to it after the heaviness of our previous conversation.

"Before we go," Reika started, "try this." She shoved a small flask under my nose. Knowing what she had been collecting, my stomach roiled.

Pinching my nose, I tossed the contents back, refusing to contemplate what the ingredients could have been. I swallowed quickly and nausea immediately rose as the concoction flooded my throat. Reika watched me like a hawk, waiting until I swallowed for the last time before she clapped once in satisfaction.

"Good, good. Now." She reached into the burlap sack that hung from her shoulder and pulled out the *shiomitsu-tama*.

Seeing the flow-tide jewel without its kin felt wrong. She shoved it into my hands and my knees immediately buckled as vertigo overwhelmed me. *Shiomitsu-tama* tumbled out of my grip as I tried to roll onto my hands and knees, heaving. From the corner of my eye, I saw Pea launch her small body through the air. The sounds of shouting were like an echo through the ringing in my ears.

"Reika!" Cheuksin snarled. "*You* are the one who said we were running out of time. Then you pull this? Setting us back even further?" She bent down and helped me stand, propping me up with a shoulder.

"She needs a *kami's* power if she's going to go up against a god." Reika hurled the words back at the goddess.

"Fuck, that was worse than the last time I shifted," I gasped.

"You're part of the problem," Lala spat at Reika, stepping in front of me. "Why would Cam ever ask for help when she's used to getting help from people like you? Really? I knew she was working with you, but this is your idea of training? Oh my God. Get fucked, you hag." She turned to me and shoved her shoulder under my other arm. The two of them helped me over to a large rock and settled me down on it.

"It sucks, but I need to do it," I rasped.

"Seriously?" My friend raised an eyebrow while Cheuksin stood back on her heels, arms crossed. "This was the method you guys decided to try? Maybe ask the friend who suddenly developed *ki* in high school but never managed breasts. I was already the weird Asian refugee kid. Then everyone started losing their minds when I was around because I had no control over my power, and no idea why everyone's emotions were whipping into a frenzy. High school hormones were bad enough, then the Universe threw a Perigean like me into the mix. It was *learn to swim* or *drown*. Ask me for help, you absolute sheep."

"It's—"

"Don't you even dare say it's not the same. You're trying to manage a new-to-you *ki*. Full stop. Period." She threw Reika a filthy look over her shoulder. The *yamauba* rolled her eyes as she collected the jewel and placed it back in her sack. "This is going to get you killed that much faster. You will be fine on this trip. We might be down one weird deer dude, but you still have two deities on your side. We'll start practicing once we get back to Washington. C'mon, we need to get this search off the ground already." She walked back to her pack and hauled it on. She adjusted the headlamp she had pulled out while going through her pack earlier and shortened the straps to accommodate her head instead of the ruined helmet.

I took three deep breaths, trying to quell the waves of nausea, then went back to my gear. Lala gave me a nod as she held out her scent article to Phally, whose ears pricked with eagerness. I did the same with Max. Soon the K9s were off, scenting the area, looking for any trace of the *kariudo*.

Moments later, both K9s dropped to the ground and sounded their alerts.

Lala and I exchanged a startled glance.

"That was far easier than I expected," she said warily.

Then a tremor rumbled through the valley. All manners of supernatural avians flew from the trees, leaving the forest shivering with their flight.

Cheuksin eyed the fleeing wildlife. "Toyotama has found the *kami*. And managed to piss him off, it seems."

The countdown was on. Toyo had warned us before we had left that once she found Orochi, we had one hour *maximum*, two minutes *minimum*, to get Rafael out. If we took any longer, the danger increased exponentially. What that meant when time didn't exist here was an utter crapshoot. But the fact that we hadn't even set foot on the trail Max and Phally had scented was the worst-case scenario imagined.

We released the K9s from their alert and took off after them, protocol being shoved by the wayside in favor of speed. Max and Phally bolted through the brush, the two K9s understanding the urgency of the moment. Aches and pains were forgotten. Cheuksin and Lala took the lead as they pounded through the forest flora, setting the pace for Reika and me. I consoled myself with the thought that the way back would be easy enough to find with broken branches leaving behind a clear path.

A roar sounded through the valley as we began making our incline. The sound reverberated off the mountains that surrounded us. An answering bellow rebounded through the trees. I mentally sent every wish into the Universe that the *kami* would listen to his Thread. I wasn't hopeful though, based on his mental state when I had last seen him.

Then the K9s skidded to a halt at the edges of a clearing. A whine emitted from Max. Lala stumbled to a halt, catching herself on a branch. Cheuksin drew up before she ran into them.

I watched as blood leeched from their skin, paling at whatever sight they had beheld, and I felt a piece of my heart lodge in my esophagus. Reika and I slowed down and approached them cautiously.

No. Not them. *Him.*

A vile stream of curses fled the *yamauba's* mouth.

My eyes took in the sight before me and the fragments of my heart dropped into free fall, with exception of the one that remained lodged.

Rafael Sugiyama squinted at me through his swollen eyes. "What the fuck are you doing here, Baki?"

CHAPTER TWENTY-THREE

Rafael hadn't expected to wake back up to the sight of an ashen Baki in front of him. Let alone the others that accompanied her. His dream and nightmare were coming to fruition simultaneously.

He cradled a broken arm to his chest while he leaned back against the tree the *onna uo* had left him by, fire lighting up his back with the pressure. Was this what she meant by *your time is coming*? Rafael hoped not.

"I didn't go through all of this just for you to get captured and killed, after all," he hissed through the pain. Baki's hair was a mess, falling out of a braid she had woven at some point. The blue-black hair fell inches longer than the last time he had seen her. Months had passed then, if not years. Debris and…ashes?…littered her scalp. He fought back a smile when he saw movement within her jacket, followed by Pea's snout poking out from under the hem. A few short moments later, he held back a groan as the little *shikigami* scurried onto his chest and placed her one forepaw on his chin, pulling his face down in an assessment. A pink glow surrounded him, but it did nothing. Pea hissed in displeasure and the glow brightened.

"Save your *ki*," he said softly to the *shikigami*. He let go of his fractured limb so he could stroke her soft body, ignoring the stabbing sensation as the shattered ends of his bones ground against one another, carving the wound from the compound fracture even further as his arm dropped. It was worth it when the opossum he had once been at odds with slubbed against his good hand, clicking with worry.

His gaze lifted and he watched as Baki swallowed, his eyes following the path of her slender throat. Behind her, he vaguely noticed a flurry of movement as the females began pulling items out of their packs.

"I'm offended that you think I could be captured so easily," she retorted, though a tremor rang through her words. "Why aren't you healing?" Her eyes had a strange look to them as they trailed over his body. She shivered, then shook the tremor and the look in her eyes away.

The *kariudo* scoffed and then groaned when the act caused pain. "I seem to recall you falling into my ruse easily enough." Regret filled him with the barbed words, but every cell in his body needed Baki to leave.

"I let you capture me." How had he forgotten the way his barbs slid off this one, like water off a duck?

"Sure." He attempted to wink and failed abysmally. "We'll go with that story."

Baki raised an eyebrow as she pulled off her jacket and tossed it on a branch behind her. "Pretty sure I would have succeeded in escaping you eventually, if you could die. Besides, Orochi is currently quite occupied in an ex-lovers' quarrel. Yomi hath no fury like an Asian female scorned. It should know. It houses the ultimate scorned female."

Rafael startled into a cough-hack. "I do believe Izanami would take offense to that."

"She's busy collecting souls with your grandfather."

He wasn't even going to ask.

"You never answered me, and we're on a time crunch. That body of yours is going to slow us way the fuck down. What's with the failure to heal?" Something more than impatience underlined her words as she ripped her long-sleeved top over her head, cursing as it pulled twigs from her hair.

Bewilderment filled him at the sight. "I never realized beat-up males was your kink, Baki." He couldn't answer her question, but he did motion to the image seared into his chest, covering the grayed out *haetae*. Now the image was of an *oni* skull with antlers for horns. Red positively bled from the image, mimicking the blood as it seeped from the skull. He knew the others would have captured a motion, too fast to register for Quote eyes, as the crimson drops rolled down his chest.

"You wish," she retorted. Her face grimaced. "No, no, that didn't come out right."

"Kill me already, Baki. I know you want to." He closed his eyes with exhaustion.

He could hear shuffling and movement in front of him, the sounds riddled with hesitation. The slap of flesh meeting flesh. A body stopped in front of him. He knew it was Camellia without seeing her. At some point during their time together, his body had become intimately familiar with the rhythm of her movements, though they had often been at odds, he realized with alacrity.

"There's justification. I can come back whole and then you don't have to keep wincing with guilt every time you make me laugh and inflict pain," he reassured the *haetae* when nothing happened.

"Please. I can't help it if I'm funny." He grimaced at her statement. She really wasn't.

"How do we go about this? Do you prefer decapitation? Suffocation? Stabbed through the heart?"

"Oh, for Quotes' sake." The *yamauba* grew louder as she approached, and then a blade was driven into his chest.

Yeah. Getting stabbed in the heart would do the trick quite nicely.

Shouting filled the air below him as his body began the work of dissembling itself. Moments later, he found himself in the midst of a whiteout. Snow fell heavily, barely revealing dark shapes moving through the blinding cover of snow. His words still sealed by the geas, he waited until he caught his grandfather's attention. In the meantime, he did his best to make out the shapes. Izanami was indeed present, along with an assortment of other death entities who were roaming the area. She noticed his presence first and alerted Anhangá.

"Again?" The stag shook his head, then retethered him in less than a moment. "I'm busy. Off you go. Baki's coming for you." Anhangá's voice faded as Rafael was catapulted back to his physical body. The urge to shake his grandfather was strong, knowing the stag was likely the reason why Baki was here.

Voices were the first thing that let him know he had returned to the clearing.

"You were wasting time. Look. His body is healing. We need to move."

Floating above his body, he noticed what he hadn't before. Tremors shook the forest as the entire valley *shifted*. Yelps rang out as the small group fell over from the sudden tilt. The *yamauba* stood close to Baki, while the other two remained at the edge of the clearing, tension yielding stiff bodies. Odds and ends sat at their feet, including a gong and zither. How they had gotten a *jing* and *ajaeng* here, he had no idea. Granted, after their visit to Oliver, confusion about what she chose to pack on hikes were the least of his worries. Anxiety wore Baki's face as she stared at his body like she was willing it to rise.

She probably was. Either that or she was fantasizing about stabbing him herself.

Rafael shoved himself back into his body, the action dispersing it entirely. Pea dropped to the ground when his body disappeared out from under her, and she clicked with uncertainty. Power gradually returned to him, absorbing the death that lingered in the air, allowing his intrinsic self to heal.

Death? The presence of it led him to realize it had been entirely absent while imprisoned in Orochi's valley. The smell of rotten blood filled his awareness. A mix of copper and the sickly scent of decay. He reformed where he had been left, whole once more, and took in details of the scene before him.

In the mere moments he had been gone, Baki had dropped her glamour. The female stood before Reika, who held her *deba*, the blade polluted by the *haetae's* blood. Her forearm dripped blackened crimson sludge at barely a trickle, despite the severed artery. His stomach lurched, not only at the smell of her blood that evidenced the creeping approach of Death, but the visual evidence of what the mixing of two *kis* had done to her. Gazing at Baki was like looking at a jigsaw puzzle pieced together incorrectly, leaving you itching to just *fix it*. Except he knew he couldn't. He had only compounded the damage.

A quiet fury at the deceased *kami* began to fill him. His regret in this moment? That Ryūjin was gone and Rafael couldn't personally bring the *kami* to bear witness to what he had done to his own Thread.

A black mist—the missing piece of his soul—wisped in and out of the fragments, splitting into tendrils that dove in between several different spaces at once. The way it moved was almost inquisitive in nature, as if it was constantly assessing and testing Cam's fragments.

What that meant, he had no idea.

The *yamauba* adjusted her grip on the blade and sliced through Cam's other forearm. His own arms pulsed in vicarious pain at the sight. It wasn't a smooth slice, despite the honed edge. It couldn't be, with Cam's body broken into pieces. The *deba* slid through flesh and the raised keloid scars like they were air, then caught on the void between the fragments. Every time the blade caught, a quick flash of agony would pass over Baki's eyes, but she remained otherwise still and silent.

Reika gave her a nod and Baki began walking around his body, droplets of her rotting blood forming a circle around him, pitching occasionally when the ground rolled under her. While she formed a circle of blood, Reika, Lala, and Cheuksin spread out, forming three points. Cheuksin held the *ajaeng*. Reika, the gong. Lala held onto the two K9s, preventing them from interfering. Pea gamely followed Baki's footsteps, imbuing the droplets with power as she tried to catch up to the *haetae*. Her tail swept from side to side in agitation, as she kept trying and failing to reach Baki, though the *haetae* was going no faster than a slow walk.

The world around them had become inconsequential. It was just the two of them as sounds faded with Baki's approach.

She stepped into the circle, approaching him, and shook her wrists, splattering his bare chest and tattered pants in a methodical motion, flicking each wrist to maximize the little blood that was left. She began at his head and ended at his toes. The blood burned, as if it was a living flame, followed by a soothing wash, like an ocean's wave. finally absorbing through his skin like it had never been.

Then his gaze strayed from the tears in her forearms, that were already closing, to her hands.

He blinked, trying to ascertain if what he saw was reality or if he had descended back into a nightmare. Her right hand was missing a pinky. He swallowed thickly at the sight when Baki raised her intact hand and dug into her body, between the crevices of her fragments, sinking up to her wrist, then her forearm. She dove further and further into herself until she finally jerked back. A whimper of pain escaped her lips, but she clamped down the sound and continued to pull, withdrawing her arm. Horror filled him as a large unidentifiable fragment, discolored with decay, separated from her with a piece of her soul attached. His senses expanded to include the rest of the world again as he heard a mournful hiss leave Pea while she climbed up Baki, the *shikigami* radiating grief. Pea perched on a shoulder and threw a pink glow around the Thread of her former *kami*.

Before he could react, Baki shoved the flesh into his mouth. He swallowed reflexively from the shock of the action, fighting against the urge to cough as he felt the hardened, rotting lump move through his esophagus. Pain pulsed through his body with the effort,

Reika dug into a pouch that hung off a shoulder and handed Baki a mortar and pestle. The *haetae* accepted it dispassionately as if she hadn't literally torn a segment of herself out of her body and fed it to him. While he had been busy trying not to choke on her soul, another small object had appeared in her hand.

The missing digit. He had no idea when the amputation had happened. He thought he had only been gone for moments. But in that duration, Baki had the time to detach a part of her body from her hand, discard more clothing, and slice her forearm open. He wondered how the hell time worked here, and whether this was a normal occurrence.

A sigh gusted out of Baki, bringing his attention back to her as her eyes flashed jade. A moment later the pinky burst into blue-and-white flames, quickly burning away any flesh that remained on the finger. She grimaced and dropped it into the mortar, then began grinding. Occasionally she would stop to open the wounds in her forearms, allowing the black blood to drain into the bowl, before she resumed. The unpleasant noise of bone against granite filled the air.

He had so many questions and no words to frame them. He glanced at the other females to see if they had anything to say about these circumstances, but they just watched on without interruption. The expressions on Cheuksin and Lala's faces were particularly grim, both of them clearly holding back things they wanted to say, knowing nothing would change the course of events.

Baki held up her left hand for a moment and stared at it as she turned it from side to side, inspecting the way it looked without the digit, then shrugged and dropped her hand.

"It's not like I'll need it soon," she muttered to herself. She knelt on the ground at his side and gathered the tattered remains of his pants, tearing the fabric down each leg. A finger dipped into the paste she had made from her blood and bone. He couldn't help but focus on the way her brow furrowed in concentration, noticing how the fine lines formed slightly off-center. A shiver shuddered through his body as she began to cover his body in *hanja*.

A moment or an eternity could have passed by the time Baki sat back and set the mortar aside. He watched as she closed her eyes and took a deep breath.

Ki filled the atmosphere and Baki transformed.

Rafael didn't know if he would ever stop being in awe of her *haetae*. In this shape, her body was complete, as though no damage had ever happened to it. The only evidence was in the unnatural state of her soul.

The small wings on her back rustled and she drew in heaving breaths, looking unsteady on her feet.

Then the beating of the gong began.

CHAPTER TWENTY-FOUR

The deep bass of the percussion began at my feet and rang through my soul. The rhythmic beat that Reika drummed against the *jing* helped to steady me through the vertigo. No one realizes how much we rely on the beat of our hearts to stabilize and regulate ourselves. A soft slow beat for relaxation. A pounding fast beat for fear. A quick flutter for excitement. When it goes away, your body loses all sense of its natural pace. For a moment, I allowed myself to relish the pseudo-experience of having an internal rhythm again.

The loss of my heartbeat had been the hardest thing for me to come to terms with after *Hyakki Yagyō*. After eight counts, I opened my eyes. The *kariudo* lay below me, his gaze full of questions, confusion, anger, and sorrow. I was relieved when his body had returned whole. It was one thing to imagine it in my dreams; it was another thing altogether to see it in the flesh. The sounds of the zither begin to flit through the air, giving me my cue, Cheuksin's lyrical voice filling the space between notes. My body clumsily moved in the steps I had practiced with the goddess during our nights in Alaska. They were surprisingly easy to translate from two feet to four. What wasn't easy to translate was the appearance of grace. I held back a cringe as I rocked, twirled, and stomped to complementary sounds of the gong and zither.

With each step I took, the world around me froze, until Rafael and I were alone in this ritual. Sound faded, only the dance remained. A brief flash revealed Seokga watching from outside the circle, allowed into Orochi's dimension through the power of this ritual. He stood, legs set apart wide and arms crossed over his broad chest.

My gaze shifted back to Rafael. In this moment, I truly let go of the sense of time that bound us to our realms. The clock that had been uselessly ticking in the back of my mind after Toyo had encountered Orochi disappeared. Instead, I lost myself in Rafael's wondering stare.

Emotions hit me hard. I had thought I had done a good job processing my feeling of betrayal over the past months. I was wrong. Hurt rose up within me, strong, throwing me back to the moment I woke in Ryūgū-jō's dungeons. My steps grew in power, rage leaking from my body. Sorrow filtered through the eyes that held me through this journey. A small incline of the *kariudo's* head snapped the shield of my rage, as he acknowledged the wrongs he had done. The words he didn't voice were conveyed in that small gesture.

I am sorry. I regret my actions. I yield.

Anger petered out in favor of hurt, my steps becoming featherlight, cautious, as though I feared the forest floor was responsible for that emotional pain. I twirled, like I was avoiding the stinging bite of a whip—a hint of desperation underlying the maneuver— my eyes meeting Rafael's without fail when I finished the spin. The emotions shifted to *desire*. The desire for this life of suffering to end. The longing to be able to fall into the appreciation I saw in this *kariudo's* expression. The need to touch him.

Exhaustion filled my body as I cycled through the steps again and again. Anger, hurt, acceptance, grief, sorrow, need, desire. They came, they went, they returned with a vengeance. My soul fed the power of the dance, each step becoming increasingly *ki*-laden. Until they reached a threshold of power.

Then the slave bands clicked open.

SOUND CAME RUSHING back in. The *jing* reached a crescendo, and the ajaeng faded. Rafael's eyes remained riveted to me, entranced, with no knowledge of the enormity of what had happened. The scar tissue surrounded his bands held the obsidian fast to his arms, but I had heard it. The soft *click* that was somehow quiet and deafening all at once.

I recognized the sound from once upon a time. *I* knew what had happened. I shifted quickly and rushed to his side, despite the vertigo. The rocking motion of the land aided my movement, throwing me left when my body tried to dip to the right.

I crashed to my knees next to him and held out a hand. Reika's blade slammed into it. I held his forearm with my other hand. *Kamis* above, the feeling of holding something without my pinky felt wrong.

"Bak—" Rafael's eyes widened as he saw the tiny crack in the bands, revealing raw, red, tissue beneath it. Terror rimmed his eyes, afraid to hope, but hoping nonetheless.

Time may have no meaning here, but I still hurriedly took the *deba* and sliced through the keloid tissue covering the first band on his left arm. The tip dug under the obsidian and I *wrenched.* Sound of flesh ripping from its source replaced the sounds of the instruments, as the band gave, taking with it the skin it had adhered to so well. As soon as it was divested of Rafael's presence, the band vanished.

Rafael's body began to tremble, as I worked my way down his left arm and then his right. I refused to look at him, to look away from my task, but I could feel the palpable tension in the air.

Finally, the last band fell and disappeared from our sight, followed by Seokga's exit. A huge shuddering inhale shook the body I held and then released in a sob.

The ground rolled once more, but this time it was accompanied by the motion of the trees closing in—no, *folding*—into themselves. The physics behind it broke my brain as the forest and cliffs simply collapsed into themselves without being destroyed, like they belonged in a pop-up book.

"Hurry," Lala shouted, throwing my pack to me.

I yanked the *kariudo* to his feet with the hand I still held, and caught the heavy pack with my other, throwing it over my shoulders. I dipped down and snagged Pea, tucking her under my arm like a football.

"Run" was all I said before I bolted down the broken trail we had left behind. Max galloped at my side. Pea climbed my chest and wrapped herself around my neck, clicking at me to *run faster.* Rafael was at my heels, despite taking a moment to rip the shreds of his pants from his body, leaving behind black boxer briefs that hugged his form. My mouth suddenly went dry and I looked away quickly, focusing on the path before me.

A large, unusual shape snagged my attention and I turned my head. My pace stuttered and I nearly slammed into a tree as a massive *onna uo* watched our progress, uncaring of the folding dimension around her. She made a shooing motion with her fin and nodded in the direction we were going.

I shook my head out, strands of my hair catching in my mouth, and put the image behind me. Max barked frantically at me from a few feet ahead, telling me to get my ass in gear. This time Rafael grabbed my hand as he gained purchase and powered in front of me, dragging me along.

Phally slammed through the invisible wall that separated this dimension from the Quotidian realm without hesitation. Cheuksin, and Lala followed right behind him. A few moments later, Rafael, Pea, Max, and I hit the wall and were spit out on the other side as a sucking sensation filled the air for a moment then abruptly stopped.

The mountain range that had been behind us a moment ago was gone. Max and Phally were barking up a storm, snarling at the empty space behind us.

I fervently hoped none of the SAR teams were searching in the range before Orochi shifted back into his human form.

Pea climbed from my neck at a speed no opossum should be capable of while I leaned over, hands on my kneecaps. I reached for her with my other arm and cradled her to me.

"Hey, would you look at that? We match now." I held my hand with the missing digit up against her missing foreleg, my breath raspy with exertion.

Pea hissed at me in admonishment and snapped her teeth at my fingertips. I gave a breathless chuckle and surveyed our group, stiffening when I noticed our numbers.

"Reika?" I stood, my fragments smashing into one another with the movement, still trying to settle in place from our race against Orochi's transformation. Flakes of snow drifted around me lazily, sunlight trying to break through the clouds. I spun around, searching for the *yamauba* amid the unfamiliar surroundings.

Lala had a hand propped against a boulder as she tried to catch her breath. "She stayed behind. She threw her pouch at me and told me to go. We didn't have time to argue. She just told me to do my damn job with you and warded herself so we couldn't drag her along."

Words fled me as I stared at Lala. I didn't get along with the *yamauba*, but she had been a staple in the Pacific Northwest for over a century. The fallout from this choice would have ripple effects throughout the Abbie community.

I focused on Rafael instead, shoving my worries down. There was nothing I could do about it now. The *kariudo* stood behind me in his underwear and covered with the *hanja* I had left on his body. His eyes fixated on his forearms, his left hand rubbing his right forearm again and again. I had been the same, once upon a time. The faded blacks, grays, and vibrant colors of his tattoos had been erased from his body, leaving a blank slate behind. The deep divots of missing flesh that resulted from tearing the bands from his skin were now filled with the glowing pink of healthy new tissue, his healing no longer obstructed by Orochi's commands. Max turned away from the missing landscape and gave a deep happy *woof* at Rafael's presence, jumping up on the male and throwing him off-balance, startling him out of his reverie. A long tongue whipped out and slurped half of Rafael's face. He laughed and shoved the Saint Bernard back down, his attention redirected to where I stood.

"How?" The word was whispered. It reminded me of another time, on Mount St. Helens, when he had asked the same question, afraid to hope. We had made it to the other side of that conversation.

I shrugged tiredly. "Helps when you know a Korean deity or two," I said offhandedly.

Cheuksin scoffed. "What she isn't telling you is that she bargained on your behalf. So, you better not fuck this up for her."

At her words, Rafael sucked in a breath. "You bargained? Why? After what I did to you?"

I shrugged again, getting a hiss from Pea in my ear for the motion. "Sure, you put me through hell. But you also saved me. You saved my friends. You saved my K9s. And you sacrificed yourself to keep it that way. That counts for a lot in my world. I'm kinda like Olly that way."

The corner of his lip lifted in a wry smile. "Pretty sure everybody else would have happily searched for a way to kill me instead. But not you. No…Camellia Kimoto hunts down a way to give a wayward soul a second chance. Why am I not surprised?"

I shrugged again. Pea bit my ear in retaliation. Fuck, I needed to stop doing that, but there was nothing in these realms I hated more than being given more credit than I needed or wanted. "Been there, done that. Wasn't as satisfying as I had hoped when you popped back to life."

His face lifted to the gray skies, and the laugh that rolled out of him was deep and genuine, his shoulders shaking in mirth. The sound warmed my heart and melted a small piece of me I hadn't been aware was frozen.

"What do I even do now?" he mused, glancing down at his body and its lack of commands in fascination.

"Well"—Lala slapped a hand to his bare back, the sound loud in the quiet space—"our attempt to rescue you wasn't entirely altruistic. We do still need your help putting the pieces together with the disappearing guardians and the overall state of the realms. But we've got a nice apartment back in Blue Bear with your name on it."

He nodded. "We do have work to do, don't we?" He glanced down at his body again, which now had a slight sheen from the snow melting on it, smudging the *hanja*. "But first, where are we? And what is the date? Is it winter already? Have I been gone that long?"

"It's August." A slight grimace furrowed his brow as I said the words. "We're high in elevation in Alaska and Yuri's out here somewhere. Hence, the snow. As for the exact answer to that question… Gale?"

The little gremlin popped into existence on Lala's shoulder. "You found him! Theo and Yuri aren't too far from you. Trying to get through the *kodama* forest set them way behind you guys."

Lala's eyes practically bugged out from the information. "That has to be at least seventy-five miles as the crow flies from where we were. How does that even work?"

"I mean, we were on a live dragon, not an actual mountain," Cheuksin said with a muffled laugh.

"Ugh. Does that mean we have to go through a *kodama* forest to get back?" Lala was asking the important questions.

Gale snickered. "No, my father and I mapped out a new path for the return. They're probably about two hours behind you. It's been two days on this side since you vanished into Orochi's realm."

Two damn days. It had felt like a lifetime, and only minutes, while we were in Orochi's world. As a memory surfaced, I separated from the group and pulled out the satnav phone that Whiz had upgraded to be cross-realm compatible. "Hey, Whiz?"

The gremlin answered in my mind, "You can't ask Gale for whatever you need?"

"They're talking to the rest of the group right now. Can you pull up the image of the leshy who went missing real quick. The one of him in his natural form?"

Whiz let out a put-upon sigh, but the image of the environmental lawyer popped in my mind, both in his human and Abbie form. I winced. "Thanks, Whiz. That was all I needed."

Lala cocked her head at me questioningly and I held up a finger indicating I needed a moment. She nodded and returned to the conversation she was having with Gale about logistics, Cheuksin listening closely to the details. Rafael, however, was watching me intently. I turned away from the group and made my way toward a rivulet that cut through the rocky terrain—just far enough for a semblance of privacy—and began dialing.

"Danly." The answer was clipped and strained, sending my hackles up immediately.

"Hey, Jeff, it's me," I responded cautiously. "Your leshy." The image of the head with the eerie blue eyes and branches protruding from his skull flashed in my mind. "He's dead. Like the others."

"Oh, I know. His headless body was found on your living room floor."

CHAPTER TWENTY-FIVE

"*OH, I know. His headless body was found on your living room floor.*"

Jeff's words rang through my head, the two sentences repeating on a loop like I could make sense of them if only I said them enough times. Rapid fire clicks came from my jacket as Pea crawled back up, gripping my collar to perch on my chest and listen in on the conversation.

"What do you mean his body was found on my *living room floor?*" I choked out. Rafael came up beside me, full of concern. I shook my head at him, needing more details before I could even begin to process the words that had just come out of my mouth.

"Exactly what it sounds like." Danly's voice was grim. "I'm in your home looking at it right now." I heard footsteps and then a door shut behind him as he moved through my house. My. House. Where I wasn't right now. Maybe that was for the best. I shuddered at the thought of my sanctuary being violated, silently grateful that Vicky and Woody were with Kenichi and not at the house. "Someone called in a disturbance at your address. One of my deputies responded, found the door smashed in, and entered the house to find our missing person decapitated on your floor. Now, how did *you* know he was dead?"

"His head was used to form a *gashadokuro* not all that long ago," I said numbly.

"And you didn't call me right away?" he demanded. Pea's tail thumped against my chest in indignation at his tone.

"I was a little busy with gods and death and a rescue mission," I snapped back, anger breaking through the numbness. I stroked the *shikigami's* fur to calm her down. "Wait. You don't think this was me, do you?" The little body under my hand stiffened at my words.

"Of fucking course I don't, Cam. The first body was found when you were off being a hero down in some undersea kingdom. But try telling the Quotes that. You have been the one who's found nearly every body since you returned. Not your team. You."

"That's because of Max!" I protested in chorus with Pea's vicious hiss.

"You know that, I know that. Tish knows that. Everyone else? They don't have a clue."

"Why would I lead everybody to the bodies of people I killed? Common sense would suggest that I would make sure they could never be found again."

Common sense would be the fact I was a haetae *and I didn't leave bodies behind.*

"Listen. Everybody and their mother watches true crime documentaries these days. They figure you to be a serial killer showing off their work. The FBI is involved now. I'm shocked they didn't step in sooner. Your agency's reputation is taking a shit-kicking. My advice that you didn't hear from me? Don't come home until Tish or I give you the all clear." Danly hung up.

I stared at the dead phone in my hand. What the hell was I supposed to do then? Pea yanked it out of my grip with her tail and attempted to throw it before I stopped her. We needed the technology more than we needed to vent our frustration.

Rafael cleared his throat. "Trouble?" he asked delicately.

I snorted, still shocked. "That's the simplest way you could boil it down." I took a good look at him again. "We gotta get to Theo so you can borrow some of his clothes. Sorry, all we have of yours is a dirty sock and one of your cuffs."

His eyes sparkled. "I'll pass on the dirty sock, thanks all the same. And I think I'd like to admire these scars for a bit longer." He held out his forearms yet again, twisting and turning them in the soft light that filtered through the clouds. Then he dematerialized into a cloud of mist before reforming in the next moment, fully decked out in the trekking clothes he had worn for our trip to Olly.

I eyed him. "So that's why all your pants are molded to your ass like they were glued on," I muttered under my breath.

He let out a light laugh; they were coming freer and easier now with each one. The realization helped to dull the edge of the worries that were eating away at my mind. "It's okay, Baki, you can say it louder. I know you appreciate them." Then he winked at me. Rafael Sugiyama, the former *kariudo*, winked.

"Who abducted you and replaced you with an alien?"

"Considering how the three of you yanked me out of a different dimension, I would say you ladies. Reika, included, even if she didn't eject me from Orochi's realm herself." He nodded at the phone I had rescued from Pea. "Why is there a headless body in your house?"

It didn't matter how many times those words were said out loud, they still felt unnatural. I motioned for him to follow me back to Lala, Cheuksin, and Gale. Lala, in particular, needed this information with the way it was apparently rocking Blue Bear Search and Rescue's reputation.

"Gale, could you give the crew a call, please? The whole gang?" I asked, reaching them.

"Sure, let me go give them a heads-up to take it first," they said with ease, and then popped out of our view to do whatever they did to make the connection. Not getting snark and sarcasm when I asked for something technical was still weird, much as I loved Gale. I was too used to their father.

One by one, holographic images of the team that made up BBSR appeared in a semicircle around us.

"Hey, Theo," I said to the *dokkaebi*. "Stay where you are for now. We've recovered Rafael and are a couple hours from you. We'll catch up and go from there."

Theo and Yuri looked worn out. Dark circles underlined Theo's eyes. Yuri's regal posture was drooped. Their jackets were torn and hung from their bodies in shreds. At least Lala was the only one who needed to worry about exposure to the elements in this crew. Either way, we'd have to put in a new order for jackets when we got back to Washington. If the agency still existed, that is. I felt a little bad that they had gone through hell and back for nothing, really, but they had volunteered for this part.

"Not going to lie…taking a break for a couple hours sounds like heaven," he admitted. Yuri nodded in agreement. "Didn't think I'd ever say this, but glad to see you, Sugiyama."

Rafael smirked. "Same to you, *dokkaebi*."

Scott and Leilani were next, their faces solemn. They knew then.

"Emma and Hideki won't be calling in," Scott said, his words tight. "They're at the sheriff's office right now being questioned."

"Excuse me?" Lala burst out.

I held a hand up. "I'll explain in a moment."

Finally, Aidan and Toyo's image joined the others. Aidan looked like he had gone through a hurricane, his eyes still wide from whatever he had witnessed. And then there was Toyo.

Toyo had an unconscious Orochi thrown over her shoulder. A scarlet rope tied his limbs together.

Suddenly I understood why Aidan's eyes were wide, because I felt my own try to bulge straight out of my skull.

"Uhhh. Toyo, right?" Leilani said hesitantly. "Why do you have someone trussed up and unconscious?"

"It's Orochi," Toyo said calmly. "Figured it would make things easier for all of us if we had him in our hands. I cut a frayed Thread from myself to tie him up; he's not going anywhere."

Well, I guess we knew why the mountain range had folded in on itself and disappeared then. It was weird to think that Reika was somewhere in him. And I had no idea you could simply *cut off* a piece of your own damn Thread. Then again, I wasn't a *kami*, or the daughter of the *kami* who had figured out how to sever Threads, so there was that.

"We're all here, Cam. Spill." Lala's boot tapped in impatience.

"So…thedeadbodyofourmissingpersonwasfoundinmyhouse," I spat out in a rush.

"I'm sorry, what?" Aidan asked. "It sounded like you said our missing person was found. Sans head. In your hyuse."

Scott and Leilani nodded to confirm his statement.

"What the royal fuck??" he exclaimed.

"Hideki and Emma have been taken in for questioning, given that our agency is the one that found all the bodies. Leilani and I are next. The FBI SAC is frothing at the mouth wanting to know where you are, Cam. Goes by the name of Solomon Park. He's new. Evidently, he was put in charge of our region and he's one hundred percent a dick," Scott answered.

Toyo looked positively ready to eat people. "Why are you being targeted, Cam? It doesn't seem all that random that these bodies have shown up in your backyard, in the middle of your involvement with Orochi, in the spring. Now one is dropped in your damn home? Whoever is responsible for this is taunting you."

"Yeah, well, what the hell am I going to do about it until we know more?" I grimaced. "We're not heading back to Skamania after this. We're going to the Neskowin territory. I want to keep as many people away from the situation as possible."

"You could always stay in your home in the Abstruse realm," Cheuksin pointed out. "You paid a hefty fee to have access to your home in either realm."

"Neskowin gives me more freedom and access to Ryūgū-jō." I gestured to the unconscious god. "Quotes know that we're never going to keep him contained on this side. I'm assuming you planned to put him in the cells below the palace. Neskowin also doesn't put Danly in the position of knowing I'm in his jurisdiction and not bringing me in."

Toyo gave me a smile filled with malice and teeth.

"You don't think it'll look even more suspicious that half of the agency just…isn't there?" Aidan questioned.

"Well, I'd rather look suspicious and stay out of jail than show up thinking it proves my innocence, all while not having enough proof to clear my name and our agency's name," Lala retorted.

Yuriko pointed at Lala. "What she said." Her face looked positively disgusted by the prospect of being enclosed in a space with people she didn't know or like.

Relatable. Theo nodded in firm agreement.

"Alrighty, well that's decided. Moving on then. It's been two days since we were last in the realm. So that made, what? Six days to get to your location, Theo?" I asked.

He rocked his hand back and forth to indicate the approximation.

"Swell. So, about a week to get to the bay to meet up with Anhangá to get back to Neskowin, providing he's done with the souls. Hopefully, it doesn't take them that long to put the *gashadokuro* to rest permanently instead of leaving it dormant."

"Scott and Leilani, you good?" Concern laced Lala's voice. Scott was her younger brother. As her only other Perigean sibling, they were both long-lived and looked like they were in their thirties, as opposed to pushing their fifties and sixties.

"Don't worry about us." Scott waved off her concern. "We've got things handled down here. Danly and Tish have been keeping us in the know."

"Yeah, I can't wait for them to call me in," Leilani said with a slow, wide smile. I felt sorry for this Solomon Park agent.

"Alright, so our plan is essentially the same as it would have been if it had taken another week to locate and rescue Rafael," I summed up. "Hideki, Emma, Scott, and Leilani hold down the fort in Skamania. We'll be on the coast in the Abbie realm, instead of Alaska, with a *kodama* forest that actually likes us. We all good here? Scott, Leilani, call me if the situation changes at all."

"Sure. It's the same. With the exception of, I don't know, clearing your name and the reputation of our agency," Leilani snorted. "What's our plan for *that?*"

"Given that I can't possibly have been at the same time and place for all of these people I don't even know, receipts. Lots and lots of receipts." And I'm hoping we could pull it off, given how much time some of us spent in the Abstruse realm that the Quotes didn't even know existed.

"Whiz? Gale? Can you find out what the approximate TODs were and see how many of us have legitimate alibis for them? I don't want to involve Tish or Danly here; I just want to be prepared in the event we need it."

"Bet," Gale responded.

Whiz sent a thumbs-up emoji and a text stating that he was already digging up alibis for Emma and Hideki. No wonder he hadn't appeared with Gale.

"I mean, one of the first bodies was someone from Brazil. How the hell does the FBI plan to tie you to that when you've never even been to the country?" Scott commented. "Their theory might as well be Swiss cheese for all the holes there are in it."

Excited barking filled the air when Yumi suddenly launched into the group in a cloud of black mist. Max and Phally danced around the newcomers, reveling in the reunion. I was glad to see the experience hadn't scarred Phally. Max was, unfortunately, used to these kinds of adventures, but I still worried. Seeing them prancing around warmed my soul. Pea hissed at the pile of K9s when one came precariously close to crashing into us. A moment later, Anhangá materialized next to his grandson, along with Toyo, Aidan, and an unconscious Orochi. I had never seen the stag look tired before, but the entity's head drooped and his eyes were world-weary.

"Thought a lift back might be helpful, considering everything my grandson just relayed to me," he said.

I glanced over at Rafael, but he just gave me a good-natured shrug, though a vein had popped in his forehead upon seeing Orochi. "I haven't recovered enough to jump to Neskowin. And I'm not up for a six-day hike."

"Whatever you want, it's yours." Lala whooped. "I could kiss you for saving us the trip. Both of you."

I'd pass on the stag, but the idea had merit.

CHAPTER TWENTY-SIX

Abruptly our view shifted from mountains and glaciers to the Ghost Forest peeking up through the Neskowin sand. Anhangá departed immediately after dropping us off to fetch Theo and Yuriko, then planned to return to his lands to recover.

Blessedly, the heat wave must have broken at some point while we were away, and I took a deep breath of the fresh sea air, silently appreciating the territory that had been my sanctuary once upon a time. Max bolted through the waves with glee, drenching himself in the salt water before bounding back to us. A blue glow shone about a hundred feet offshore, made more vibrant by the darkening skies. Skeletal birds swooped into the waves, sweeping herring from the ocean's surface and throwing them into the air. Beaks snapped at the falling fish before they plummeted back into the ocean, limp, their souls consumed by Murry's retinue.

"Well, I'm off." Toyo waved, Orochi still hauled over her shoulder. "Gotta get this one in the dungeons before he wakes up," she said gleefully.

"I wouldn't relish being Orochi right now," I commented, watching her shift into a massive sea turtle before she hit the waves then paddled out to sea. It wasn't her favorite form, after the events that led to our meeting, once upon a time, but she still pulled it out every now and then. She met up with the blue glow that encompassed Murry, and the light slowly vanished as they made their way to the snare.

Cheuksin snorted in agreement, whereas Aidan and Rafael cringed.

"I should be thrilled by the prospect after what that *kami* put me through, but honestly, I think I feel sorry for him," Rafael remarked.

I didn't.

"C'mon, girl." Aidan waved to Yumi. "Let's go see your favorite great-Uncles."

The group of us turned as one and began trudging up the beach to the parking lot where the Uncles had left a vehicle for us, just in case. We crammed into Cheuksin's old Subaru, Pea clicking unhappily at sharing the space with a soggy Saint Bernard. Four humans, two K9s, an opossum, plus three packs, made for an exceptionally uncomfortable drive, no matter how short it was. The car reeked of wet dog and rotting muskeg. Cheuksin complained the entire way, and I promised to get it detailed as I leaned my head out the window the entire way home. I didn't care that my back was getting soaked by Max, who warred with me for space in the window. I was just glad to have something keeping my body semi-upright. An eternity later, we turned down the dirt road and passed the *kodama* who actually liked us.

Howls and yips greeted Cheuksin's Subaru as she parked next to a gleaming vintage Mini Cooper. I nearly fell out of the car as I threw the door open and found myself at the bottom of a dog pile, tongues and paws everywhere. Pea screeched in outrage and did her best to scamper out from under the pile as my body was pummeled by the combination of Max, Woody, and Vicky, and she beelined for the front door. A laugh of joy squeezed out of me as a heavy pair of malamute paws pounced straight onto my diaphragm, leaving me gasping for air. I finally managed to sit back up and did my best to throw my arms around all three of them.

Rafael stepped out of the Subaru, now that there was space in front of the door, while the rest of the group had already clambered out of their respective exits. Cheuksin was well on her way to the house; Aidan and Yumi headed into the woods, leaving us to our reunion.

Vicky let out a long howl and darted for Rafael, leaping high with absolute trust that he wouldn't let her fall. He managed to catch her, despite the unexpected welcome, stumbling back against the frame of the vehicle with the force of her impact.

I smiled as Woodrow dragged his tongue up my face while I hugged him to my side. "She missed you, you know."

He carefully held her to his chest, holding her tight in a hug. "I missed her, too," he admitted.

"She's your heart dog," I said simply. "You don't really have a choice; the two of you belong to one another now."

The expression on his face encompassed a thousand emotions and none at all. It was wonder and awe, accompanied by sorrow and pain, shining through the cracks in a wall of detachment. The thoughts racing through his mind were nearly tangible as he looked at Vicky with reverence. She grinned a happy dog grin and reached up to lick him frantically. Laughter rang from him, free and clear, as he sank to the ground with the pup who had experienced horrors at the hands of men, sharing in the joy she now held. The laughter turned into silent tears as he clutched her to his chest and buried his face in her fur.

Echoes of the turmoil he was experiencing thrummed through my body, and I stood to leave, feeling like a voyeur under the circumstances. Max and Woody flanked me as I entered the front door and closed it gently behind us.

The sounds of a shower running upstairs filled the silence, and I took advantage of Cheuky's absence to raid the kitchen. Max and Woody stretched out on their sides in the living room. I'd have to mop the floor later. Pea climbed to the top of the refrigerator to watch over us all. If Rafael was anything like I had been, he would need time and space to process his abrupt and unexpected freedom. Comfort food always helped with the aftermath, in my experience.

As I debated the offerings in front of me, I heard soft footsteps and turned to watch the male quietly pad out to the Adirondack chairs from my nightmares. Vicky jumped up lightly and curled into a ball in his lap. I handed a glass of *sikhye* to Pea. "Take this out to him?" I figured he could use the sweet rice drink to give him something else to focus on while his emotions went haywire.

She regarded me with a solemn face, her gaze pointed at my hand, before wrapping her tail around the glass. I sighed. "You know it was the only way." She chattered at me—*scolded* me was more accurate—before she hoofed it out the door after Rafael. I scrubbed the filth from my hands in the kitchen sink, watching as she crawled up the chair Rafael had repositioned to face the ocean and deposited the glass on the wooden plank that made up its arm. His hand came down on her back, stroking her once before the huntsman lifted the tiny *shikigami* to his shoulder and rested his cheek against her face. The beverage sat forgotten as the three of them comforted each other in silence.

As they sat, I allowed my vision to shift. Nausea, vertigo—and a new sensation?—unbalanced me, but I held my wet hands tightly to the counter as I focused on Rafael's heart. I breathed a sigh of relief when I beheld the organ maintaining a normal rhythm. The squirming mass of parasitic Evil had been pushed back even further from when I had last seen the *kariudo*. My sight shifted back to normal and I braced myself against the counter until my equilibrium returned. The new tightness that cocooned my body faded with the other symptoms. My shoulders dropped at the realization that my condition was progressing.

Comfort food. I needed comfort food. I dried my hands, then pulled out the flour and salt, threw them in a bowl, and poured in some water. Kneading the dough gave me something to focus on, too, as memories of how the fragments of my heart had thumped with the sight of Rafael's. The memory was ephemeral and my body strained to recreate the moment, needing my heart to work the way it should, especially in the wake of the tightness.

I set the mixture aside to rest and did my best to put my yearning for a heartbeat aside. Instead, I placed a block of frozen broth on medium heat to begin melting it in a stockpot while I began sautéing some marinated beef that had been in the refrigerator. The action was a piss-poor distraction.

I had no idea where to even begin with that single beat. My heart had been a useless organ pinballing inside of my body until that moment. Was it Rafael's soul doing weird things to me? Was it a signal of how close I was to dying? Like how some Quotes dying of tuberculosis experienced a surge before death? An aftereffect of some horrid concoction that Reika had made me swallow?

I shook my head like it would send my thoughts flying from my mind. I had been lost in my thoughts so long that the frozen block had turned liquid and was beginning to boil. I turned my attention to chopping vegetables to add to the broth and tossed a portion of them in, along with a few seasonings.

While the ingredients melded together, I returned to my dough and rolled it out, attuned to the changes in my grip as I worked the rolling pin. I had never realized how much my pinky contributed to my grip before. I did my best to put aside the feeling and folded the dough over, then sliced noodles off with the knife I snagged from the block. It was madness to try and figure out the beat of my heart when it could be any number of things, but my mind kept wandering back to that *thump*, trying to dissect the cause behind it.

In reality, I knew I just wanted that *thump* to come back. To give me a rhythm once again. Experiencing a solitary beat was a tease, as though the Universe was taunting me with what I had once been.

Dueling snores resonated from the living room, providing a soundtrack to my thoughts, almost mocking in the rhythm the two K9s established with their breath. Needless to say, I wasn't going to find any answers today. I separated the noodles carefully and dropped them into the broth, along with the zucchini I had held back. A few moments later I sampled the soup and threw in a few more seasonings to elevate the taste. Maybe I couldn't solve this problem, but I could still cook a mean *kalguksu*.

I left the noodles and zucchini to cook for a few more minutes and washed the dishes I had used. Delicate footfalls sounded behind me and Cheuksin peered into the pot.

"I could've made us some food," she stated. "I just needed a shower first."

"I needed something for my hands to do," I professed. "My mind was going in circles and needed an outlet for the energy it was creating."

She nodded in understanding and pulled out soup bowls and spoons. A ladle appeared in her hand and she began dishing out the meal. I added the meat I had sauteed earlier and green onions to the top.

Cheuksin placed spoons in two of the bowls and held them out to me. "Try to get him to talk. It'll be good for both of you."

Feelings. Quotes above, I hated talking about them. But I accepted the bowls and used my elbow to slide the glass door open. It was officially time to ambush the male.

CHAPTER TWENTY-SEVEN

"I STILL think saving me was an unnecessary risk," the former kariudo said softly when he heard me approach. His stare remained steady on the sun setting over the ocean.

I sighed and handed him a bowl before I sat in the chair next to him. The same one I had sat in months ago…and every night in my dreams. "Can you just be grateful to be free from your bands and we can put off this fight for another day?"

Rafael shifted, causing both Vicky and Pea to grumble. The *shikigami* climbed off and opted to perch on the back of his chair instead. He set the bowl of *kalguksu* on the arm next to the *sikhye* and spent an uncomfortable length of time studying me. "It's not that I'm not grateful, Baki. I just would rather take on this burden a thousand times over than for you have the tiniest possibility of being subjected to this hell for a second time in your life." He took a deep breath and rubbed at his forearms with more force than usual, as if he was trying to convince himself they were truly gone.

My jaw clenched. "How did you know?" I hadn't planned to tell him the terms of the bargain. I knew I had a time limit on my life. I figured my life would expire before the possibility of being enslaved again came to pass, in the event I failed Seokga's tasks. It was one of the reasons I had agreed to take them on.

"My grandfather filled me in."

I shrugged. "Well, unluckily for you, free will is a thing and I chose differently. Besides, you're borrowing trouble for a future that might not even come to pass."

"Don't expect me to stand by and accept it if that version of the future becomes reality," he warned.

"Why would I expect you to listen to me? The entire course of our relationship has been rife with one of us ignoring the other's advice."

"Correction. It has been rife with *you* ignoring *my* words. I have always considered yours."

I winced. He wasn't wrong. "I'm sorry," I admitted. "I wanted to hate you at first, and I did, but the more time I had to think about the situation, the more time I had to realize that I actually don't. I hated the way the events had to play out. You were in a terrible spot and tried to do the best you could to work around your restrictions. Don't get me wrong, I still resent the hell out of you for what you did, but we were both victims of circumstance. I should have stuck to your plan rather than going off script when it came to facing Orochi. It was a moment of recklessness with costs that were far too high."

The words were so much easier to say now after my dream conversation in Alaska.

Rafe waved me off. "You were coming face-to-face with the visage of your Thread and your enemy in the same being. I'm pretty sure anybody's common sense would have fled from that encounter."

"It's not a good enough excuse. You have spent literal months trapped by Orochi. It's actually been keeping me up at night."

A mischievous gleam overtook his haunted expression momentarily. "So you admit to thinking of me while in bed at night. I'm flattered." His gaze darted to my bedroom window before returning to me. I would have missed it had I not been watching him so closely.

I would swat the male, but it felt too soon after the destruction I had seen wrought on the body that had just healed. I settled for a mouthful of noodles instead. A long exhale gusted from him and he began eating. His eyes closed in appreciation as he chewed silently alongside me.

With that soft sound, and our placement, I was transported back to the night where I had run my fingers along his skin to inspect his tattoos. My fingers trembled at the memory, and I quickly set my bowl down so he wouldn't notice. What would it be like to run my fingers over his bare skin now? To follow the planes of his torso instead of images inked in cruelty. What would change, with Rafael Sugiyama being a male who was now in charge of his own actions? A shiver passed through me as my mind ran wild with possibilities.

You just rescued him from a traumatic situation, Cam. Give the male time to readjust before you contemplate jumping his beautiful body.

"What were you thinking about?"

I choked on my noodles and thought frantically. In a move that stank of desperation, I gestured wildly to the space around us. "I was wondering how you were coping with everything."

Sure, Cam. He bought that. He doesn't know that you were wondering how well he was coping because his body was occupying your mind. Stop that. Thank the Quotes he can't read my thoughts like Anhangá.

A furrow appeared in his brow, and his right leg began to bob restlessly, making Vicky grumble and readjust her body. The small action gave me hope that he hadn't noticed my awkwardness, even as I fought the urge to fidget myself.

"I don't know who I am on my own," he finally confessed. "My entire life I've been bound either by duty to my grandfather or by slave bands. What do I even do with this freedom? Do I go back to working with my grandfather? I don't particularly want to. I'd like to find out what *I* like and what I'm good at, outside of threatening and killing."

I frowned at the setting sun. "You're not out of the woods yet. We still have a wannabe world destroyer to tackle. But…what do you imagine for yourself?"

"That's the problem. My mind is blank when it comes to that."

"Where would you be and what would you be doing right now if you could be doing anything in the world?"

"Honestly?" He nodded his head at the dog and opossum that surrounded him. "This. Being able to be just sit and be me, surrounded by a beautiful landscape and others who don't judge you for who you are."

Silence followed his words. I waited him out.

"I'm not worth it, you know. My life has been spent in darkness." Rafael finally said, his words a whisper that barely carried over to me.

"I'll have to disagree with you there," I said, swallowing thickly at the self-hatred this male held for himself. "You literally just waved off my actions that put you in the position for Orochi to identify you as a traitor and to find out your secrets. The consequences of what happened to you because of the way I reacted is going to stick with me for a while, no matter what you say. And don't excuse them away again. I *need* to remember that my actions don't only impact me.

"Besides which, I saw your heart," I continued. "You managed to give Evil a shove off a cliff. Did it catch a branch on the way down? Yeah, it's still hanging in there. But somehow, you're still winning, despite all odds."

Rafael held out a hand and watched as wisps of black mist rose from it, curling around his forearms, inspecting the scars the bands had left behind before darting to Vicky. Vicky tried to lick it, only for it to dissipate before she could make contact, reforming a moment later. "You have a unique outlook on life, Baki," he murmured. "I don't know if I've ever met someone quite like you."

"That's me. One of a kind. Last *haetae* standing," I joked weakly, taking hold of his hand and bringing it down. Warmth suffused me with the touch, and I watched, fascinated, as goose bumps rippled down his arm. Black mist rose from my own arm, intertwining with his. I felt a pang of sadness thinking it was returning to become whole with Rafael once again, but it somehow remained separate.

I squeezed his hand and let go. "Which, I will remind you, it's only because of you I'm still standing, despite whatever you may have done to me in the past. Keep that in mind when you wallow, okay?"

I got up from the chair and gathered our empty bowls, waiting until his eyes met mine once again. "I wasn't kidding. I want you to remember that. I am the worst ever at letting others in, but when I do, the feeling of relief is incredible. Don't be like me. Talk to someone. I don't care who. Vicky. Pea. Me. Cheuky. We've all been through some shit; we can all relate."

He smiled as he looked down at the dog that was still curled up in his lap, and I melted a little at the smile. "Vicky is a pretty great talking buddy."

"Don't I know it. She doesn't sass back like the others too. Once upon a time, you questioned talking to dogs, so look at how far you've come. There's hope for you yet." I rested a hand on his shoulder for a moment, then bent down to whisper in his ear, "And take a shower. You reek."

Rafael threw a pillow at me. "You're not any better, *haetae*."

I snorted. "Where the hell do you think I'm going?"

His eyes darkened at my comment and his gaze dropped to my lips. My mouth went dry as his opened to say something. Heat flooded through me and I rushed into my house to escape the confused feelings that had resurfaced from that one look.

CHAPTER TWENTY-EIGHT

After I searched every inch of my bathroom for the *akaname* and came up empty, I relaxed and ran my shower. Wet wipes only did so much for someone when you're covered in the ash of Abstruse remains, on top of the dirt and sweat from our adventure in Alaska. There was nothing like the first hit of scalding hot water to cleanse the trauma from your skin. I sank down and sat on the river rock that made up the floor of my shower, exhausted. I dropped my glamour and allowed the water to run through me, soothing sore muscles and running in wild patterns due to the unusual landscape of my body.

A sigh of relief gusted from me as the spray hit a particularly painful spot along my quad. A shard had rotated badly, leaving its edges catching against two others. The pain was like sitting on the serrated edge of a knife, but nothing was there. It had first happened on a call-out for one of the bodies about a month ago, and I had gotten good at turning it into white noise, but this trip had wrenched it even further. I had been doing my best to hide the increased pain. So far, no one had noticed; not that I was aware of anyway.

An inquisitive chirp sounded from the other side of the water. I smiled at the sound. Except for Pea. Pea noticed everything, except when she was curled up in a ball, hiding from the world.

"I'm fine, Pea. Just tired. Thank you for checking in." A series of clicks and hisses followed my comment. "It's okay, I know you wish you could fix it. But you already did everything you could possibly do to fix me when I first broke."

A brief blast of red *ki* shot from her body, incinerating a stack of folded towels on the rack. I was glad she had passed the grief stage for the time being, but her rage was wreaking havoc on my linens.

"Please don't ash my towels. I like those towels. They're the perfect size and have the fluffiness factor down just right," I commented mildly. I winced as I stood, pain roaring to life in every part of my body now that I was safe at home. I ignored the empty space from the bit of my soul I had ripped out. What was one more missing part of my body when I was trying to get the grit of the past few days off.

Pea sniffed and turned her back to me, ambling over to the counter. She climbed up, then reached over to the door handle with her tail and unlatched it. Every door in my home had handles instead of knobs, as well as something to elevate Pea to the appropriate height. She had as much right to enjoy the entirety of our home as I did. Her *ki* might be capable of a vast number of skills, but one thing it wasn't was dexterous. She slipped out the door with her tail whipping behind her, conveying her offense at my request.

I snagged the surviving towel from the hook next to my shower, and stepped out, vigorously drying off my body then twisting my hair up in the same towel, since I didn't have a second one available. I bypassed the mirror. The pain told me enough about my current state. Whether this would be my new baseline or simply a flare would reveal itself eventually. Instead, I strode out to the bedroom.

Before I could collapse face down on my bed and melt into it, a motion caught the corner of my eye. The bedroom door was ajar, and a frozen Rafael stood in the middle of the four-inch crack Pea had left. His hair was wet and the white tee he had thrown on clung to every ripple of his still damp body. I swore the male had no idea how to wear an item of clothing poorly. Navy joggers hugged his thighs, and I threw a hand over my eyes like *he* was the naked one and not me.

Why did my common sense escape me around this male? I hadn't even been like this with Ryūjin.

More unnerving than my stupid impulsive motion was the fact that I could feel a myriad of emotions that weren't mine but Rafael's, judging by the expression on his face. First surprise, then a tinge of shame—that was a confidence booster for a naked female. But that was quickly nudged aside by stronger emotions as I felt his gaze peruse my body.

Shock and anger dominated. No, that wasn't right. *Anger* was the dominant emotion. By far. But then, it shifted to desire. I wasn't entirely surprised, not after our shared experience in Orochi's dimension, but experiencing someone else's desire for me was still foreign.

I finally snagged the throw from the foot of the bed and threw it around my body, my ability to think rushing back at long last.

He closed the door silently behind him, the soft *snick* of the latch sounding loud in the room. His gaze narrowed on me, his focus laser-sharp, and his steps were quiet but determined. He only stopped when he neared enough for me to feel him exhale across my bare shoulders.

"You are stunning," he whispered. It wasn't in the tone of a male telling his mate how much he desires her. Despite his quiet tone, his words were stern, as if he was expecting an argument from me. He wasn't wrong.

I scoffed, looking down at the ruins of my body not covered by the towel. A deep crevasse carved my chest now, ruining the tattoo I had done in remembrance of my Thread and as a reminder to myself of what I had survived.

Rafael tipped my chin up with a crooked finger. I watched a droplet of water trail down his face, echoing the path of a teardrop. "I came by your room for two reasons. The first, and trivial, reason was to ask about the *akaname* in my bathroom. The second was because I realized I hadn't truly thanked you while we talked on the deck. I didn't realize how badly you were injured. I should have. Quotes above, I should have." He paused as he appeared to gather himself and his chest heaved on his next breath. "Baki. *Thank you.* There's no language that exists in these realms that could possibly convey how much I need to thank you." His words ended on a sigh as he watched himself run his fingers along a void. A tremor ran through my body, the phantom touch giving me chills despite the absence of anything solid beneath it. My hands twitched with desire to reciprocate the action.

"These are a story of your life. One full of trials." A finger traced the cracks that ran between the shards. Then along the scars on my forearms, evidence of my time as a slave. "And your triumphs." His hand came back to rest just above where my heart should lay beating, covering most of the crevasse with his large hand. I watched as his gaze widened at the realization that no heart pounded beneath his touch. I ached for that one *thump* with everything I had as nothingness filled the empty space where there should have been some form of reciprocation.

"Is this because of what you gave up in the ritual?" he asked softly. Pain washed over his face at the thought.

While I might not have had a whole heart to race at the *kariudo's* touch, my breath still grew shallow. His face dipped as he concentrated on the rise and fall of my chest, a deeper furrow forming between his brows.

I covered his hand with mine, ready to remove it, uncomfortable with the thought of him feeling my lack of a heartbeat. Instead, Rafael laid his other hand over both of ours, and met my eyes once again, his face a hair's breadth from my own.

"I haven't had a heartbeat since *Hyakki Yagyō*," I admitted. Pea and Whiz were the only ones who knew that truth. Not even Murry had known. Whiz only did because he monitored our vitals and fabricated a heart rhythm for me so no one else knew. A pang of guilt shot through me at the realization it was yet another secret I had kept from my friends.

He cut off whatever he had been about to say, his gaze studying mine intently. I could only imagine what he saw in them. What he felt through this unintentional bond that was created with my death.

"That night back in May," he murmured. "When you died. I had assumed you did, because there was no heartbeat."

I gave him a crooked smile. "Pretty sure I did. I did get hit with sap after all. This"—I motioned to where my heart should have been—"isn't exactly a good barometer for life or death in me anymore. That girl cracked with the rest of me over a century ago."

His fingers thrummed along the space as he tapped them thoughtfully. The sensation was strange...but not unwelcome. The fact I could even feel anything was a wonder. I surmised that what I was experiencing was probably his sensation of touch as opposed to my own.

"Your soul started to dissipate," he said finally. "But it hadn't fully detached. I kept doing my best to retether it as Pea worked on healing you. I think you were dying, but perhaps, not fully dead."

"Woo." I let out a weak, fake cheer. "One thing went right for me this past spring. Maybe I didn't die!" I pumped a fist in the air and proceeded to lose the blanket around me in the process.

Amusement rode his mouth, but his gaze grew hot, though he was a gentleman and kept it above my chest.

"Baki," he murmured, leaning in close. "Why do you seem to always lose clothes around me?

I shivered at both his words and the breath that had rushed over my ear. He reached down, maintaining his gaze on me, and began wrapping the throw around me once more. His eyes flashed black fire before returning to their deep burnt umber as he tucked the tail of the blanket between my breasts. He had barely pulled away and his face was achingly close to mine, his breath minty from whatever toothpaste he had used. My breath caught as his hand reached out once more and his fingertips grazed my clavicle. His eyes searched mine.

I gave the barest hint of a nod and his mouth curved up in the smallest of smiles as his head dipped. His lips lightly brushed against mine and a soft moan escaped me, releasing the air that had been held captive within me. Once again, my world was narrowing to this male and this male alone. My free hand lifted of its own volition, wrapping around Rafael, coiling into the soft, damp waves of his hair as I deepened the kiss.

A sense of urgency rode us both. For the first time in over a century, I felt truly alive. Not only did I feel alive, but I *wanted* to live. I wanted to experience all that Rafael had to offer with my entire being. His desire fed my own as the kiss transformed, and he adjusted his grip on the throw, using his hold on it to tug me closer still as his lips trailed down my neck. My head fell back, exposing my throat to him as I reveled in the sensation. The throw finally slipped from my body for good, unable to stay secured with our movements. His hands ran down my sides, uncaring whether flesh or emptiness met them from underneath.

"I've been wanting to do this since that thumb war," he murmured.

I gasped as his fingers played lightly along the edges of a fragment millimeters above my hip bones, his words washing over me and failing to register under the assault of sensation. It was one I had never experienced before. Rafael was the first I had ever allowed to see the truth of me. But there was not even an iota of self-consciousness. There couldn't be with what I saw in his gaze.

My thoughts, my ability to reason, all the reasons why this was a bad idea, fled from me as his lips wrapped around my breast, softly sucking at the flesh as his hand moved to tweak my other nipple with the just right amount of pressure. My body arched under his touch, begging for more. The hand upon my hip trailed further down, tantalizing in its light touch, feathering closer and closer to where I needed it the most.

Instead, his touch left abruptly, and a soft protest left my lips that turned into a gasp. He rested his forehead against mine, breathing hard.

"Soon," he said with promise, his fingers trailing up my throat before he rested his thumb against my lower lip, tugging it down slightly.

My mind was in a fog as I processed his words, protests still reeling through my thoughts, then I heard what had stopped him. Footsteps. A group of them. And voices growing louder.

I dropped down to my bed with a groan. *Quotes, we had been so close.* "Back to saving the world we go."

"Haven't you heard? There's no rest for the wicked." Rafael's eyes sparkled before he dematerialized from my room.

Well, that was convenient. I grimaced. At least I wouldn't have to explain why the male was leaving my bedroom with his hair a mess and his shirt askew.

CHAPTER TWENTY-NINE

took my time getting dressed, needing a few more minutes to myself after being around people nonstop for several days. I braided my hair before I tugged a comfortable old shirt over my head. The shirt dipped past my shoulder, its collar long since worn-out, but I didn't care what it exposed of my scars.

Fuck it. I was in the comfort of my own home and in the Abbie realm. A pair of joggers completed my ensemble. I pulled open the door and headed in the direction of the voices.

Abbies had taken over my living room and kitchen. The Uncles were settled on the floor. One was squishing Max's face and cooing sweet nothings at him; the other was in his raccoon dog form, a blur of salt-and-pepper as he darted in between Woody's legs, the malamute reeling about, trying to catch him. Yuriko and Toyo, who must have returned sometime after I went upstairs, were chatting quietly on the couch facing the bay windows. Willa lay contentedly at Yuri's feet, flat on her back, paws in the air.

In the kitchen, Aidan leaned against the counter, one hand playing with Yumi's ears while the K9 gave Cheuksin imploring eyes. Lala was seated next to Aidan, Gale on her shoulder, and the four were chatting with Theo, who was trying and failing to help Cheuky in the kitchen. Pea sat perched on the refrigerator once more. I sent her a suspicious glance, and she stared at me with wide, innocent eyes.

I might not be able to prove it, but I knew the *shikigami* had left my bedroom door ajar on purpose.

Rafael stood on the fringe, practically on the back porch, and you could feel the uncertainty radiating from his body. Or maybe it was the fact that I could sense his emotions. Vicky sat, leaning against his hand, unwilling to leave his side.

I caught his eye and nodded to Lala's K9, who was asleep in the corner, and wandered up to him.

"*That's* why he's named Phallus," I said in a side-whisper to him. Rafael cocked his head and studied the German Shepherd mix again and a twinkle reached his eyes as he took in the sight before him.

The K9 had his head tucked under himself, flat against the floor. How he breathed, I had no idea. The floppy ears he had inherited from whatever he was mixed with rounded out the top of his head. The folds of his scruff were layered *just* right. His forelegs were tucked tight under himself, as were his hindquarters, only leaving a wide round base that was accentuated by the way his tail wrapped around his rear.

In short, the K9 looked like a German Shepherd–colored dick.

Lala sidled up to us, a bottle of beer in hand. "He's slept like that ever since he was a puppy." She grinned. "How could I name him anything other than Phallus?"

"Valid point," Rafael agreed on a chuckle. "Areola and Phallus has a certain ring to it as well."

She bumped him with a shoulder. "I knew you'd get it. C'mon. Aidan's been regaling us with tales of the *kotengu*, and I have a feeling he's been exaggerating his fight with the bird. Be his fact-checker. Gale's useless. There's no footage since his nanos got knocked out of commission by your mojo."

Rafael gave me the imploring look of the introverted at a party as Lala pulled him over to the kitchen counter. I gave him a little finger wave instead. There was no use in fighting Lala; you learned to go along with the flow—it was easiest not to resist. Bonus was that she unconsciously eased any social anxiety with her *ki*, so she really was the ultimate extroverted friend to have in a gathering. The male would be fine. Plus, he had Victoria to ground him.

I flopped down next to Yuriko and Toyo on the couch, and instead of melting in my bed, I became one with the sofa as I leaned my head back and stared at the beams that ran across my ceilings.

"It's been a week, hasn't it," Toyo commented.

I groaned and rubbed my eyes. "How are you holding up? That's the first time you've come face-to-face with Orochi while you were in your right mind."

Her pupils lengthened into narrow vertical slits and her nictitating membrane drew across her eyes—once, twice, three times—then a vicious smile filled with crocodilian teeth spread over her face. "Seeing as he was the one unconscious at the end, and is now in my father's dungeons, I would qualify it as…satisfying." Her words themselves were confident. Her tone? Not so much.

"Have you spoken to him yet?" I asked.

"No, I left him to rot in the temporal snare that runs a hundred years to one of our days. He'll have some time to burn off his rage before I try."

A chorus of howls rose as all the K9s, except Vicky, leapt from their current placements and began dancing around the back door. Vicky just sat back and watched from the kitchen.

A few moments later, a giant mantid stood behind the glass, bottles of tequila clasped between the pincers of his forelimbs while he manipulated the sliding door with the tarsi of his middle limbs until it slid open. He raised his limbs in victory.

"I brought the good stuff," Kenichi shouted as he ducked under the doorframe, the bottles clinking against one another with alarming force. The K9s started prancing around him and I hurried over. To rescue the tequila. Not the *kamikiri*.

"How you manage to get into your Mini Cooper, I'll never know," I teased, grabbing the bottles and giving him a kiss on the cheek as he bent down to give me a hug with his forelimbs. "Thank you for bringing the pups, Chi-chi."

"You know I love watching the doggos, Cam." He patted my shoulder with a tarsi before he shrank into his human form to better fit in the space. "Tish gave me a heads-up about what was happening. I packed them up as soon as I heard and we headed out here. Figured you wouldn't want them around that in their own home. Although, it looks like you lost another one, did you?" He nodded to Rafael and Vicky with concern in his eyes.

I lifted a shoulder, my shirt slipping a bit further down the arm as I did so, and I caught the *kamikiri's* horrified look, though he hid it quickly. It was nearly identical to everyone else's expressions when they saw me, except for Rafael and his grandfather.

"I'm okay." My reassurance held a double meaning and Kenichi nodded seriously. "This one felt right. They belong to one another, and it makes my heart happy instead of sad. I never thought Vicky would fully trust a male again after what she lived through. They're good for one another."

I headed to the kitchen with the bottles and set them on the counter. "Rafael, Kenichi. Ken, Rafael."

Lala made grabby hands for the bottles as I attempted introductions and shoved Cheuky away when she approached. "Absolutely not. You might be a household goddess, but I tasted the margarita you made earlier and you are fired from margarita making. At least it's good to know that gods still suck at some things."

Ken's arms folded across his chest and inclined his head to the former *kariudo*, though his shoulders shook slightly from holding his laughter back.

Rafael winced. "I've never even met you and yet I owe you an apology."

Theo coughed into his hand, choking on his beer. "I'm pretty sure you owe thousands of people apologies, *kariudo*. Including people you haven't met."

Rafael's shoulders sank.

"Former *kariudo*," I corrected, leaning against the refrigerator. "Luckily, we're long-lived, so he has ample time to make the apologies. Starting with one in particular."

"I threatened your life in an attempt to coerce Camellia to work with me," Rafael began. "It felt wrong, and I knew it was wrong. I didn't have to do it, it wasn't something that was inked into my skin, but I knew threatening loved ones was a pressure point that worked for most. Fortunately for all of us," he continued in a dry voice, "Cam doesn't play with threats. I deeply regret and apologize for my actions. I plan to do better from here on out, once I figure what *here on out* means."

Kenichi studied Rafael for a long time, tense moments passing in silence, even from the living room. Finally, he held out a hand to the taller male and pulled him in for a hug, yanking an unsuspecting Rafael off-balance. "I accept. On the condition you never pull that shit again, unless it's on *Cam's* behalf. And only because you sacrificed yourself for her. If you hadn't, we'd be having a different conversation."

I snickered at the deeply uncomfortable look on Rafael's face. "Chichi's a hugger. Like Lala, you get used to it. If you're going to be part of this weird, jumbled-up family, you don't have a choice."

Aidan threw an arm around Rafael's shoulders after Ken let him go and gave him a good-natured hug. "He's a pretty cool guy, Ken, once you get to know him. Granted, he was a little off-putting at first, but he grows on you quickly. Like mold."

Hooves on hardwood floors sounded behind me, and Anhangá stood next to me, watching the group. "You gave him something I never could, *haetae*."

Turning, I arched an eyebrow. "And what would that be? Choices? A sense of belonging? Affection? *Laughter*?"

The stag smiled. Although it was still unsettling to see a cervid with fangs smiling, I was growing used to it. "A family, Chun-Hei. As strange as your family might be, it's still a strong one."

I looked at the group as well. Pea dropped from the refrigerator, trusting that I would catch her, and I held her against my chest. She hissed softly at the stag but settled into my arms. "It wasn't that hard. Just takes a little perspective." I nudged his soft shoulder with my elbow. "You should try it sometime. You might end up with a family, too."

CHAPTER THIRTY

The high-pitched *whir* of the blender faded, and I tapped a spoon against the margarita glass I held once Lala finished pouring. I waited until everyone had a glass in hand, whether it be a margarita, beer, tea, or water, and then raised my own. "Here's to a successful call-out that ended with a live person in relatively good physical condition. *Kanpai.*"

Everyone in the house raised their glasses and cheered.

"I wondered why everyone had a celebratory attitude when you have a body in your house and an FBI agent looking for you," Rafael commented as he sidled up to me, sipping on his beer.

"When you're an Abbie, dead bodies become a dime a dozen over the centuries. Less so for Perigeans, but Lala and Scott have their own history that has desensitized them to the experience. Finding people alive? Now that's something to celebrate."

We hadn't done so after finding Misaki, who turned out to be Toyotama. But everything had been upside down by that point, and no one had felt like celebrating under the circumstances.

"It feels wrong to be present at a party celebrating a missing person when I was the missing person," Rafael admitted.

I took a sip of my margarita, hiding my smile behind the glass, because I agreed completely. I would've felt the same in his shoes.

Lala set down her drink and clapped her hands together. "Alright, people! Now that we're done with that, we have an agency's name to clear and a director's freedom to save. Gather round and let's figure shit out. Whiz, whatcha got?"

"Scott, Hideki, and Leilani are all clear for alibis on every single case so far," Whiz said projecting into the room with our SAR members in Skamania. The three cheered with relief. "It's because you guys are pickleball nerds and spend your life on the courts and at tournaments. I wouldn't be celebrating if I were you."

Rafael did his best at turning his snicker into a cough. And failed abysmally.

"Emma is…*kind of* covered," the gremlin continued. The *nukekubi* made a face. "She needs to get a life outside of staying in her apartment or here all day. But so long as a digital forensics expert authenticates all the time she spends on computers, she should be fine."

"Whiz really just slaughters all of you, doesn't he," Rafael whispered to me. "Athletes, computer nerds. What comes next?"

"Theo might as well undergo a transformation and adopt a new identity. You're worse than Cam. Get a debit card already and stop paying in cash so I can track your shit. And Yuriko? Girl. Get off that mountain once in a while for something other than a deployment. Quotes above, what do the members of Blue Bear Search and Rescue have in common? *They have no lives.*" Whiz threw his hands up in the air.

"And you." He pointed a long, thin finger at Lala. She shrank back into the stool she had snagged from the kitchen. "You are my favorite. You actually have friends. You go out and do shit. People like you and will corroborate your story. You have social media and photos that prove that you're where you said you would be."

Lala somehow managed to slump even further on her stool without falling off, this time in relief.

"Aidan is my second favorite. He was in Neskowin for the majority of the time, rehabbing with Yumi and his Uncles. And in the short time he was here, he had a one-night stand nearly every night. Solid work."

I elbowed Aidan, who stood on my other side. "Who knew being a fuck boy would come so in handy?"

"And you!" Whiz actually materialized into the room for his finale and his voice boomed, a sound much too loud for his small body. He shoved his finger in my face, accompanied by the full force of his Disappointed

Dad Stare. Gale squeaked and hid, despite the fact they were at least six feet away. "You are a carbuncle on my ass. A wet sock in a leather shoe. The soggy kitchen scraps that you have to clear from the drain. You are my *hell*, Cam. Because not only do you suck at leaving the house, but when you do, *you happen to be in the same vicinity* as a solid percentage of the people with no heads!" He ended on a crescendo, throwing both hands in the air, which flung the flash drive he'd had in his hand clear across the room.

I had been withering from his string of insults, but a disbelieving "excuse me?" squeaked out of my mouth with his last statement. Everyone in the room straightened at his words.

"*Oh yeah*," the gremlin drew out sarcastically. "The leshy? He was at Powell's browsing graphic novels while you were picking up a stack of romcoms. The *iwana bōzu*? He purchased a permit for daily parking on Sauvie's Island when you were cruising through U-Pick-It farms. And the kicker? The *curupira*? The male from Brazil, of all places? You just *happened* to be in the same city as him for a training, when he took a vacation, for once in his life, to Hawaii. There's more! But I think those examples are enough to ram it home."

Aidan whistled through his teeth. "Who the fuck did you piss off, Cam? Because they are gunning for you like nobody's business. How are we going to get you out of this one?"

"How?" I asked, bewildered, feeling myself list slightly to the side, unable to keep up the pretense of not being in pain while under shock. "Have they been watching me closely and they just plucked a guardian that happens to be near me at the time to frame me later? Are they somehow manipulating my fate to be in the same place as their chosen victims? Or manipulating their victims? Just…*how?*"

"Beats the hell out of me," Whiz ranted. "But you know what I do know? They kept this hidden from the public for obvious reasons, but each victim had a small flower burned into a bone. I'll give you one guess what that flower was."

Everyone's eyes shot to either my chest or the bay window where the camellia tree stood.

"You got it." Whiz pointed finger guns at me even though no one had actually said anything. "A fucking camellia."

"Wait. *What?*" The word exploded out of me. "Danl—"

Whiz shook his head. "Jeff was taken off the case, given that you're his landlord and friend. So was Tish. The new FBI SAC had an outside consultant come in to review the autopsies and *that's* when the flowers were found. Tish has been placed on a suspension pending an investigation for allegedly missing them."

"Because that's not suspicious as fuck," Leilani said, frustrated. "All of a sudden, out of nowhere, someone new walks in and *boom* here's a huge clue that everyone missed, and because of that, everyone who may have been a support for Cam in this situation is taken off the case? How do we know it wasn't fabricated? A lot of shit can be achieved with *ki*, including inflicting a wound on a dead person to look like it was done while they were alive."

"Yes, well, the Quotes don't believe in magic, now do they," Whiz deadpanned. "So, what are we going to do with that?"

Someone slid a chair behind me and took me by the shoulder to sit me down. I dropped my head between my knees, dizziness overtaking me with the news.

"Do *not*"—Whiz stabbed me with his finger again—"I repeat: *Do. Not.* Come back here until I give you the all clear, do you understand? It's not safe for you. Actually, don't fucking leave the Abbie Realm, period."

"I can't just—" My weak protest was cut off by Cheuksin.

"You fucking can and will," Cheuky said fiercely. "You hid yourself from Orochi for over a century. The Quotes? They'll be a walk in the park in comparison."

"But...I have tasks," my words trailed off as it was dawning on me how impossible this situation was.

Burn it all to Yomi. My options had been whittled down to enslavement or death.

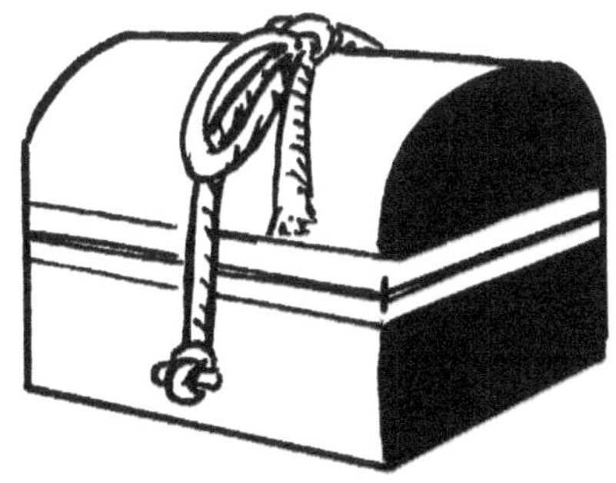

CHAPTER THIRTY-ONE

Shouting filled the house as I contemplated my choices. I had made my bed, now I had to sleep in it. I went down the road of enslavement once. It wasn't one I was willing to go down again. With that in mind, I shifted just enough for a claw to break through the tip of my index finger and used it to open my liminal pocket. Everyone quieted at my actions, the tension building in the room.

I ignored them all. Instead, I focused on my task as I gingerly lifted my *tamatebako* from the sera where it had been hidden. The jade box glowed with an eerie pale green light that flickered like fire, the material sourced from the armor of my thorax. Gold from my horn was inlaid in the jade and depicted intricate illustrations that should be too small to have so much detail, and yet, here we were. Images of fire, war, judgment, and pestilence decorated the walls. The top of the box was an Old World *haetae*. Not one seam marred the box. Only the right *ki* would open the *tamatebako* and release me from this world.

"Cam…" Toyotama's hushed voice broke the silence. I couldn't address her yet. The hand on my shoulder tightened painfully. Rafael.

Instead, I faced Anhangá, who transformed to his human form. His expression was solemn, already knowing what I was going to ask. I handed the *tamatebako* to him and he took it into his grasp reverently before it vanished in black mist a moment later.

"I trust you," I said, my eyes unwavering from his gaze. "Everyone else here is too close to me in some way to ask this of them. But you understand the need. You will understand *when*."

Perhaps Theo might have been willing in the end, but I couldn't trust that his intrinsic need to see karma through would prevent him from opening my *tamatebako.*

"You underestimate yourself, little *haetae*, if you think you haven't endeared yourself to me…but I understand. And am honored." The slightest twinkle appeared in his eye and he winked. I cringed. Somehow it was even worse when he was human. "Whoever thought you'd trust me in this lifetime?"

"Please don't wink again," I said, wrinkling my nose. "It doesn't suit you. Not in that form anyway." I took a deep breath and faced the rest of the room. A dust mote would make more noise than this group. "Relax, guys, no one is dead. Yet." I smiled weakly. Black humor for the win.

Max whined and shoved his soft muzzle under my hand, lifting it from my thigh, while Woody growled at me. Pea had vanished. She would be at the camellia tree, if I had to guess. A small lick at my ankle made me smile as Vicky looked at me with concern. Not having been around us long enough to have quite the same level of understanding as Max and Woody, she only sensed the turmoil in the room and reacted accordingly.

I would have to make arrangements for them. Victoria had Rafael now. But Woody, Max, and Pea… I should have made a plan long ago, considering how close to Death I teetered, but denial had always called my name instead.

"They'll be okay," Cheuksin said softly, sensing the direction my thoughts had gone. She gave me a sad smile and a side hug.

"Come on, guys," Lala demanded. "All of you are acting as if death or slavery is a foregone conclusion. They're two possibilities out of potential millions. Let's take them and shove them where the sun wouldn't dare to shine and get these tasks done. Look around, for Quotes' sake. In this room alone we have a Death entity, two goddesses, a demigod *oni*, a *kamikiri* who is basically immortal—given the amount of hair he has amassed—a *dokkaebi*, gremlins, a *yuki onna, tanukis,* and a Perigean. And that's just in this room! Somewhere in this house is a *shikigami,* and then you guys in Skamania. Are you really trying to tell me Death is the most logical conclusion? Please!" She threw her hands up in the air. "I swear, you Abbies are so melodramatic. What are the tasks?"

"You've already done the *gut*," Cheuksin said thoughtfully. "So you're down to two tasks at least."

I snorted. "Yeah, which are to somehow fix what's broken in not only me, but also Orochi."

"To be fair, no one has tried to *fix* Orochi," Rafael pointed out, his hand still lingering on my shoulder. "No one even knew he was Orochi until recently, so we don't know how difficult the task might be."

"And we've already cut out half the battle, thanks to Toyo," Aidan added. "He's accessible to us. It's a little hard to fix a *kami* if you can't catch him."

"This is the only time I'm going to say this, but I wish Reika was here," Toyo muttered. "Why hasn't she left his dimension yet? It's not like she's trapped there."

"I mean, she is a little, considering Orochi is in a cell," Aidan pointed out.

"No point in hoping for something that might not come to pass," Uncle said pragmatically in his deep baritone voice. His Thread nodded in agreement. "We need to split up—one group to tackle the FBI and clear Cam's name, another to work on Orochi, and the last to figure out how to put Cam back together again."

I didn't want to discourage them, but I had spent over a century with Pea and Murry trying to figure out how to fix myself to no avail. It was the reality of that particular situation that had led me to passing my *tamatebako* to Anhangá. Still, my heart warmed at the sight of my friends coming together for me.

Ken rubbed his hands together. "Put me on the Clear Cam's Name team. I can put my gossip trade to good use there."

Whiz and Gale let out identical long-suffering sighs and eyed one another. He nodded to them and a 3D holographic board took up the entire expanse of my wall. Everyone quieted as Whiz began handing out instructions to every person in the room, determined to set things straight.

CHAPTER THIRTY-TWO

"**A**BSOLUTELY not." Lala wagged a finger in Rafael's face when he took a step toward me. The crew was breaking up after spending hours working out plans. "You've had your time with her. It's my turn now." She grabbed my hand and dragged me out the back door, our K9s and Rafael trailing behind us. "You too, Toyo! You know your father's ki better than anyone," she called over her shoulder.

The princess sighed and heaved herself off the couch. We made our way around the deck until we came into full view of the ocean. The pitch of night was lifting, midnight blues beginning to lighten in the sky and cast a soft eerie glow over Lala's cheeks.

I groaned, thinking wistfully of my bed. Not of sleeping and the nightmares that would be lying in wait for me, but of resting my aching body on something soft and clean for the first time in days.

"Oh hush," Lala scolded, knowing where my thoughts had gone. "You think I wouldn't rather be in bed, too? But *no*, someone had to go make a bargain with a god when they had no business doing so, particularly since you have almost no control over either one of your *kis*. Now none of us get any sleep. Sit." A series of thuds surrounded me as all four K9s sat. Too bad she hadn't been referring to them.

My ass hit the deck as she shoved me down with sadistic glee. Toyo hurriedly sat next to me before Lala had a chance to accost her. I could see the slight smirk on Rafael's face from the corner of my eye as he leaned his body against the railing, his form lengthened by the pose. A light slap on my cheek redirected my attention to the little dictator in front of me. "No. No getting distracted by sexy males. You need to master this *ki* before it kills you if you want any hope of fixing yourself. Whatever that means."

She pointed out to the sunrise as she settled down to the deck. "You see that view in front of you? I want you to sink into it. I want you to drop everything else around you and focus on the sunrise."

I raised an eyebrow. "You're not going to tell me to close my eyes and breathe?"

Lala snorted. "No."

"Why not?" Rafael asked curiously, moving from the railing to sit on my other side, the three of us now forming a small semicircle facing Lala. Vicky curled into his lap like they had been doing this routine for years. "That's usually the first step Abbies take when they come into their *ki*."

"And how has that been working out for Cam over these hundred-some-odd years, hmm?"

He inclined his head to her, conceding her point.

"Then what?" Toyo asked. "If breathing isn't working and everything Reika put her through was for nothing?"

"Once upon a time, when my family resettled in the United States, we had the option of choosing our names," Lala began.

I knew this story already, though I didn't know how it related to the topic at hand. Rafael and Toyo didn't, however. Toyo shifted uncomfortably, rolling the shoulder closest to me as though she was shrugging off someone's hand. She probably was.

Lala continued, "My mother had just given birth to my little brother and lost our father to pneumonia nearly all in one fell swoop. To say nothing of the traumatic delivery she had just undergone. She was lost to a trifecta of postpartum depression, PTSD, and grief, not that any of us knew it back then. But we still needed names. She let us choose our own. That was fine for my older brothers. They chose *normal*,"—she bit out the word like it was sour—"names. David. Adam. Daniel. But she also left my name to six-year-old me.

"By the time we had resettled in America, Scottie was smaller than the average infant and was diagnosed with failure to thrive. I wasn't in school yet, unlike my older brothers, and was with my mother for all her medical care. I had heard the word *areola* being thrown around while I played in the corner of the exam room, and I thought it was the most beautiful word in the world. My brothers all begged our mother to make me choose a different name, but I was stubborn, even then. It was Areola or nothing. I was so happy when I won the battle."

Lala whirled to Rafael even though he had made no comment or facial expression. "I love my name," she said fiercely. This I knew. She went by Lala to avoid having to tell this story every time she introduced herself, although her nickname didn't fly under the radar either. "But the judgment began the day I entered the public school system."

I stilled. She had alluded to bullying here and there, but that was par for the course for most Asian kids. "I came home crying nearly every day. It wasn't the other girls. Not yet. It was the teachers and the comments they made. It was the gasps of mothers, as they hurried their daughters along, not wanting them to learn the word so young. I didn't understand why I wasn't allowed to play with other girls. Why no one wanted to play with the poor little refugee girl.

"Then came my preteens. We all started learning what the word meant. For the first time, I was ashamed of my name. Boys could be called Dick, but Quotes' forbid a girl be called *Areola*," she spat. "And then my *ki* developed." Phally crept up to his companion and laid half his body over her lap. He gave her a quick lick on her cheek and her hands began to play with his ears.

Lala leaned over the K9 and the three of us unconsciously leaned forward with her. "Do you know what it's like for your *ki* to develop—not only *ki*, but more specifically, one that influences emotions—as a prepubescent child who's being bullied? I had no idea what was happening. I had no idea why fights would break out around me, why our mother would break out sobbing, even though we had all thought she was doing better, why my brothers would get into violent brawls, ones where they intended to hurt one another. I knew I was the common denominator. That I made everyone around me angry, or sad, or hurt each other."

Her attention shifted to Phally's ears as she continued to rub them, her voice becoming distant. "Then my mother slit her wrists when I was in the next room." Toyo sucked in a gasp next to me while Max nudged his big head under my hand to diffuse the tension that was building in me. Rafael watched Lala with a steady gaze. A gaze of understanding from another child who went through life with a mother lost to grief and trauma.

"I found her and called 9-1-1. They got there just in time and she was hospitalized, first for a blood transfusion and surgery to repair her wrists, then admitted to a psychiatric unit. That night I came home; my two oldest brothers stayed at the hospital with our mother. A lot of the night is missing in my memories, but I suddenly found myself standing on the rooftop of my school. I was good at that by then. Sneaking out of my house and finding my way into restricted places. My subconscious might have led me there, but I knew why I was there. I was ready. All I was good for was hurting other people."

My breath stuck in my throat at the image of a preteen Lala with no hope left, and I swallowed thickly.

"My feet were dangling over the ledge while I built up my courage, and out of nowhere a voice spoke behind me. I almost fell off instead of jumping. It was this deep male voice. The pitch of it just…resonated in your soul. I could feel myself being soothed with every word he said."

A soft smile overtook her face with the memory, despite its tragic beginning. "You know what he said? He sat calmly next to me, dangling these legs the size of tree trunks over the roof's edge, and pointed out the sun beginning to rise, like finding a twelve-year-old girl sitting on a rooftop was an everyday experience.

"He asked me what color the sky was. He said he was colorblind, and while he could appreciate the base colors of the sunrise, he couldn't pick out all the hues. He asked me to describe it to him in excruciating detail while his feet thudded against the side of the building. We sat there, me describing every shift of color in some way that didn't use hues, until the first school employees began trickling into the building and he vanished. A teacher saw me and screamed and chaos ensued. I was yelled at and suspended for being reckless and trespassing.

"That afternoon, when I dropped by the elementary school to walk Scottie home, there he was. Huge and jolly. A redheaded kid a little older than Scottie was holding his hand. He gave me a wink and disappeared with the crowd of parents leaving with their kids."

"Did you ever learn who the male was?" Rafael asked curiously.

Lala sniffed, her eyes reflecting a tender sort of affection in the fine lines that formed around them. "I stalked the elementary school while I was suspended. It was supposed to be a punishment for me…picking up Scottie. Little did David and Adam know that I *wanted* to pick up my little brother, if only to figure out who the male was. A couple afternoons later, I saw the redheaded kid again, though he was being picked up by a different male, and followed them home."

"Ehhh, are you trying to ruin my reputation?" An amused voice—a deep voice—reverberated over us. "I come back for my phone, and instead I find my spitfire here telling tall tales." Uncle ruffled Lala's hair.

"Uncle?" I asked in disbelief.

Lala scowled good-naturedly as she ducked out from under his hand, doing her best to fix her ponytail without having to take the whole thing out. "They're not tall tales if they're true," she pointed out.

Uncle settled next to her, crossing his legs, his tree-trunk-thick legs, in front of her. "Fine. Grossly exaggerated tales."

She ignored him. "It turned out to be the Uncles visiting their sister in Fresno to help out after finding out she had a terminal condition. They introduced me to Aidan, and I spent the better part of the year with them, until she passed and they took Aidan with them back to Hawaii." Lala leaned her head against Uncle's shoulder. "I would be there for every dawn and every sunset, and I would pick out the subtleties in the colors to describe them to their family. In return, they taught me about *ki*, Abbies, Peris, Quotes, and I began to gain control over my *ki* over the course of several months.

"After they moved home, I kept looking for the colors, the shifts, the tiny changes happening around me. And I began to learn that the more I did it, the more people stayed calm around me. And that while I might aggravate emotional outbursts, I couldn't influence thoughts that weren't already there." She took a deep breath. "My mother's attempted suicide wasn't my fault. Though my uncontrolled power wasn't helping matters, her own grief and depression were unmanaged, and she had no tools to cope with them then."

"Proud of you," Uncle said, wrapping an arm around her.

"I'm proud of me, too." Lala smiled, before placing her attention back on me. "You have spent a century *fighting* Ryūjin's *ki* rather than letting it settle. Even if you weren't aware of the fight at all times, your *ki* was in the background battling it. I want you to actively draw your *ki* forth and sink into that sunrise and exist in it."

I cringed at the thought of drawing my *ki* forward. Lala stabbed her finger in my face and I fought back an urge to bite it. "That. That right there. You've reached a new low where you're actively fighting *both* of your powers, even the magic you were born with."

She waved the finger at Toyo next. "This one didn't even use her *ki* for a century, until she regained her identity, and still she's fallen back to it with little issue."

"You have a lot of balls to be talking about a *kami* this way in front of them," Toyo commented.

"Please. Don't insult us females. They're ovaries, not balls," Lala scoffed.

"Great big ones," Uncle added with a smile.

A muffled cough sounded to the side, and I glanced over to find Rafael holding a fist over his mouth, like that did any good covering the smirk that was taking over his face.

A warm presence began crawling up my back and soft, scolding chitters echoed in my ear as Pea joined the group from wherever she had been, wrapping herself around my neck. I sighed. "You're right. I dread using my own *ki* now, let alone trying to find a way to work with Ryūjin's. Every time I use it, his draws up, and the combination of the two makes me feel like I have the flu while on a ship in the world's greatest storm. I lose all of my equilibrium and it takes everything in me not to puke my guts out." I made a face.

"And who would want to continue to do something that made them feel like hell," Rafael said quietly.

"Exactly," Lala nodded. "This is one of those situations where you're going to feel worse before you feel better, but you will eventually feel better."

I nodded. They didn't need to know that it had taken me thousands of years to gain control of my natural *ki* the first time around.

My eyes closed and I took a deep breath. A soft whack hit me upside the head. "You can't describe the shifting colors of the sky if your eyes are *closed*," Toyo scolded.

I scowled at her, rubbing my head. "I was trying to release some tension first."

"Won't get a chance to *release your tension* if you need to use your *ki* in an attack," Lala singsonged.

Because I'd have time to describe the sky if we were attacked?

"I didn't see any of you complaining how fast I was able to use my *ki* against the *gashadokuro*, thank you very much." My glare shifted to Lala.

"*Gashadokuro?*" Rafael asked, straightening.

"No." At least I wasn't the recipient of Lala's finger this time. "If you're going to be a distraction, you can just fuck off, right on to bed. *Without* Cam."

My face went up in flames. Rafael's was overtaken by an enigmatic smile. And then there was Uncle, cackling and shaking the whole damn deck with his laughter.

"Anyway," I said hurriedly. "The sunrise?"

"You know, I find that flush you get whenever sex is brought up enchanting," Rafael murmured to me as he rubbed Vicky's velvety half-mast ears. "Funny though. It didn't seem to happen when you mentioned the topic around Aidan. I might have to study the effect further. For science."

I was absolutely sure it wasn't possible to burn any hotter. Millenia old, and still, here I was acting like a juvenile with her first crush. Why was I even doing this in front of an audience?

"You. Get the fuck out," Lala demanded.

Rafael's smile widened and he leaned back, resting his weight on his palms, which were flat against the deck. "Sorry. No can do. My lap is currently occupied."

A low growl emitted from Lala. Uncle covered her mouth with a large hand that nearly covered her entire face. "Tell me, Niece. Tell me about the colors I can't see."

I took a deep breath and began.

CHAPTER THIRTY-THREE

Remarkably, falling into the sunrise was far easier than I anticipated. Unremarkably, getting my *ki* to do what I wanted was not. Regardless, I did my due diligence in trying to describe the dawn to Uncle. It was the least I could do for the *tanuki* who had saved one of my best friends.

"The pinks are settling among the clouds like the way a much-needed fire wraps its warmth around you." Fire was one thing I understood beyond a shadow of doubt, the one metaphor I could use to explain a color to someone who had never seen it. "It clings to your skin, before permeating beneath, but its warmth can only go so far, before it fails to reach the rest of you. What remains on the other side of you is like the deep lavender of the sky, a cool color, struggling to feel that warmth, like the underside of the clouds over the ocean."

A sigh came from beside me and I could hear Rafael settling deeper into his position, leaning back against his hands, face straining for the sky and its warmth. I imagined it had been an eternity since he felt it kiss his skin. Uncle had turned his back to us so he could watch the sunrise as I described it. To my surprise, his Thread had joined us at some point, and Uncle held him in his *tanuki* form, stroking the soft salt-and-pepper fur. His Thread watched the sunrise, just as rapt as Uncle. It occurred to me then that his Thread had never truly seen the iridescence in Uncle's hair and fur. The look of adoration they passed between them was a testament to how little it mattered to them.

I continued with a determination to make the dawn come alive for these three males. The *kis* within me stirred but otherwise remained repressed. "The fire reaches new heights, the sky lightening to oranges and yellows in the same way a bonfire increases in intensity when fuel is added to it. The dark blues and purples flee from the heat, unable to fight it off, and the sky is filled with brilliant flames that encompass everything around it. The ocean reflects the fire's twin. The one in the sky is elegance and grace. Its sibling in the ocean—mirth and mischief, as it dances along the waves, one that whirls, frolics, and skips along the water."

I carried on with my description, trying, but not, to allow the *kis* to rise within me. The concept of letting something happen organically without forcing it when your very life depends on it was contrary at best, and impossible at worst. My voice faded as the sun rose fully into the sky, and my frustration rose with it.

Uncle's Thread reformed into his human shape and shook his finger at me, sensing my despair. "Ehhhh. You will stop that voice in your head now, Niece. Do you think any of us"—he gestured to our whole group—"learned to harness our *kis* with one simple meditation?"

"I know I'm not likely to get it on the first try." I sighed. "It doesn't mean I couldn't hope that something more than *nothing* would have happened."

"Ah, but did nothing happen?" Uncle asked with a professorial air, his great heft turning to face us. "Look into your body and ask yourself, what is different?"

"Eh. Don't ask yourself, tell us," his Thread urged.

"Now you can close your eyes," Lala said with some amusement.

I shot her the finger before closing my eyes. "I..." My voice faded out as I tried to catalogue the differences I felt in my body. "The noise in my body has quieted. I don't ache as much as I did before," I admitted.

The Uncles nodded. "The pain keeps you—" one began.

"—from being able to reach your true potential," the other finished.

"The pain is taking up too much of your attention," Rafael said softly. He massaged his left wrist. "It keeps you from being able to access the resources you need to acknowledge your *kis*, let alone accept them."

"It's a built-in defense mechanism," Toyo added bitterly. "One that ensures my father's *ki* wins out over yours because your attention is too split to try. His fail-safe."

Pea hissed long and low at her comment.

"But what does killing me with his *ki* accomplish," I protested, reaching up for Pea to grasp my hand with her remaining paw in support. "It's not that I don't believe you, but more so the fact that it seems futile, and your father hated futility above everything else."

"It ensures you remain a vessel for his power and nothing more," a quiet voice came from behind us. "A protected vessel. Because when Ryūjin's *ki* takes over, nothing of you will remain to oppose it, and then his daughter will be able to wield it."

"As if I would be willing to wield my dead father's magic after it killed my best friend," Toyo snarled.

"Would you not?" Cheuksin settled herself into an Adirondack chair, her voice still a near-whisper. "If it came between saving an entire realm or using the power housed in your dead friend, would you still refuse?"

Toyo's nictating membranes flickered several times as she tried to control her anger.

I motioned down my body. "How will I be a vessel to his power when this vessel is crumbling from the effort of holding a foreign *ki*?" Pea clicked rapidly at me, alarm riding the coattails of her vocalizations.

"Your liver is still intact though." It was a statement, not a question, from the male sitting beside me.

Unpleasant shock filled me from those six words. I had known, of course, that my liver had remained whole despite the impact of my Thread severing. I had known that it still remained intact as the *kis* warred within me, at least until the *gut* ritual. But it had never occurred to me until now why that might have been important. I had been too busy hiding it from those who wanted it for the power it housed.

"A Thread is simply a fated mate," Uncle said thinly, his knuckles turning white as he gripped his Thread's hand, who had shifted with Rafael's revelation about my liver.

"It doesn't equal love," his Thread continued, the cords of his neck strained with tension. "It does not mean loyalty above all."

"It doesn't mean that your Thread cannot betray you." The pain in Toyo's voice was acid thrown in our faces.

"Just because I loved *him* doesn't mean he loved me in return." It was my turn to be bitter. Pea's tail tightened painfully around my neck, but I couldn't be bothered to care about the way she was choking me.

Rafael reached over and gently unfurled the opossum from my neck and cradled her to his chest. "It doesn't mean he didn't love you; it simply means he didn't love you *more* than the fate of his realm." I was only able to bear his statement by the matter-of-factness of his tone. Had it leaned a millimeter to reassurance, I would have broken.

Toyo scoffed. "Because that's better, *kariudo*?"

"*Former*," I snapped. "Former *kariudo* because he is not bound to whatever plot my Thread enacted who knows how long ago anymore." Max whined at my distress and forced his big head under my clenched fist. I forced my hand to relax and focused on the motion of stroking his soft fur, watching the mahogany fibers part to white beneath my fingers before I struggled to stand.

"I need some air," I said, even as my thoughts raced thinking of what a *stupid* saying that was. How could you need air when you were surrounded by it? No. I needed my lungs to stop seizing in grief and rage. I needed my Thread to not be a betraying asshole of immense proportions. I needed away from the pitying looks that surrounded me. It wasn't air I needed at all as I turned from the group and practically ran down the stairs and into the woods.

CHAPTER THIRTY-FOUR

The sun had risen fully by the time I slowed to a stop by a burbling hot spring hidden deep within this realm's version of the Siuslaw and settled on a boulder, wrapping my hands around my knees. Max and Woody had followed, Pea clinging to Max's back. The two K9s hopped neatly onto the boulder and curled up on either side of me as Pea detached herself from Max's fur and hurried over to me, chittering away in a scolding tone.

"Not right now, Pea." I curled into a tighter ball, resting my cheek against my knees. "I'm sorry for running off, but I just…couldn't anymore." A tightening around my wrist let me know that Pea had wrapped her tail around it to offer comfort. A corner of my mouth lifted in a parody of a smile. "Thank you, friend."

I let out a gust of air and tucked my chin between my knees, gazing out at the hot spring. A cloud passed overhead, then a brilliant array of light sparkled across the forest as a flock of *bonghwang* gracefully dropped from the trees and onto the banks, the avians each a slightly different conglomeration of birds. The one nearest to me preened as it bathed in the warm water. The sun reflected off its feathers, which were wrapped in reds, yellows, and greens, with hints of black and white, which served to further accentuate its colors. It had the deadly head and talons of a Steller's sea eagle with the body and plumage of a ring-necked pheasant.

The K9s' ears pricked as they watched the spectacle before us, but they stayed steady at my side, content to watch from our vantage point. We sat in silence for over an hour, watching the fowl preen and splash in the waters, before they took flight back into the treetops that towered far above us.

"You can come out now," I called.

Vicky leapt lightly onto the boulder and curled in a circle three times before settling into Woody's side. Rafael stepped out from the trees and stood facing the hot spring without meeting my gaze. After a few moments of awkwardness, he shoved his hands into his pockets, like he had no idea what to do with them.

"You knew?" he asked.

"You may be silent, but she isn't." I nodded to the multicolored ball of fur. Besides, that little piece of soul we shared between us had clued me in to the trailing male even as I had wandered the woods. Just his presence, not his emotions. He must have put up a shield once we realized what we shared.

"I was trying to give you space," he replied, a light flush overtaking the back of his neck.

"If you wanted to give me space, you wouldn't have followed me." I watched in fascination as the pink overtook his ears.

"I said space, not privacy," he retorted. "I just…"

"You just?" I raised an eyebrow.

"I just wanted to make sure you were coping, but I didn't want to crowd you."

I sighed and laid back on the rock, watching the fluffy clouds cross the sky. Pea unraveled her tail from my wrist and scrambled up my side before stretching out on my stomach. "Don't you have something better to do than to make sure I'm okay, like, I don't know, sleep?"

"I'm not looking forward to my nightmares greeting me when my eyes close." The words were quiet, barely reaching my ears on the hint of a breeze.

"That's fair." The cloud that lingered to the left looked like a *chollima*, its equine shape in a full gallop with wings widespread. Or Godzilla. It really depended on how you turned your head. "Nightmares are a bitch."

"That they are," he agreed. Scraping noises sounded against the boulder, and I turned my head to watch Rafael clamber up the rock.

"You could've materialized up here, Sugs," I said, amused. That little black wisp rose from my body, filaments branching off its main form and dancing in the air, like a puppy overcome by excitement to see its owner.

"Eh, where's the fun in materializing everywhere and not actually using this physical form?" The corner of the male's lip curled at the sight of the wisp, before he laid back on the other side of Woody and Vicky, his hands intertwined behind his head. "Is that Godzilla?"

"I can't decide between Godzilla or a *chollima*."

"Definitely Godzilla. That isn't a wing, that's a blast of radiation. So, are you?"

The whiplash this male gave me sometimes. "So am I what?"

"Coping."

I stayed silent for several moments, the wisp twining up my arm. "If you call complete and utter avoidance with a dash of denial *coping*, then yeah, I'm coping." Avoidance and denial had yet to let me down. "In this year alone, I have been hunted, betrayed, nearly killed, fragmented, accused of being a serial decapitator, and now betrayed yet again. Only instead of it being a virtual stranger, it was my fucking *Thread*. If the past few months hadn't been uncommonly sunny, I would think a *hong'aek* was following me like I was some *haetae* version of Eeyore, cursed by a cloud of bad luck. I'm pretty sure the most well-adjusted person in the world would be burying their head in the sand right now. I would think you of all people would be able to relate."

There was a snort. It could have been from Rafael. Or it could have easily come from any of the three K9s currently occupying this rock.

I picked up Pea and placed her on Woody's back, rolling onto my stomach so I could prop my face on my hands. "I would just like a month where I went on a search and actually found someone alive and didn't have to worry about how my fate has been twisted by deities with far more power than me. I don't think a month out of a millennia of existence is too much to ask for," I admitted.

"One would think," Rafael mused with his eyes closed. "I don't think a quiet life is in the books for beings like us, Baki."

"Speak for yourself. I'm still holding out hope."

"Hmm. What are your nightmares about?"

"What is this? Bare-my-soul-to-the-male-who-betrayed-me hour?" I asked defensively.

"I feel like my betrayal pales in comparison to the betrayal of your Thread, but that's just me."

"Rude." But not wrong. Apparently I had a type. I flopped back to face the sky, holding back a groan as my fragments protested the movement. The black wisp burst into mist before reforming and settling on my chest.

"I'll tell you mine," Rafael began. He propped himself up by the elbow. "You. They are solely composed of you."

"I'm sorry?" Even though Rafael Sugiyama was the main star of all my nightmares lately, I hadn't expected to feature in his. Pea crawled back on my torso, careful to avoid the ever-widening cavity that was my chest, her ears upright and alert.

"In every one of my nightmares, I am frozen in place as I watch the *kami* render you to pieces. Or I watch helplessly as your body and soul are finally unable to hold themselves together and burst into ashes."

"But you hardly know me." Rafael starring in *my* nightmares made sense to me—he had gained my trust and threw it away. But I couldn't imagine why I would be important enough to be his recurring night terror.

"Oh, Baki. I knew you long before I met you." I watched as his face softened, the harsh lines smoothing out to a semblance of a smile. "I don't think you realize the number of souls you have touched in your lifetime." I recoiled at the thought. The desire to sink into a black hole was strong as I thought of all the innocent lives I had ended during my time enslaved.

He continued, "I encounter the departed everywhere I go and have met thousands who were impacted by your role as *haetae*. Not only Abbies, but Quotes and Peris. Olivia for one."

Vicky's ears perked up at the sound of her old owner's name. My next inhale lodged in my throat as anxiety crashed over me. I swallowed around the lump in my throat. "Olivia who?"

He played with Vicky's ears. "You know which Olivia."

"No. She *just* sent me a text..." My voice trailed off as I recounted the months.

Rafael nodded. "She passed away in February. Did you know she was of Brazilian descent? I happened on her when she decided to visit our afterlife to vacation with some of her relatives."

My next word was forced. I didn't want to know, but I couldn't *not* know either. "How?"

Vicky rolled over and he rubbed her velveteen belly. "It wasn't her ex-husband. But you obviously knew that. She had cancer and they caught it late. She knew she would never see Vicky again, but she was happy. So happy. She had made friends and her own family. She married a Quote who treated her like the queen Livvy was until she passed away seven years ago. Olivia joined a knitting club and a book club. She taught everyone she knew about insentient romance and omegaverses." The last sentence was said wryly.

"That included me, by the way. Do you know what it's like to have a Quote in her eighties telling you all about *knots*? And she told everyone she knew about the woman who saved her life when she was a young woman, to say nothing of her heart." Tears rolled down my cheeks as he continued. "Olivia knew. She heard of her ex's disappearance once he was paroled early. She never worried that he was coming for her. She knew his disappearance meant that you had taken care of him for her. She was one of many stories about how your intervention spared so much pain. No matter the number of your misdeeds, you made up for them by far when you rid the world of evil after evil.

"Everything indicated you were in America. So, I avoided the Western hemisphere to the best of my ability. So long as I didn't know where you were, I could avoid my task. Until I was ordered to find Orochi's Thread and found myself in your path."

"You already knew," I said slowly, every fragment of my heart aching in a chorus of grief. "You knew what Vicky's origins were like when you asked me about them."

He inclined his head. "I brought Livvy with me when I first came to your facility. She was delighted with the way you treated me. And she was overwhelmed when she saw Victoria and how happy her heart dog looked. I wish you could have seen the smile on her face. Livvy never thought she'd see her beloved dog live to be so old. She returned to her afterlife thrilled." Silver rimmed his eyes before he blinked it away. "You never did tell me that Vicky was in her fifties."

I smiled and wrapped my arms around the K9s that flanked me. Woodrow gave a soft *woo* of protest, while Max leaned heavily into my back. "She's just a baby. Maxwell is a couple years shy of a hundred, and Woody will be ninety this year. If you already knew about Vicky, then why did you ask?"

Rafael shrugged. "I wanted to hear it from your perspective. Livvy was pretty unimpressed with the way you understated their rescue." His face hardened. "For sure, you understated the severity of their assault for her abuser to actually be sentenced back in the nineteen seventies."

"That was all Woodrow," I said, repressing a shudder at the memory of Vicky and Olivia's injuries. The malamute's fluffy tail wagged, happy to take the credit for his role in finding Olivia and Vicky.

"Woodrow may have found them, and Pea may have healed them and extended their lives, but you're the one who intervened and gave them the opportunity for a new life in the first place, Baki."

He took a breath. "I met a thousand versions of you, and yet thousands more before my eyes ever rested upon you."

I closed my eyes, my skin feeling too tight against my flesh at the realization. "You met thousands of *idealized* versions of me. You barely know *me*."

CHAPTER THIRTY-FIVE

A light little chuckle turned into a roar of laughter. I sat up, unseating a hissing Pea, and glared at the male who was now beset by undignified giggles, accompanied by an occasional snort.

"I truly fail to see what's so funny here," I said in the dryest tone I could manage.

"You—" A laugh burst out of him and he had to get his hysteria under control before he could continue. "You think that those thousands were idealized versions of you? Oh, Baki. I met many, many souls who utterly loathed the mere mention of you. That only made me like you more."

"That tracks," I muttered. "And now that you've actually met me?"

"I find that each and every account has been like a diamond settling into the place of a beautiful statement piece, and seeing it in all its glory is stunning. You'll have to excuse me if the thought of you no longer being in this world horrifies me."

I didn't know what to make of his nightmares. He had put me on a pedestal of impossible standards, pieced together by others' stories, when the real me was so much uglier. He had only known me for mere days in comparison.

He nodded to the black wisp, fully acknowledging it for the first time. "I may have only known you for a few days, but my soul connected us. Over these few short months, I have gotten to know you more intimately than any other in my life."

"Well, that's entirely disturbing." I glared at the little traitor still curled up on my chest. "You didn't have to narc me out to the rest of you, you know."

A little ripple ran through the wisp the motion oddly reminiscent of shrugging. Figuring out how to put up mental walls would be on my to-do list. Right after fixing my body, mastering two *kis*, finding an Abbie serial killer, and evading the FBI. No big deal.

"For real though." I kept talking to the piece of Rafael's soul like it was sentient. "You gave up all my secrets to that guy but didn't bother to share any of his? The audacity of you."

The smile in Rafael's voice was practically blinding when he responded. "Did you really expect it to?"

I considered that for a moment. "You're right. No. Being a is traitor part of you after all."

He raised an imaginary glass to toast the air. "Luckily for you."

What kind of tragedy had my life turned into for me to be *thankful* for a male betraying me. The Fates could go fuck themselves. And I had basically eaten his face last night. It took everything in me to not palm my own face at the memory.

"I don't know where we go from here," I admitted.

Rafael shrugged. "This is a start. This is actually beyond my wildest expectations." He held his forearms to the sky. The leather cuffs he normally wore were nowhere in sight. He twisted his arms, studying the scar tissue. "I never thought I'd see my arms bare again. I didn't think it was possible. So, Camellia Kimoto, you have far exceeded what most would think possible. How about that?"

"That's hard to remember in face of all my failures."

I eyed the deeply bronzed arms as the sun hit the keloid scars that rung his flesh. "How are you even keeping yourself together right now? After I got free, I isolated myself to a cave for two hundred years before I was ever willing to interact with another person."

"I assure you, I am freaking out internally." He reached for his wrist and rubbed his right forearm as he dropped them back down. "But I have been surrounded by people who care since you removed my bands. I'm not going to lie, Daki, the concept is baffling to me. I have no idea why they would care after all I had done. It's a new thing, and uncomfortable to the nth degree, but I find that I don't want to escape it."

I laughed. "Sugs. You saved Aidan's K9 and Uncle from the *kotengu*. You have a friend for forever in him. Once he decides he likes you, you can't shake him. Same with the Uncles. You saved Olly's life; he doesn't take that lightly. You brought Toyo back to me. You may have had no idea she was Toyotama at the time, but you brought back one of my oldest and dearest friends. And Lala was going to love you from the moment you didn't make fun of her name. Either one of them. We all understood that you had no choice because of the bands. Does that mean I didn't feel betrayed? Of course not, but I got over it. I hate to break it to you, but your years of doing everything on your own are over. Welcome to the club. I'm still not used to it."

"You know. Before I met you, I never had any other name than the one given to me by a stranger and the last name of a monster," Rafael said slowly. "Sugs? Rafe? Those are people entirely separate from who I was."

I reached over Woody and the sleeping Pea to shove him lightly. "Just imagine what Rafe and Sugs might be able to accomplish now that he's not bound to someone. The options are endless."

The sudden panic that filled the air was palpable. It stuck in my throat as I watched Rafael finally fall apart. His nostrils flared rapidly and his eyes dilated until they were entirely black, while the rest of the former *kariudo* froze in a deadly stillness.

"You're okay," I said softly, my words slow, in time with my breath. His eyes tracked mine, something I was only able to tell by the way the sun reflected off of them. "You're not with the *kami* anymore. You're in Neskowin. You're safe."

Vicky gave a low whine, and despite the lethality that the male next to me exuded, crawled across his chest, laying her entire body against him. She lapped his face and gave a quick, sharp *yip*. His gaze shifted to the K9 staring at him earnestly with her tail wagging and he lifted a hand to stroke her back. Slowly his breathing and eyes returned to normal, and the fear that had riddled the air dissipated.

"You've got a good one in her." My heart broke a little, knowing she had split from me, but how could I begrudge their relationship? "She's good at that."

Rafael let out a long breath as though he could exorcise his demons through his lungs alone and gathered the K9 up in his arms, burying his face in her neck, and she wiggled with happiness, seeing him return to present time.

"Take your time," I said, squeezing his shoulder before making my way off the rock. Max and Woody got up along with me, Woody careful to avoid disrupting the sleeping demon on his back. Rafael's body language screamed with the need to be alone right now. "You have all the time in the world to figure out who Rafael Sugiyama and all his iterations are now."

"I may have time, but not with you."

I pretended not to hear the soft words following me down the trail.

CHAPTER THIRTY-SIX

took my time wandering home, lost in my thoughts. Rafael and I had spent the entire day out by the hot springs and the air was turning cooler as the sun began to set. Woody and Max trotted alongside me, pausing occasionally to bounce into the brush when they thought they spied something. Pea had long since ditched Woody in favor for my nonbouncing body. The wisp of Rafael's soul danced around me, diving between my fragments like they were an obstacle course.

"I can't keep thinking of you as Rafael's *soul*." The wisp perked up and rose to face me, the top portion cocked to the left and somehow managing to look exactly like Woody when he was actually listening to me. "I shall dub thee…Seymour."

Pea clicked disapprovingly at me and whacked the back of my shoulder with her tail. "What? He likes it." Seymour was dancing around my body, practically radiating happiness with his new moniker.

Whiz materialized onto the trail about five feet ahead of me. Today he had fashioned overalls made from screen protectors. I sent up a prayer to whatever gods were listening that he wouldn't turn enough for them to become transparent.

"What is it with you and old man names?" he asked. "Maxwell, Woodrow, Seymour." He ticked off each name on his fingers.

I stopped walking and eyed him warily. "You rarely deliver good news when you pop in like that."

"Don't expect me to start now. FBI guy found your property in Neskowin. He's on his way."

I groaned. Apparently I was never going to see a bed again. "How much time do I have?"

"Like…eight minutes. Give or take."

"Whiz!"

"What? Don't blame the messenger. I flagged it when I saw his account register a purchase at one of the gas stations between here and Portland. I'm not omniscient here."

My nose wrinkled. "Do I hang out in the forest and let Cheuky deal with it, or do I answer the door."

Whiz put his hands on his hips and glared.

"I apparently have no alibis," I hissed at him. Or a lawyer for that matter. The only one I knew was a prosecutor. And currently suspended.

"And you think disappearing off the face of the Earth after a headless body was found in your home is a good look?"

"*You* told me to stay in the Abbie realm."

"So sue me. My opinion changed when I got more facts in front of me."

"Fucking hell." I scrubbed my face and sighed. "Alright, let's go do this."

"Ah…."

"What?"

"Maybe do something about all that." The gremlin gestured to my entire body.

I glanced down. Somehow I had forgotten about the glamours I had dropped. "I don't know. It might be fun to fuck with the agent and answer the door like this."

"Please don't. You're already in enough hot water as it is. Now, *git*."

"I'm going, I'm going. Thanks for the heads-up, Whiz." I started up the steps to my back deck, throwing my glamours on as I went.

Whiz waved me off and vanished again.

The doorbell rang as I entered my home. Eight minutes, my ass. Pea hastily climbed off me and waddled into the house ahead of me.

"I've got it," I called before Cheuksin could answer the door. She resettled on the cushion she was sitting on and resumed the game of *Koi-koi* she was playing with Aidan and the Uncles. Lala and Toyo were nowhere to be seen, and I assumed they were sleeping, like I should be doing now.

I paused and closed my eyes, shifting to the Quotes' realm. Max and Woody followed, having long since been attuned to my *ki*. The bonus of having a home that straddled realms was that it simply took a mental nudge to cross over. It was worth every ounce of gold it had cost me.

The bell was on its second ring when I swung open the front door. The agent on my doorstep was noting the camellias that were exploding over my walkway. Fan*fucking*tastic. He looked to be somewhere around his fifties with a nice mix of salt in his dark hair and a figure that was likely slim under the well-traveled suit he wore. The slightest hint of age spots decorated his tanned skin, like he spent a lot of his time outdoors. I couldn't detect a drop of *ki* in the agent. A Quote, then.

"Can I help you?" I propped a hip against the doorframe, blocking the entrance and the view into my home. Not that he'd be able to see Cheuksin and the Uncles, given that they were still in the Abbie version of my house.

"Ms. Kimoto?"

"Who's asking?"

He reached into the pocket of his rumpled suit and pulled out his badge. "I'm Agent Park with the Federal Bureau of Investigation. I have a few questions for you, if you don't mind, ma'am."

I released a heavy sigh and swung my door open the rest of the way. The agent's eyes widened slightly at the sight of Woodrow and Maxwell, who had been hidden by the door. "This about the dead body in my house?"

"Are they friendly?"

"Well, they're not growling or snapping at you, so that's something at least." I began walking back into the house.

He cautiously made his way past the K9s who tracked his movements with their eyes, which made it all the more unnerving. I didn't feel the need to rectify that in any way. A breeze blew a swirl of camellia petals behind the agent before he could close the door.

"If you don't mind me asking, if you know about the dead body in your home, why are you out on the coast?"

"I found out about it an hour ago," I lied as I took a seat on a kitchen stool, leaving him standing and looking around what he could see of my home. "I just got back from being off-grid for the past several days to beef up my wilderness training. Came back home to find my cell blown up with messages."

"That's rather convenient." He took up post in front of my refrigerator. I marked his height a couple inches shy of six feet, based on the height of the appliance.

"You'll have to excuse me if I disagree. I don't think a dead body in someone's house is convenient for anyone."

"And were you planning to come back to Skamania, if that was the case?"

I eyed him. Max and Woody trotted into the kitchen and sat down, each one flanking my side. A loud hiss sounded by Agent Park's ear. I had to hand it to him; he hardly startled at the sound. "Agent Park, meet Pea, my opossum. I might step away from the fridge if I were you. She's been known to chomp on facial features."

He hastily took a long step to the right, well out of the *shikigami's* reach.

"Of course I was planning to come back to Skamania," I said in answer the question he had posed prior to Pea's interruption. It wasn't technically a lie…I just hadn't planned on returning to the Quote's version of Skamania before I was no longer a person of interest. "Why do you ask?"

"I find it interesting that you found out there was a dead body in your house and you're still on the coast."

"Should I be calling a lawyer?" I asked calmly. "Because God forbid a girl take her first shower in days before booking it several hours across the state."

"That seems a bit dramatic for a simple question."

"Turns out it had a fairly simple answer. If I had headed back to Washington right away, you would have missed me anyway, so I guess this works out well for you."

"Indeed, it does. And I was under the impression that you already knew a lawyer anyway."

I tilted my head. "I do know the difference between a district attorney and a defense attorney. Thanks for assuming I don't though."

"And why would you think you might need a defense attorney?"

I snorted. I couldn't help myself. "Please, Agent Park. A dead body was found in my house, of course I'm a person of interest. Why wouldn't I think I need a lawyer."

He nodded to concede the point. "Where were you this past Wednesday between the hours of 0300 and 0700?"

I gestured behind me. "In the Siuslaw National Forest."

"Can anyone corroborate that besides your K9s?"

"I can," Lala's voice rang out from the middle of the staircase.

I let out a silent breath of relief at the sound of her voice while the agent was turned to see who was talking.

"And who might you be?"

"Areola Moua."

I clocked the double-blink Agent Park did at her name with a smile.

"Ah, the co-director. Is this something you do normally? Train together so neither director is at your facility?"

Lala hitched herself onto the stool next to me, leaving the agent standing like I had. "Our crew is more than able to direct themselves. The title is basically in name only; it allows us to sign off on business and legal documents. Cam and I usually pair up on SARs, so it makes sense for us to train together."

Agent Park hummed to himself, his gaze alternating between the two of us. "I don't suppose there is any concrete evidence of this?"

Lala pulled out her phone and tapped for a few moments before turning the screen. There we were, in blindingly pink tees with the BSSR logo, mugging for the camera in the forest. It was time-stamped three days ago. She scrolled through a stream of photos, swiping up on each one to show the agent the geolocation and time of each photo. I recognized the photos. We had taken them five years ago while actually training in the Siuslaw. I had much shorter hair back then, but our helmets hid it. Lala, on the other hand, has had the same hairstyle since the moment I met her. I didn't touch social media, being what I was and Lala never posted anything related to BBSR on hers, so I knew there was no other trace of these online that would contradict the dates and times.

Kamis bless technologically savvy gremlins.

A muscle clenched in Agent Park's jaw as he took the phone from Lala to study them further. An eternity later, he gave a sharp nod and handed the phone back to Lala.

"And how about the last week in July?" he asked me.

Both my eyebrows raised in feigned surprise. "The remains we pulled from the river?"

He said nothing, simply waiting for me to reply.

"I can't account for the entire week, I don't think anybody could, but I think you'll find that I was on the SAR for the person the remains belonged to when he was first reported missing. There should be a whole host of deputies, volunteers, and my own staff who can account for the majority of that time. Of course, I also had to sleep, and I live alone, so there's that."

"And your disappearance in May?"

Fuck. He had dug deep to find out about that. I wondered how he found out, but it didn't matter in the long run. He knew about it, period. Lala sat straighter next to me.

I gave him a cold stare. "I don't see how this relates to anything you might be looking into."

"Indulge me, Ms. Kimoto."

"Thanks, but I'll pass. You can stop by SORO SORO on your way back into Portland for a mean tiramisu if you want to be indulged." I hopped off my stool and began walking back to my front door, my cue for him to leave unmistakable.

I opened the door wide and gestured through it. "If you don't mind, Agent Park. I have things to catch up on."

"I hope one of them is returning to Skamania sometime today." Agent Park paused on his way out to look back at me. "By the way, Ms. Kimoto. Your hair is dry."

"Have you never heard of a hair dryer? Dyson makes some really good ones. I can recommend a few if you want, for that thick hair of yours." As if he thought he could catch me in that lie.

He smiled, though it didn't meet his eyes, the crow's feet alongside them remaining perfectly in place. "I'll look forward to meeting you again."

"I won't," I muttered as I shut the door after him.

CHAPTER THIRTY-SEVEN

waited, watching through the frosted glass at the top of my door until his vehicle began backing down the driveway. I turned around and sagged down the door until my ass hit the ground, returning to the Abstruse realm as I did so.

A small round of applause greeted me. Cheuksin, the Uncles, and Aidan were now joined by Rafael and Vicky.

"And the Oscar goes to Camellia Kimoto," the Uncles cheered. I gave them the finger and they laughed.

"Jesus fucking Christ." I groaned. "Whiz, what do I owe you? Anything you want, no matter how impossible, I will get for you, you absolute gem."

He popped into the room with an evil grin on his face. "Let me update the servers again."

"You say that like I would ever refuse having an upgraded system."

"You're going to have to go back to paper reports with the upgrades I have in mind."

Aidan let out a whimper of protest from the living room.

"You can have a whole year to upgrade the system for what you pulled off."

He shook a flash drive at me. "Those photos just put doubt in his mind. It doesn't mean that you couldn't be working with an accomplice."

"I don't even care. I'll take any doubts we can create. How are the Danlys holding up?"

The grumpy gremlin actually grinned. "Remind me never to get on Tish's bad side. She's raising absolute hell over her suspension. She especially likes pointing out how finding a tiny camellia etched into one of over two hundred bones is stratospherically unlikely."

"How did they find that anyway?" I asked curiously as I stood back up.

"Flesh sloughed off the *iwana bōzu's* toe; decomp accelerated way fast after he was pulled out of the water."

"Girl's got a point," I noted. "Who would think to check the bone of the big toe if the cause of death was pretty obvious."

"Which leads one to wonder how they even noticed in the first place," Rafael commented. "Even if they found one on the *iwana bōzu's* foot, why would they think to check all the bodies they had available?"

"So someone's feeding them information," Lala said slowly.

"Probably the same person who reported them missing in the first place," Aidan chimed in with a dark look on his face.

"No doubt. And now we have to move up the timeline for Orochi, seeing as how I'm supposed to be having an appropriate reaction to a dead body being found in my house." Fatigue weighed me down, making each limb feel like they weighed a hundred pounds each.

"Go to bed," Lala ordered. "We can do that in the morning. The man already questioned you; you don't have to ride his bumper all the way back to Skamania. Vambi can transport you back—he won't even know that you spent those extra hours out here."

Rafael's eyebrows shot up, and I watched as he silently mouthed *Vambi* to himself.

"Now shoo." My diminutive co-worker grabbed my arm and began dragging me up the stairs.

"Is dragging your new thing? Because you keep dragging me everywhere lately," I asked on our way up.

"Herding is for dogs. This is far more effective." She dismissed me as she opened my bedroom door and shoved me in. The door shut in my face before I could say anything else, and I blinked at it for a few seconds, processing the fact that I had been locked in my own room in my own house.

"And stay in!" Lala's voice yelled through the door after the scraping sounds of what I assumed was a chair under the doorknob stopped. My assumption was proven correct when the door whipped open and Pea scurried in before it was slammed back shut, the doorknob clattering as Lala positioned the chair back under the door.

"I think we just turned into Cinderella and got locked in our room by our evil stepmother," I informed Pea as I fell onto my bed face-first. I turned my head to look at Pea. "You must be my version of Gus Gus."

She sniffed at my audacity, then climbed the blanket to curl up on the pillow next to me. I wanted to resist sleep and everything that laid in wait for me when I closed my eyes, but the traitorous things refused to remain open, and the battle to stay awake was lost in mere moments.

MY NIGHTMARE STARTED out the same way it had for the past two months. On my back porch, in the two Adirondack chairs Rafael and I had used in the spring. Me with the red pillow. Rafael with the blue. During this particular dream, Rafael was the one picking at the threads and staring pensively out into the Siuslaw.

"Well, color me surprised," I muttered from my chair. "As soon as I close my eyes, I end up here. Every. Damn. Time."

Rafael peered at me, interrupting his stare-down with the forest. "What do you mean, every damn time?"

I ignored him. "What's the conversation topic tonight?"

"Baki. Please. Answer me—what do you mean by *every damn time*?"

I rolled my eyes and waved a hand at our milieu. "Every nightmare I've had for the past eight weeks or so has started out on this deck, in this setup."

His hands stilled on the thread he had been picking. A gold thread this time. "I don't think..." he started slowly, before stopping like he was choking on the words. He cleared his throat and tried again. "Baki. I don't think those were nightmares."

My head whipped to him. It was my turn to ask "what do you mean?"

"My dreams always start this way as well. They don't end this way, as you know, but they always started with us having a conversation together. About everything and anything."

"So when you asked about my nightmares..." My voice trailed off. My face felt like it was on fire as I recalled how I had guilelessly grabbed his hand and initiated a thumb war with the male, and the way his hand had unerringly found my most vulnerable spots. The embarrassment increased tenfold when I remembered his comment in my bedroom.

He nodded. "I suspected. I asked because I wanted to confirm that we had shared them."

"And when my nightmares ended with you being pulled away from me or in pain?"

Rafael flinched in his seat. It was the smallest movement, a mere flutter, but I still clocked everything I needed to know. My mind flashed back to that first nightmare on my deck.

I WAKE UP, twisted in sheets that are unpleasantly soaked with cold sweat. Woodrow's ears are flat against his head, his eyes wide. I flinch as I remember the nightmare, the burning pain of the sap coursing through my body, then the abrupt sensation of nothing that followed. A soft woo *leaves Woody's muzzle and I give him a pat on the head as I throw back the sheets, carefully placing my feet on the other side of Maxwell's prone body. A faint thought that never reaches the forefront of my mind wonders where Victoria is as I stand. A flash of crimson streaks across my vision, like blood arcing across a wall; an* oni's *skull is covered in the splatter. I shake my head, as if I can so easily shake off the vestiges of the nightmare I just had, and pad out of my bedroom, hoping the cool night air will clear my brain. Pea hisses softly from her perch on the back of the couch as I slide open the back door and freeze.*

A silhouette of a figure sitting on my deck is softly lit by the full moon. Their feet are propped on the railing, their head resting against the back of the chair, staring up at the stars.

A cloud passes and the newly exposed moonlight illuminates their face. Rage ignites through my entire body, like a wildfire through a dead forest.

The absolute fucking arrogance of this male, to simply show up in my territory like this.

I storm out, slamming my sliding door shut. The fact that the glass doesn't shatter should be my clue that all is not as it seems, but the action barely registers through the anger flooding my system. I don't register how difficult it is to maneuver through the atmosphere, it only antagonizes me further. I try to temper my anger, knowing that he saved my life in the end. Another splash of crimson blinds me for a moment, reminding me of the nightmare I had just had, of Rafael's blood spraying across the throne room as he was speared.

But my life wouldn't have been at risk if it hadn't been for his machinations, *the devil on my shoulder whispers into my ear.*

"Get the fuck *off my land." The words snap out of my mouth before I'm even aware of speaking.*

He doesn't turn or even look my way in the slightest. Instead, his gaze remains focused on the stars as a slow smile spreads across his face, small wrinkles crinkling at the corners of his eyes.

My vision begins to shift with my anger, splitting from the gestalt of the world before me and into the most basic of its parts at the sight of that fucking smile. I rein my ki *back in as a cushion goes up in flames, internally scolding myself for allowing this male to see any hint of weakness.*

"Hello, Baki." His voice is cool. Smooth. Calm. Everything that I am not.

His head finally turns and, still, he doesn't meet my eye. Instead, his gaze wanders my entire body, including the empty space around me, and a small furrow forms in his brow.

My eyes catch on a small movement. Victoria is laying at his feet, content, though alert, and I try my best to push back my feeling of betrayal, and fail as my heart splinters at the realization that Rafael is truly Vicky's person now, and I no longer claim the title to that privilege.

"You're not welcome here," I hiss.

He shrugs. A pained expression flits across his face before he quickly hides it and returns to stargazing. "Seems like you're the reason I'm here, not me."

"Excuse the fuck out of me?"

"Do you honestly think it would be so easy for me to get away from Orochi after I went against him?" He pats the arm of the chair next to him. "Sit."

"I am not a dog for you to command," I snarl.

He snorts. "As if. It was an invitation to join me, but if you prefer to stand, far be it from me to stop you."

I stiffen and fold my arms across my chest. His body seems to deflate as he sighs when I remain standing. "Do you ever wish things could be different, Baki?"

I have to work to keep my jaw from unhinging at the gall of his question. "Are you for real right now? Unfortunately for you, you can't change the past."

His head drops back down and he stares pensively into the dark forest ahead of him; his fingers steeple against the arm of the chair. I can't place what it is exactly, but something seems off *about his fingers. "There's so much I would do differently if I'd had the choice."*

"It's too bad for both of us that you didn't, now isn't it." I spit the words out like they taste awful.

"But I wouldn't change my choice to save you," he says softly, ignoring my last comment. So softly that I almost miss the words.

"Fucked that one up nice and thoroughly, didn't we though. Wouldn't have had to save me if you hadn't put me in the position to be saved in the first place." I finally voice the refrain that has been thrumming through my head on repeat since the kariudo *first betrayed me.*

"Hmm." A slight flinch rattles through his form, like my words were a physical force against his body. With it comes an odd flickering effect, like a hologram struggling to maintain its image.

I drop my arms and finally sit. The thing nobody ever really talks about is that you can only maintain peak levels of anger for so long before it drains you. Was I still angry? Absolutely. Was I still ready to light everything on fire?

Well, yes. But maybe while sitting instead of standing.

"Why are you even here, Rafael? What purpose could your presence possibly serve? And don't tell me you're here because I want you here, because that's complete and utter bullshit. I can't think of anyone I would want to see less."

He doesn't answer me. He just continues to stare into the forest, though I can see the muscle in his jaw fluttering with tension.

Right as I'm about to give up and go back inside, his mouth opens as if to say something, then closes without releasing his words. I stand, unwilling to listen to more excuses. "Just tell me where you are so we can finish this and you can get the fuck out of my life, once and for all."

His face contorts into a scream. Vicky scrambles to her feet, growling and snarling at an enemy I can't see. Rafael's face melts away leaving him a blank slate, before it flashes back into place, his face in utter agony.

A sharp crack *shatters the silence of the night. And I watch in horror as the glamour holding Rafael together drops and I see his broken body in front of me. His femur at an impossible angle. His back, flayed open. Fingers twisted in unnatural positions. He drops to the deck like a marionette whose strings have been cut…before he vanishes as if he was never there.*

Except for the pool of blood glistening by the light of the moon.

And I wake up. Twisted in sheets soaked with sweat. Woodrow now standing on the bed, nudging at my body again and again until I lift a hand to calm him.

CHAPTER THIRTY-EIGHT

"I WATCHED you be tortured," I said flatly as I resurfaced from the nightmare. Memory. Some unholy combination of the two.

"You watched me be tortured," he agreed.

"Awesome." My head thunked against the wooden back of my chair. "Just what I always wanted. Because I haven't witnessed enough torture in my lifetime. Fuck." Night after night, I had seen his body contort under the damages it suffered. My nightmares would be all the more awful with the realization that the images weren't imagined...but *real*.

"Considering the circumstances, I would think you might've enjoyed the sight."

I glared at him. "Just because I was pissed at you doesn't mean I wanted to see you *tortured*. That kind of shit leaves a mark."

"Tell me about it," he countered.

"Besides," I continued as though he hadn't said anything, "I might have killed you a time or three, but I wouldn't have tormented you. I'm not that kinda gal."

Rafael threw his head back and laughed. "I'm glad to know you have boundaries, Baki."

"I'm violent," I grumbled, sinking deep into my chair like that would hide me from his judgment. "That doesn't mean I'm a sadist."

The smile remained on his face. "Never said you were. Just violent. I do enjoy a violent female, particularly during thumb war."

As I assumed the shape and color of a cooked shrimp, like I could hide from my embarrassment, my body protested, fragments crashing and grinding into each other. It wasn't fair…that even in sleep, I had to live with pain. Another thump from my chest and I rubbed at my sternum absently.

"So what is this now? Some fucked-up version of *Inception*? A dream within a dream? An out-of-body experience? Lala spiking my drink with psychedelics?" I asked.

The corners of Rafael's lips quirked as he tried to fight another smile. "Out-of-body experience would be my best guess. A meeting of our sub-consciousness somewhere in the liminal sera seems a bit more accurate, though more wordy."

"So I get to blame you for never feeling rested when I wake up."

An eyebrow raised. "You got to sleep and wake up rested before all this happened? I'm jealous."

"Fair point," I conceded. "I don't know when the last time I had a restful night of sleep was."

Just call me Ol' Raccoon Eyes at this point.

I massaged my chest again as a *thump* rose from it and realized two things: My chest was whole again in this dream—or liminal sera, wherever we were—and my heart was beating like it had never stopped in the first place. Stunned, I rubbed harder, as if I could will my heart to keep beating after I woke back up.

His gaze fell to my hand and he nodded at it. "That's new," he said softly.

"Tell me about it. I haven't felt it beat like this since *Hyakki Yagyō*." Then his words registered. "Wait. You can hear it?"

My hearing might be ultrasensitive, but I still couldn't hear someone else's heartbeat.

Rafael shook his head. "I don't hear it. I can *feel* it."

I stared at him. "What do you mean you can feel it?"

His hand drifted to my throat. I tensed automatically; the idea of anyone's hands anywhere near my throat was enough to incite violence. His fingers drifted down the curvature of my neck and stopped over the newfound pulse in my throat.

My heart might be beating, but my lungs had stopped working at his closeness. Rafael gently grabbed my hand with his free one and laid it over his heart.

"Do you feel that?" he asked. I watched in fascination as his Adam's apple bobbed, his neck flexing, almost like it were a reflex, before his words sank in and I paid attention to the rhythm of our hearts.

Or I would, if they could be differentiated.

"What the fuck?" I whispered, the words fueled with the last vestiges of air in my lungs before I dragged in an enormous inhale to make up for my lack of breathing.

A smile broke across his face and he dropped his hands. "What the fuck indeed, Baki."

"Why are our hearts beating to the same rhythm?" I demanded. Not that I was complaining about my heart beating. It just seemed like it would be better if I had my *own* rhythm.

"I very much suspect that it has something to do with the fragment of your soul you gifted me, and that." He nodded to Seymour as the wisp spiraled around my forearm.

"Seymour?"

"See more what?" Rafael asked, bewildered.

I retracted my arm back to my chest. "Seymour. That's his name."

"You…named my soul."

"Obviously. I couldn't keep thinking of him as Rafael's soul when you're right there. It was too confusing and inefficient."

"You gendered him as well?"

I threw my hands up in the air. "Why wouldn't he be a *he* if he came from *you?*"

"Because he's a soul?" Rafael asked, amused.

"How do you know souls don't have genders? Have you ever asked? Are you a *he?*" I whispered that last question to Seymour, feeling a little guilty about assuming its gender. Seymour simply nodded his wispy head and split into tendrils of mist that spiraled down my hand, weaving between my fingers.

"I rest my case," I said in triumph. Too bad I couldn't ask my own soul what gender it was, but I wasn't the one who could perceive souls. Only this little bit of one that was literally wrapped around my remaining little finger.

Rafael shook his head. "Seymour it is," he said with a smile. "Why that name?"

"Because he reminds me of Audrey II from *Little Shop of Horrors*, but Audrey doesn't fit him. He looks like Audrey II but acts like Seymour." It made perfect sense in my head.

"I— You know what. I'm not even going to ask how the fragment of a soul can act like a character named Seymour, I'm just going to trust the way your brain works on that one. But between my body containing a fragment of your heart, and yours a piece of my soul, I suspect your heart might be syncing to mine in an echo of the connections we now share, considering it didn't used to work."

I scrunched my nose, unsure if I liked the idea of our hearts being in sync. At least that's what I told myself. In reality, I was too afraid to hope. Too afraid to ask the question that was flashing in neon lights at the front of my mind. I changed the subject instead, like a coward.

"So I guess I forgave you in real time," I mused. "Well, maybe not so much real time, but real interactions at the very least."

"That was rather enlightened of you."

I smirked. "Not expecting that from me?"

The male hummed noncommittally.

"Orochi though…" My voice trailed off as Rafael's right leg began to bounce, betraying his agitation at the sound of the *kami's* name. I cleared my throat. "Orochi can burn, for all I care."

"What do you plan to ask him?" Rafael asked curiously.

I grinned wickedly as I heard my name called in the distance. "Who said anything about asking? You joining us?"

"I wouldn't miss it."

FOR ONCE, I woke up to dry sheets and no horrific images of blood and contorted limbs. Instead, I opened my eyes and nearly screamed at the sight of Toyo's unsettling eyes double-blinking at me, inches away from my nose.

"It's time," she intoned.

"Why can't a single one of you ever *knock*," I grumped. "It's a good thing I wasn't naked."

"Why? It's nothing I haven't seen before," she retorted. "For Quotes' sake, how long have you been in America for? When was the last time you visited a *sento?*"

"Listen," I started as I swung my legs over the side of my bed for what might have been the third time today, if we counted my dreams. Max bumped my calf from where he was sprawled on the floor, checking in with me. I reached down to give him a quick scratch behind the ears. "It's been over a century. I'm not gonna say I don't miss communal bathhouses, but...*I don't miss communal bathhouses.*"

A shudder that wasn't altogether sarcastic ran through my body. I'd been a loner for far too much of my life to appreciate communal *anything*. It wasn't about mutual nakedness; it was about needing space away from people.

Toyo shook her head at me and threw a clean bra and shirt at my face. "How else do you stay up on gossip if you haven't been going to one all these years?"

"That's what Kenji is for. He gathers all the hot goss, and I reap the benefits without having to be present for when said hot goss is occurring. It's the best of both worlds. And I get to enjoy my steam shower, by myself, alone, in peace." Pea hissed. "Alone except for the *shikigami*," I amended, tugging off the shirt I'd worn all day yesterday and hooking my bra around my chest.

"So what I'm hearing is that there will be no *onsens* for us in the future." Toyo tossed a pair of pants onto the bed.

"If it's just us two, sure. I'm down to visit hot springs," I said with fond exasperation, my voice muffled by the T-shirt as I pulled it on. I knew she was doing her best not to think about the task ahead of us, and I had no problem with that. Ancient Abbies—the true professionals in the game of avoidance.

"You better be." A pair of socks bounced off my head while I was bent over, stepping into my pants. "We have a hundred years to catch up on. That's going to be at least three days' worth of *onsen*-ing."

A pair of slobbery socks dropped at my feet with a soft thud, Max accompanying them as he sat, his tongue lolling out of his mouth. "Thanks, buddy." I cringed as I lifted the wet pair and gave Toyo a look that cried for help.

She rolled her eyes and threw another pair at me, the first item of clothing I managed to catch so far. I set the wet pair gingerly next to me on the floor and gave Max a solid pat to reward him for his efforts, then sat on the bed so I could pull the dry socks on.

I ducked as a hairbrush was the next missile aimed for my head. "Could we maybe not give me a concussion before we go interrogate the alleged former love of your life?"

"Please. As if anything could get past that thick skull of yours to rattle your brain."

I gave her a shove as I went into my bathroom. The *akaname* were back, one crouched on the ceiling of my shower, the other hunched in my toilet bowl. I gave them a friendly wave and hesitated as I grabbed my toothbrush. What were the chances they hadn't licked it yet?

I was holding the toothbrush in my hand, debating the merits of hunting down a brand-new one, when Toyo showed up in the doorway. She did a double take. "You have *akaname*, Cam."

"I'm aware."

She reached over and pulled the toothbrush out of my hand and threw it in the trash. A crepey limb stretched from the toilet bowl, dripping water on my tile, and snatched the toothbrush from the trash. The *akaname* immediately stuffed it in their mouth like it was a lollipop.

"You were actually going to use that?" Toyo asked with a grimace on her face.

"I didn't want to hunt down a new one."

"Oh my gods. Cheuky!" she yelled over her shoulder.

"What?" came the faint response from somewhere in the house.

"Where are the new toothbrushes?"

"Who do you need it for?"

"Cam!"

A moment later a new electronic toothbrush appeared on my bathroom counter. Complete with UV sanitizer. I shrugged and began unboxing it.

"Thanks, Cheuks!" Toyo yelled again.

"She was gonna use the old one that's been sitting there for months, wasn't she." Cheuksin's voice was much closer now as she appeared in the doorway, though she still stayed a good two feet away from the actual threshold. I wasn't sure when she'd willingly entered a bathroom last. She didn't need to use one as a deity, and she always bathed in a nearby spring.

"I wasn't aware I was going to have a whole-ass audience for the spectacle that is me brushing my teeth," I complained as I applied toothpaste to the brush and began the process of ridding myself of morning breath.

"Cam. It's not so much an audience as it is supervision," Cheuky said primly. "Someone has to keep standards for you."

"In the grand scheme of things, my toothbrush hardly rates as important right now," I said, my words muffled. I took a moment to spit and continued, "Besides, that toothbrush was probably the cleanest one in the house after they ate everything off of it."

Cheuky and Toyo wore matching looks of pain on their faces.

"What? I'm not wrong." The one on the ceiling crawled down the mirror and sat on the bathroom counter next to me. I gave them a pat on the head. "Thanks for keeping the bathroom clean, buddy."

"Is anyone else going with you guys?" Cheuksin asked.

"Rafael. I think that's it. Pretty sure he's asleep right now, so why don't you go bother him instead?"

"You sure about that?" Toyo commented with an amused look on her face.

"Yeah, why?" I replied, a little confused by what was amusing about that statement.

"No reason," the two deities singsonged.

I squinted at them.

"Just saying." Toyo held up her hands. "How would you know for sure if he was asleep?"

"Rafael and Cam sitting in a tree—" Cheuksin started.

They ran away laughing when I threw my toothbrush at them.

CHAPTER THIRTY-NINE

The aroma of breakfast rose as Max, Pea, and I descended the stairs a few minutes later and the Uncles came into view. Cheuky sat on a kitchen stool, a mildly anxious look on her face as she watched the Uncles absolutely destroy her kitchen. Some of us clean as we cook…not the Uncles. Dirty dishes were everywhere. Pancake mix, in both dry and batter form, was scattered on every available surface *and* the floor. Slimy trails of where Aidan's most enthusiastic Uncle had cracked eggs a little too hard led from the stovetop to the trash.

His more sedate Thread was at the stovetop wearing an apron, at the very least. He poked at something with a spatula, then flipped a hamburger patty while he stirred a pot of gravy with the other arm. Uncle bumped him out of the way with his wide body, snatching the spatula out of his Thread's hand to flip a bevy of fried eggs.

Organized chaos was the only way to describe the scene. The electronic sound of a machine attempting to replicate music joined the fray, the notes of "Amaryllis" doing its best to let everyone know that the rice was done.

"Oi! This is not how you cook pancake! Look at this. Bubbles! You need *puka*! Give me that!" Uncle's Thread snatched the spatula back during his scolding and waited for approximately a nanosecond. "Look! You see? *Puka!* You wait until there are holes *before* you flip. See how nice?" A golden pancake flipped in the air, landing neatly in the pan.

A plate of rejected pancakes sat to the side, with a group of K9s, including Woody, staring at them longingly. Max joined them and Pea climbed from his back, up the kitchen drawer handles, then began tossing them to each K9 with her tail. The Uncles ignored them as they continued arguing.

Aidan lifted a hand in a half-assed greeting while Theo nodded his head at us as they both ate their breakfast on the couch. The dining room table was forgotten. I didn't know why I ever bothered with one when everyone sat everywhere except in the dining room to eat.

Cheuksin's face turned to despair. I snickered as I took a seat between her and Toyo.

"Why so glum?" I teased. It felt good being able to get her back.

"They are using a *metal* spatula on my pans," she moaned.

"Just gives you an excuse to upgrade them to stainless steel," I noted, pouring myself a glass of POG that the Uncles must have brought with them this morning.

She brightened. "That's true."

Toyo snatched the glass of juice I had just poured and chugged it, then held it out for a refill.

"Rude."

She shrugged.

"Cam!" the Uncles chorused when they realized I had entered the room. Uncle busied himself with assembling two breakfast dishes together, his enormous body still looking incongruous in Cheuky's kitchen. Before long, Toyo and I both had a plate of *loco moco* in front of us, along with pineapple macadamia nut pancakes. "Go," he urged. "*Kau kau.* Eat."

The Uncles in their natural state might be my favorite version of them, especially when they made food like this.

His Thread nodded approvingly as we stuffed our faces, while Cheuksin sipped on a cup of coffee. "By the way, Cam. Did you know that FBI agent is staking out your house Quoteside?" he asked nonchalantly.

I choked on my POG and barely managed to swallow instead of spraying the kitchen with sticky juice and adding to Cheuky's distress. "He's still there?"

"Yep." Cheuksin couldn't contain herself anymore and rattled her spoon against her mug. A moment later, her kitchen was immaculate again.

"We were gonna clean that," the Uncles chorused in unison.

She waved them off. "I've been switching between realms to give the appearance of someone being home so he doesn't think you somehow snuck past him."

"Even though we're going to do exactly that," I said in amusement.

Suddenly the clatter in the living room fell silent as the TV began to blast. Lala had joined Theo and Aidan and was holding the remote, still clad in her PJs. "You guys, they found them."

"Search and Rescue has recovered their missing team members and scientists in Wrangell–St. Elias National Park. When the Alaska National Guard set out to run their search this morning, they were stunned to find the terrain completely reverted to the way it had once been. The missing are being treated for exposure and dehydration. Many have reported sightings of creatures they have never seen before, and all described a shared experience of their world collapsing in on them. Doctors are calling it a collective hysteria due to the unprecedented level of gases released by the decaying land, though they had no explanation for the decay itself."

"Fabulous," Aidan muttered. "The *kami* couldn't have done this in the Abbie realm? At least then we wouldn't have to deal with the Quote conspiracy theories that are going to spring up from this."

I silently agreed. At least the jellyfish had attempted to go ashore in our realm once they had congregated in Icy Bay and wouldn't add to the unusual happenings occurring in that region for now.

Theo snatched the remote from Lala and rewound the program until it flashed a photo of the missing people. "Reika's not there."

Lala sniffed. "Please. As if the *yamauba* would allow the Quotes to find her. She's either still in Orochi or has gone off to claim one of Alaska's mountains as her own now."

The three of them continued to bicker over their theories over where Reika might be and why she had chosen to stay behind. We turned back to our meal and ate in silence for a few minutes.

"You ready?" Cheuksin finally broke the quiet and asked the question like we were about to go out for a walk in the forest. Toyo and I shrugged in unison, matching her intensity.

A *swoosh* interrupted the relative silence of the kitchen, and all activity suspended as everyone waited for our answers. Rafael stepped through the open door, his dark hair made darker with the rain that dampened it. His navy Henley clung to his chest, outlining his torso. Drops of water went flying as he shook himself like a dog. Vicky padded in behind him, leaving muddy prints, then proceeded to shake as well. Woody and Max bounded over to greet them, now that the pile of pancakes had been decimated.

Cheuksin pushed her coffee to the side and slumped over, her arms wrapped around her head. A soft thud repeated itself as she beat her head against the granite. The goddess was clearly ready to have the home back to herself again. I patted her on the shoulder.

The Uncles wrinkled their noses. "Still raining?"

Rafael nodded, like it wasn't obvious.

They chuckled and I peered at the couple, wondering what I was missing.

"Yuri and Gale are out on a mission to make the FBI agent as miserable as possible," one of them started.

"Gale damaged his car. Not so badly that it can't run and leave us be, but enough so that it leaks when Yuri drops the temps and makes it rain," the other added.

"Then Gale messed with the stereo system so it's only playing talk stations in foreign languages," the original Uncle concluded.

A wide grin wreathed my face. I had the absolute best friends.

Pea waddled over and climbed up my body to wrap around my neck, her weight a comfort against the knowledge that we were about to interrogate a *kami* that had posed as someone we had both loved for so long.

"You ready?" I echoed the Uncles' question, directing it at Rafael.

"As ready as I'll ever be." His smile was vicious.

"No, you aren't," Uncle's Thread scolded. "First, you'll sit down and eat some food. Nobody goes into a situation like this without their wits about them, and you need to have fuel to keep those."

He wasn't wrong. Even if I felt like vomiting from sheer nerves, despite how delicious their food was.

Rafael took the fourth stool, on the other side of Toyo, and Uncle ladled brown gravy over the bed of rice that had a hamburger patty and a fried egg stacked on top. His Thread shoved a short stack of pancakes in front of the male. Rafael dug in, consuming his food in the way only those who'd starved in the past could appreciate.

After a few minutes I was the only one who hadn't finished, and I rushed to swallow my last few bites. As soon as I shoveled it in, Cheuksin stood up.

"Alright, everybody out. Shoo. Go do your respective things and leave me in peace."

"It's like she doesn't even love us anymore," Aidan joked to his Uncles as the goddess literally shoved them out of the house.

"You have your own den to dirty!" she shouted after them.

"Thank you for breakfast!" I yelled.

The Uncles raised a hand in acknowledgement then shifted into their *tanuki* form and scampered home, Aidan following behind them at a stroll.

"What about me and Lala?" Theo asked in amusement.

"Go to the beach or do a hike somewhere. I just need some nonpeople time so I can straighten all this out," Cheuksin said.

"C'mon, T. Let's take Phally to the beach and see what kind of tracking we can do with him there." Lala grabbed the *dokkaebi* by the hand and dragged him out the front door, her K9 following behind.

"That leaves you three." Cheuksin gave us a pointed look.

"We're leaving, we're leaving." I scurried out the front door, Rafael and Toyo on my tail, before she could shove us out.

"Is she always so rude?" Toyo asked as we piled into Cheuksin's Subaru. She waved as we passed Theo and Lala.

"You try living for millennia with people vomiting, urinating, and defecating on you, and you would probably only be able to stand people for a limited amount of time, too," I said mildly as I shifted into gear. Mentally, I gave thanks to the gods that we were in the Abbie realm and wouldn't have to chance the FBI agent seeing us leave for the beach instead of heading back to Washington.

"Fair point."

The three of us passed under the ever-watchful *kodama* to face a *kami* who had done us all harm.

CHAPTER FORTY

"A RE you sure this is a good idea?" Murry asked for the fifth time as he carried us to the spatial snare.

"Definitely not," Toyo muttered.

Rafael snorted. His shoulders had been creeping closer and closer to his ears since we had left my home. He looked about as uncomfortable as person could look while riding the skeleton of a whale.

"If nothing else, we do need to check in on Reika," I said. "She was a mainstay of the Pacific Northwest *yōkai* and I'm not sure what they'd do if she never returned."

The other two glared at me while I got soaked in the indignant plume of water that Murry blasted from his spiracles. A second later, we vanished into the snare and were spat out into Ryūgū-jō.

"*Cam.*" Toyo's voice trembled as we looked out over the realm.

We had stood here less than a week ago, and in that time, Ryūgū-jō's situation had worsened drastically. I blinked back tears as I struggled to find any trace of life in the realm.

Toyo dropped to her knees and dug her hand into the ocean bed, seeking a connection, any connection, indicating Ryūgū-jō was still alive.

The faintest vibration greeted us. It was so weak it didn't register any movement in Murry's air bubbles.

Rafael's head bowed, his voice silent. I placed a hand on his shoulder. "It's not your fault," I said, hushed.

He looked at me, eyes blazing. "How could you say that? I served that *kami* for near on a century and never realized what was happening to this realm or that he was an imposter. Ryūgū-jō deserved better."

"You're right, Ryūgū-jō deserved better. But it's not your fault. It's not even Orochi's fault." Much as I wanted to claim it was. "It's the fault of whoever began this chain of events." I reached down to pull Toyo to her feet. "So how about we try to find out who that might have been and then get this *ki* out of me so the realm can heal at last."

Toyo straightened, wiping the tears from her eyes, and nodded once with determination. "Let's interrogate that asshole and find out who this motherfucker is."

WE ARRIVED AT the gates that led to the dungeon far too soon. I swallowed thickly, memories of the last time I was here riding me hard. My flashbacks weren't filled with Ryūjin this time around. Instead, visions of a spear obliterating Rafael's chest filled my vision with red. I shook my head in a quick, violent action, grounding myself in the present moment. From the look of them, Toyo and Rafael weren't faring much better. I wasn't sure if having them with me was the wisest choice, but I was damn glad they were here.

I took a deep breath and swung the gate open, remembering a time when Ryūgū-jō had been strong enough to swing them open for me, and we began to descend the steps. The mold and mildew that had been restricted to my leaking cell had spread since May. Streaks of black and gray crept up the steps like a blanket of death. Small puffs of dust arose with every step we took, the denizens of the dungeon padding our steps over what used to be a stone floor.

Toyo took the lead, her steps purposeful, until she stopped in front of a wall. I watched as her shoulders squared, her eyes closing for a moment, before she began etching *kanji* on the wall, then stepped behind us once more.

Creaking echoed through the dungeon as the wall groaned then vanished. A darkness consumed the space until our eyes adjusted to find an eye, easily as large as a human, staring at us in return. The vertical slit disappeared momentarily as the dragon blinked. Then it drew back as it rose, now joined by fifteen amber orbs that blinked at different times.

The effect was entirely unsettling.

Orochi stood to his full height, his immense body vanishing in the space behind him, the cell having adjusted its dimensions to accommodate his size. A mountain range had sprung up inside Ryūgū-jō's dungeon, courtesy of the eight-headed *kami* before us.

An immense dragon's head dipped back down, not the same one who had spotted us when we opened the door, but a neighboring head.

"You make me wait nearly two centuries for your audience, little *hae-tae*?" Amusement rolled over the gravel in his voice.

"Why does everyone call me *little*," I muttered under my breath.

"Because you are," everyone said in varying tones.

"Finally." A different voice echoed through the chamber, then a ghostly figure emerged from the darkness. Her bone-white skin shone eerily in contrast to the pitch black, with two piercing eyes the color of dried blood.

"Reika." I wasn't sure if I had the ego strength to be berated by the *yamauba,* but I was still happy to see her well. "You haven't aged a day."

"I haven't," she agreed. "Even after you guys left me in here for two hundred years to rot."

Toyo raised an eyebrow. "As far as I'm aware, you chose to remain behind, hag."

"Mmm. It's a good thing, too." She nodded to the dragon behind her, waiting patiently. "I've done what I could with him."

What the fuck did that mean?

Before I could ask, I noticed Rafael, stiff as a board next to me, and barely breathing. Panic that wasn't mine rode me hard, leaking through the mental barriers he had put up. "You don't have to come in with us," I said softly, in a tone only he could hear.

"Ah. You brought my pet." Rafael flinched at the chorus of voices that came from the heads in unison.

I was going to make this hurt. It wouldn't be enough, but it would be a start for that flinch.

"Orochi." The heads whipped to the side as Toyo stepped to my right.

"My Thread." The *kami's* tone was reverent, not the disgust he had had when she had still been in the form of Aoki.

"I'm not your Thread," Toyo said, head held high. "You ensured that eons ago and lost the right to call me as such."

"Be it as it may, you are still my Thread, even severed." The eyes blinked asynchronously, leaving me dizzy. "This was all for you. I bent my knee for you."

"I never wanted it." She spat on the floor. "I could have held my own. I have *always* held my own. And now you justify how many lost lives in a bid to protect me?"

Hissing surrounded us as the heads drew up in anger. I braced myself. There was still a wall of *ki* shielding us, but I didn't know how strong it could still be with the state of Ryūgū-jō.

"Calm yourself," the *kami* on my side of the wall barked. "Or never see me again."

A head ducked down, back to our level, and peered at Toyo, dilating as it took her in. "You think you could hide from me?"

"Apparently I did well enough for a century."

A *tsk* sounded from the *yamauba*. "That was a one-time deal, Princess. Don't expect me to be able to wield that kind of power again. I had to save for centuries to manage the feat."

I was tired of this. And Rafael's panic wasn't receding. "Enough. Do you know why I'm here then?"

"I do indeed, little one."

"And do you consent?"

"The *yamauba* has counseled me to do so."

That was something at least. A pulse of *ki* singed my hairs with the depth of its power, then a male stood before me. I had never seen Orochi in the flesh, only him imitating Ryūjin. He stood tall—taller and broader than Rafael—his hair long and wavy. His skin was dark, to Toyo's light, similar in tone to my bronze. Unlike Ryūjin, Orochi's features were rugged, like the jagged peaks of a mountain. He wasn't classically handsome, but his features gave an aura of strength. His feet were bare against the stone floor, this chamber void of the mildew that had taken over the rest of the dungeon.

The *kami* stood, his arms spread out to his sides in an open invitation for me to pierce his heart.

CHAPTER FORTY-ONE

The moment Rafael blinked to attention with the realization of what was about to happen distracted me from the dread that overtook me whenever I shifted. The panic that had piggybacked my own feelings subsided, replaced with anger at himself and concern for me. I did my best to ignore it and braced myself for the transformation, fervently hoping it wouldn't be my last.

Ki rushed through me, and despite the fact I now stood on four feet instead of two, I was unsteady as a newborn colt. Rafael held a hand against my side, like he could prop me up through sheer will alone. I did my best not to lean too much weight against him, not wanting to flatten him with my size.

Reika *tsked* again and shook her head at my apparent failure to fix my *kis*. A look of concern passed over Orochi's face, confusing everything I knew about the *kami*, but the moment was fleeting as he steeled himself. I took one staggering step forward, then another, slowly stabilizing until I had passed the wall of *ki* that allegedly kept Orochi or Reika from leaving. I had my doubts. My suspicion was growing that the two of them were exactly where they wanted to be. Rafael followed me with each step, taking care to ensure I didn't fall.

My eleventh step brought me just shy of the *kami*. He gave me a solemn nod, and without further fanfare, my horn pierced his heart.

MY JAW UNHINGED in a silent scream as the Evil rushed through my horn. It went against all reasoning that piercing a willing heart was so much more painful than the unwilling. I was only grateful that most hearts fought every step of the way. I trusted that Rafael would be retethering the *kami's* soul as I went. I didn't know if I could kill a god this way, but I didn't want to kill Orochi due to my inexperience. We probably still needed him.

I pushed through the pain and skimmed through Orochi's life, taking a moment to note he had no knowledge of how he came into being. Eons flashed me by until the moment the plan that resulted in our presence today was seeded. My breath seized as I experienced My Thread again, though in another's perspective.

A group of five Abbies stand in a circle arguing. Well, three stood, two float-ed. Ryūjin, Reika, and Orochi shout, while Murry and an onna uo look on from above. The look in Orochi's gaze is pleading as he begs Ryūjin not to take his Thread away, but the sea kami *is stoic. Ryūjin motions back to the onna uo and informs Orochi that he won't be the only one to lose his Thread, and all four double down against the eight-headed dragon on the necessity of the action, reassuring Orochi that he will be reunited with his Thread again one day.*

A fragment of my heart cracked in two at the realization that Murry had indeed known about everything from the very beginning.

Time skips ahead once more, and I see Ryūjin with Orochi in what will become our bedroom. A flash of power knocks the kamis flat on their backs, unconscious. When Orochi wakes, I gasp and rewind Time back to compare the change in Orochi's eyes and understand. While the severing of a Red Thread left my body shattered and opened an all-access highway for the dead to enter Toyotama's mind, it had split Orochi's soul into eighths, leaving behind eight distinct personalities.

Another flash forward, and I see Orochi willingly submit himself to a god, no longer caring what happens to his souls after Toyo left him for his actions, so long as she is protected. The memory is unclear, as though someone has gone through and purposely blurred the kami's *recall of the god.*

Time and time again, I watch as Orochi receives his instructions from the god. And then it happens. After hundreds of times over the years, the god makes a mistake and neglects to hide himself from Orochi's memories and reveals his face.

I sucked in a huge inhale, my horn withdrawing from Orochi's heart in my shock. I bent over, coughing, my hands braced against my knees as I tried to process what I witnessed. After I finally caught my breath, I looked up to find Orochi's expression sad but knowing.

"Keep going, child." He waved to his chest, like there wasn't already a gaping hole left in it. "Wouldn't want you to leave any of that rot behind."

With grim intent, I pierced his heart again, the pain far worse for both of us this time. Now that I knew Seokga's identity, I could see the god clearly in Orochi's memories.

I recognize the chaos in this memory. Citizens of Ryūgū-jō scream in panic as oni *mow them down and the streets run with blood. And then I witness the fight that led to my Thread's death. If it could be called a fight. Ryūjin arrives with Pea, in her phantom form, to a field on the outskirts of the realm, the field where I will eventually find him. And he* stands *there and does nothing when Orochi disables him, then marks his body with* kanji *that drain the sea* kami's *life force. Every motion Orochi makes is weary and done with clear reluctance. He leaves before I show up, finding what I had found when I had run through the streets of Ryūgū-jō.* The dragon nearly collapses when he sees Toyotama and Tamayori lying prone, but manages to make it to the sisters, heartbreak taking over his movements. He gently rolls Tamayori to the side and lifts Toyotama in his arms, ignoring the bedlam around him, *and carries her to a temporary spatial snare where he gets her to Reika to be healed and changed. He leaves before he sees his Thread take a breath, unable to take the sight of her body any longer, and returns to Ryūgū-jō, his body shedding the shape of Orochi with every step, until he is no longer himself, but Ryūjin, aided by Seokga's power of trickery.*

Seokga grins as he commands Orochi to take Rafael's father as his kariudo, *despite Orochi's hatred for the male and the way he treats Toyo. I can see the sick thrill that ripples through Seokga when he has Orochi order the genocide of the* haetae. *Then Seokga discovers the existence of Rafael and abandons his project in Rafael's father for the grandson of Anhangá, his hands rubbing in glee at the thought of having such a creature under his command. He orders Orochi to have Rafael commit atrocity after atrocity once he is* kariudo, *but Orochi does what he can to mitigate the damage, taking care to leave his orders just ambiguous enough that Rafael is able to work around them, hoping against hope that the* kariudo *is smart enough to recognize the loopholes where he can.*

My stomach churned with horror when image after image is revealed to me of all Orochi has borne over the millennia. I skim the fight from spring, knowing well enough what happened, then paused on the moment before Orochi summoned Rafael, needing to take a breath before seeing the images that were already ingrained in my brain of Rafael's torture. Except what is revealed to me is even more horrifying.

Because the god is wearing a glamour, fresh from his recent exploits. And the glamour the god is wearing is none other than the visage of Agent Park.

The FBI agent sitting outside of my property at this very moment.

CHAPTER FORTY-TWO

withdrew my horn from Orochi and his wound healed before my eyes. Before I could say anything, I shifted and turned to the side Rafael wasn't supporting and vomited. Wriggling, maggot-like parasites, the color of pus and bile, along with streaks of black, rotting blood purged from me over and over again, rather than simply passing through my *ki* to be purified. Instead, the Evil that my body consumed from Orochi's heart was consumed by an unnatural fire until not a speck remained. I shuddered as I continued to heave, panic adding to my inability to control it. The pain racking my body as my fragments split further apart made it that much harder to collect myself, even as I desperately tried to rein it in. We had to leave this realm *right fucking now.*

"Seokga...Agent Park," I attempted to explain between heaves. "Neskowin...we—" I gasped. "We need to leave...*right now.*"

Rafael, bless him, figured out my meaning instantly and scooped me in his arms and sprinted for the gates. I would kiss this male with everything in my being after this was over. And after I had brushed my teeth.

"What is going on?" Toyo yelled from behind us. Orochi and Reika followed. I didn't give a fuck *who* was with me, all I cared about was getting back to my territory—my *people*—in time.

"Seokga is the god responsible for all of this," Rafael shouted over his shoulder. "And he's the agent sitting outside Cam's *kamis-damned* driveway."

A sharp intake of air was all I needed to hear to know she understood the severity of the matter. Murry was waiting, doing a whale's equivalent of pacing in front of the spatial snare. Because he knew. Of course he fucking knew. I didn't know what I would do about the *bakekujira* if I survived the battle to come. Reika was one thing; I wasn't close to the *yamauba*. But I had been friends with Murry for thousands of years, since he had been a calf.

The snare spat us back into the Neskowin waters, and we swam for our lives until we hit the beach and sprinted for Cheuksin's Subaru, back under my own steam. I slammed into the driver's seat, the remainder of our group not far behind. The tires burned rubber as I spun out of the parking lot before any of the doors could even close. Toyo let out a yelp as she nearly fell out of the vehicle, but she righted herself immediately and slammed the door shut behind her.

Even from the beach, I could see the smoke rising from the hills where my territory lay. I smashed my foot down harder, like that would coax anymore speed out of the Subaru. Only the curves of the road kept my eyes off the rising plumes, knowing that Pea, Max, Woody, Vicky, and nearly all of my friends, to say nothing of the refugees, were somewhere in it.

I screeched to a stop, the engine protesting, and leapt from the car when I was met with a wall of *kodama* who were all focused inward and not permitting me passage. I said an apology under my breath and began lighting select branches on fire, just enough to create a tunnel through the forest spirits. Those in my party that could shift had already done so, as an antlered *oni*, a massive crocodile, and an eight-headed dragon charged ahead of me. I cursed as Reika and I sprinted after them, the *yamauba* holding her *deba* in hand.

I stumbled and nearly fell when my *eomma* appeared in front of me. Reika continued on, unaware of her presence.

"Hurry," *Eomma* urged.

"Thanks. In the middle of trying to do that," I said through gritted teeth, doing my best not to scream in frustration.

"Your friends…they do not know."

"I know they don't know, *Eomma*. That's why we returned."

"No," she insisted. "The trickster, Seokga. He wears your face. Their minds, he confuses them."

I slowed for half a step. "What?"

"The god! He is pretending to be *you*. And he has confused their minds so they are all fighting each other!"

Renewed panic quickened my step. Suddenly the *kodama* refusing me passage made a sick kind of sense. As a god, especially a *trickster*, Seokga would be able to mimic me down to the essence of my *ki*, even if he couldn't truly replicate my magic.

I skidded to a stop upon seeing a living nightmare. Everything around me was on fire. I seized onto it with all the power I possessed, wrenching it under my control and guiding it away from those it hovered too closely to, and others who were already on fire. I could do nothing for the already dead. An *ushi oni* bleated, then succumbed to the burns. The shards of my heart hurt, recognizing the mate of the one whose life had been forfeited to her *tamatebako* a few short days ago. I gathered the fuel the fire provided and ripped a hole in the liminal sera, gathering my *wakizashi* from the pocket.

I nearly swallowed my own tongue when I saw the Uncles fighting viciously against the other, unable to recognize each other. Their forms shifted nearly too fast to track as they morphed from one *yōkai* form to the next. I ran through the fray, doing my best to evade blows, screaming to try to get their attention the entire time, slashing with my short swords when the opportunity provided, avoiding fatal injuries when possible. Before I arrived, they were stymied by gently glowing shields preventing them from reaching one another.

"Pea," I panted. The *shikigami* dropped from the branch she had been perched on above the mayhem, into my arms. "Thank the fucking gods. You're okay."

She clicked, chirped, and hissed too quickly for me to understand, but her tone was enough.

"Seokga. Where is the bastard?" Her tail lashed with rage, and she stabbed her one foreleg in the direction where the roars of several dragons sounded. An explosion of power sent *yōkai* flying as Orochi grew in size. A clone of myself grinned wildly at the *kami* and I began to run in their direction.

A howl cut through the noise, a sound I would hear anywhere in the world, and I ducked as a *kanabō* went flying for my neck. A second later, Woodrow tackled the forest-green *oni* that had nearly crushed my skull. A vicious growl tore out of him as he ripped out the *oni's* throat, and I lit the club and the *oni's* mask on fire. The light died from his eyes as I destroyed the source of his *ki* and he was unable to heal from the wounds Woodrow had dealt. The malamute was drenched in blood, his hindquarters shredded from where the *oni's* tusks had caught him. I kicked the body away from me, wishing I could kill him again, even as I watched Woodrow's wounds knit close. He glued himself to my side as I continued my path to Seokga.

A deep rumble announced Maxwell's arrival, and I watched, unable to breathe, as he bounded into the path of a *futakuchi onna*, too far from my reach, and too close to the *futakuchi onna* for me to ignite without hurting him in the process. I desperately wanted to shift, needing to be a form more powerful than this human body so that I could do *something* as I watched one of my beloved K9s throw himself at a deadly *yōkai*. But I needed to save my shift for when it could do the most damage, because I had no idea if it would be my last. Maxwell's teeth tore the cords of hair from her head, leaving her without weapons. He leapt over her body and joined the three of us.

Any hope that I had fell when Orochi shrieked in a chorus of voices, and I watched as Seokga used his power, using Orochi's split soul to his advantage, and causing them to fight among themselves.

A skull with antlers rose above the fighting *yōkai*, clear across the melee, and I said a silent prayer of thanks when I saw Victoria at Rafael's heels, snapping at the feet of anything that ventured too close. I had no idea how he had gotten so far so fast, but I wasn't going to question anything if he had found Vicky in the process. I blasted a *bakeneko* with fire when they nearly made it past the pair and blocked a blow from a whipping branch of thorns the size of my forearm with my *wakizashi*.

Pea let out a shriek as she was ripped off my neck, and I whirled to find her held in the grasp of Cheuksin, wrapped tightly in the curtain of the goddess's hair. My friend's once colorful clothing had faded to a soiled white nightgown, and her eyes had gone opaque as she embraced her curse. Boils exploded across the faces of anyone within a ten-foot vicinity, and *yōkai* howled in pain, dropping to their knees to claw at their skin. I couldn't give a single fuck about the pain that had exploded across my body. I dealt with horrific pain on a daily basis, this was just one more as I ducked under the reach of her hair and spun, slicing her hair off to the nape of her neck. Pea scrambled out of the coils, hissing at Cheuksin, and threw another shield over her to prevent the goddess from hurting others and getting hurt in the process. The *shikigami* had to be running out of power.

I gathered up the small opossum and threw her under my shirt to protect her from any further grabs, then picked up my swords and continued to fight my way to the god, Maxwell and Woodrow guarding my flank. I saw Theo evade a blast of ice from Yuriko along the way and passed Lala doing her best to subdue Aidan, their empathic powers only serving to cancel the other's out.

My fires began to rage out of control as my attention faltered with fatigue and distraction, and the natural forest around us began to flicker as the flames began to consume them, eating through the fuel I had provided. I didn't have the time to pull it back as I slashed my way to Seokga, until at long last, I stood before the god who had destroyed my family, my Thread, and a realm.

CHAPTER FORTY-THREE

There was something inherently fucked up about facing a copy of yourself that's wearing a sadistic look of glee, prepared to do what is necessary to cut them down, knowing you are only a *haetae* fighting against one of the rulers of this world. The ruler responsible for the corruption and Evil that infected it versus me, armed with only two *wakizashis*, and backed up by two K9s and a *shikigami* in a juvenile dead opossum.

"Why?" I croaked out, my voice hoarse from screaming and exhaustion. Meanwhile, my mirror image looked as fresh as someone who had never experienced a hardship in their life.

"Why?" Seokga responded. "*Why?* Because I *can*. Because I won this world from Mireuk long ago and I can do with it what I please. Destroying the guardians that try to circumvent my power is my *right*."

"You cheated in your game for control of this world," I sneered. "And Mireuk is a coward for not even contesting it and leaving us with you. Neither of you deserve this world." The world had borne the consequences when the creator god abandoned it and allowed the scales to tip further and further into chaos and evil.

"I won," he insisted. "And Mireuk knew it. He left the world to me to do with it what I wished. And I did, until the other gods began interfering."

"All I see is a whiny little boy in front of me who couldn't contain his own jealousy when Mireuk created something beautiful, so he stole it just like any other bully that has ever existed. You're not special, you have just created millions of versions of your selfishness in the process, all because you didn't know how to cope with your own feelings of distress."

Seokga's smile grew unnaturally wide, splitting my face in half as he bared his teeth at me. "Isn't it wonderful? And now I get to claim Yeomra's prized possession. His last *haetae*. The one that holds not only the power of the *haetae* but also the *ki* of a sea *kami*…and the soul of a descendant of Anhangá. I have allowed you to develop like a fine wine, and now you're all *mine*."

With his last word, he dropped the glamour and took on his own image, spreading his hands out before him. The obsidian slave bands that had once trapped Rafael materialized and dropped into the outstretched hands.

"Your debt is due, *haetae*. And it appears you're unable to pay in full. You remain broken…and mine to reap."

I would die before I allowed that to happen, and so I lunged for the god, Woodrow and Maxwell leaping for him at the same time. The bands vanished at once, in favor of a *hwandudaedo* that he wielded in front of him. Instead of a dragon or phoenix, the ringed pommel of the sword featured a magnolia, the flower Seokga had stolen from Mireuk and won the world with.

My K9s yelped and dodged the swipe of the god's sword before it met mine in a *clang* that reverberated up my arms. His straight sword had double the reach of my blades and were fueled by the strength of a god, whereas I held two weapons to his one, and rode a wave of rage with nothing to lose if I lost this fight to him.

A burn screamed across my torso as his *hwandudaedo* landed a blow, and I resisted the urge to bend into it, blocking and throwing his blade back at his face. I took the opportunity to dip beneath his arm, using my short stature that everyone commented on to my advantage, one *wakizashi* parrying his blade while the other slashed under his arm. Seokga hissed with pain and pulled back for another strike. I leapt back, barely avoiding the strike that would have halved my torso from my body, and spun toward him, missing my own attempt to sever his hamstrings as he pulled his sword back. A sick feeling washed over me, making me stumble backwards, and I realized he had poisoned his blades with the sap of an ulleungdo hemlock. A soothing pink glow surrounded me as Pea clung to my waist and tried her best to heal my wound and draw the poison from me.

Woodrow and Maxwell came rushing back in, aiming for the god's shins, forcing him to dance back to avoid tripping over the K9s. My world narrowed to the battle before me, all other noise from the chaos that Seokga had wrought blocked. I swung again, taking the opportunity my K9s had given me and sent a blast of fire toward the god's face, when suddenly my world went black.

THE SOUND OF footsteps and growls neared me, though I couldn't see. I held my attack, not knowing where Max or Woody were. Pea hissed in rage and a blast of *ki* shot out from her, shattering the darkness that surrounded me.

Rafael stood before me now, his *oni* skull warped with fury as he sprang toward me, the spikes of his *kanabō* humming with magical enchantments, Seokga nowhere in sight. I recognized the enchantments; they were the same as the ones that were locked away at BSSR's facility, because they prevented a wound from healing. Betrayal filled me, turning my rage into an inferno. The forest fire surrounding us responded to my heightened emotion and the flames leapt ever higher into the sky.

It didn't matter, I was already poisoned, and I was used to betrayal. I bent backwards, avoiding yet another club aimed for my neck. A bellow broke into my concentration, and I turned against my will, seeing a second Rafael fighting his way to me. Confusion struck me for a moment before I realized Seokga was using his power to render me more suggestive to his illusions. But I felt nothing from the Rafael in front of me, whereas the devil throwing bodies from his path filled me with his determination to get to me.

A sudden crushing blow sent me stumbling back until I hit a hard surface. Seokga's *ki* had done its job in distracting me, and I looked down to find a simulation of Rafael's *kanabō* mutilating my torso, a dozen spikes pinning me to the tree. Rafael's face broke into a slow smile above me. Ice spread down my body when obsidian rings materialized into his hand, the knowledge that I had failed all of us the only thought at the forefront of my mind.

I could see Rafael fighting his way to get to me, disadvantaged by his efforts to avoid fatal blows, when the *yōkai* had no such compunctions, their minds now warped by Seokga's deception. I felt the moment he died on his way to me, and then when he was retethered nearly as quickly, his body returning to its last location perfectly whole once more. He was choosing death over injury, to keep himself in fighting form, and everything in me wanted to protest.

How could this male possibly think he was unsalvageable when he did things like this?

Desperation racked my body with the *clink* that signified my final sentencing.

I screamed for Anhangá in my mind, playing my final card. Maniacal glee was written over Seokga's face, the god knowing that he had cornered me at last.

Utter revulsion rolled through me with the heaviness of the obsidian settling into my skin, into the scars where they had once been. Before Seokga could utter a single command, Pea soared from shoulder and into his face, and I shifted for one last time.

CHAPTER FORTY-FOUR

Fear flooded Rafael's system as he watched his grandfather materialize at Baki's side. Even though it had never been voiced in words, he knew what the action meant. Pain ripped through his body as an uncontrolled shift overtook him, and he transformed to his human form for a moment before his oni tore back out of his body once more. Vicky snarled and snapped at a hanzaki that threatened to swallow them whole.

He no longer cared about whether the person in his way was a friend or foe. If they were in his path, his mind catalogued them as an enemy, and bodies went flying as he barreled through them in his need to get to Baki *now*. Vicky darted behind him, never drifting from his heels, unless it was to ward off Abbies trying to take him down from behind. Not for the first time, he cursed the limitations on his ability to travel, wishing he was back to his full power once more.

In his soul, he knew. He knew that he would be too late. That he wouldn't be able to save her this time. But he would be damned if he wouldn't die trying.

His heart caught in his throat as he watched Baki shift, her *haetae* worthy of taking his breath away every single time. Pride radiated from him as he watched her raise her dragon's head despite the sickness that ravaged her every time she shifted. Gold glinted red as her horn reflected the fires around them, and her beautiful, small cobalt-black wings expanded, the feathers attempting to ruffle in a bid to help her gain her balance. A gleam caught his eye, and his breath stopped as he realized her slave bands had transferred to her wings, shackling them from spreading to their full span.

Time slowed as though the next events occurred over the next few seconds, rather within the same moment. He witnessed Baki's lunge forward, using her unsteadiness to her advantage for once. She allowed herself to fall into the god that wore his face and had caused so much damage over millennia. Time stopped altogether as her horn punctured Seokga,, pulsing with the Evil it was siphoning, the burnished gold, slowly turning the color of rot.

Then he saw the cracks. Once upon a time, not even so very long ago, her *haetae* had shown none of the damage Baki had incurred when her Thread had been severed. But now he watched as the cracks expanded. And fragmented. Shards of her jade thorax began to crumble into dust, whisked away in air, ceasing to exist, and they were swept into the inferno around them, unable to contain the Evil of a god. Her tail whipped wildly with pain, even as bits of it disintegrated, the spade crashing to the ground as its link to her body vanished, before it, too, faded into dust.

Rafael's mouth dropped in a scream of protest as the realm resumed its normal speed and a *tamatebako* with inlaid gold materialized in his grandfather's hand. Its lid opened for the first and only time in its existence as Anhangá touched the jade box to the spade that was disintegrating on the forest floor. Rafael heard an echo of a muffled scream join his and distantly recognized it as Pea, the *shikigami's* jaw locked around Seokga's face, viciously tearing at the flesh there, fully believing that she could take on a god. Vivid colors flashed dizzyingly as the opossum threw all of her *ki* into her efforts.

His body continued its forward movement, though he no longer felt it. Horror and awe competed for attention in his mind as he watched *ki* made of jade and gold rise from the box and surround Baki. The image of the *haetae* cocooned in her own power would be forever imprinted in his mind, even as she began to disintegrate into particles of *ki* that joined her magic in the air before it gently vanished, the flames around them extinguishing as the final mote winked out. The slave bands plunged from the air without flesh to carry them and shattered upon impact.

Rafael dropped to his knees, his momentum carrying him into the space where Baki had been. Seokga fell a moment later, a soft thud that was discordant to the damage the god had caused. With the god's fall, the mayhem quieted, until cries of confused Abbies filled the air, but he paid the noises no attention, his mind singularly focused on the empty space in front of him. He distantly noted his demonic hands desperately grabbing the air around him like he could pluck her back out of the air and put her back together, the way Pea had done once upon a time. His soul joined him in the act, the tendrils of black mist straining to find something, anything. But unlike the last time they were in Ryūgū-jō, there was nothing for him to latch onto. Nothing but a translucent *ki* dancing in the air like water.

Reika approached, her face solemn instead of snide for once, and opened the pouch she always carried with her. *Shiomitsu-tama* and *shiohiru-tama* floated out, rising to join the *ki* that lingered in the air. A moment later, both jewels burst with a soft *pop*, the power they had contained now freed to join the rest of itself. A moment later, Ryūjin's *ki* speared away and vanished as if it had never been present.

A high-pitched keening filled the air next to him, and his eyes widened as body and mind rejoined at last to fully realize what happened. The wail was joined by the howl of Baki's K9s, including Victoria, as they circled the space her body had been, trying to find their friend and companion.

Rafael wanted to stay, he *needed* to stay, to remain where Baki had lost her life, but there was nothing left for him here. Yet there was still a little *shikigami* who had just lost her bond. Before Pea's *ki* rebounded completely and rendered Ryūgū-jō to rubble and their allies to their final rest, he grabbed her, the small opossum looking even tinier in his larger-than-normal hands, and vanished.

He might not have been able to save Baki, but he would save her *shikigami* and their friends for her if it took him the rest of his endless eternal life.

EPILOGUE

A rhythmic pulse surrounded me, soothing in its low vibration. Occasionally it changed its pace, sometimes slowing, other times racing. But it always came back to this tempo, which I liked best. The pulse cradled me, leaving me with a feeling of peace and security I don't think I had ever experienced in my long life.

Confusion reigned over me as I fully registered what was happening. I hadn't expected to sense anything once I died. Anhangá had opened my *tamatebako*, freeing me from the constraints of my life—I shouldn't exist. My Thread had been severed after all. I had nothing to tether me across realms anymore. Even so, if I did still exist, where was I?

There was no sense of time in this current state of mine. It may have taken an eternity, or it may have taken a second, but I was eventually able to see. If you could call it that.

A void stretched all around me. Maybe I had died, and this was where those of us without a Thread went for our final rest? "Ryūjin?" I called out tentatively. I didn't know if I wanted to see my Red Thread again after everything he had done to not only me but his realm, his daughters, and his *shikigami*. I broke a little when I realized I couldn't feel Pea anymore. But why would I? Despair overwhelmed me at the realization she probably didn't survive my death. One severance? Sure. But two? I didn't know of any *shikigami* in history that could have survived that. I refused to let myself think about Max or Woody.

The name I called was swallowed by the void, as though I had never uttered the word. There was no echo, no resonance. I realized I hadn't even heard the sound of my voice within my own mind. The absoluteness sent a twinge of panic through me until I felt the vibrations cocooning me once more, and the sensation calmed the feeling of nothingness, with the reminder that at least this beat existed.

The pulse that surrounded me picked up the tempo by a beat, then another, the way I had subconsciously recognized previously.

"Ah. She joins us at last."

The end...*for now.*

THE SONG
OF THE
CREATION
OF THE
UNIVERSE

In the very beginning,
Many, many years before you or I existed,
The earth and the heavens were one.
Until, one day, a god named Mireuk divided the two,
And created an idyllic world,
A world where mankind blossomed and prospered.

The trickster god, Seokga, saw all that Mireuk had created,
And he became envious.
The trickster proposed a competition.
To the winner—the right to rule Mireuk's world.

Thusly, three trials were assembled.
The first: a tug-of-war at sea.
Mireuk won.
The second: freezing a river.
Mireuk won.

The third trial, Seokga suggested,
Would be to bloom a flower in their lap.
This, he said, would demonstrate their ability:
To care for the world,
To love the world,
And to be patient with the world.

But during this trial, Mireuk fell asleep!
Despite this, a beautiful magnolia still blossomed from his body.

Nevertheless, Seokga was a trickster god.
When the flowers he grew withered in his lap,
The trickster crept to the god's body
And stole the magnolia for his own.

When Mireuk woke,
Seokga showed him the beautiful blossom.
He had bloomed it himself, the trickster claimed,
While Mireuk grew none.

The creator god knew Seokga lied,
But he conceded the trickster's victory.
Rule over the earth was granted to Seokga.

And so, the creator god abandoned the world he had created.

But the world was cursed.

For Seokga's dishonorable actions,
Evil and corruption infected the earth.
Leaving hatred, greed, envy, and war
To become a part of it forevermore.

ACKNOWLEDGMENTS

We made it! Past Me would never have believed that Present Me not only wrote an entire novel, but we also successfully completed a second one only a year later. It has been an absolute adventure, and I hope everyone has enjoyed coming along on Cam's journey with me. (And that we're not too mad at me for that ending.)

That being said, this book would absolutely have never happened without the support of my amazing husband. If you ever need a cheerleader, he is the one who will be right up front and center supporting you the entire way. Plus he's the artist behind all of the beautiful chapter headings in this series.

Holly, I cannot appreciate you enough for all the work that you do editing my manuscripts. Especially having to sort out my inability to remember where commas go outside of the Oxford and direct address commas. I fear I will always be hopeless with them, so thank you for saving my butt each time.

Rena, thank you again for such a GORGEOUS cover. Both times you have taken my hopes and dreams and far exceeded them. I get countless compliments on the cover for Mountains, and I'm so excited that my readers get to indulge in the visual art you produce yet again.

Cheree, best beta reader, friend, and trauma bonding buddy. I relish all the screaming reactions I got while you read the very rough draft and I'm not sorry for any emotional damage I might have caused.

Readers, I love every one of you for taking the chance on this series and sticking it through for Fragments. I hope this book did the first justice. *Thank you* from the bottom of my heart.

Now, what's next to come? Stay tuned for Cam's final book, *The Tether, the Thread, and the Way Back Home*. And as a bonus, I plan to release a novella to accompany the final book. Which I better get back to writing now.

With much love and appreciation,
SM Hyun

ABOUT THE AUTHOR

SM Hyun is a Korean-Japanese American author who currently lives in the great frozen north of Alaska, though she spent a great deal of time in the Pacific Northwest. She resides with her very own book boyfriend as her longtime husband with a giant floof of a dog and a void kitty, who are the greatest supporters while being the biggest distractors. She grew up on fairy-tales handed down from her Japanese grandparents and folk songs from her Korean mother. Her favorite genres are epic and urban fantasy and she loves the growing representation of diversity in literature. So she decided to reach for the stars and give it a try.

FOLLOW SM HYUN

@smhyunauthor @sm.hyun.author @sm.hyun.author @smhyunauthor SM Hyun

JOIN SM HYUN'S DISCORD GROUP
AND BECOME AN ABBIE

NEWSLETTER
sm-hyun.com/subscribe

GLOSSARY

K - Korean, J - Japanese, P - Portuguese,
T – Tupí, H – Hawaiian, H* – Hawaiian Pidgin

Aigoo (K), Terminology: Conveys sympathy or pity.

Aish (K), Terminology: Conveys annoyance, frustration, and/or anger.

Ajaeng (K), Object: A traditional Korean bowed zither.

Akaname (J), Being: A *yōkai* that licks the scum that accumulates in a bathroom.

Anhangá (T), Being: A Tupínamba entity, guardian of the forests and the creatures within them. It either guides souls to *Guajupiá* or torments them. His usual appearance is a massive golden stag.

Ani (K) Terminology: No.

Aoki (J), Terminology: Green tree.

Aokigahara (J), Place: The Sea of Trees. A forest in Japan dubbed The Suicide Forest due to the deaths associated with it.

Appa (K) Terminology: Father, Dad.

Atuikakura (J), Being: An enormous sea cucumber *yōkai* known for wrecking ships.

Baka (J), Terminology: Idiot, jackass, fool

Bakekujira (J), Being: The spirit of a baleen whale in the form of a skeleton. It is commonly seen with strange fish and birds. Known for destroying ships, bringing plagues, or natural disasters.

Bakeneko (J), Being: A feline *yōkai* associated with omens. Also able to shape-shift.

Baki (J), Terminology: The sound of a branch breaking. Camellia's nickname given to her by Rafael.

Banchan (K), Food: Small side dishes that accompany a Korean meal.

Bibimbap (K), Food: A rice dish mixed with marinated vegetables, meat, *gochujang*, and served with an egg. Most often cooked in a *dolsot* for a crispy bottom.

Bijin (J), Being: Beautiful person, but generally directed toward women. The Pacific Northwest *yōkai* use this word to refer to a mysterious woman found on Mount St. Helens.

Bitan (J), Being: A large *yōkai* appearing as a hybrid of a steer with a fishlike body.

Bonghwang (K), Being: A phoenix-like avian composed of the body parts of different birds.

Bulgae (K), Being: Firedogs from Korea. Known for chasing the Sun and the Moon.

Bulgogi (K), Food: A marinated beef dish.

Chabudai (J), Object: A low-set table, generally with folding legs, used for dining.

Cheuksingaksi (K), Person: Outhouse Deity Maiden. She was cursed to dwell in outhouses by her family.

Chīnouya (J), Being: The spirit of a woman with large breasts who provides nourishment for the spirits of children.

Chollima (K), Being: A winged horse.

Curupira (T) Being: A guardian of the rainforests known for confusing anybody trying to damage the creatures within it.

Daeji bulgogi (K), Food: A dish of spicy BBQ pork.

Deba (J), Object: A traditional Japanese knife used in the kitchen.

Dokkaebi (K), Being: A goblin. There are different types depending on whether their interactions with humans are positive or negative. Known for being associated with karma.

Donburi (J), Food: A rice dish served with a variety of toppings that may include meat, vegetables, seafood, or eggs.

Eomma (K), Terminology: Mother, Mom.

Futakuchi onna (J), Being: A female *yōkai* characterized by having two mouths—a normal mouth with her human face and a grotesque mouth split on the back of her scalp with an insatiable appetite. In some myths, her hair functions as additional prehensile parts and/or are limb-like.

Gameshirō (J), Being: Similar to the *kappa*, they are ocean-faring, clawed, and possess a *sara.*

Gashadokuro, (J), Being: A giant skeleton formed by the bones of those who have died in anger.

Gochujang (K), Food: A Korean chili paste that is sweet and savory and made through fermentation.

Goguma (K), Food: A Korean sweet potato.

Guajupiá (T), Place: Land Without Evils.

Gut (K), Terminology: A spiritual ritual that is traditionally performed by Korean shamans.

Habu kurage (J), Being: Viper jellyfish (scientific name *Chironex yamaguchii),* a highly venomous and deadly box jellyfish. The *habu kurage* in Ryūgū-jō are deadlier than their Quotidian counterpart.

Haetae (K), Being: Known for their lionlike bodies that are covered in scales with a horn upon their heads. Camellia is an older version of the *haetae* and possesses a dragon's head.

Hai (J), Terminology: Yes/I understand.

Hakama (J), Object: Traditional Japanese pants styled from the *samurai*.

Hanafuda (J), Object: A deck of cards featuring beautifully illustrated natural scenes. This deck contains 48 cards in 12 suits that represent the months.

Hangul (K), Terminology: The Korean alphabet system.

Hanja (K), Terminology: Korean language written in Chinese characters, predating *hangul*.

Hanzaki (J), Being: A giant salamander *yōkai* which grows far larger than its Quotidian counterpart. As they grow, they may begin eating livestock or humans.

Hihi (J), Being: A *yōkai* that resembles a baboon and has long, flappy lips. They are characterized by their distinctive laughter and are known for consuming wild animals and the occasional person.

Hong'aek (K), Being: A cursed cloud that renders misfortune.

Hwandudaedo (K), Object: A straight sword with a pommel that ends in a ring.

Hyakki Yagyō (J), Event: The Night Procession of One Hundred Demons.

Ikebana (J), Terminology: Style of floral arrangement.

Iwana bōzu (J), Being: An enormous freshwater fish that walks upright and can shift into a human form and protect their waters from overfishing through lectures.

Izanagi (J), Being: Japanese God of Creation and brother-husband to Izanami.

Izanami (J), Being: Japanese Goddess of Creation and Death and sister-wife to Izanagi.

Jing (K), Object: A traditional Korean gong.

Jorōgumo (J), Being: A female *yōkai* that possesses arachnid traits. She is soulless and is known for preying on young, handsome men.

Kalguksu (K), Food: A broth soup made with knife-cut noodles and vegetables.

Kami (J), Terminology: God

Kamikiri (J), Being: A large mantid *yōkai* known for cutting hair.

Kanabō (J), Object: A spiked club.

Kanji (J), Terminology: Japanese written characters.

Kanpai (J), Terminology: A toast made while drinking. Translates to "dry cup."

Kappa (J), Being: A *yōkai* known for dwelling in rivers and lakes. They are known for their *saras* and may be a deity or demonic.

Karakasa obake (J), Being: A *yōkai* spirit that takes the shape of an umbrella with a single foot.

Kariudo (J), Terminology: Huntsman.

Kau kau (H*), Terminology: "Eat!"

*This Hawaiian pidgin term originates from the Chinese language

Ki (J), Terminology: The magic that the Asian Abstruse derive their power from. May also be spelled *gi* (Korean) or *qi* (Chinese).

Kijibae (K), Terminology: An affectionate way of calling a female friend a bitch.

Kimengani (J), Being: A crab *yōkai* that has a samurai-face on its shell due to being possessed by a *samurai's* soul.

Kimoto (J), Terminology: One who lives beneath the trees.

Kitsune (J), Being: A many-tailed vulpine *yōkai*.

Kodama (J), Being: A Japanese spirit that dwells within trees. They are benevolent unless they have been torn from their tree and cursed.

Koi-koi (J), Object: A Japanese card game that features beautifully illustrated *hanafuda* cards and is centered around obtaining specific card combinations.

*Kosodate y*ūrei (J), Being: A female Japanese spirit who has died in childbirth. Their afterlife is spent trying to find and ensure the well-being of their child.

Kotengu (J), Being: A large birdlike *yōkai* that possesses human traits as well. Known for their destructive and violent ways.

*Kuro b*ōzu (J), Being: A dark, shadow-like *yōkai* that spreads disease and steals the breath of their victims.

Kuso (J), Terminology: Shit.

Loco Moco (H), Food: A Hawaiian breakfast meal composed of a hamburger patty and fried egg on a bed of rice with brown gravy.

Maemmae (K), Object: Stick or other object used for spanking.

Magana (J), Terminology: An ancient Japanese writing system.

Michyeosseo (K), Terminology: Crazy.

Mireuk (K), Being: Korean God of Creation who ceded his rule to Seokga.

Misaki (J), Terminology: Beautiful bloom.

Mukwa (K), Title: Korean military office in the highest class from the Chosŏn era.

Namazu (J), Being: An enormous catfish *yōkai* capable of causing earthquakes.

Nhanderuvuçú (T) Being: The Tupí-Guarani creator entity.

Nukekubi (J), Being: A female *yōkai* with a head that detaches from her body. Known for drinking blood.

Nure onna (J), Being: A female *yōkai* with a snakelike body and the upper torso of a woman. They are vampiric and are found near bodies of water.

Obaasan (J), Terminology: Grandmother.

Okaasan (J) Terminology: Mother.

Oni (J), Being: A bearded demon with tusks, typically with blue or red skin.

Oni baba (J), Being: A demon witch known for looking like an elderly woman or hag-like.

Onikuma (J), Being: A demon bear known for being far larger than their Quotidian counterpart. They are typically solitary but have been known to eat humans.

Onmyōji (J), Being: Diviners with a connection to Wood, Fire, Earth, Metal, and Water.

Onna uo (J), Being: A massive fish with the head of a woman. They are known for their prophetic abilities.

Onsen (J), Object: A hot spring that is used for communal bathing.

Puka (H), Terminology: Hole.

Que caralho (P) Terminology: "What the fuck?"

Rokurokubi (J), Being: A female *yōkai* with an extendable neck.

Ryūgū-jō (J), Place: The undersea realm of Ryūjin.

Ryūjin (J), Being: The Japanese God of the seas.

Sama (J), Terminology: An honorific that implies a rank higher than oneself. May also be used for deities.

Samgyetang (K) Food: A broth-based chicken soup made with dates, ginseng, garlic, rice, and game hens. Often served in hot weather to replenish salt.

San (K), Object: Mountain.

Sansin (K), Being: Mountain Deity.

Sara (J), Object: Saucer that sits on top of a *kappa's* head and holds their strength-giving water.

Sento (J), Object: Traditional Japanese bathhouses.

Seokga (K), Being: Korean Trickster God who stole the realm from Mireuk through deception.

Shikigami (J), Being: A small spirit known for possessing small objects or animals. They are bonded against their will to *kami* for their power.

Shiohiru-tama (J), Object: Ebb-tide jewel.

Shiomitsu-tama (J), Object: Flow-tide jewel.

Shirikodama (J), Object: An outdated belief that there was a ball-like organ called a *shirikodama* at the opening of the anus that was coveted by the *kappa* and was the reason why *kappa* would snatch humans and drown them.

Shishi (H*), Terminology: Urine or to urinate.

*Technically a word from Hawaiian Pidgin/Creole stemming from the Japanese word shiko/shito or the Portuguese word xixi.

Sikhye (K), Food: A sweet, fermented drink made from malt and rice and often garnished with pine nuts.

Sinhwa (K), Place: Hell realm.

Ssam (K), Food: A style of eating meat wrapped in a leafy green.

Ssamjang (K), Food: A dipping sauce often used when eating *ssam*.

Ssitgim-gut (K), Terminology: A Korean shamanistic ritual to help purify the soul and guide it after death.

Sua puta (P), Terminology: "You bitch."

Suītopī (J), Terminology: Sweet pea.

Susano'o (K), Being: A son of Izanami and Izanagi and the God of Seas and Storms. Once defeated Yamata-no-Orochi.

Tamatebako (J), Object: A small box. When opened, it will bring Death to immortal *yōkai*.

Tansu (J), Object: Antique Japanese cabinetry.

Tanto (J) Object: A Japanese short sword.

Tanuki (J), Being: A *yōkai* that takes the form of a raccoon dog. They derive their power from their scrotums, which they use for all manner of things, including shape-shifting.

Tatami mat (J), Object: A soft mat made from grass and straw that is used for flooring.

Toki (K), Animal: Rabbit/Bunny/Hare.

Torii (J), Objects: Traditional gates, often found at the entrance of a shrine.

Tsubaki (J), Terminology: Camellia.

Tsuchigumo (J), Being: An enormous purse web spider.

Umami (J), Terminology: A delicious savory flavor.

Umibōzu (J), Being: A massive black humanlike being found in the oceans. Known for destroying ships.

Ushi oni (J), Being: A *yōkai* with an arachnid body, though they have six legs and an ox's head. Known for their violence.

Wakizashi (J), Object: Japanese short swords.

Yamauba (J), Being: Near synonymous with *oni baba,* these witches are known for being mountain hags.

Yariman (J), Terminology: Slut/whore.

Yeomra (K), Being: The Korean god of the underworld

Yōkai (J), Being: Oftentimes, this word is inferred to mean monster or demon; however, in its truest sense, *yō*kai is used as a descriptor for eerie and supernatural phenomena that may range from cryptids, spirits, demons, ghosts, monsters, and sprites, to things that go bump in the night.

Yomi/Yomi-no-kuni (J), Place: The Japanese underworld realm.

Yuki-onna (J), Being: A Japanese winter witch.

www.ingramcontent.com/pod-product-compliance
Lightning Source LLC
Chambersburg PA
CBHW051309130726
47987CB00004B/1725